VERY FINE PEOPLE

SCOTT GANNIS

ATLATL

Atlatl Press
POB 521
Dayton, Ohio 45401
atlatlpress.com
info@atlatlpress.com

VERY FINE PEOPLE

It would be a tragedy to spend your whole life desperately wanting to be something that you already were, all along.

— David Berman, "Clip-On Tie"

1.

NOTES FROM THE UNDEREMPLOYED

I SPENT THE last few hours of my mother's life half-comatose on oxycodone, rooting for a terrorist attack to splatter me across an art museum. Even on that last full day of her bout with leiomyosarcoma—even though the house had sunk into foreclosure, and I hadn't seen my father in months, and my brothers had just bong-ripped their way through high school—life made sense.

Well, no, of course it didn't. But that, too, made sense. In a sense. We were poor, and my cousins drank Coors Light unironically, and I didn't have a single relative who had a college degree or had ever left the country, so nothing was expected of us. Or, at least, of them. Nothing but laughing at network television and slapping toddlers in public. Calling the police when Dad shattered Mom's eye socket. Mocking Jews and cripples and queers. Fearing anyone who wasn't white. Or an alcoholic. That I would, within three months, attempt to teabag the president-elect of the United States while a platoon of anarchists wielded dildoes and lobbed lube outside these very museum galleries—becoming, once a bomb went off, the most wanted American fugitive since the Harrison Ford movie—seemed at least as unlikely as a reality-TV star being elected president. Or a Midwesterner doing something interesting.

We'll cover all that later.

For now, from this shed in what might be Canada, starving to death next to a skating rink plastered with used candy and condom wrappers, honking-off to keep warm, I need you to know something:

I do regret point-blanking two U.S. Marshals, stealing their DOJ van and blasting up 72 toward the Northwest Angle, but I don't regret making Gavrilo Princip look as smart as the UNAbomber. I just wish that, before we elected a rapist real estate game show host as POTUS 45, I'd kissed my mother her last conscious morning and thanked her. Said I loved her one last time. Squeezed her hand and cried with her, maybe even prayed with her, instead of hollering about improv comedy and graduate school, then slamming the door on "Fuck this" before twelve hours of non-stop hunger and back pain around quiet-framed works of art.

More than anything, though, I probably should have battered Stephen Scheisskopf to death with a three-ring notebook when I had the chance.

BEFORE ALL THAT, before Scheisskopf re-entered my skid-marked boxer brief of a life, before I ended up a fugitive domestic terrorist in this North Woods utility hut, I was a security guard. And, humorlessly, a standup comic. And before a gig as the latter, I had to grind out a living as the former. Which is why I stood in the Minneapolis Arts Organization Institute, eyes twitching like roadkill, making $13.72/hour to endure a Friday night jamboree—September 2nd—before Mom bled and wheezed and wet herself to death on September 3rd.

Even now, my hands spasm as I write the dates and symptoms.

The MAOI bullshit ended at 9:00. *Passionately in Love with Passion*, the marketing staff branded this evening, our pre-opening, the millennial-centric premiere of the Eugene Delacroix retrospective. If I made it to 9:15 without garroting myself, I would then suicide ideate onstage and—

"Jude?" my boss shouted. "Jude, are you okay?"

"I'd eat the ass of every coal miner in the country to be someone else," I called back from the Cargill Family Commemorative Grand Staircase. The strobe lights and craft beer puddles and pulsing indie rock eclipsed his response.

A beardo wearing clown shoes and Lululemon humped a Chin dynasty vase. I blinked, dropped my head in my hands.

It was 8:46.

As a preschooler, I did not dream of developing plantar fasciitis at America's thirteenth best public art museum. Standup was my vocation, according to a college career counselor, and I fucking hated

2

it. If I'd been more successful, I wouldn't be writing this memoir. Every second on stage, at least until my fame level supplanted my ego, twisted me into more bitterness. More jealousy. More envy that Mom was dying instead of me. Because I needed to be the most successful class clown in my high school's history but played half-empty rooms in Dinkytown for two pints of Surly and the rush of screaming at racist Wisconsinites. Because I had childhood eye cancer and people like Stephen Scheisskopf bullied me into nihilism, yes-ANDing, podcast hot-takes, and whippits. Because as much as I hated slumping against a stool, sucking from a flask, and slurring social justice buzzwords to a few dozen strangers, I would rather lose a seven-year war of attrition with leiomyosarcoma than spend another blink wearing a clip-on tie at the MAOI. Fame and standup could cancel out all the shittiness. Pepto-Bismol for the diarrhea of my backstory.

The hipster rubbed his nipples on the vase. Nehemiah bellowed over the din, probably asked me to "conduct a patron-interference maneuver," but I was too high and self-centered to care.

I thought I saw two women from my alma mater. Having my throat slashed with a fortified wine bottle sounded like more fun than running into acquaintances. Since graduating a year ago, I'd been boozing alone in my childhood bedroom and chauffeuring Mom to appointments. Oncologists, otolaryngologists, neurologists, Geek Squad technologists. This was her third bout with cancer; the first made her blind in both eyes (whereas, when I developed the same cancer at six weeks old, I only lost the one). Her second, when I was a toddler, generated $50,000 in medical debt she tried paying off with a $9.00 hourly wage. Now this, the grand finale, brought us to all sorts of exotic surgeons and chemotherapy infusions, sticking needles and knives in her face, her ears, her arms, her chest. You will be pleased to learn that the vomit of cancer patients bridges the entire color spectrum. Human suffering is an inclusive thing.

I squinted through the opiate fog, scanned for status anxiety accelerants.

8:47.

Desperate to escape Minneapolis, I did the most selfish thing a poor kid can do and followed my dreams after college. June 2015, as Mom started dying in earnest, and my standup career started producing tens of dollars, I accepted a job in New York. Doing the Lord's Work, I was tasked with shitting out listicles and packaging

GIFs for one of those millennial click dungeons. Move to Bushwick, Ridgewood, some indistinct fecal-heap and price out people who actually needed to live there. Scramble across boroughs to ten, twelve, fourteen open mics a week. Either "make it" or belly-flop off the Williamsburg Bridge.

Twenty-four hours before my first day, the same day Scheisskopf's demagogue scooted down the golden steps of his penthouse and declared his candidacy for president, I backed out, saying something came up. It had: Mom's smooth tissue cancer, which had metastasized into her bone marrow, now settled into the lungs. The liver, kidneys, lymph nodes were next.

8:48.

I stepped away from the staircase, the porcelain-thruster. Tore at my cuticles, hid. I wondered what Mom was doing—yelling for help from bed? wondering why my younger brothers always smelled like skunk?—and felt the pummel of percussion, the orgasmic plume of Percocet.

"Ohmigod!" my college crush, Madeline Einstein, shrieked. "Is that Jude Glick?"

"Blow me up," I muttered to myself, not making eye contact. "I wanna blow up."

"That is!" Nala Bashir, who'd co-edited *The Hegemonocle*, my college's humorless comedy magazine, informed Madeline. We'd gone to K-12 together; she knew me when I wasn't this. "That *is* Jude Glick."

The MRI-machine clunks leaking from the DJ decrescendoed into X-ray machine hisses, or whatever passed for music in 2016.

Five years after giving my high school commencement speech in front of 10,000 people, one year since a graduation wrist-slit with my Phi Beta Kappa key, less than 24 hours to the motherly heave-and-shrivel, and here I was: cowering in my black cardigan and khakis. Damp blazer limp like a noose on the Cargill Family Commemorative Bannister. Gagging then swallowing four *more* stolen opioids with spit, finger-banging my earpiece, and clenching my teeth until they squeaked as chino-clad data analysts and the soon-to-be date-raped social media managers dry-humped and booze-whispered. And now this.

Madeline and Nala were laughing at me. My life the punchline. The set-up? These were the future boat-owners of America, the NPR-donors, the people who were better than me, my friends, my family by dint of having novels in the house. Doctor-lawyer-professor run-off, the folks who matriculated at their safety school and never stopped class-shaming the economic and/or racial diversity admits. Forty-hour work weeks on top of a "rigorous, multidisciplinary education in the collaborative bonhomie of St. Paul, MN" and what did it get me? A post-bacc job that didn't require a high school diploma and a prose style encumbered by rhetorical questions.

"Wow," Madeline said as Nala blushed. I offered a low-wave, reverse-pivoted behind a potted plant, slouched back toward Nehemiah.

"J.G.," he said. "Are you okay, baby?"

"Do you think I'll get in trouble with HR if I kill myself at work?" My college classmates wandered toward the bar, amped to pay $14.00 for a hard cider.

"What?" he said. "Did you run into Mac kids or . . ."

I nodded. He stubble-rubbed.

A white woman with dreadlocks hoovered a shot of something brown and then hacked it onto a caterer's face. Nehemiah shook his short afro. He was the smartest person I knew, somehow not choking with rage, and if I wasn't nominally straight I would've fallen in love with him.

"I was saying earlier how I want to be somebody—"

"Say no more," he said, re-clipping his tie. "I heard you. It's just bullshit. You don't wanna be anyone else. You just wanna be yourself on your terms. That's all anyone wants. The issue is that they've divided us when there are basically only two categories: the fucking and the fucked. Which is why those fuckers from college . . ."

As I swung my head from Nehemiah, I took in the scene, the scenesters: the white bros in Hawaiian shirts scratching turntables their parents had paid for. The whiskey snobs practicing their whiskey snobbery. The moustaches who worked from *artist lofts* and wrote screenplays about screenwriters in *artist lofts* to impress, screw, and then screw-over women. The phalanx of twenty-and-thirty-somethings who listed their occupation as "writer" on Facebook. The woke progressives who were either planning to gentrify a coastal city or had just returned home to gentrify a non-coastal one. The trust-fund kids who drove to work in a car without trashbag windows. The spawn of college-educated middle-classers who could afford to one day retire. The hipster gentry who didn't feel seppuku-inducing shame when catching up with acquaintances.

The fucking.

Then my glance traced the periphery: co-workers sweating through linen shirts and wool sweaters on Labor Day weekend. Asking their demographic peers to keep arms-length from the gift shop. Eyes bouncing from Ralph Lauren t-shirts to Louboutins to Rolexes as we shuffled along in Kmart dress shoes.

Finally, sufficiently focused on suffering, I thought of my blind mother: the hours of medical transcription and carpal tunnel. Medical bills the only constant in life. My cancer. Her cancer. Unsure if each cough was the last. Sliding under a bedpan in her soon-to-be foreclosed house. And how, despite already missing her, the horror of small-talk scared me more than what would happen when she died.

The fucked.

I geared-up for a public cry, but Nehemiah couldn't see, I guess.

". . . I mean, you wanna be *that* dude?"

He pointed at a Fu-man-chu'd jabroni in aviators tapping his foot offbeat and sucking an IPA from a crazy straw. A hard-on jousted from his sweatpants.

"I bet he makes more than $13.72 an hour," I said, all I could muster without breaking.

The radio crackled and sputtered. We both ignored it. Wendy, Sandy, Lindy, Mandy, one of the lifers rambled about a short gentleman defacing the Koran in area 23, but we assumed it was standard, low-roil Islamophobia. This was (white/Christian) God's Country; a neo-fascist who wanted to build a wall between the U.S. and Mexico, or maybe just a normal Republican, was running for president on a platform of cracker nationalism, and with Mom's living room a hospice center, Nehemiah was the only adult in my life who asked about my day, who lip-bit when I refused to say anything positive about myself, who suspected I was addicted to prescription painkillers. I needed this conversation.

He did, too. He'd been my English professor once, an adjunct, before heroin addiction tarred-and-feathered his course evaluations. If I could blink through the endorphin storm drifting down my limbs, if I could rip my eyes away from the crowd, we could talk shop, talk Schopenhauer.

8:51. My standup gig—emceeing an orchestra benefit—started at 10:00.

So we ignored the squawks and my tics. Until a woman with

dreadlocks tumbled down the Cargill Family Commemorative Grand Staircase and busted her head open on the Best Buy Foundation Lobby before sliding and bouncing across the Mondale Memorial Marble into a support column.

"Shit," Nehemiah said.

"Blood," I said.

We waited, unsure if this would transform into a medical emergency or just an eventual AA anecdote.

Then the call came: *10-19, need captain's immediate assistance.*

"Yeah, Nehemiah, er, Dr. Weaver if you prefer, guard in 21 here, y'know, one floor up from the lobby?" said John Coogan, a man who had worked at the MAOI since the Kennedy Administration. "The second floor? As in, uh, above the first? Altitude-wise. Height. Not to be confused with length or volume. To say nothing of width. Not dissimilar to the 'hotdog is a sandwich' paradox. Anyway, and this is John R. Coogan, call-number six, by the way, reason I'm radioing, Nehemiah, is that 11, area 11, see, if you're familiar, y'know we split the museum into numerical regions and the lobby is 11? Well, it appears to have an injured patron."

We both looked to John, halfway down the stairs, close enough to register his semen-and-vinegar essence. This job was mostly walking past the same few thousand priceless, worthless watercolors, statues or furniture installments, and staying off the airwaves in a possible crisis. Coogan still hadn't mastered it.

"Okay," Nehemiah said into the radio.

"This is Coogan, to be clear."

"Right."

"That's John as in Jonathan. C-O-O-G—"

The concussed woman's friends, or some people who allowed her to get literally, mind-numbingly plastered by 8:52 p.m., gasped, tugged at Nehemiah's sleeve.

"Our friend is hurt," one of them said, no more than twenty feet away from their hurt friend as Nehemiah inched through the crowd toward their hurt friend. "Please hurry!"

"Cover me," he called over his shoulder.

"I don't know what that means," I shouted as the morass swallowed him.

"Sounds good," he said.

A few other guards in the lobby, colleagues who must have been working past 9:15 or still labored under the delusion that this job could be performed well, circled around Nehemiah and the casualty. I exhaled, waiting, rocking from side-to-side, checking my pants for piss leaks, scraping crust and blood and hair from my scalp, certain something bad would happen, was happening. A few thousand people, active oppressors or active oppressor-adjacent, rich kids with BFAs that cost several times my mother's yearly income, or else self-described liberals who supported presidential candidates endorsing forever war in the Middle East. The sort of crusaders whose familial wealth extended beyond a Social Security check for $688 a month and still enthusiastically wanted to vote for someone willing to slash Social Security. Meditation-appropriators and the speciously thoughtful flannel-wearers who wanted to bone them. They all fancied themselves safe from the horrors of the world they'd created and, thus, were teed-up for a mass-shooting, a pressure-cooker explosion, no? If it took a box of nails to my already cancer-scarred face to clean house, well, maybe utilitarians could rationalize it. Maybe my name would trickle across the CNN ticker.

Or maybe another acquaintance would touch eyes, immolate me with inadequacy.

Marketing and Communications, whatever that means, expected 1500 to 2000 yuppies to scuff our marble and clog our toilets tonight. This meant the likelihood of even more people I knew—people who were more successful than me—ass-grinding and molly-dipping in these unfriendly confines registered as, like, likely. So I shouldn't have been surprised when I heard my name.

"Jude Glick!" someone said as the music trickled to silence while the dreaded lady snored. "J.G.!"

"Don't hide," another voice said.

"It really is him," a final voice said.

I stutter-stepped, found my best friend, Addison Bockenhauer, arm-in-arm with Madeline Einstein and Nala Bashir, hopping over blood, beer, and vomit. The radio groaned for an ambulance. The public address announcer asked for a Stephen Scheisskopf to come to the main lobby, Stephen Scheisskopf please come to the main lobby, thank you.

"Um, hi," I said, brain flooded with opioids, anxiety, apocalypse. *Stephen Scheisskopf?* I fake-smiled at Nala and Madeline, made sounds of vague shock like we hadn't made eye contact five minutes earlier. Then I radiated hate toward my closest friend. "Addy, shouldn't you be . . . at the Downtown Library? Where your public relations firm is hosting a benefit for the orchestra?"

Addy was the entire reason I'd taken the gig later. I could make more money (i.e., any money) at the Comedy Underground near the West Bank, but she was already over budget and had guaranteed me open bar access. I told myself this was what a good person would do. But really, a good person would head straight home to their cancer-stricken mother, wash her forehead and massage her feet.

"Oh, I just Uber'd over for, like, ten minutes? Fun event!" Addy looked good, maybe even great, backless dress and toned legs befitting a weekend CorePower instructor who knew men viewed all women as cum receptacles yet swiped right on life anyway.

But my eyes, or at least my good eye, traced Madeline Einstein's B-cups. I'd hooked up with more men than women in my life, considered myself voluntarily celibate, but I'd taken up comedy to spend time around Mads, who organized campus-wide sketch shows and open mics, and had spoken to me exactly once. In Nehemiah's class.

"Didn't know you still lived here," Madeline said. Per Facebook, she was an urban planner and Nala in law school. Per Instagram, they resided in Williamsburg, sipped expensive cocktails, lived in a high-rise with a rooftop pool. Per Twitter, this was not nearly as interesting as it sounds. On the other hand, they wore dresses I recognized from Urban Outfitters commercials while I self-loathed in Willy Loman's clothes. I bet they weren't even on antidepressants.

"He's actually doing comedy at my event tonight," Addy squealed, smiled.

"Oh," Madeline said.

"How do y'all know each other?" I asked Madeline and Addy. "*Do* y'all know each other? Can anyone truly know another—"

"Our fathers went to med school together near Boston."

"Mmm," I said. Nala Bashir scratched her neck. She volunteered for CAIR and had a crush on me, allegedly, when I'd captained the high school football team, worried my way to salutatorian. All three women had doctor fathers, but at least Nala, who had been born in Somalia, knew struggle. The American Medical Association (i.e., a cartel) hadn't licensed her dad for decades, so she grew up in the projects near our high school. Just like Malik, Ulysses, and all my other friends of color. "And Nala, what's new with—"

"I'm just here so I won't get fined."

We all pretended to laugh.

"Ah," said Madeline, who I had liked since sophomore creative writing class. Her leopard-spotted belt, her unpronounceable jeans promised a life of normalcy, loving in-laws, maybe a handjob. Of course, I never made a move. I'd planned on never seeing these people again despite harboring resentments and obsessions for years. If I achieved B-list celebrity, my chronic thoughts of death and memories of Dad pummeling Mom would be worth it. Would somehow absolve these people of *also* contributing to my misery by not liking me as much as I, an unbiased and objective party, thought they should. Or something.

"Will we see you tonight?" Addy asked them. Nala had been my first kiss, mid-7th grade, after *Rent* the movie. We'd hardly spoken since. She became cool in college, gyrating in warehouses to EDM, organizing interfaith dialogues on Israel-Palestine, sucking-off the scions of NBA ownership groups as I splintered under the pressure of high-deductible healthcare.

"J.G.?"

"Huh?" I could not concentrate. 8:55 now. It felt like I was body-surfing. Disorienting, as I had never been body-surfing.

The house lights flickered. The PA screeched. An ambulance whined. Nehemiah crouched, popped up, waved a stretcher through the glass doors. My colleagues parted the crowd. The gig, my soon-to-be standup debacle, emceeing the gala then closing out with thirty minutes of working not-too-blue, seemed further away than our ten-year reunion, our college commencement, our deaths. I cleared my throat. "You aren't . . . why are . . . what . . ."

"I ran into Stephen Scheisskopf and his sister here," Nala said, eyes locked on the ground. "You guys knew him in high school, right? I dunno if I ever actually talked to him."

I shook my head as Addy nodded. We both knew him. Well.

"Small world," Madeline said to Addy.

"Earth's circumference is 24,901 miles," I said. "It's 81 times bigger than the moon."

"He's, like, a really big deal," Madeline said. "The opening act for a guy who might be the freaking president. From, sorry, but middle-of-nowhere Minnesota? Can you believe it? I mean, we're all liberals, of course, like, *We're With Her*, but he's donating, I guess, to the Delacroix Exhibit? Or the campaign is? To defend Western Cultural Values? So Nala and I were maybe gonna get drinks with him and then—"

"There he is," a voice rumbled behind me, my shoulder now

clamped. "The man himself, doing what we all thought he'd be doing: working as a museum security guard."

Scheisskopf extended a hand; I refused to shake it, knowing some juvenilia awaited.

"Oh, c'mon, Judy," he said. My eyes narrowed, trying to explode his balding head with telekinesis. He pocketed his paw, undoubtedly coated with spit, jizz, or Reagan's cremains. "It's been like six years, I'm in town for one night, and Mr. Liberal-Arts-College won't show love for his old preschool cubby partner. Unbelievable, Addison, no?"

"You went to preschool together?" she asked. We never discussed Scheisskopf because we both despised him.

Stephen and I had, in fact, attended the same preschool. Calvary Lutheran Church, the only one in walking distance from my house. His grandparents, working-class scum like me, lived around the block. But with his dad running the subprime mortgage department of some Fortune 100 monstrosity and his mother hoping to parlay philanthropy into a state Senate seat, little Stephen deigned to spend three days a week in Mr. Glick's Neighborhood. Tuesdays and Thursdays, some nanny shuffled him from some lake house, but for a while, Teeny Stevie still endured a pseudo-humble upbringing. But not too humble. Given my blind mom and drunk dad, I often trudged to Calvary alone. Because Scheisskopf's family refused my mother's pleas for a ride even once a week.

This was the peak of our relationship. Nowadays, after a European Studies degree and being born rich, white, and male, Scheisskopf—miraculously—turned his parents' connections into a Senate internship, a cable news contributor contract, a communications post with the aforementioned real estate mogul presidential-ish candidate.

"Love trumps hate, remember?" Scheisskopf said, yukking and eyebrow-vaulting for Addy, Nala, and (judging by the arm hovering toward her ass) especially Madeline.

"No, it doesn't," I said, scoping out a clock.

Maybe this place shriveled your brain. Maybe Coogan couldn't help it. Ten months of rotating from gallery to gallery. Fifty hours most weeks. No accrued time-off. Triaging the same bullshit each day: spilled juice box, separated child, lost school group, homeless man holding-up the gift shop with an erection. Trapped in a dead-end gig at 23. Pacing the hardwood. The pavement. Printing

Berryman poems at lunch. Or following the campaign horserace on my often-confiscated-by-management phone. And still I hadn't memorized the floor plans. Audacious I considered myself superior to anyone. These people were attractive and wealthy. They could afford to disguise their sadness with yoga.

My phone. Duh. Was I that high? At 8:58?

The paramedics hoisted the drunk woman, the lacerated lush, by the cocktail dress and strapped her into the stretcher. I could hear Coogan's mouth-breathing from the stairs.

"Ask a holocaust survivor if love trumps hate," I said. "Ask my Jewish granddad who took shrapnel on Omaha beach."

"Easy, buddy, I'm just joking. You wouldn't get it, though. Everybody's a comedian, even you, I hear, but nobody's funny, especially you, I hear. No need to wear your insecurity on your security guard sleeve."

Madeline laughed. It occurred to me they would fuck tonight. Nala withheld the truth, obviously; they'd all traveled together. Proximity to power more important than anything, regardless of ideology or yard-sign. Had they ridden on *His* plane? Kibitzed with *His* third wife, the Slovenian model, while Scheisskopf did punch up on that week's stump? And poor Addy, vacuumed into more than a pleasantry-exchange when she simply wanted to warn me.

The campaign had launched from New York City, where Scheisskopf introduced The Mogul in a speech. Back when people—idiots—thought America was better than a perma-bankrupted slumlord heir winning a major party's nomination. He and Scheisskopf and their shared xenophobia kept rising in the polls as my mother's white blood cell count kept cratering, my self-esteem, too. Meanwhile, the candidate anyone left of Ayn Rand supported, for the party that historically championed the working class by process of elimination, had decided to run on Love and Kindness.

Love and fucking Kindness.

Where was the suicide bomber?

Love doesn't trump hate. Love doesn't trump anything. Money does. People like Scheisskopf, even like yuppie-liberal Addy, don't see that. Maybe you don't either. Because you've never spent your spring break stuck in a dorm room, a blizzard whipping the Twin Cities, public transit suspended and your blind mother hospitalized, heat in the dorm turned off because they figured everybody fled Minnesota. Nobody could live off Rolos stolen from a smashed vending machine at the *U.S. News & World Report*'s most progressive college in America, an institution with a billion-dollar endowment. Nobody except Julian Glick.

"Fuck off, Steve," I said.

He jumped back, pretended I'd stabbed his heart. Six inches shorter than me, sixty pounds lighter, and I had pictured his face when pumping out another rep on the bench press, or when I felt like puking after playing both ways. He won the first few rounds of life, I almost knocked him out in high school, but now his combos pinned me to the ropes.

I waited for the announcement so we could shovel these cretins into their Lyfts and Ubers, and return to our meaninglessness in the privacy of our own disappointment.

"Okay, so you might be at Miss Bockenhauer's fundraiser, I take it?" he asked. Addy tapped her work-phone. "Lotta nerve, Glick. Lotta nerve. Debasing yourself for a champagne flute. We might make it. At least me and Mads, assuming my cunt sister Gwendolyn didn't break her skull. Again."

"I'm gonna get going," Addy said. "So nice to see you, Madeline! And, Nala, let's catch-up soon." She cheek-pecked both ladies. I cracked my knuckles, glared at Stephen.

"See ya in an hour, Addy," I muttered. Everyone ignored me. If you could spontaneously combust from social awkwardness, the smoke had started to billow.

"I forgot you were that funny, Steve," Addy said. He reached out for a hug, kissed her forehead, smacked her ass as she scurried away. Nala and I touched eyes. I thought of Stephen in junior high, dragging some distant cousin or mail-order-relative to semi-formals, while my friends—never me, but my friends, especially my best friend Malik—would bump and grind to Kanye or Soulja Boy. Me, I watched Scheisskopf drink punch and scowl. Whatever influence and fame he'd cultivated in the last eighteen months owed something to the neon lights and thump of those cafeteria dances. Malik gone, my mother next, I wondered if Stephen thought of the past as often as I did.

He caressed Madeline's bare shoulder. "You wanna head to my suite at the Loews? It's only a four-star but, then again, J.G. is a one-star, so we'll round up to five."

"I am dying of laughter," I said, very much alive and not laughing. My blood wasn't boiling at this point. A boil isn't hot enough. The cliché not angry enough. All the oxygen surged from my limbs to my brain—mixing with the pills, the lack of serotonin, the dying mother—and ignited. Supernova, solar flare. A bluepoint flame careening from my amygdala to my cocked right fist. My left foot creeping forward and hips swiveling. My arm and toxic masculinity and pride swelling into my elbow and . . . promptly dropping as John Coogan toppled over the staircase bannister, flailing foot flicking a fire alarm in the process.

Sprinklers gushed. Patrons screamed. Glasses smashed. Drunks sang "It's Raining Men."

As Madeline and Nala scattered, and Addy clomped ahead of the stampede, Scheisskopf, leaning into his cartoonish evil, his sadism, winked at me.

"You'll be seeing me. I won't be seeing you."

Coogan groped for his walkie-talkie as Stephen pocketed some beers. High-heeled women tripped and scraped knees. Shouts and retching filled the galleries. My stomach whinnied, ached. Smiling for the first time all night, I caught Nehemiah murmuring into his rosary beads, probably visualizing the Dorothy Day poster in his locker; this was supposed to be his night off. He felt my gaze, stared beyond the DJs flinging vinyl like frisbees and the ex-frat boys slipping in their Sperrys. Looked on with tired eyes as I play-acted the thing every socially immobile American wants to do: I stuck a finger-gun to my head, cocked it, and splattered my cerebellum all over the Dockers-decked-dipshits who had somebody to pay their rent.

2.

APROPOS OF THE SPECIAL SNOWFLAKES

UNFORTUNATELY FOR YOU, me, and the dignity of the United States, my suicide attempts never quite took. No surprise, I guess. I find a way to disappoint everyone, most of all myself.

The hunger never diminished though.

Before the museum, in college, I gagged at the thought of sex, kissed a man or two, but talked too much about basketball for an invite to Queer Union, to float the nickname Ace. The football team I played on hated me because I openly hated football. Baldwin, hooks, Lorde, Letterman (never Leno), Carson, Friedan, Feynman, the Black Guy at *The Atlantic*, never fucking, knapsack unpacked—this made swilling Schlitz and spitting slurs with my cousins impossible. But I'm too angry, too normal-looking-ish despite the kiddie cancer, too obsessed with Randy Moss to have had a chance with the Cultural Studies majors, the families that grew up with Jane Austen novels, the classmates who always hit WITHDRAW and never BALANCE. But the snarl, the brooding, the comedic rule-of-three felt unearned, too. Appetite never vanquished. As my dorm neighbors moaned and sprayed body fluids on each other's faces and assses, as my friends from high school grinded their middle-class social capital into gravity bongs, as another year went by with a blank resumé and no hope of a bailout from some family friend, the hate fossilized, sure, but self-consciously. With how much harder every other group had it in this exploding science fair experiment, I wondered if I was the only white guy in the Midwest who didn't feel

15

entitled to his anger. But even that's self-pitying, self-congratulating bullshit. And all the while Scheisskopf landed some op/ed in the *Times*, the *Post*. Some feature on the local news, where he spouted his pro-market, anti-minority, unfettered-failure-for-anyone-other-than-rich-white-people agenda. And with Mom sick and the house fucked and nothing to look forward to but climate change boiling all the poor people (while we still popped out more kids), it made me hopeless. And hungry. With Mom next-to-dead, and my work alienation/schedule—to say nothing of my pay rate—I'd taken to eating once every 24 hours, replaced most meals with substance abuse. Two, three days without nourishment if I wanted to catch a movie, or refill my prescriptions.

Everything, even Scheisskopf, even domestic terrorism, comes back to hunger.

Summer before second grade, right after the divorce, I sometimes ate fast food or TV dinners as my sole meal of the day. Mom had enough trouble keeping us housed; food became a luxury. Unfortunately, it turned out that even with free or reduced-price lunch, me and the smattering of working-class kids—our high school's future football, basketball, and teen-pregnancy stars—couldn't always afford to eat.

So seven-year-old Jude, woozy and tired from listening to Mom cry through the walls and/or being slapped for interrupting her braille Bible study, shows up the first day of school jazzed like Richard Simmons because I might put on weight instead of lose it.

In line, scooching along the cement, I watched the sons and daughters of salaried employees unpack their home lunches, the meals someone—probably a Caribbean nanny but still—had the time and energy to curate: pita wraps and hummus and kale salads, shit I didn't even know the name of until I fetched that liberal arts degree. I grabbed my tray, riffed about fuzzy math or Britney Spears' inevitable head-shaving or sham-marriage. Already a precocious and seething hater, the only positive thing I inherited from my father. I dug around the freezer for chocolate milk, plopped it down. Shuffled along the conveyor belt. Opted-in to popcorn chicken or meatloaf and fries. Received laughs and/or covert middle-fingers from Scheisskopf and his goons, then moseyed to the cashier, gave my pin number, and produced a glare and shake of the hairnet.

"Not happening," the lunch lady said. "I'm gonna need to take that."

"Take what?" I said. "My mom says I have free lunch?"

"Doesn't matter. You're negative."

I heard Scheisskopf bounce up from the bench, start the "Oooooooh!" The seven-year-old vegans whispered, pointed, giggled from across the cafeteria.

My tormentor cleared her throat.

A stamp hovered over my hand, big and red and inky: NEED LUNCH MONEY.

She branded me.

"Gimme that tray," she said. "You can have a PB&J. But that's it."

We were now holding up the line. The heckles and taunts dissipated, the volume faded as hundreds of elementary schoolers watched my distrust of authority harden in real time.

"No. This is what I want to eat."

I started walking toward Nala, the side opposite Scheisskopf, but the lunch lady tugged my collar, jerking the unopened milk carton to the floor. It skipped, caromed off a wall, and oozed on the ground.

"Cyclops dropped his milk!" Scheisskopf screamed, gelled hairs like a pitchfork.

The lunch lady snapped her rubber gloves off, shook her head at me.

"Now look what you did!"

She stripped the tray from my tiny hands, marched to the trash can, and spiked my hot meal into the garbage.

"Get a warm rag and clean up your mess," she bellowed, tossing her gloves at my face. "And tell your mother to pay what she owes."

Everybody was looking at me. Staff too. Even then I sensed it, wanted more of it, hungered for people to talk about me. I craved fame. Or at least infamy.

"Fuck you," I said.

"What?" the cashier said. Walkie-talkie static. Skittering feet. Gasps. Hall monitors hustling over.

"I said: 'Fuck you.' I want a hot meal. Why can they have one and I can't?" I pointed at Scheisskopf's side of the table.

"Those are the rules!" the lunch lady said. "Are you too special to follow the rules, you one-eyed twerp?"

"Go to hell. All of you. Go fuck yourselves," I screamed at her, at the whole lunchroom, voice cracking and eyes twitching. "I just want a real lunch. I just wanna be normal."

"Then tell your delinquent mom to pay up," she said.

"Fuck that. I just don't wanna be hungry!"

"Jude, apologize!" said our gym teacher, Mr. Ronholm, neck veins twitching behind his white turtleneck. He was an ex-golf-pro who, according to rumor, gave Scheisskopf free personal lessons.

"Apologize?" I said. I was full-on crying now. "Fuck you, too. I just wanna—"

Ronholm grabbed a fistful of sweatshirt and pulled me toward him. I tried anchoring myself to the checkout counter but one yank and I was sliding across the lunchroom as girls shrieked and boys pointed, the first moment of real violence many had ever seen. I thrashed and tried to break his wrist, cussing him out and screaming about popcorn chicken until he got tired of the abuse, swung me over his shoulders in a fireman's carry, stomped out of the cafeteria, and plowed by open classrooms, my sobs and pleas petering out into soft and dejected pants. We turned a corner, saw more heads swing to the bizarre scene, overtook the library, the social worker, the staff lounge, and then burst through the principal's office doors, beelined for a back room. He whipped me into a chair and slammed the door.

"You don't treat people like that," he said.

I tried to mumble another string of obscenities but couldn't overcome the snot.

"Stop crying, you pansy, and listen: I don't care what's happened at home, or if you're having a tough time. You're a man. Now act like it."

More tears. I saw that he wanted to slap me. He and I both knew he'd get away with it.

A quick pivot and he flipped the lock on the door, looked up at the ceiling for cameras, then turned his gray crewcut and lineman-build back to me. Like a guy pushing a piece of furniture, he extended both arms, rammed his palms into my chest, and sent me and the chair hurtling toward the wall where, me still seated, he pressed his giant hands on my collarbone and thrust harder and harder, my upper back digging into the chair and my head scraping the wall.

I looked up at him. He was maybe three times my size, much bigger than my father, even now he'd lord over my 6'2" and 220 lbs.

He gave a shake, banging my neck and skull. GOT MILK? posters and student paintings of the Edmund Fitzgerald clanked and shook in their frames.

"You are a goddamn man. Not some special snowflake," he said.

"Not. Some. Motherfucking. Special. Snowflake."

He slapped me, front-to-back. I crumpled like wet paper. Too coursed with realization and rage, I didn't see him rip me by the scalp to a seated position, but I felt it. I opened my eyes. He shook me, shook his head, spat, and left.

The eventual three-day suspension was the first of many K-12 punishments. And the stamped hand, the lunch shaming, the trashed hot meal happened a few dozen times, too. Worst of all, Scheisskopf's nickname for me—Cyclops—stuck, entangled with my blow-up, at least until high school. But my vengeance then, just like my vengeance now, should've been beat out by Ronholm and left in that chair.

It wasn't. Instead, I've stayed hungry, foolish. And since the wet snow continues to pelt the tin roof, since the holidays are long over and winter isn't coming but is here, since the ice caps are melting and polar bears will soon need to grow gills, since we're just standing by idly—especially me, now—as the U.S. finally welcomes the strongman con artist, the TV autocrat that is so normal in other countries, all I can do is look back, shudder at looking forward, and watch the slush cover my ice rink while I finish my edgy, voice-driven first-person narrative and feel bad about everything.

So let this be a story apropos of the special snowflakes.

COUPLE HOURS POST-work, slumped and seething since leaving the museum, still shivering from the sprinklers, I gulped my sixth rum-and-coke and shook the thousand-yard stare from my unshaven face. Thirty seconds out from the worst set of my life, heart still rumbling like a basketball in the trunk, alternating between rage and, like, self-directed rage, Reid Scheisskopf—yes, Stephen's distant cousin, my oldest living friend, the unofficial co-host of this party, a guy who did seem to love me yet I hated anyway—had the temerity to stumble toward my corner of this downtown banquet hall.

Here for Addy, I mumbled to myself, here for Addy. Her PR firm threw this benefit to, uh, benefit the locked-out Minnesota Orchestra. It was Labor Day weekend, remember, and I called myself a leftist, belonged to SEIU 26, so when her original emcee—Gunnar Peuschold, a late-thirties schlub who lived with his dad in Spooner, Wisconsin and prided himself on not swearing—backed out to audition for some reality TV show, I agreed, but would not commit to working clean.

That was a mistake. I bombed, hard, repeatedly, could not manage to introduce the guest speakers and silent auctioneers without a murmur and tinkle of silverware in place of laughter. As Reid lurched closer, whiskey breath announcing his arrival, I closed my eyes, exhaled, tried to calm down. We didn't talk much anymore. He had dated Addy in high school and college, cheated on her a couple years back, and when it came to choosing sides, I went with Addy because Reid is either a psychopath or a libertarian.

"I know this wasn't easy, maybe, with, like, the people here, so, uh, thanks, bud. What'd ya think?" he slurred, his tuxedo brushing my flannel. Couple hundred people milled around this big marbled waste of taxpayer money, some of Addy's millennial dipshit friends, and high school acquaintances who couldn't escape the Midwest, but mostly violinists, cellists, donors, intelligentsia, people with informed opinions on wines and graduate schools and what's best for poor people. Light jazz polluted the air. I recognized some of these benefactors from museum fundraisers. In every major city, the same sorts of pretentious whites circle-jerked the same sorts of literary organizations or philharmonics or theater trusts while poor people crowdfunded their medical care. What humanists. Maybe Mom should've realized that *writing saves lives*. Or maybe escapism is fundamentally selfish.

"The hell do you think I think? Think about it," I said, squeezing my glass so hard my forearm tickled. "Thought you loved thinking, methinks."

"You were fine, dude. I think. But I wanted to ask you something. Couple thinks."

"Why?"

"It's . . . well, first, um, thing, is, is your mom okay? Maybe that's . . ."

I waved him off, fished for my emergency flask of Bacardi 151.

"You sure? People are starting to worry about—"

"What people? You, when Addy tells you to? You a grief counselor now?" I dumped the 151 in my gullet and choked it down. "Nobody gives a shit, Reid, and that's fine. Life is a pointless toil for 99.9% of the people on this planet. At least be honest about it."

Watching my mother—my relentlessly loving single-mother—live off a feeding tube and oxygen tank for six months (after seven years of chemo and disfigurement) had been awful, yes, doubly so because I was 23 and already teetering between ruining my twenties and not making it to 30, but I could compartmentalize her imminent death from all the other bullshit. After radiation at six weeks old, I never had the privilege of life containing *bumps in the road* or *rough patches* or *ups and downs*; life was nasty, brutish, and way too fucking long. But when people like Reid—Ivy League despite dabbling with everything from blow to full-on-pissing-himself alcoholism since high school, ending up some numbers wizard who dabbled with everything from blow to full-on-pissing-himself alcoholism at Hamilton Adams Asset Management, healthy parents who loved each other, good looks, no trauma, no anxiety, no problems other than late-capitalist malaise and whatever relationship failures people opt-in to for unconvincing biological reasons—faked the solidarity, the fellow traveler in suffering schtick, it made me want to slash their aortas with safety scissors. My mother was born in a barn, my father was adopted, and, hell, even I considered myself lucky. Good Old Malik never knew his dad, while his mom smoked crack like cigarettes. Suffering Olympics is pointless, yet another wall between people, but, still: I had actually suffered.

"J.G.?"

"I'm fine," I said, looking for Addy. "Perfect."

"Good because there was something else I wanted to run by you," he said, a hand ruffling his faux-hawk. "I think I might quit my job. It's too demeaning. I can't take it."

Like a proxy war between two imperialist nation-states, Reid and I used the trajectory of our lives to fight about public policy. How fun! An investment banker, he had carved an interesting/insufferable niche for himself at parties by playing the WHITE GUY WITH AN ECON DEGREE WHO IS JUST ASKING QUESTIONS, whereas I earned social capital on top of my quasi-manufactured GUY WHO IS SO FUCKED-UP AND EMOTIONALLY VOLATILE THAT IT IS AMUSING/ANNOYING front by developing a POSSIBLY PERFORMATIVE, BUT NONETHELESS _WOKE_ WHITE DUDE shtick. We were very chill people. He read the sociopathic finance blogs; I read the social justice verticals. He advocated market-based solutions to the degradation of unions and factory jobs; I went to a Wobblies meeting for three minutes then cranked to Madeline Einstein in my car. Smoking American Spirits on the porch, huffing Old Style and looking at the Mississippi from the house he and a bunch of our friends shared in Minneapolis, Reid would lecture and condescend to the rotating cast of pals and drunks just looking to get lit if they absentmindedly endorsed the Fight for Fifteen or the public school system. He wanted more wonkery in politics, more means-testing and Bloomberg Terminals. The dude called HTML/CSS "the future universal grammar." He hated the rise of the The Mogul, a man whose three divorces and vagina-yanking and gold penthouse fed on anti-intellectualism, but *despised* the "unreflective, economically illiterate policy-making" that propelled Him to the Republican nomination. And because Reid went to Dartmouth, and all our friends, other than me, went to Big Ten state schools and majored in Day-Drinking with minors in Applied Beer Pong, people just let him gesticulate until he moved on. Or they just didn't give a shit about politics. Probably that one, actually. Maybe the only thing we shared in common anymore was that we both hated his cousin. After all, hate trumps love.

"I'd vote Republican for your salary," I said as I plucked a mystery drink from a cocktail table, cashed it. "Hell, I'd even respect your fascist cousin for enough money."

"That's the thing, man. I just helped make 400K in profit on this corporate restructuring and what's my year-end bonus gonna be? The same $50,000 every other analyst makes. I mean, why do I bother? Some house in the suburbs? Retirement at 35 and then drinking myself to death? Is this all there is? Really? Least Steve is inflicting himself on the world, y'know?" He snatched his own flask now, slugged, dropped it to the marble with a ping. "Me? I drink seven nights a week, I cheated on the only woman who ever loved me. My only hobby is making lists of hobbies."

"Quit bragging. Snowflake."

"What?"

"You're lucky. How can you not see that you're lucky?"

"Me?" said my rich/white/cis/able-bodied/straight/male pal. "Lucky?"

I found this boring in real time. But it was his turn to dramatically and pensively sip alcohol, and I was ostensibly a good friend. Or at least wanted to present as one. So I listened to him sigh and kvetch as he rubbed his nose and looked at his Audemars Piguet. This was *Mad Men* without the sex and fitted suits. *Sad Men.* A wholly original series dedicated to the existential despair of white boys, media's most underrepresented group. What, nobody wants to touch their curving needledicks? Is that what this is about? They, like literally every other socially constructed group of people, find life a bummer? Poor things. If John Updike were still alive, I'd choke him with anal beads until he renounced Rabbit Angstrom as a stumbling dildo without anything important to say. In high school, Reid knew he would enter finance and knew he would hate it; I knew he'd leave the Midwest, knew we'd grow apart, knew he'd lack the fortitude to either endure the death march or make a change, and knew we'd end up hating each other but never admitting it.

But, if I'm honest with myself—and I'm not sure humans can be—I didn't know how, or what, life would look like without Mom to cheer me on. And I *was* scared. So rather than admit this fear, I did what men do: ingest whiskey and painkillers while radiating anger.

"Any idea where your former life partner is?" I asked, cutting off another stream of self-flagellation and stock tips. Reid and Addy had fucked several times since the breakup, but lately they spent more (i.e., some) time together in public. Hence, Reid's role as first lieutenant of this white collar hellscape. Depending on which of our friends you asked, and, yes, all of our friends were mutual and pretty much from high school because we were provincial Midwestern sludge (and even the people who hated our status quo didn't hate it enough to challenge it), this thawing of relations was either suspicious or a klaxon for the Second Coming. Addy frequently plumbed for inside info, assuming my skills as a bro-whisperer still resonated with Reid, but if I scraped myself out of bed at all that summer it was either for the MAOI, a gig, or the sliding-scale psychiatrist in St. Paul.

"Oh, I'm not interesting enough for the hunger artist, eh? Mr. Volcel and his band of neuroses can't ace an empathy exam for old Reid Scheisskopf."

"Funny."

"I can turn a phrase, too, jackass." I rubbed a thumb and middle finger across my eyes and pinched the bridge of my nose. When I opened them, I spotted Nala Bashir, alone, sipping champagne. She escaped. Or maybe Stephen Scheisskopf was diddling Madeline Einstein in some limo, leaving Nala to self-deport from a bar or hotel where rich people buy self-esteem. "But you know what the real difference is between you and me, J.G.? It's not the politics or how shitty your childhood was or how you ended up poor and—"

"Oh, now this is some lesson you can teach me? Some parable from Spreadsheet Jesus? Or are you gonna call my childhood home

Foreclosure Factory again and—"

"You make an economically stupid choice, you have to live with the consequences."

"Remind me of what happened to the guys who created the Great Recession? The dudes who turned a generation of college-educated, would-be Yuppies into Lacan-quoting baristas?"

"You aren't a would-be Yuppie. You aren't even a bohemian. You're a museum security guard who's pissed off because he'll never be Lenny Bruce. You aren't special."

"Et tu, guy who got a 5 on both AP Calc exams?"

Reid spat, sipped, spat again. A few suits and gowns turned our way. Nala included.

"You gotta drop this artsy bullshit," he said, cracking his knuckles. The pianist broke into "Someday, My Prince Will Come," and I decided it was time to detonate the conversation, find Addy, and drunk-drive back to Mom's. "Or at least the pop culture references. Become Excel certified. Learn to code. Get a gig writing ad copy and someone androgynous to pork."

"No," I said, swigging, almost smiling at the hollowness and stupidity of life, the shit drunks argue about. We'd yelled and slurred about this stuff so often the content wrote itself, like a hack newspaper column. Or suicide note.

"All I'm saying is you, specifically, have a choice to not be such a goddamn downer all the time, such a relentless fuck-up."

"That's rich from your alcoholic ass. Your rich alcoholic ass. What were these choices I made? My mother made? Or you made? Or anyone made?"

I glanced at Nala again. This time she looked up from her drink, smiled, offered spirit fingers that suggested sexual possibility. Or not. My stomach growled. I was malnourished, maladapted, and prone to malapriapisms.

"Listen, man," I said. "I—"

"No," he said, not listening. "I feel like you're trying to—"

"Hear me out—"

"What?"

"Listen, if you wanna get real, how's this for real: I hate my life. Really. And I'll trade places with you. With anyone at this shitheap party, this waste of fucking liquor, if it meant—"

"Listen, dude: listen to yourself."

"What?"

"What is this about? You're so hostile. You're coming unglued."

"Where?"

"This."

"Who's on first?"

"Huh?"

"You want the truth? My Mom'll kick any day now and it's got me fucked up."

"Christ," he said before offering platitudes and a pat on the back. Both of us sufficiently uncomfortable now, I felt up my pants pocket and produced my fentanyl gummy bear, a very bad idea that I chewed then washed down with an unattended beer. I'd been high since work, but now decided to press the substance issue. 100mg of hydros, twelve or so drinks, the strongest medical opioid, empty stomach, fuck it.

"She can't leave the couch, Reid. Can't speak above a whisper. Needs 24/7 observation, but my brothers are too goddamn stoned all the time, so it's on me. Of course. Oh, and I ran into your cousin at work. He was with folks I know from college somehow, one of whom is here and also from Hopkins and staring at us as I say all this, thus prompting me to check-in with your schtup-buddy and get the hell out of Dodge."

"Don't you drive an Oldsmobile? Are you—"

"Your problems don't exist if you don't exist," I said, stumbling away, drunker than I realized. "Take it from a comic: the first step is admitting you need more alcohol."

"They've got a rally in Duluth tomorrow afternoon," Reid shouted as I lurched through the crowd, the fake-laughter, the cheese nibbling, the wine. "Food trucks. Steve'll hook us up. Text me."

I kept my eyes on my Chuck Taylors, felt the sweat in my socks when I found Addy, finishing up with the Mayor's Chief of Staff at the bar.

"We will pass this info on to Betsy," the woman said to her. "And thank you, and your firm, for a mostly wonderful evening." The operative stared at me, tight-smiled, and scurried off.

"There you are. It's been so long since we've talked," Addy said as I staggered toward her. "You were so good!"

I gestured to the bartender, ordered two shots of tequila, slammed them both, blinked. Of course, you are not supposed to mix opiates with alcohol, but you also aren't supposed to walk in on your father raping your mother at knifepoint as a five-year-old, so whatever.

"You wanna explain to me why you came to the museum? And/or why Nala Bashir is at a VIP-saturated fundraiser despite—"

"I haven't seen you since—what?—May? God, we've all been worried about you, Jude. I wanted to make sure you weren't gonna bail on me. I mean, Reid talks about you all the time, and I got a heads-up that Stephen was in town and wanted to—"

"To flap those social butterfly wings and cocoon me between three people I hate?"

Addy frowned. "Nice to see you, too, J.G."

She sipped, side-eyed, smoldered.

"So what's new then? Anything? I miss you."

"Nothing. Nothing is ever new. Other than cancer cells in my mother's vital organs."

"Is that it? Is she . . ." Addy reached out, put a hand on my forearm.

"It's fine," I said, thinking of Mom struggling to swallow the pills that kept her not dead. Addy squinted, frowned. I slugged the beer I couldn't remember ordering. Perhaps there was something to these booze-and-pills warnings. There was something to everything, I guess. Isn't that something? "I miss you, too, Addy. So let's talk about you, please. Are you happy with the night?"

"Of course not. It was a freaking disaster."

"Did I—"

"Stephen Scheisskopf donated. Publicly. With a statement. The Orchestra couldn't accept, of course, but it's a friggin' PR nightmare. You were fine, Jude. Don't worry."

"Are you fine though?" I didn't want her to ask any more questions. Too difficult. My blinks creeped along like the tarp being tugged over a baseball diamond. I felt my neurons line up at the punch clock, yawn as the shift ended. *This* was new. Perhaps I drank too much to safely abuse substances that aren't ever safe to mix.

"It's just, I . . . maybe you'd know what this is like. The more I take on at work, the more I get paid and people talk about me, and the more that I, like, kick-ass on the outside? Columns in *Minnesota Business* now? Radio on Wednesday? The hollower it feels when I go to bed at night, I guess."

"Mmm."

She tucked some black hair behind her ear and exhaled.

"Reid has been great, actually, and I know my friends would hate it if we got back together, so it's not like I have all that many reasons to feel sorry for myself, but—"

"Addy, you're great. You're pretty and charismatic and energetic and you never feel sorry for yourself, unlike the drunk comic we all know and despise. If you wanna get back together, well, life is a cascade of suffering anyway, and if it makes you two marginally less miserable, then who cares. I certainly don't. I just want someone to kill me."

"What? Are you okay?" she asked, her hand squeezing my hand. An afterglow hovered behind her earrings. The room wobbled like a bad punt.

"I'm kidding. Go on. Ours is the best of all possible worlds."

"If you ever need to talk, J.G., you can always—"

"No," I said, as my ears boiled. "I wanna catch up."

"Well, so—I really hope you're feeling alright?—I've been having this dream that feels significant, I guess? Every night. I'm backstage. It's like a product launch or I'm giving a speech to the Women's Business Association or something. Maybe I won an award. Whatever it is, it's a big deal. Auditorium. Convention center. Buzz in the air. So I peek out from behind the curtain and it's my show: I'm the one with the dressing room, it's my name on the marquee, but the crowd? This huge crowd? They start chanting someone else's name. Maybe Stephen's, or someone who was bitchy to me at the U, or some sorority chick, but every night, they're chanting a name that isn't mine. Are you listening? Okay because . . . well, whatever. It's my name on the tickets and the program, but something is wrong. They keep howling for someone else, and it morphs. This is supposed to be my big moment. So I ask the house staff, then call my boss or dad or Reid or you, and the chanting for Stephen or whoever gets louder and louder and pretty soon I look down and I'm wearing all black with workgloves. And I'm running around, trying to get the staff to listen to me, but then the curtain goes up and I get yanked away while someone else comes out to a standing ovation, and when I ask a lighting tech what happened, this guy says: 'All the world's a stage and you're a stagehand.' And then I wake up. And holy shit, Jude, are you sure you're fine? Your eyes are like—"

"Uh-huh," I said.

"I think you might be sick." The hand was now covering her mouth.

"All the world's a stage, and I'm gonna go the bathroom."

I swung around and almost pancaked a woman and her champagne flute. The neurons were in their beds, lights off, watching the *Late Show*. On my high-step to the toilet, I thought I saw Nala, thought I heard her gasp, but I blinked and found myself over the sink, at the mirror, the Bad Eye, the childhood cancer eye, rimmed red and hot, leaking a line of something gross. I dry-heaved. People always lied, said it looked fine, claimed they couldn't even notice the asymmetry. My pocket buzzed. Mom. My phone, I believed, had been dead. Or had I just called her? She was the only person who could, however briefly, make me feel okay about my looks, my self-annihilation, my self. But the voice on the other line just slurred, groaned, mumbled, total incoherence, not language. Or maybe the universal language: pain. I shouted for her to slow down, to call Tom or Chris or Aunt Lydia or even Boris, my figureless father, but more yips, inhales, sobs, moans as I paced circles on the tile, vomit, or maybe just stomach acid, now caking my shoes, a line of blood trickling from my bad eye, me now screaming her name but just a suck of air from the other line, like a pneumatic tube as I spun to the handicap stall and the line went dead, the infinite beep, the last seconds before coma, the emptiness. Nothing, nada, zilch, no more Paula Glick, I figured, just Paula Glick the hunk of flesh, and I didn't know it then as my knees buckled and launched me chin first into the toilet bowl, but I was right: this was the last chance I'd have to talk to my mother, or even hear her voice, my last conscious impression on her—me drunk and delirious and overdosed, my final statement to the only hero I've ever had, the strongest person I knew, the parent I wanted to take after, the only person able to stop me before life transformed from hellish slog into my particular brand of American carnage—and I was a drug addicted, forever-starving joke.

3.

A HEARTBREAKING WORK OF
STAGGERING BULLSHIT

MAYBE THE ONLY useful advice my father, Boris, ever gave me—
outside of how *not* to rail coke—is that most halfway houses sit
within staggering distance of bus stops.

"Why?" seven-year-old me asked in the basement of his, uh, halfway house during our bimonthly visitation session. The social
worker was upstairs mixing a paper cup of Kool Aid. A couple years
removed from what the Al-Anon literature called Boris' *Rock Bottom*
(i.e., the Wholesome Midwestern Fun of Mom screaming and Boris
panting and me trapped in the basement while he leveled up on the
abusive husband RPG and used fists and knives and his cock to un-
lock PTSD for his soon-to-be-ex-wife and estranged children), Child
Protective Services decided to pretend people are capable of change,
rendering me the lab rat. My brothers, Tom and Chris, at three years
old, would attend the supervised playdates, the ones at some off-
hours daycare facility, Mom and Hennepin County staff small-talk-
ing behind two-way glass as the Glick Boys played Candy Land or
faked loving each other. But only I would ride with Mom to 5th and
University, enduring sixty minutes of my father while she knitted in
the CPS car.

"Because," Boris said, lighting up below the NO SMOCKIN!
sign, eyes on a game of pool and not me, jamming *Capital, Volume II*
back into his sweatpants, "how else are you gonna get to work-

release or the liquor store?"

"I am seven years old," I said.

"Sure. Right. Thing is though, Jude? The county, the state, no, The Fucking *State*, man, doesn't realize that homeless guys, drug dealers, drunks? They congregate near public transportation, too. At least in the Midwest."

A man with face tattoos struck the cueball, scratched. Homophobic slurs proliferated. An unfamiliar odor escaped Boris' hand-rolled cigarette.

"Dad?"

"Ergo—do you know that word yet? Your great uncle Sholem loved it when I was his ward—ergo, if you ever need cheap labor or a gram of something, look for the helpers. Just like Mr. Rogers said. Late at night, drunk mornings, in-and-around a bus stop, you will always find people who are helping."

So, as the traffic cop shook me awake in my puke-splattered backseat, swinging my keys like a proto-fascist hypnotist while a headache tackled my brainstem, I had to ask:

"Where's the nearest bus stop?"

"Eh, sir, you are illegally parked dere," said the man, Lt. Donglefritz per the badge, his overhanging gut and tan forearms distracting me from his left-listing goatee.

"Mmm."

"If you are indeed Mr. Julian Gladden Glick, or his mudder, per our title records, would ya kindly move your gotdang car? Or'm I gonna have to breathalyze ya? Maybe somethin' worse. Department policy says my body cam isn't—"

"Don't you have something better to do?" I said, lurching out of the car and grabbing the keys, and my parking ticket, from his sausage-link fingers.

"Yes, actually. There's a whole friggin' ordeal down at the MAOI, er whatever they're callin' themselves nowadays."

I sat down in the driver's seat, head pulsing from either a hangover, or withdrawal symptoms, or karma. It was Saturday and, despite my irregular schedule, I always worked Saturdays.

It now appeared I would not be working Saturday.

"What time is it?" I asked. The sun shone overhead. Brunch-goers and bicyclists leaked out of Trader Joe's and SmartCars. An Elite East Coast Magazine™ recently labeled Minneapolis a "miracle" and "the best city in America." Less than a year ago, less than a mile away from the coffee shops and art spaces and redlining of this very Warehouse District, a cop executed an unarmed black man in front of hundreds of people. No charges filed, of course. Our Twin Cities, three million-ish white dullards whose ancestors slaughtered Natives and then named shit after them as recompense, loved to tout its pockets of diversity—the Somalis of Cedar-Riverside, the Hmong of Summit-University, the latino South Side—while ignoring that these were some of the poorest neighborhoods in the country. Blue Cities, Blue State, income inequality shooting up in tandem with heroin addiction, adjuncts like Nehemiah making more money guarding art than teaching liberal brats, foregoing follow-up treatment for my own childhood cancer so we could afford another $30 hospice copay. *When They Go Low, We Go High! And When We Go High, 85% Of Income Created Since 2008 Went To The 1%.*

"Time for you to get a glass of milk and get yer crap together, bub. Ya look like hell. Avoid Lyndale in both directions, and be thankful whoever dumped you here knows it's legal to be lit in yer car as long as the keys ain't inside."

"But I live off Glen—"

"They're infecting the country, bub. If a place like Minnesota starts falling apart, what's next? Either with us or against us, I say. Choose carefully. Oh, and maybe work the steps, ya friggin' drunk."

With that, he waddled off.

I slumped against the headrest. Bee stings lined my skull. My stomach gurgled like an engine sans oil, backache so demented Dante's Inferno seemed only mildly hellacious. It hurt to blink, but I groped the glove compartment for my phone, my pills. I needed to combat junk sickness to endure calling in sick.

My pill bottle was empty; an oregano shaker had replaced the charger in my cupholder; and, alas, my phone was dead. Maybe Mom was dead, too.

I shook like a wet dog drying off and jammed my keys in the ignition.

"C'mon," I said, heart pitter-pattering, "c'mon, baby."

She revved, coughed, would not start. The motherfucking car would not start.

I hammered the steering wheel, kicked up at the engine, pounded the center console like Donkey Kong and turned the key again.

It started. The gas light flared red, but the Oldsmobile started. I needed gas, drugs, and, most importantly—but impossible without the first two—to get back, to check-in with Mom.

So the Oldsmobile trundled across side streets and bike lanes, heading for the halfway house on 5th and University, just across the river, where I hoped to trade spices for a phone charger, a gallon of gas, and, if necessary, a bus pass. The end of the month, direct deposit not processed until Tuesday, I knew I just got lucky. Everything was awful, would forever be awful, but I was white and not under arrest when I should have been, and the cratering mood of last night stabilized into an almost tolerable ennui. Mom's call rattled in my shriveling brain, but I could be home—and high—within twenty minutes. She wouldn't die without me there, would she? I passed a big white van like the one my dad drove. The hospice nurses claimed the cancer-ridden body just gives out at some point, not unlike my Oldsmobile. But the car had started, and the Third Avenue bridge bled into University, so what did they know about Mom's, or my sedan's, resolve? I smiled. Mom could do this. I could do this.

And then, as my engine lurched and warning lights flashed and dinged, I heard Scheisskopf arguing with a familiar voice on Minnesota Public Radio.

GROWING UP WITH a Boris who didn't offer child or emotional support led to two paradoxical facts.

The first: I despised authority figures, especially men, anyone with higher social status than me, whether rabbis, priests, defensive line coaches, or English teachers. Or the rich, speciously impressive popular kids dotting every large and middling Midwestern public school. Really anyone who did not entertain suicide as a best-case scenario. Ergo, I was a "smart aleck" and a "sauce-box" and, according to Boris, a "meshuggener." A grade-school nihilist who commandeered projectors to mock teacher handwriting, who purchased an industrial-size vat from eBay and invited an entire lunchroom to eat Frosted Flakes from it, who started unprovoked Gregorian chanting when taught by substitutes.

I was a real asshole.

But it was either the funnyman posture or the more vulnerable, and more likely to end in violence, tortured-artsy-weirdo posture, and if people were laughing—if I was riffing away my anxiety, the chronic thrum of suicide ideation, the intrusive terrors of Boris and Mom screaming at each other—then I knew, in real time, I wasn't worthless.

Which leads to the second fact: I looked for validation everywhere, especially from authority figures, a Harlow monkey clinging to wire, hungry for nourishment that Mom was too stretched, too depressed, too preoccupied with keeping us housed and fed and clothed to provide. Any time an adult, or even older kid, treated me, like, as a sensitive human being doing his best, I folded. I would grasp and grovel, do whatever they said, whether a puff of weed at thirteen, or getting drunk and sneaking out at fourteen, or lending the little money I had to Malik—my best friend other than Reid—so he could take a Greyhound to Duluth to try and bone a grad student.

So although my dead mother taught me to fight like hell, through the retinoblastoma and domestic battery and recesses spent in silent tears, through eye surgeries and skipped proms and dysmorphic celibacy, through the third of my life she spent stiff-arming death and the loss of everything that followed, the lesson that solidified my self-schema as special, as a snowflake, as the future owner of a well-stocked and notable Wikipedia page, came from a deranged high school administrator and not Mom.

Her name was Patty Schmidt, JD, EdD, and she fucked me up as much as anyone.

Spring of 11th grade, Malik long gone. Reid strolled up to my locker one morning with a group of fellow stoned white boys: Sam, Connor, Mike, Dylan, Rory, etc., dudes who played in Jazz Band, kvetched about their professional-class parents, unironically enjoyed Animal Collective and/or eating Taco Bell. We proceeded with the usual dick quips, regaled each other with harrowing masturbation tales. We talked about weekend plans (i.e., lack of weekend plans). We riffed, ass-slapped, smirked. Even though I was now a varsity football player, having filled my empty weekends with a Spartan commitment to exercise and bitterness, and even though White Boys et al. sniffed coke and chomped edibles and tried to blur the lines of consent with dreadlocked future rave kids—stuff I avoided because I could not yet accept I was Boris' son—we ragged on jocks, toga-party-throwers, future healthcare executives and copywriters hand-jobbing and finger-banging poolside while we laid in wait, until the real world, when we'd show them. Whatever that meant. Uncooly, we were convinced we were cooler than everyone else. It was pretty cool.

Then someone nudged into the circle. Our high school was an

33

abandoned mall, somehow, and, creatively, they called the giant common area beyond the entrance The (Abandoned) Mall, so this registered as normal. Thousands of adolescents flirting and mean-mugging and rap-battling and loathing on blue tile. More lockers and hallways spidered from this atrium; the classrooms, deep and nestled together, resembled shops; our cafeteria lay across the remains of a food court. But most folks—whether Crips or Bloods, future neu-rosurgeons or anesthesiologists, pot dealers or pot smokers—con-gregated where the fountain, the escalators, the kiosks should have gone. We all hung out in The Mall.

People bounced from literal social circle to literal social circle. My friends and I were not popular, but I was popular-adjacent; the People's Champ, they called me. The near-extinct, unclassifiable weirdo who found books *and* sports compelling. Friendly with soccer play-ers, poetry readers. I did my best to treat girls as humans, not objects to "get with," which, until I could bench press 225, got me called Faggot. In the mornings, our phalanx of white jabronis served as an on-ramp to the horrors of the day; at lunch, we'd branch out and mingle with Addy and her friends. Around this time I learned of Nala's crush on me, but I hadn't done anything about it. Maybe that explains what happened next.

Stephen Scheisskopf, a year older than us and friendly with D&D players and Stormfront readers, squeezed by Reid into the circle. The conversation immediately petered out.

I nodded at him.

"Steve," said Reid, submitting a lazy salute.

None of us liked Scheisskopf, of course—I would never forgive the Cyclops moniker, the recess football league he prevented me from joining on account of him bringing the ball—but ours was a cold war. A louse who ran for student body president and lost three times, a dweeb who got cut from the cross-country team and threat-ened to sue the school district when he couldn't join the girls team, a performance artist, a proto-troll before that word entered the zeit-geist, Scheisskopf was infamous and pathetic. Balding and bitter, he frequently asked girls out with roses and chocolates, only to find the bouquets crumpled in trash bins.

"Did I hear you guys talking about me?" he asked.

"No," Reid said.

"Yes," I said.

The awkward silence spread like a fart. Reid and I touched eyes.

"Are you lying to me?"

"Yes," I said.

"No," Reid said. Scheisskopf squirmed toward me, his head at my shoulder. "Dylan just said the blimp you rented to ask Addison Bockenhauer to prom with was a worse disaster than the Hindenburg."

"Oh, the humanity," I yelped.

"Sorry, Steve." Rumor had it Addy and Reid had been sexting since homecoming, but Reid refused to divulge details. Which steamed me, as he'd shared everything (down to the toe-curling, the shape of nipples, the lack of pubic hair) when he lost his V-card to Annabelle Birkeland-Bergeland a couple years back.

"You should try elementary schools, Steve," I said with a laugh, "maybe they'll mistake you for a grandpa."

"Ah," Scheisskopf said, a vein wiggling across his forehead, "I guess you're too cool to go to prom, Captain Fag-tastic? Or too afraid of girls?"

"Stephen," said Reid.

There was something to this. I found hugging too intimate, too likely to end in calamity. I certainly had no interest, had never displayed interest, in sex. All romantic or sexual contact, hetero or homo or whatever, came from Spin-the-Bottle, Truth-or-Dare; I wouldn't lose my virginity until deep into college. Still, Malik and Reid used to drag me to these parentless parties—strip poker and hot tubs—until *my* tag-alongs put the kibosh on *their* invitations. Self-conscious of my eye, and confused at how easy getting sucked off seemed for everybody else, even the theater kids in QU, I recoiled, avoided the topic, experimented with the Wikipedia page to *Dukkha*, let Malik and Reid and whoever else ditch me to nut on Erin McDonnell's sweater or dry hump Addy Bockenhauer. My sex life, my eye, my mother, and what happened to Malik were the only things I considered off-limits, and Reid knew it.

"Maybe I am afraid," I said, opening and closing my right fist, "maybe both. Or maybe I don't need to rent a tuxedo to find out that getting blown by some 9th grader drunk on wine coolers is no way to treat a person."

"Daaaaaaaaaaaaaaamn!" White Boys et al. shouted.

I glanced for a clock. A few dozen bystanders encircled our group. First block wouldn't start for seven minutes.

"All the whey protein and one-liners in the world won't change the fact that you're overcompensating," Scheisskopf said. He must have been bullied, too, I realized, his hair thinning since junior high, his neo-con parents publicly supporting unpopular wars and white supremacy in one of the most progressive and diverse school districts in the Midwest. But I didn't start this, he did. He and his people. F. Scott Fitzgerald, that emotionally brutalized hero who grew up ten minutes from my house, wrote about the Stephen Scheisskopfs, and I wanted a slice of the action.

"Me, overcompensating? You're a 5'5" eighteen-year-old rapist who's only going to Dartmouth because your dad did."

"Oooooooh!" the growing crowd wailed.

"You're such a creep Radiohead built a career off you, ya GWB-slobbing, Hitler-without-the-looks lookin' boy."

"Ahhhhhhhhhh!"

"Scheisskopf is so weak he can't squat my ACT score."

"People's champ! People's champ!" the audience, in the hundreds now, chanted. Soon, I knew, the paraprofessionals, maybe the school cops with loaded guns, would break up this almost riot. It occurred to me that I wanted two people, Addy Bockenhauer and Nala Bashir, to witness this. Somebody, probably my buddy Ulysses "U.P." Patterson, Mal's cousin, a bench-warming defensive tackle who sold stolen Snickers and K-Swiss out of his locker, blasted the instrumental to "Shook Ones, pt. 2," from the final rap battle in *8 Mile*.

"Scheisskopf really is a sex symbol in that having sex with him symbolizes the worst night of your life."

"Fammmmmmmmmmmm."

"Scheisskopf is so stupid he thought 9/11 sold Big Gulps."

"Bruuuuuuuuuuuuuuuuuuh."

"Scheisskopf's brain is so smooth Rob Thomas wrote a song about it."

"Well," he screamed, hands fluttering at his sides and face the color of cranberries, "at least my fucking parents went to college. And my mom isn't a fully blind, half-retarded fundamentalist who buys furniture she can't afford with Social Security checks."

I scowled at Reid, who planted his eyes on his Converse, his lanky arms drooping. "Do it to 'em, J.G.!" some football players yelled. "Fuck his rich ass up!"

"Don't talk about my mother," I said. The mob inched forward, shoved me a bit as someone—a girl's voice—called to be let through.

"Fine," Scheisskopf said, "you want me to talk about your cancer, you cancer? How you aren't some fucking visionary because of your ugly-ass eyes? The fake one? Faker than you? How you're ugly and awkward and this whole outsider identity, this whole 'I'm above it all!' pose is bullshit because you aren't, you're just a momma's boy pussy who pretends he's hard. You're more blind than your mother."

"Steve!" Reid said, trying to grab his polo while I brushed my ocular scars and nodded. The Mall went quiet now, or maybe this was like a big fourth down play where the mind clears and anger flows. Whatever happened in that millisecond, in the next I had Scheisskopf by the back of the head and started bouncing him against my locker like a basketball.

Boom.

Boom.

Boom.

Boom.

Boom.

My left fist connected with his left temple, once, twice, and then with both hands, I gripped him by the collar and slammed him against my locker again, busting his head open, blood and teeth puddling on the floor. His body at my feet, I grabbed a notebook and rolled it into a club, then stretched the wire spine into a shank, unsure if I should go for the right eye or just jam it down his esophagus and make him choke on his tongue. As I looked down on him, curled and fetal, he was mumbling something.

"Malik . . ." floated off his swollen lips. "You killed Malik. You killed Malik. You loved Malik, and you killed him . . ."

That was it, my amygdala decided, raising the notebook like an axe, not certain how I would eliminate my Scheisskopf problem but convinced this was my chance, when someone wrestled me from behind and kicked my ankle, spilling me backwards into the arms of two cops and a para, who I swung and kicked at as they lugged me like a barbecue spit to Schmidt's office—Scheisskopf shrieking gay slurs and promising vengeance and carnage the whole time—then jerked my shoulders back, slashed zip-cuffs around my wrists, and dropped me on the carpet-covered cement.

The first block bell rang.

My heart bonked with panic attack intensity. I couldn't catch my breath.

Schmidt, unequivocally the most interesting person any of us knew (or would ever know), just sat on her desk in the lotus position and thumbed through a copy of *Dissent*.

She didn't even look up.

"Principal Principles" had been an All-American power forward at Penn State, deployed to Vietnam as a Marine in the late stages, joined the anti-war effort soon after and picked up a law degree from the U. Within months, she'd been fired from the Hennepin County DA's office for refusing to prosecute drug crimes and then was disbarred altogether after threatening to self-immolate as a public defender. Teaching Civics, and eventually becoming the radical, mindfulness-practicing administrator constantly defending her eccentricities from the school board and No Child Left Behind, soon followed. At our 2400 kid school, 50/50 whites and students of color, housing projects and million-dollar-cul-de-sac developments within a mile of the football field, nobody agreed on anything other than our basketball team being the best in the five-state-area, and Patty Schmidt scaring us more than death. She had called my mother several times that year, as I frequently mouthed off to English teachers fumbling through "Comic Rhetoric" or Pre-Calc instructors who couldn't explain why any of this was worth learning, but I'd never actually met her. She avoided the hallways, delegated discipline to her assistants, manufactured a personality cult that had gradually increased test scores, decreased suspensions, and earned her Minnesota Educator of the Year six times in two decades. Mom defended my behavior reflexively, even when she shouldn't have, but she still admired Patty Schmidt.

"That woman is a fighter," Mom would say, "and that's the most important thing to be."

Maybe so, but I had just committed felony assault in front of hundreds of people.

So this fight, I guess, was different.

"Staggering synchronicity here, young man," Schmidt said, still reading her magazine, as I struggled to my feet and plopped into a bean bag chair, "in that Juana Mariana, Spanish Jesuit and hero to the Catholic Left, a topic of interest to your mother, incidentally, is featured prominently in this tyrannicide essay written by Father Daniel Berrigan."

"Okay," I said.

She kicked her legs out like a child on a swing-set, tossed the magazine toward a plastic plant, and locked the most exacting stare I've ever seen on my quick-blinking eyes.

"Of course, as with your blowup today, a rubric of justice is wielded all the time for unjust means. Look at the War on Terror. Or the proliferation of 3.2 beer at Midwestern gas stations."

"Dr. Schmidt—"

"Say what you will about his motives, his allegiance to industrial capital, but look at Lincoln . . ."

Instead, I looked at the ground. U.P., himself a constant trouble-maker without the grades or melanin to get away with it, often mentioned that making eye contact with Schmidt is more dangerous than staring into the sun with binoculars.

"She talks a buncha bullshit, bruh bruh," U.P. would say in the locker room. "Like a wizard in a fairy tale or something. It's all a riddle with Dr. Schmidttle."

The rugged berber was also, uh, rug-covered. A red afghan in front of the desk, a long and woven thing next to the floor-to-ceiling bookcase along the left wall. On the opposite side, sixteen screens with live footage of The Mall, various hallways, the library, the most popular places for violence and/or sexual activity.

". . . but Bronstein said that fascism is nothing but capitalist reaction; from the point of view of the proletariat the difference between the types of reaction is meaningless. Ergo, John Wilkes Booth. Or, if you aren't a Tankie, ergo, ice pick."

"Right," I said.

She stood up now, just inside my peripheral vision, picked up an empty mason jar from her desk, lit two incense sticks with a zippo—lavender?—and swung it in slow circles, her combat boots, black tights, and polka-dotted tunic evoking a gray and militant Ellen De-Generes.

This was extremely fucking weird.

"This is extremely fucking weird," I said.

My stare ventured no higher than her shins. Schmidt hadn't said anything for a full minute when she, and the incense, inched toward my beanbag.

If you rounded up, ever since the divorce I'd been a Bad Kid, escaping the label because of perfect attendance and straight-A's and white skin. I'd been suspended a dozen times in my career, ejected for class clowning at least once a week. The appetite for attention never sated, which meant Mom wasted hours she didn't have, and pride she couldn't swallow, on sit-downs, and screaming matches with teachers and deans. Sometimes an aunt drove her, sometimes a friend, sometimes, like the time I mocked a health teacher for having us play Sexual Monopoly and convinced the class to belt her with condoms, even Boris. I never fought, though, and generally loathed violence. Too much of it growing up, too closely tied to my distrust of men, of masculinity. I saw physical domination, like football, like my good grades, as an instrument of survival, of reorienting my fork-lift-driving destiny, yet an instrument I had little interest in practicing. That morning was the first and only time I started it.

"Am . . . Am I in trou—"

"Of course you're in trouble!" Schmidt shouted, throwing her hands up, dropping the mason jar, and thus ripping my eyes from the floor. She stamped out the incense before it ignited the room and then lifted my chin to meet her gaze. "You are obviously suspended for two weeks, and if you weren't well-liked, it wouldn't surprise me if Scheisskopf's parents sued you and the goddamn school district. Jesus, Jude, there's a responsibility that comes with being a man, and especially a man of conscience, because they don't make many, and to have you crossover into that cro-magnonism is disappointing crap. You aren't your father, I hope?"

"You know—"

"Of course I do. I know you better than you do. Your mother is a real card. A ham like her son. And I'm a vegan. But she's intimated—and this is why Father Berrigan is relevant—that you have a lot of directionless anger, which appears to have landed on Stephen's face this morning, Satan Bless Him."

"His . . . his teeth? Are his parents—"

"The coward has a single fake that pops out when he gets punched. You aren't the first, Jude, but that's not why I brought you in here."

"Okay."

"You are a special young man. Do you know that? Has anyone ever told you that? Your mother, maybe?"

I nodded. Mom told me that all the time, explained that one day I'd be rich, or at least famous. That she could not retire and needed me to be rich, or at least famous.

Schmidt swooped away from me and teetered, foot-to-foot, in front of the bean bag, hands clasped behind her back.

"You're not normal, Julian," she said, now leaning toward my face. No blinks. No smiles. "And, y'know, that's okay. It's overrated, being normal. You end up a very successful but forgettable high school principal if you're normal, yes? Most days, I regret how normal I've become. I'll give it up one day, get back to the fight, but now? I am normal."

"Normal?"

"Normal. But the thing with you, Jude, is that, outside of being *ab*normal, you are a nobody. Has anyone ever told you *that*? Maybe that departed Malik of yours?"

I tried to look elsewhere, but she snapped my head back into place. Her lack of irony, her cardigan, her stare prevented a response.

"No," she said. "I guess they haven't told you that. Well, I am. You think you're brilliant and unique and have lived a life unlike most kids your age, most people my age, but that doesn't matter. Your suffering is immaterial. For now. Because you're a nobody. Correct?"

I tried to say "agree to disagree," but my throat felt like sandpaper.

"Are you familiar with Horatio Alger, Jude? The American Dream myth?"

"Sure."

"Stand up, son."

I obeyed. I was 6'2" in 11th grade, but the only time I felt smaller in my life was bedside as my mother heaved to death.

"It's a lie," she said, laying a palm on my shoulder. "Hard work and perseverance don't really matter. Your mom, how hard has she worked to stay alive and feed you and your brothers, and what does she have to show for it but a furious oldest son who is too self-conscious to engage people without a veneer of irony or cynicism, who so far has frittered high school and will probably fritter college without ever making anything but the tiniest impact? I am so very tired of angry young men allowing anger to ruin their potential. I figure you would be too, given personal history."

"My mom said—"

"How else could I explain you to the staff you exploit for laughs? The ostentatious cries for help you produce every other day?"

"What is going on right now?" I said, wavering on my heels. "Things like this don't actually happen in real life. Authority figures don't just impart wisdom like in some movie or—"

"Of course they do, child. American life makes no sense if you view it as a logic puzzle. That 'moral arc of the universe bends toward justice' drivel? There is no arc. In my lifetime, I've seen our

41

best politicians taken out. Or shamed for the color of their skin. Yet who's the most revered? A braindead, objectivism-humping actor who doubled the national deficit. We'll do our best to keep the suspension in school, Jude, but I need you to understand something."

"What?"

"It doesn't get better."

"Aren't you supposed to tell me it does?"

"No. Not you. Others, maybe. Not you. In your lifetime, things will deteriorate into sheer horror. Personally and politically. And, more importantly, they'll get stupid. And that's where you come in."

I had, and have, no real idea what she was talking about, and in hindsight she might have been drunk, but I remember the next part more clearly than anything I've ever heard. I don't really buy epiphanies. I try not to buy anything because I have limited disposable income. But I don't buy epiphanies because you learn the world is a hellscape in creeping pieces; you learn from the outset; or you never learn. What wisdom could a *Brothers Karamazov* dialogue impart that wasn't already cemented by a shitty childhood and beyond. For years, I'd been the 'A' student who huffed attention to avoid suicide (and sometimes punched holes in walls). And after this, I was an 'A' student who huffed attention to avoid suicide (and sometimes punched holes in walls). Thrashing upstream in the day-to-day whitewater rapids of being an adult, of being miserable, delusional, or impotent, change is imperceptible, if change is real at all, anything but circumstantial weirdness and ill-informed choice. Still, this moment with a silver-haired principal in the Spring of 2010 deformed me, altered me genetically, changed my capabilities. Peter Parker's spider bite sans unitard or narrative cohesion.

She put her hands on both sides of my head, held my gaze in place. Then, with those eyes, she nudged the launch-point, started the countdown that, depending on how this all turns out, might have imploded my life.

"You're brilliant, Jude. You can and will inflict yourself on this stupid world. But here's the problem: there are only the pursued, the pursuing, the busy and the tired. Choose wisely."

"YOU PEOPLE ARE policing, and thus oppressing, my people for thoughtcrimes. Any proposed 'Muslim Ban' is simply self-preservation," Scheisskopf said as I floored it on University toward Boris' old halfway house, my closest and least-bad option.

"Multiculturalism is erasure. If racial and ethnic minorities can rally around their identity, why can't I rally around mine? White separatism is about protecting what we've built. Is this any more discriminatory than, say, moneyed Jewry protecting their gains by frowning on miscegenation? Than Muslim-Arabs who—"

"First: your fascist's haircut is just a mullet in reverse. No character. Balding in the back, racism in the front," said Principal, or I guess ex-Principal, Schmidt. "Second: calling you out for being an idiot is not the same thing as being oppressed, my child. You can say whatever you want, and I hope you do, Stephen, because you'll either get smacked in the jaw like high school, or continue to look like the pasty, privileged pinhead you are. And, still, you won't see it. This is the first time in U.S. history that people are forcing you to be self-reflective, but you are too self-absorbed and too sociopathic to reassess your inconsistent worldview. Why? Because you and 'your people' are lazy, Stephen Scheisskopf. And I'd know, having written a letter of rec for you. Per Arendt, it explains European forays into colonialism and even slavery. Racism, the heteropatriarchy, these ostensible liberal arts buzzwords are real things, are verifiable instruments of capital, denigrated by white dudes in suits like you, no? Work to you is cruising Reddit and praying to Jordan Peterson."

"This is PC language policing," Stephen said as my car sloweddown, the gas gauge flashing at me. "And, look, Dr. Schmidt, by your logic, these ad-hominem attacks—"

"The third thing, Stephen: maybe my personal preference is a multiracial, multicultural coalition centered on class, but to equate your cultural preservation with my cultural preservation, even as a white, queer woman, let alone the cultural preservation of a people so systemically disenfranchised as the African-Americans or post-Shoah ethnic Jews, is ahistorical. The history of so-called Western Chauvinism is inextricable from destroying other peoples' cultures, no? Minority pride is different than your pride because your pride is pride in telling me, and my black allies and brown allies and poor allies and queer allies, that we shouldn't have any pride. The question is: can you care about lives that have been different than yours? If you can't, you're a shitty person."

Crosstalk. Paper-shuffling. Something about *Call of Duty 3*. The host, the useless schmuck, yelped about listening to both sides in an atmosphere of mutual respect.

My car groaned to a halt a couple blocks from my best bet at securing drugs, gas, or a phone charger.

"Mutual respect?" Schmidt screamed over Scheisskopf. "What is there to respect? These fascists all want the same thing: me to not exist. Why should I respect that? This movement is empowering a bunch of lonely and demented men who believe themselves to be white, these twentysomething virgins who sit around on 4chan all day, edging to Nazi memes, these entitled and failed pick-up artists who picked up racism when nobody wanted to touch their white supremacist genitalia. Ergo, to overcompensate for their butchered masculinity, which is a social construct just like race by the way, they cling to Helter Skelter fanfic and an anti-civil-rights agenda. I am to respect this? No—no, Stephen—me and my comrades will piss on it, thank you. And, you know what, NPR, MPR, and any liberals listening? Whiteness isn't real anyway, you fuck-stick child."

"I am twenty-four," said the future Senior Adviser to the President.

The broadcast cut into a screech-and-buzz of technical difficulties. Then my car did, too.

I stepped away from the vehicle, jogged southeast on University Avenue, the main drag of UMN's campus, home to de-certified frats and the halfway-housers who supplied them whippits. My headache abated. I needed to exercise more, genuinely enjoyed it when I did, but fifty-plus hours a week on my feet and knees without cartilage, and an arm I could not raise above my ear, conspired to make stealing painkillers and reading Schopenhauer and Kierkegaard the most realistic option. Besides, I'd been losing weight for months, and—as I suddenly felt dizzy and noodle-like—I didn't eat enough to sustain an active lifestyle, or whatever people with disposable income call it.

I panted into a trot, crossed 5th Avenue SE, and waited. I had assumed the halfway house was still here, given all the bus stops lining University, but I wasn't sure until some graying codger with a braided beard crept toward me. Boris, between hits of bagged wine, had always insisted felons were the nicest people in the world.

"Hey, brother," he said with a Deadhead's gregariousness. "You got a light?"

"Got more than that," I said as my stomach rumbled.

The old man rubbed his neck. "I'm sober, brother, if—"

"You smoke weed?"

"Of course," he said, cackling with a creak in his leather jacket. It looked less Meth Murders and more Military. "Said I'm sober, not stupid, y'know?" I handed him the lighter. "Maybe weird, brother, but you look just like some guy I knew in the workhouse fifteen years prior. Lived in this house in the late 90s, too."

"Mmm." We stood in silence as he lit the American Spirit.

"Fella had a weird name. Odd duck, that one."

"Right," I said. His jacket said *Hess*. I plundered my brain for the next thing to say. "You ex-military, my man? My gramps was 101st Airborne."

"Marines. Like some fucking Springsteen song. Heard 'bout this shit on the radio, *Hillbilly Elegy*, and it made me so mad. I grew up on the Range, near Cloquet, not that you give a hoot, but anyway, them stories these rich kids tell themselves about working people, military people, even if they come from our neck? Makes a man sick."

"I know the feeling," I said, not sure if I knew the feeling. "So, grunt-to-grunt, I got a question. My Olds is tapped out, y'know, and I s'pose we could come to a cash-free arrangement if you don't got—"

"What do you need, Boss?" The term *code-switching* entered my brain. It did not surprise me that Boris had relapsed here. If I weren't a white guy in flannel, none of this would be happening. "Gas? Or you lookin' for—"

"An android phone charger, too? Like, for a car? If—"

"Here," he said, tossing me exactly what I needed. "Pilfered that from a meth-head farmgirl at the Women's Unit in Nordeast."

"Oh." Seemed Boris had been right about something for the first time in my life.

"But let's stroll down toward the Stone Arch, so I can introduce myself to your friend."

So we walked toward the Mississippi, my heart rattling against my ribcage. Malik and I used to sell oregano as weed all the time in junior high, but that was ten years ago. And this bandana-clad ex-addict was not a 7th grader.

"You hear 'bout that shit over Whittier? Some attack or whatever down by the MA—"

"Here it is," I said, shoving a pill bottle into his hand. We'd moved less than two blocks, stood between an arts organization parking lot and subsidized lofts that priced out long-time residents but allowed folks like Addy to feel cool. I had considered living here myself if Mom died and the house was repossessed, though

$900/month on rent, even if subsidized, seemed steep.

He unscrewed, sniffed. "What is this?"

"A dime."

"No, buddy, what the hell is this?"

"It's, uh—" coughing into my hand, scraping for something abstract but not corny, hating myself for not thinking this through and just walking the six miles home—"Commercial Fiction. Outta Humboldt."

"What?"

"Yeah," I said, smiling at my cleverness, thanking Mom and Boris for my wit. "It's extra palatable. Fun. Laid-back. Clean. And, best of all, leaves no stink."

He sniffed it again, held it up to his face. "You sure this ain't oregano?"

"This stuff is medicinal, y'know? Might not smell dank, but you'll get knocked on your ass like there's nothing to it."

"Commercial Fiction, eh? Ain't never seen weed like this. Brown and sticky like opium."

He scratched his beard and stared at me. A charger without gas wouldn't help me much, I thought, but I could always ditch the car and call an Uber, maybe put it on my credit card, or, if things were deathbed-bad with Mom, and not just emergency-room-bad, Tom or Chris could pick me up, or lend me money.

The biker was tapping my wrist. "Sorry?"

"I said you seem spacy like some college fuck."

"Uh."

"But you're different, I can tell, you ain't no fake tough guy," he said, clapping my back twice. "Facial scars and thick forearms, y'know? So let's go see 'bout that gas can."

AS I CAREENED through a stop sign onto Highway 55, a North Minneapolis main drag, bisecting a neighborhood famous for some of the most egregious redlining and predatory lending in U.S. history, a car shaped like a hotdog, a Wienermobile, skidded to a halt. It did not leave a trail of mustard. I swerved, tried to pass it, but then stomped my brakes and saw why we were parked in the middle of the road a few blocks of West of Downtown.

Pumping signs and chanting, hundreds of marchers clogged the street. Dozens more stood with locked arms in front of me and the Wienermobile. I looked over at the driver. He shook his head, dug into a pocket beneath the red cursive of his uniform, and sucked from a flask. He tipped it toward me, a peace offering. I cranked down my window, caught his toss, swigged, and lofted it back to him. Proletarian solidarity. A random act of alcoholism. Two guys stuck behind a Saturday march for social justice, one trying to get to work and one trying to get on with the worst day of his life. Maybe America wasn't doomed.

"America is fucking doomed!" an organizer blared from a bullhorn. I recognized the voice before I felt the eyes. It was Principal Schmidt, shouting down -isms and the cops who had showed up to protect the -isms.

Pocket rumbling. I cut the engine, excavated the phone. Aunt Lydia, Mom's oldest sister.

"Hell—"

"Where are you?" she asked as protesters surrounded my car, the Wienermobile, and the idling cops.

"I'm stuck behind a—"

"Holy Mary, Mother of God. Julian Glick, you gotta be kidding me. You went to that crap? Did you get your mother's message? I rushed over from Dawson in the middle of the night."

"Yeah," I said, watching a group in all black rock the Wienermobile back-and-forth, "I'm going to be there soon. I'm on my way. Is, ah, is she . . ."

"Just get over here."

Dial tone.

Principal Schmidt, I gathered from her ranting, was now some sort of radical with the National Lawyers Guild; this explained her NPR appearance and leadership role. There was an anarchist element, an antifascist contingent, Black Lives Matter folks, and other people with convictions and/or nothing better to do on a Saturday morning. The hotdog tipped on two wheels and plopped back to the asphalt. The driver, probably fearing a Reginald Denny rerun and/or listening to too much conservative talk radio, jumped from his cooked sausage and barrel-rolled to the curb.

I stepped out of my car, tried to follow along with the "Hey Ho!"s and "Gots to Go!"s.

A police chopper whipped in slow circles overhead. It appeared my commute was postponed indefinitely. I jostled and bumped and large-white-manned my way through the throngs, hoping to find my fellow blue-collar bro, or at least avoid being seen by an acquaintance. Anything to avoid reinforcing my loserdom.

A few yards from the median strip, from the chance to sober up on the grass or maybe even start walking to my mother's deathbed, a hand yanked me around.

It was Nala Bashir, from high school, from college, from last night. I was being seen by an acquaintance. I was reinforcing my loserdom.

"Jude! Didn't know you'd be here," she said over the bedlam. "Have you seen Fuck-and-blow-her?"

"What?"

"I said, have you seen Porking-power?"

"Huh?"

"Bockenhauer. Addy. I lost her in the crowd."

"Oh, right. Yeah. Nope. Addy?"

"Can you believe what Scheisskopf and the campaign said?"

"Uh."

"I know. It's insane. What's gonna happen if he wins? It's ludicrous. It'll be like this every day for the next four years."

"Listen, Nala, I—"

"Surprised you made it," she said, shoving us toward a pocket of space back near my car. Most of the protesters linked arms with the other linkers. "I heard you had an interesting night."

I flipped through my mental file cabinet and couldn't locate any memos involving Nala and last night.

"You don't remember seeing me," she said.

"At the museum? Because I don't work there. Not really. Last night was—"

"No, at the fundraiser? Addy's thing? Where you did comedy? I ditched Maddy Einstein, who, oh my goodness there's a lot I could say about her since we graduated, but, anyway, I wanted to see you do standup, and you don't even remember seeing me."

The Wienermobile commander rushed past and shrieked as his frank crashed to the road. Glass and bits of plastic scattered at our shins, at my car.

"Of course I do! I know this is hard to believe, but I like to abuse drugs and alcohol."

I was wearing what I passed out in: t-shirt caked with dried blood, grime-covered corduroys, dark flannel with the "Ask Me About My Social Anxiety!" lapel pin.

The hotdog prole wandered away from the action and stood near us. The wall preventing traffic flow hunkered down and sang "Kum-bah-yah" as riot police adjusted their elbow pads. My phone buzzed once, twice. I snuck a glance. Two texts from Aunt Lydia. As I put it back in my pocket, one each came from my younger brothers. Christ.

"I thought your stuff was hilarious. It was a real hit," she said. "Addy was telling me you seemed pretty bummed about it though." Addy. How'd she end up here? And why? And why did I care?

"Well," I said, stealing a peek at words like *advance directive* and *what the hell*, "I don't know how much value there is in art, especially political art, y'know? It's all about who has power. The only artists with power are already part of the establishment."

I had no idea what I was talking about, or if I even believed what I spewed. People like me, people who don't actually know anything worth knowing, spout off believable-sounding bullshit and hope we aren't cross-examined. Nala, though, had suffered a helluva lot more than I had, but didn't let it deform her emotionally. She grew up in Somalia, came over as a refugee, toiled with eight siblings in a one-bedroom, and graduated with highest honors. Her dad was a neurologist, actually, now worked at the same hospital Mom received chemo, but he'd driven a cab for fifteen years while the spawn of overpaid, shitty doctors used their trusts to become overpaid, shitty doctors. She'd endured Al-Qaeda quips and hijab-pulling and watching her parents languish without bitterness.

Me, I wanted revenge, so I lifted six days-a-week, ran a 5K every morning, and fell asleep furious at the kids who spit on my years-old shoes and asked if my Goodwill clothes came from . . . Goodwill. Childish. Hack. Michael Jordan without literally anything else resembling Michael Jordan.

A heartbreaking work of staggering bullshit.

Nala, a good person, wanted to improve the world and herself. She went to our Very Liberal alma mater and interned at Planned Parenthood, and then the White House. Tried to stay a good Muslim, realized it wasn't for her, ditched the hijab for good, shtupped, drank. Pretended it was for her around her family. Could fake it. Not some New Atheist dickweed like me. We'd Facebook chat or DM sometimes; I always liked her. Maybe because I barely knew her. But still. She organized and rallied and grew as a person while I moved on from sports I didn't enjoy to self-medicate with dick jokes and thumbing through *The Chomsky Reader* (i.e., stuff I didn't enjoy).

Maybe I said the right things and thought the right things, but I had never done the right things.

"... yeah? Like, with so much on the Left, there are shades of gray," she said. "The choice isn't always yours; we don't all have the ability to participate in direct action, but we can affect change in different ways. Your political comedy fits somewhere. And it wasn't even why people were upset at you, at least I don't think."

"Huh?"

"You aren't a fuckboy, or anything."

A cease-and-desist warning echoed from the riot cops. Another helicopter rumbled above. A couple of anarchists breached the Wienermobile and started hucking cheddarwurst. Two old hippies started fencing with jalapeño dogs. Principal Schmidt taunted the police, begged them to make her a martyr.

My phone kept buzzing.

"I should really get going," I said.

"Is it . . . maybe this is too forward but Addy said something about—"

"Nope. Yeah, no. Everything is fine. Well, everything is bad. Life is perpetually bad, but everything is adequate. It's chill."

"Right."

"It was good to see you," I said, frozen, trying to decide how much physical contact would be construed as normal. "Again. Like last night. Which I remember."

She leaned in, squeezed, made the decision for me. I hugged back, lightly, pretending to feel warm and casual around another human being, a friend.

Mercifully, it ended.

Then the phone vibrated.

"Hey," she said as I peeled away, "whatever you're doing, make sure you don't talk that crazy stuff like last night though. That hotdog, sandwich stuff."

"What?" I said. Some deeply embedded flight-or-fight reflex flipped on. I felt the Wienermobile driver's eyes. I wanted to get high.

"That was the problem. The politics stuff, I thought, went well. It was that other joke."

"What other joke?" My eyes bounced from Nala to the cops to the bullhorn to the crowd.

"How messed up were you?" she laughed.

"Um."

"Dude, Jude, you lost the crowd when you went on this insane rant about how a hotdog is a sandwich. You yelled at people, roasted them, you seemed just as angry about that as you did about the rise of American fascism."

"Well, I'm not."

"I know."

"I'd like to get more politically active. Maybe. I gotta do more. Enough talk. Well, could talk it out over coffee. With you. Or not. But I'd like that. Probably."

"Sure."

"Nonetheless, a hotdog is absolutely a sandwich."

I didn't have time to brace myself. The clotheslining Wienermobiler cracked me in the neck and sent me sprawling toward my car. I banged my shoulder on a hubcap just as the riot police charged the wall of protesters, bashing them with shields and pepper-spraying all of us. A stun grenade burst near the hotdog/sandwich. Principal Schmidt screamed a Yeats poem into the bullhorn as they yanked her into a paddy wagon. Mere anarchy was loosed upon Highway 55 as nightsticks cracked heads in full daylight, stun-guns zapped anti-racists into submission. Aunt Lydia called again. I let it go to voicemail and waited for things to calm down, like Mom had done my entire life and wouldn't be doing much longer.

"ARE YOU GONNA charge me for a consultation?" I asked the paramedic who was demanding I go to the emergency room. "Like, you could just diagnose the thing here?"

"Buddy, you've got a dislocated shoulder. You need to see a doctor."

"What happens if I don't?"

"What? This is all treatable, but you have to have it treated."

"So, I dunno, maybe 24 to 48 hours before things get really bad?"

"I dunno. Maybe. But this is your health. You can't put a price on it."

"I can't," I said, trying and failing to raise my arm, "but the Fairview Health Center can. They think my health is worth a couple hundred thousand dollars if I need surgery with general anesthesia."

"There could be lasting damage. You could—"

"I've endured worse."

Right hand poking around my collarbone, left arm limp at my

side, I cupped my shoulder and shoved it like a fork into an electric outlet. The paramedic's gum tumbled from his mouth. I raised both hands above my head and high-fived myself.

"That thing is gonna hurt so bad you'll—"

"Well," I said, grinning, "do you have anything for pain?"

"Yeah, but I'm not gonna—"

"Fine, I'll do it. I'm experienced."

This is how I found myself shooting morphine into my wrist as I continued to ignore Lydia's phone calls. Once I insisted via text that I was almost home (yet not almost home), I turned my phone off and wept. I preferred hydros, preferred not shooting or snorting, but the human spirit is indomitable. Still, this stuff was harsher, sludgier. I could still tolerate life, of course, but morphine came with fuzz, a buffering stream-of-consciousness. And yet! Body billowing out (what I, embarrassed-owner of a Saharan dry-streak, a never-enjoyed-it as much as enjoyed-it-being-over sexual history, remember as) an orgasmic glow, the loss of self, once the traffic and stragglers cleared, I headed home. Extremely fucked-up.

This ended up being less than ideal.

We lived in a neighborhood we couldn't afford. We couldn't afford not to. Until I dabbled in local celebrity during high school (and later through standup), my mother (and thus her children) struggled to generate self-worth.

Ergo, consumption.

Ergo, citing her children as her best friends, her only purpose in life.

Ergo, Evangelical Christianity and Oedipal subtexts with her sons.

I inched, grandma-style, on backstreets. The Oldsmobile groaned past the houses of graphic designers, professors, journalists, dogs. Doctors weren't uncommon. We endured split-levels and four-season porches. Ramblers. Sport courts with official dimensions. We were the only foreclosure I could remember. A neighborhood screwed by the Great Recession, I guess, but on a plane I couldn't theorize. Roth IRAs. Health Savings Accounts. Index Funds. Pensions. Had to retire at 65, not 62. Couldn't buy that boat.

We weren't "street" poor, or even "owns a dangerous dog" poor, but we were "above ground pool/melted cheese on Doritos" poor. PTA mothers called Mom white trash; Mom's family called her a libtard. In elementary school, she bitched out a teacher for throwing a holiday party. Something about the heavy casualties lost in the War on Christmas. In junior high, after Malik and I planned a foodfight then an "ironic" hunger strike then a coup, she screamed at an assistant principal for suspending my black friends longer than she suspended me. Mom found gay marriage immoral, disgusting, and phonebanked against a proposition to make it illegal in Minnesota anyway. Until she landed a gig typing up medical reports, she bounced from McNugget manufacturer to lunchlady to the only female line cook at Minneapolis' Cheesecake Factory. All while riding public transit blind, without even a seeing-eye dog (because we couldn't afford it). Years of bending, chopping, and dishing led her to trade slipped discs for carpal tunnel, in addition to the second round of cancer. Life was choosing more pain or more debt. Then, to patch together the veneer of middle-class normalcy, she chose a subprime mortgage. And, even though she hated the Catholic Church for policing her divorce and her body, she tithed anyway.

Meanwhile, Dad licked envelopes and stamped checks for $8.00 an hour. Inspiring. I remember him slogging home in the same suit every day looking like a wet newspaper, sweat and dandruff crashing into his glass of Wild Turkey 101. Because Mom and I had pre-existing conditions, we couldn't access health insurance. Fast-forward through a few of my in-patient stays and her second cancer scare, and The Old Man came unglued, beat Mom like a Bobo doll too many times, divorced her, and passed on paying child support. Until it became clear Mom was dying, like really extinguishing this time, I saw him two or three times a year. He skipped my high school and college graduations. Saw me play football once in ten years. Before she died, I'm not sure my Dad and I had ever shaken hands, let alone hugged.

So it was a pleasure to see him smoking a cigarette in the driveway as I swerved onto Mom's block. Camouflage pickup trucks and battle-ready SUVs spread across the yard like acne. Boris Lawrence Glick must have walked. If my life at that time could lend itself to (interesting) narrative retelling, he might've materialized as a wraith, King Hamlet sans an arc. Instead, he double-fisted Pall Malls.

I parked behind Lydia's American-made guzzler.

"Boris," I said. "Thanks for holding the line."

He nodded, bit his lip. Probably the least sexy thing that has ever happened.

"Jude . . . yep," he said, eyes flipping between a multi-colored paper stack and the grass.

He blew a smoke ring. Top form. He'd allegedly been handsome once, and I'd seen pictures that, if they were indeed Boris, check out. A young Jeff Goldblum with a Jewfro. Now, a walrus. Maybe a dead one. In cargo shorts, flip-flops with socks, and a tall-tee that couldn't cover his gut. He was also wearing a sombrero.

My Boris diagnoses alternated between bipolar disorder and severe social anxiety. He was also, to use the clinical term, a piece-of-shit. There might have been a sprinkle of spectral autism, too. Why not. Like some ancient creation myth, I'd Rube Goldberg'd an explanation for Boris, a dash of sexual abuse, a dad with PTSD, adoption because his parents simply got tired of parenting, and, voila, the inability to love or be loved. But Mom blamed it on financial stress. And all that other stuff, too, but mostly financial stress. To her, he could have either loved his family, suffered alongside us and chiseled away at our debts, or not loved his family, not suffered alongside us, and nonetheless materially supported us with alimony and (for my brothers at least) health insurance.

He chose neither.

After a couple years in prison, during the probation/work-release portion of his sentence, Boris claims to have broken his tailbone after a crackhead colleague prodded his ass with a fork lift. The State of Minnesota, probably knowing he'd never find employment and/or wanting to avoid adjudicating a pegging incident, said "Sure!" and supplied him with SSDI. Which came with Medicare. To be fair, because my mother was blind, she qualified for SSI, which, when not messed with by Republicans or Democrats-who-are-basically-Republicans, tossed her Medicaid breadcrumbs. Nonetheless, it was not always comprehensive, not always available, or not helpful for chronic, expensive illnesses.

Boris fucked us over.

"What's going on, Dad?"

My high kept rippling, a cascade of patience, a flow of bliss.

He flicked a cigarette butt. Didn't care that it landed on my shoe.

"Where have you been?"

"Y'know, I could barely begin to tell you."

He sniffed, fired up another Pall Mall. "Want it?"

"What?"

"Well," he said, putting it to his mouth, "while you were on some . . ."

"Boris."

"Picaresque jaunt. Some meandering, ah . . ."

I sighed at him. He puffed.

". . . roundabout. Pointless detours. Extraneous rubbish . . ."

He flipped the still smoldering heater over his shoulder. I sometimes forgot that he was a helluva lot better read than me, even if he didn't graduate high school. Whereas most people love their spouse or raise children as a hobby, Boris loved being emotionally vacant and raised my blood pressure as a hobby. He never bothered to learn how to use a computer, but I suppose I never Googled "How to overcome childhood emotional neglect."

"Whatever you were you doing, which must have been nothing judging by whatserface's reaction, the sheriff came, bank is expediting the stuff, and Paula, y'know, Mom, lost consciousness, I guess."

"Are you drunk?" I asked. "The stuff?"

He shook his head. "House."

I stood, allowing the high to wash over me a little longer. It felt good, feeling good. Occurred to me I should try to feel good more often. Could be good for me. Self-care, of course, is bullshit, but maybe I needed more good bullshit instead of bad bullshit. If people, in their bulgur-and-yoga-induced bullshit, conquered life's bullshit vis-a-vis stupid but personally meaningful bullshit, maybe it wasn't bullshit.

This was bullshit. The only intellectually honest self-care is suicide. We have established this. The psychiatric records suggested Boris and I agree on at least one thing.

"Don't bullshit me, Boris."

He shook his head again.

"It's not great, kid. Life. People like us."

I nodded.

"Seems we've got ninety days."

Then I slow-blinked.

"There's also some personal and public debts Mom didn't tell you about."

Then I rubbed my chin.

"And, I guess, these are debts that children can inherit."

Then I kicked my car so hard the front bumper fell off.

Boris rubbed his scruff, pinkied something out of his eye.

"Some guy, Nehemiah, called, too. Your museum. Some incident."

It was a Saturday, Jude, you fucking idiot. You always worked Saturdays.

"Incident?" I asked, my ears filling with a metallic rattle.

"Yeah. An incident."

"What sort of incident, Boris?"

Boris sniffed, scratched his ass, sniffed again. The neighbor, Mr. Bonser, clambered from his John Deere riding mower, tai-chi'd as it rumbled in concentric circles, and bowed for his long-suffering wife when the green beast puffed to a stop.

"Incidentally," Boris said, "I am too drunk to recall."

"DEY'S TRYNA PUT in dere Shania Law here in God's country!" my wife-and-child-beating, cattle-raising, 8th-grade-educated Polack grandfather hollered over the cable news panel. I was watching the coverage in the living room when I got bored of watching my mother die in her bedroom. She was, indeed, unconscious. Each breath was a choke, a pant, then a snore. Every time she inhaled, her central nervous system weighed the pros and cons of just letting her die, but even Mom's brainstem was stubborn; she continued dying gasp by gasp. They'd moved her into the bedroom, so she could fade with some dignity. Maybe they knew I didn't want to reupholster the couch if she kept wetting herself. I could either hold her blueing hands and stiff-arm my tears, or listen to an illiterate geriatric analyze geopolitics. For now, I chose the latter. "Goddammit, it ain't right, Jude. Our peoples is strugglin' and they let more'n'more in."

"You drive an SUV," I said. I could've pointed out that my grandfather's first language was Polish, that his father came over on a boat a hundred years ago, but it wouldn't have mattered. My cousins, my giant Catholic family, the pipefitters and lead abaters, the bricklayers and housebuilders, the PCAs and DWIs, paced the composite blend carpet, opining about the Deer Opener and Gopher football season and how Mom married a kike, and why Muslims are evil.

The facts were sketchy, and nobody got hurt, but this morning, when I should've been at work by 8:15 a.m. for a donor presentation of that new Delacroix exhibit, three American citizens, Minnesotans who the media quickly assumed were Muslims because they grew up in Cedar-Riverside, had driven an eighteen-wheeler into the museum's atrium. Possibly an accident but "the situation" was "fluid." They broke some windows, scraped a veranda, knocked over a bollard. Because it was early, only a few dozen people were there.

Because a bunch of VIPs (i.e., rich white people, and a retired vice president, and a sitting senator) were there, the MPD (and news media) littered alcoves and vestibules. The truck guys panicked, jumped out of the cab and were wrangled without exchanging gunfire. CNN, which I insisted we watch despite grumbling about "Fake News," reported the trio were three mostly secular Somali-Americans seeking to call attention to the Yemen humanitarian crisis. The men said they made a wrong turn. Fox News claimed the trio were lying and really intended to blow up the museum, to destroy cultural artifacts a la the so-called Islamic State. The FBI scampered into full-on Islamophobia mode and apparently started questioning entire floors of apartment buildings, seeking a dragnet. Already in the state, already too many politically exploitable coincidences, the Republican Nominee tweeted something racist about No Go Zones and people named Muhammad. This is what prompted Scheisskopf's appearance on *Weekend Edition* with Schmidt and befuddled Scott Simon. I guess the Minneapolis Left found the whole thing un-chill.

To me, the whole thing seemed stupid. Maybe because my mother was slowly asphyxiating down the hall, but still. There were no guns, no bombs, no casualties. You could see the alt-right blogosphere bending this into A Big Deal, and CNN had just cut to the rally in Duluth, two hours north in our economically decimated Iron Range, but the men cooperated with authorities, were confirmed Red Crescent volunteers, and, after a CAIR lawyer showed up, supposedly claimed the only objective was media attention with the goal of ending U.S. imperialism and/or cutting aid to Saudi Arabia. I tried telling my grandfather, cousins, Mom's evangelical friends that white nationalist militias had taken to blowing up mosques or burning African-American churches, and it never got covered. That none other than Stephen Scheisskopf—yes, that Stephen, yes, I know, we grew up together, yes Mom was not fond of him and neither was I—considered an ethno-state viable and preferable. They told me I didn't get it, that I was too stuck in my *Chomp-skeet* books and ironic t-shirts. But man, three humanitarians with Arabic script sweaters get into a car accident, and Middle America needs to breathe into a paper bag. Everyone knew the non-psychotics and non-racists would forget about it by Tuesday, but it was a three-day weekend and shitty TV is our national pastime.

One of my brothers, Tom, slumped over, smelling like rolling papers and stems.

"Me and Chris wanna go out for a little bit," he said. "You should sit by Mom again."

"You're gonna leave? She could . . . something could happen any minute."

"Took you forever this morning. We want a break."

He shuffled toward Mom's room. I hadn't swallowed opiates in several hours, suddenly felt the urge. Mom kept her stash in a kitchen cabinet, and the kitchen was presently loaded with clucking Midwestern aunts, cousins, nieces. With nothing to do but follow backwards gender roles until my mother died, they'd taken to baking cookies, pies, cakes, hot dishes, anything to cloud out the day's realities.

I turned up the television as they live-streamed his entrance; Scheisskopf exited stage left. The Candidate waved at the frothing white folks, the bleating U-S-A chants that echoed across the airplane hangar. Machinists in red hats, phrenologists who teach kindergarten, meth-carved grandmothers following politics for the first time. White people too dumb to realize they were white people with a voice voiced the opinion he was a voice for the voiceless, a man whose dander and business acumen and willingness to bring up his penis size during a Republican debate would restore this country to . . . something. Jim Crow? Supply-side circle-jerking? No more bowling alone? My grandfather snapped his suspenders, giddy with white supremacy on the afternoon his second-oldest daughter would die. The strum of some nationalist hoedown, a spotlight trailing The Candidate as he rode the working class, the suburbanites, the neo-Nazi white light, the opioid epidemic white heat. His goons, a private security detail who sometimes wore brown shirts, took to flogging protesters, or just black people who "didn't belong there." But not today. Not yet. Still, this tension, the subtext of Helter Skelter, made his rallies even more popular, worthier of more BREAKING NEWS! coverage. American flags. Confederate flags. "God Hates Flags" flags. *Triumph of the "Will They Seriously Elect This Thrice Bankrupted Trust Fund Fossil/Racist?"* His red tie, long, too long, stretched to the inseam of his pants, an arrow pointing from his head directly to Hell. He was famous for his hair and fake tan, symbols of his absolute fucking weirdness. A frayed rope sitting on an orange bowling ball. He kept waving the wave of someone who only feels whole as the center of attention. I knew that wave.

"Folks," he said, wobbling to the lectern as the chants collapsed into murmurs. "This crowd, what a crowd. Tremendous. They say I have the biggest crowds, h-yooge crowds. But we all know that. We're the good people, okay? Smart. Smart people. Let me tell you: we know the media—very, dishonest, very dishonest, I know, keep booing, very, very, very unfair to me, folks, they, the media, fake news, they need to hear it, gotta hear it, folks, that's right—with the lies. Traitors, liars. If we—us—if we were smart? Tough? Line 'em up. Okay? Shut 'em up the old-fashioned way, the right way, right between the eyes. Enough. Enough is enough. Politics is rough. Many, many people are saying you'd get tired if you were me, okay? Except I have never been tired. Only of Democrats. Only of Democrats. The swamp, we're draining it, folks, draining the swamp. The swamp? It's now drained. Incredible. No doubt about it. And we'll drain it at that museum in Minnesota, believe me, I know, a museum getting—and my friend Stephen, you saw him earlier, great guy, great guy, very smart and very rich, even from, like, here, okay?—these people who hate us. The crime and the immigrants. Total disaster. Believe me, okay? So, when I win? And I'm a winner. Maybe you don't know, because of the fake media, who are doing a really very bad job, but I don't lose. Which means I win. And the—it's a museum. What's going on? Believe me. First place we go, okay? Minneapolis. First place we go . . ."

My grandfather yipped, clapped. He was functionally deaf, hadn't voted since Reagan, but celebrated like he'd won a fly-fishing tournament.

I skulked to my mother's death bed, found Boris reading some James Baldwin book he must have nabbed from my room. Chris and Tom had decamped. One of Mom's best friends, another evangelical Christian, was switching the radio over from 60s pop to some sermon. She looked up, started crying, and hugged me.

"I'm so sorry, Jude," she said. "It's just been so unfair. Your dad just told me about the house, too. You, Chris, and Tom will always, always have a place with me."

She lived about 300 miles away, farmed alfalfa and lima beans.

"Mmm," I said.

"And, Julian, I want you to know that God's kingdom is waiting for your mother. And—"

Boris heaved himself out of the chair and banged into my mom's desk, the desk she sat at eight hours a day for $9.00/hour and no benefits. He hacked something into his palm, inspected it, and left.

"Right," I said.

"Do you think we should ask a priest to come? And what about the advance directive?"

I did not think we should ask a priest to come. And what *about* the advance directive? The hospice nurse had swung by earlier, told us Mom wasn't totally lost yet, but we could only extend the clock artificially. Mom was always adamant that if she "ever got really sick, to get sick at home, around you boys." After digging around her purse, I found some crumpled card that said as much in legalese, with two notarizations. Earlier in the week, Mom had finalized her will—I helped proofread it—but I had no idea where she put it. The list of things to do as soon as she passed kept stretching. Like the TV fascist's tie.

"Uh, the priest—"

"Oh, good. Would your Mom prefer last rites? She told me that—"

"Whatever you think is best."

She rubbed her tear ducts, nodded, left.

I yanked a chair toward the bed and switched the radio back to the oldies that Mom, a solid and boring white person, loved. I kinda liked them, too. She would sit on the floor next to the radio and rock along, singing a Neil Diamond chorus or Marvin Gaye verse. I'd sit, too, just hanging out, an embarrassment, sometimes on Friday nights in high school when Reid, Addy et al. would drink and smoke and fuck. If I started partying I'd be an alcoholic, a Boris, so I spent the weekend watching my blind mother bop and/or tell me I just had to hang in there and things would get better.

I held her cold hand. She was so obviously wrong.

And now she'd die knowing our last conversation, the real conversation and not her organ failure-induced slurring, was an argument, our own solid gold oldie. We'd had it a thousand times. Me, miserable, suicidal and not afraid to talk about it. Her, literally dying and unable to comprehend how her oldest son—first generation college student, four years on the Dean's list, teller of jokes at shitty bars for free beer and sometimes $50, guy who got recognized by strangers in *both* Twin Cities and many inner-ring suburbs—could be so sad. Of course, she'd attempted suicide as a teenager. But unlike me, she never had the privilege of feeling sorry for herself, as a blind mother riding the bus to a food pantry or a frenzied 911 caller scrambling to get us into a battered women's shelter for a night.

I leaned over the bed, laid a rag on her forehead, and squeezed her hand harder.

A text buzzed in from Reid.

hope you're feelin ok bud. u got housed, eh? sorry 4 dumping u in car. wanted to spend night at addy's, etc. the boys are cumming over tonight to get lit. show up whenever.

He and I had a secret depression code. If either of us said, "Under Heavy Manners," it meant I was too depressed to leave bed, too depressed to drink, and that he would cover for me.

I turned off the phone and jammed it in my cords.

Mom wheezed. Sometimes a low moan, like a rusty swing, would eke out as she turned her head from side to side. The hospice nurses had told me cancer death is gradual. You lose your senses one by one, your hearing last. A person in a detente with cancer would ease out of consciousness over time, and that must have been her incoherent message, but consciousness is like a deep pool. A fully conscious person is a head above water, and maybe a dream is your head dunked a few feet under. The night before, I guess, she thrashed as if drowning. As death neared, Mom would drift to the bottom of the deep end and stay there, but she could maybe make out muddled voices, might feel death's creeping pressure through the fentanyl patch.

I squeezed both hands now and whispered: "I love you."

I SAT LIKE that for an hour, fell asleep, and woke up to everybody piling in with a Lutheran pastor. I nodded along through the bullshit, as we held hands, thirty-deep maybe, my relatives and Mom's friends crying through prayers and "Amens" while I mumbled or didn't even pretend. I hate religion, but hate myself for, you guessed it, hating it, valued it because I wish there was less human suffering, wish people, in our meaningless quest on this stupid rock could work to not hurt each other and then, mission accomplished, punch out after 60-90 years. People misunderstand cynics and pessimists, I think. I hate the human race, yeah, but mostly because the human race is such a waste of . . . human potential. We don't need be this shitty yet find new ways to ruin the world and other humans every day. When we had the go-to argument, my position of "life as meaningless suffering then death" horrified my mother, who genuinely believed God created us and all that fairytale trash. Yet, as everybody—including

Chris and Tom and Boris—filed out and left me alone with her again, I found myself praying for the first time in my adult life. I didn't want her to die, obviously, but I prayed I wouldn't forget her goodness, her total aversion to vengeance and bitterness. I've been praying a lot lately, maybe because it's something to do, but I eventually realized that either my bedside prayer wasn't answered or that my vengeance and bitterness is stronger than God.

I'm glad I don't believe in God. Because I wouldn't want Mom to see me now.

AFTER SUNDOWN, AFTER a few more hours contemplating our lives and her bravery, after meditating on how one person could suffer so much yet keep going, I needed a breather. The TV now off, I sat on the couch and tried to read *Self-Help* by Lorrie Moore while folks bustled up and down stairs, ate, drank, bumbled around the kitchen. Mom's friends and her favorite sister were bedside now, and my mind kept wandering to the obituary I might submit to the *Star Tribune.*

Paula Lucille Glick (nee Szymans) died after a really shitty, tragic life (at, Jesus Christ, the age of 51). Born to a belt-wielding Polack with an 8th grade education and his alcoholic, Swedish sweetheart, Paula and her four sisters grew up on a farm in Dawson, Minnesota learning 20th century skills like being oppressed by men and how to milk a cow. For three years, she received a couple meals, a couple beatings a day. Her parents would trundle over gravel roads, drunkenly roll through the one stoplight, and then scream at their daughters for having the audacity to play with toys. They were devout Catholics, obviously. So devout that when my mom went cross-eyed at three-and-a-half and started crying about how her face hurt, they'd send her to bed without dinner. When this kept up, they tossed her into the jalopy and had her looked at by the University of Minnesota.

Turns out she had cancer. Turns out my grandparents let that one slide. Turns out when they do that, you lose your eyesight and live the next 50 years of your life blind. Turns out being blind in 1960s rural America leads to your sisters, your mother, walking you into doors or stealing food off your plate. Turns out this gets boring after a while, so they put you up for adoption, fail, and send you off to foster care, where you'll be beat over the head with a clock so badly the city-slicking liberals in Child Protective Services remove you from the foster home and investigate the birth parents, who deny knowing anything about your back scars, or why you went blind, and continue pretending you don't exist. Turns out, decades later, this is the era they will talk about when they want to Make America Great Again.

Paula, an eternal optimist, plugged along, moved to a different foster home in the Minneapolis suburbs, 200 miles from the farms and manufacturing of Dawson, and, through charisma and grit, became Homecoming Queen at a 3,000-person high school. Like her fucked-up oldest son, she may have peaked as a 12th grader, but Paula was a good and normal person, so she logged a few community college credits, worked whatever labor gigs a blind woman in the 1970s could find and eventually married high school dropout Boris Glick, a wannabe librarian with latent mental illnesses and childhood abuse who now lives alone in a Section 8 single bedder. They grinded through two miscarriages before pumping out a son, Julian ("Jude" or "J.G."), who developed retinoblastoma at six weeks old and lost his right eye soon after. With the universe attempting to make Paula give up, Jude's surgeries came with complications and he'd live much of his life with a severely drooping, and thus mockable, right eyelid; eventually it looked abnormal but kinda fine. Unable to pay for the extensive medical costs, the universe then gave Paula a malignant brain tumor soon after birthing twins, Chris and Tom. The stress of raising three children on working class wages, compounded with the healthcare costs and Boris' unresolved issues, drove Boris insane. Months after brain surgery that solved this second bout with cancer, Boris raped the mother of his children at knifepoint and would have murdered her if not for Jude's calling of the police, a skill he'd developed through practice over his five-ish years of life.

I guess Paula probably made mistakes along the way; one might posit that marrying Boris or having three children when financially supporting only Jude proved difficult wasn't exactly wise, but fuck that victim-blaming bullshit; Boris is 100% responsible for giving Julian PTSD, and Chris and Tom an inability to confront emotions. Thankfully, and luckily, after the divorce, Paula's sisters and father completely cut her out of their lives, and she raised three boys on $8.00-$9.50/hour and some Social Security Disability help. Julian, as it stands, still remembers going to bed hungry and still remembers being made fun of for his two pairs of pants (on top of his *eye). He's an impractical dipshit and wants to be an artist (even though he went to a really good college and could've done other, actually lucrative, stuff) and is filled with shame, if not hate, for where he comes from and what he's chosen to do with his life (Comedy? Writing? What a fucking moron . . .) knowing how much his mother suffered because of money and debt. Paula, though, kept moving forward and raised her boys the best she could. She'd slap them, pull hair, gouge eyes, or punch sometimes, but on this point, her boys don't blame her.*

Fast forward to this decade and Paula, her youngest still elementary schoolers, developed leiomyosarcoma, a rapidly spreading and aggressive cancer of the smooth tissues that usually polishes people off within 18 months, 24 at most according to the University of Minnesota Medical Center's records. Paula endured seven years of chemo, radiation, and surgeries. Yes, seven. The longest battle with leiomyosarcoma in the history of the state of MN, according to the data. Her tenacity and pain tolerance and desire to live came with costs, though, and not just the healthcare debt. The cancer treatments required: orbital bone removal, a hysterectomy, a rewiring of her nose and throat system, skin grafts, a bone yanked from her leg and put in her head, the inability to eat a solid meal for the last three years of life, and around 2,500 days of unrelenting and severe physical pain. As of this writing, she is dying surrounded by friends, loved-ones, and the family who made her life unnecessarily difficult. She'll be survived by an absence that haunts her children for the rest of their lives.

In lieu of flowers, please think about how much she suffered whenever you don't feel like going to work, or do feel like bitching about the weather. Julian, her oldest (and, since 2005ish, suicidally depressed) son, keeps going despite impossible financial stress and hating every aspect of his life (yes, really, not exaggerating! Name a dimension, a point of pride you have in yourself, and he hates it so much in himself he wants to die!) because he saw her get through worse and feels he has no excuse.

Somebody called my name, waking me up from another nap. I still hadn't made it to the pill stash and began to worry I might miss my chance. But everybody had circled up around Mom's bed. The uncle I could tolerate said only: "It's time."

We held hands, all of us, me and Boris, me and Chris, Tom and

Chris, and I was conscious of not being self-conscious, even though none of us had exchanged affection, physical or otherwise, in the last decade-plus. The breathing now slowed to once a minute and came with a seize, a rattle. There are a few moments in a human life, I've realized, that you know are so important, so impossibly influential, that the action slows down and you can reflect, in real time, that you are overwhelmed. Losing your virginity, saying *I do*, the birth of a child, an event you know is historic as it happens. Scenes that unfold from behind a pane of glass, that you are experiencing, yes, but experiencing so intensely and meaningfully that you withdraw from the scene itself. Doing twenty minutes of comedy in front of 7,000 people, sticking my penis inside another human for the first time, 9-11, Election Night 2016, and the death of my mother.

She took a breath, a forever breath, chest hanging, expanding, swelling; back arching, stretching, spasming. The scratching and screeching and gurgling in her throat crescendoed, her life crescendoed, she'd never been more alive, would never be more alive, as we waited, waited, waited, waited for the exhale, waited through the orchestral swirls of dying and then . . .

She froze.

No exhale.

That was it.

She was dead.

No soul left the body, or the room, as far as I could tell. And for a second nobody cried, or heaved, or wailed. For one second we were liminal, teetering in this moment, not quite ready to cross from before to after. It's an insane feeling, intense, even rarer than the out-of-body moments, the stakes never higher but somehow not yet started, this pause, the mix of anxiety and dread and excitement at knowing you are about to face something 100% new and life-altering. And the one person I needed to get through this was cold and blue. My mother was dead. The only person I have ever loved, have ever turned off the incessant goddamn irony and riffing and nihilism for, was dead. She'd battled blindness and poverty and sexism and somehow maintained her optimism. And all it got her was a bank-owned house and a death she couldn't afford.

4.

EITHER/OR

FIVE STAGES, THEY say, but that's bullshit. There are only two stages: before and after.

As she spent the summer dying, I tried to imagine the after. A dead single mom, her oldest son, a house in foreclosure, medical debt as my only inheritance, these were the meaningless details of the most essential human story: the story of not getting what you want. But I figured that, with the Kierkegaard capstone, the strong opinions on improv comedy, the chronic suffering, I would continue to laugh in the cave of Trophonius, would manage fine, would grind teeth through the funeral, and adjust right away.

Instead, I got really high.

The first minutes of The After: her body still warm, Saturday night of Labor Day weekend for Chrissakes, I flipped into a do-er, like her, but first did drugs, unlike her, my brain floating in a jar of numbing agents, my body circulating opiate-warmth, a handful of 7.5/300, somewhere beyond the recommended daily dose blasting me into full-body orgasmic flush up-and-down my arms, legs, fingers, toes, as I called the U of M Oncology department, who had arranged to, whom she had insisted, take her body and learn something so other families not watch happiness drip from their lives like a chemo IV bag. The bonus: avoiding an open casket funeral, a plot, a stone, chiseled pith and sobbing around a pit. All this tradition you are supposed to procure lived in a distant income bracket. So this cemented the decision to have hungover grad students wheel the corpse off into the night, poke around for a couple years, and return her in a Ziploc bag. The mortuary scientists, dressed for a job interview, low-totem-polers working the literal graveyard shift, avoided my high, vacant eyes, and asked where they might find "the subject."

"Thank you for subjecting me to this," I said.

"Subject though?" they said.

"That way," I told them, my cousin Cassie, whose high school boyfriend owned a General Lee purchased with meth proceeds, rubbing my back. They jerked a stretcher to the basement side-door, suggested we say goodbye to the body. My brothers, roasting a spliff down the block somewhere, had said they couldn't handle it, had left me to endure, this time, and forever after, the vulgarities of life not as a unit but completely alone.

I kissed her forehead.

I said "I love you" one last time.

Then she was gone. My cat, my wife will never meet her. My children, should I overcome my fear of unleashing more human suffering without a priori consent, should I chance passing down the eye cancer, my personality, my curses, will never understand why their father spends so much time exhaling, eats the inside of his cheek, implodes head into hands when some toddler shouts "Mom!" on the sidewalk. It's pathetic, unhealthy, maybe deranged, but I still think of her every day, still think that if she were alive I would've chosen mistakes within one standard deviation of normal. But now, as then, as after, nobody, zero out of 7 billion, gives a shred of a single fuck about my day, my private agony, my inability to accept the shit I've been reared to shovel, my top 1% of 1% of self-hatred. Melodramatic. Pitiful. This meta-self-loathing, the incessant deprecation of my self-deprecation. Definitionally childish, loving your mother this much, hating yourself this much, admiring and missing the guidance from this uneducated, fundamentalist hick, this white Democrat, this white racist, this poverty lifer going hungry in the richest country in human history so her children could go less hungry, could wring middle-class aspirations and accomplishments out of poverty line realities. What have I done with her sacrifices? I've bitched, I've joked, I've done the best I could. Until I couldn't.

I swallowed an 80mg Oxycontin, indifferent to overdose for the second time in 24 hours.

Then I dialed her friends, my friends, as soon as the grad students closed the side door. I held it together. Laid out the facts. Told them

I'd Rube Goldberg a memorial service in the next few days, would scrape up enough money for a two-day obituary notice. This is America, after all. The sadness parade marches on.

We staggered around like drunks in detox. Like comics with stage fright. The aunts washed her sheets, stuffed medical detritus into boxes. First cousins called second cousins, who called people I didn't know and didn't want to feed after the funeral. Then I watched somebody flush her pills down the toilet. My pills. I logged it for later use but acknowledged, somewhere deep, brainstem maybe, that I would now be doing all of this sober, if not sweating and upchucking through junk sickness.

The calls and texts rolled in. I couldn't ignore them.

From Reid: *Sorry bud.*

From Addy: *Keep going. Please.*

From 889: *You've used all of your T-Mobile monthly high speed data, and will begin using the 1GB available in your Data Stash.*

Mom was not a listmaker, had not stashed much data for me, had the organizational skills of a blind, battered, bone-tired single mother. Which, like, duh. So I burrowed into cabinets and closets, yanked out Social Security cards, birth certificates, routing numbers. There was a will somewhere, a briefcase loaded with her version of foresight. She spoke of it frequently these last weeks, always in a whisper, but never explained its contents or whereabouts. The mania was useless. Gesture without motion. I couldn't file the death certificate until Tuesday anyway, couldn't access survivor benefits for my brothers without a coroner's report, couldn't decide if it was better for financial purposes to legally adopt them and declare them as dependents or to let them walk the plank of "Independent Undergraduates," braving the Student Informatics Puzzlebox they'd ignored all summer without an obvious Emergency Contact.

This whole time, as I shat out pros and cons, Googled "*Inherit bankruptcy?*" and "*What to do when mother dies early 20s?*" my dopamine-flooded synapses, returning to intellectualization as escape, considered the election (i.e., which psychopath would have earned my mother's absentee ballot). Neither, I hoped. *This* was voting in her self-interest. We hovered around the federal poverty line my mother's entire life. Last year, I made $16,242, 138% of the FPL. Even Boris, a felon who could not vote, had to move when his rent raised from $700/month to $750. Vote for the nominal liberal, you will regret it; vote for the nominal fascist, you will regret that, too; whether you vote for the nominal liberal or nominal fascist, you will regret it either way. Why would she vote for WALLS and DRAINED SWAMPS when she signed a Do Not Resuscitate order for financial reasons? Why would she vote for FOUR MORE YEARS of rationing healthcare when idiots like Scheisskopf promised WALLS and DRAINED SWAMPS? Poor people don't vote for one party or the other; the smart ones just don't vote. No campaign ads could change, or even acknowledge, that my mother worked eight to twelve hours a day for forty years, only to die $100,000 in debt on Kmart bedding.

"Beaker," Tom said, pinching my wrist around midnight. Beaker. Only Mom, Malik, and Boris' parents ever called me Beaker. Not sure Reid or Addy knew the origin, knew the nickname existed. Beaker. The shy and suffering lab assistant was my favorite Muppet. I'd cry when test tubes exploded in his face. Maybe the constant press of *What happened to your eye?* and *Why do you look so weird?* led me to sympathize with the miserable, meeping disaster magnet. No matter how poorly the experiment had gone, he'd always dust himself off and grind out another day. Just like I would when the eye questions peppered me. I'd come up with gnarly excuses—potato cannon accidents, Battle of the Bulge shrapnel—but eventually I settled on *scientific mishap.*

Ergo, Beaker.

Ergo, twentyish years of melancholy anytime someone deployed it.

"Uh, Beaker?" Chris said. "Should we move in tomorrow?"

Tom and Chris, see, had just graduated high school in June, and we'd already put a tuition payment on my credit card. They were seventeen. For a few more days.

The aunts and uncles and cousins and gramps had fanned out to their exurbs and farms. Boris crept like radiation poisoning into Mom's bed, what used to be their bed, for the first time since the divorce.

"Excellent question," I slurred, as high as I'd ever been in my life. Every rib in my corduroys, every knot in my back, felt like an erection doused in menthol.

"Should I ask Dad?" Tom asked.

"We'll do it. Just wake me up at 8:00."

"Are you—"

"Yes. I promised her. I promised you."

"But, uh, we don't need to bring Boris?"

I stared at them. Auburn hair, pimpled foreheads. Pink Floyd T-shirts and weed stench.

"I'm not your dad," I said, fighting the spins. "But, unfortunately, Boris is."

IN HIS TRUCK the next morning, Boris shifted from asscheek to asscheek, stuffed nicotine gum in his mouth. He'd been chewing it for years with no intention of quitting cigarettes.

"What?" I said.

"Nothing," he said.

We cut through downtown, dead except for bullet cartridges rolling across 7th Street, gang members sucking from brown-bagged forties, mostly empty skyways and street corners, totally empty bars. *The Wire* with less white guilt. No concerts at First Avenue this weekend, not even some 12-stepping has-been cashing checks off Prince's death. Seemed everyone was either hungover or too afraid to fabricate fun. I suppose a possible terrorist attack and the resulting Islamophobia will do that. Whatever. Fuck it. I never wanted to do standup again, had a gig Friday night anyway. I looked at Riverside Plaza, Soviet-style slabs of concrete covered in knock-off Mondrian prints. "Brutalism" they called it. "Crack Stacks" my relatives called it. The largest Somali community in the U.S., the poorest ethnic group in Minneapolis, and maybe the only folks in Minnesota having a worse weekend than me, Tom, and Chris. Dragnets and raids, even more Islamophobia. Who knew how many Muslims would die because white people couldn't police their imaginations?

"Actually, there's something I've been meaning to tell you," Boris said.

"Yes?"

"Uh."

I knuckled my temples, already feeling withdrawal symptoms.

"Look, Boris, I'm really not in the—"

"You need to be careful with drugs, okay?"

Grease and dandruff lacquered my sideburns. I couldn't remember the last time I took a shower. "You Nancy Reagan now? Is this a very special episode?"

"All I'm saying, J.G., is that you gotta be especially careful with acid."

Boris and I didn't talk. Our idea of father-son bonding was *not* throwing beer bottles at each other. But maybe people change. Maybe they would love me if I let them. Hell, I hadn't started crying until I heard Boris coughing up sobs in the bathroom.

"Acid, eh?"

"Yes, acid," he said, adjusting his sweatpants. "I know you like pills and heroin and shit, and if you ever need to score, it really does work to just, like, ask dudes under a bridge, but, seriously, you gotta be careful with acid. I'm not kidding around."

"Yeah?"

"It's serious stuff. Back in Cleveland, me and Carl Lapitus bought a bunk batch from some municipal lifeguard, and we had to see The Eagles sober."

I sighed, stared out the window, turned on NPR. Boris started to squirm, arched his back with a crack. Two hours down I-35. As we left Hennepin county, Minnesota's largest and most urban, the yard signs changed from blue to red. We bumbled past thousands of SUVs and minivans caking strip mall parking lots, account managers and stay-at-homers spending Labor Day weekend screaming at minimum wage grocery clerks. Past billboards letting us know that "ABORTION = STABBING BABIES TO DEATH! JOHN 3:16!" Past molding barns and cows fecal-blasting each other. Past Korean War veterans inching their walkers to the VFW for liver cirrhosis. How many people in the United States, I wonder, have a B.A. from a liberal arts college and a parent who grew up with this shit?

I switched off *Morning Edition*, the Scheisskopf coverage, the ominous subtext, and tried to read up on foreclosure law as Boris scratched his ass and stomach-rumbled. A self-described anarcho-syndicalist, he flipped on some braying shock jock, stuff he knows I despise, a show called "The Schtup," some flopping cock rambling about titjobs, another white guy furious with America because he can't fuck Hooters waitresses.

I turned it off.

We sat in silence. Boris farted. I cranked down the window. He farted again.

"Seriously, Boris," I said.

"I don't follow," he said, adjusting his sweatpants.

"Just say it," I said.

"Say what?" Boris said, asshole flapping and blowing sulfur.

"Jesus H. Christ."

We trundled some more. Tom and Chris sped ahead, broke up the caravan.

Boris moved wind.

Again.

I turned the shock jock back on.

"Hey," he said. "I was listening to that."

"To—"

"Yes. This guy, an audiologist, a regular. McDonalds? Says your acoustico-flatology says a lot about the, your, state. State of mind."

"Mmm," I said.

We touched eyes.

"J.G.?"

"What?"

"Or maybe, uh, Beak—"

"Absolutely not," I said, stretching my forearms, my fists.

"Now that Paula is gone . . ."

"Do you wanna talk, Boris? Like real people or—"

"Mom. She was hard on me, okay? Wasn't always telling you the right stuff. I wasn't that bad. I did my best. I tried. The money, Jude. It wasn't very easy. She was, I mean, I—"

"Shut the fuck up," I said.

"I'm just saying, Jude, that—"

"I'm just saying, Boris, that you locked me in an unfinished basement as a five-year-old while you raped the mother of your children at knifepoint in front of two toddlers."

He sniffed, wriggled into the gardening gloves he inexplicably wears when he's driving or tired. We whizzed the rest of the way to Winona without speaking.

An hour later, they checked us in. Some blond, unquestionably Norse doofus, smiling and prattling on about how excited this made him, how he'd love it if we could fill out name tags and pose for a family photo. Facebook material for student affairs.

"No," I said.

This Viking offspring, this Dude Who Thinks Baseball Is Exciting, vaulted his eyebrows then winked at Tom and Chris.

"Someone seems a little crabby, huh, fellas?"

"Fuck off," Chris said, grabbing the keys. Tom shrugged, grabbed his. The Aryan-looking cretin torqued his face into an admissions office smile.

Boris went with Chris. I went with Tom. It took us several tries to find his room. Finally hefting the fridge up six flights of stairs, watching disinterestedly as the metal base lacerated my hands and forearms, I felt good, like things would be a slog but a winnable one. I knew pain and obviously enjoyed self-laceration. Hence, the standup comedy. If I wanted the easy way out, I'd join an improv troupe.

I dropped the mini-fridge in the hall, shoved it through Tom's door.

His roommate and mother were delofting a bed. The father grumbled into a BlueTooth on Tom's would-be mattress. He wore a camouflage tie. The room was 12x12, white walls, gray carpet, sink and mirror in the corner, a place to tug-and-spurt without a pile of cum tissues.

"Hey," the man said into the BlueTooth, "listen, no, you listen, okay? The Johnson Account? Kayden and the MAOI? Don't drop this. Gotta run. Two city boys just walked in."

"Hi," I said. "Just a couple of city boys here!"

The mother rubbed her hands together, extended the right to both of us. I sensed immediately she was a real estate agent. The smile, the lilt. Minnesota-Nice-induced psychosis. Hockey pennants and a notorious red hat already covered their corner.

"So this is Tom, who wrote such lovely Facebook messages, and you must be . . ."

"Julian. J.G. The older brother."

"Ah, sure. Right. Your father, Mr. Boris, popped in. What an . . . interesting guy!"

Tom and I looked at each other. He set a box on the mini-fridge.

"What, if I might ask, Tom, do your parents do?"

"Um," Tom said. "Uh."

"Oh, a shy guy! You'll get along great with my Lars. Isn't that right, Lars?"

The roommate jumped down from the bed, whipped his hockey hair, said: "Sup."

Tom and I both sensed Lars wouldn't last long here, would join a frat, steady his nerves for rape with Smirnoff Ice, and eventually sue the school before doing community service for premeditated sexual assault. This double would soon be a single, and Lars would never go to jail. Cool country, cool system. Maybe he's born with it; maybe it's the patriarchy.

His copy of *American Rifleman* teased an interview with Stephen

Scheisskopf. Whatever *it* is, it certainly isn't smart.

"Is your mother around?" Lars' mom said as her husband answered a call and strode from the room, bumping me. "I was thinking us moms might have a little pow wow!"

"Our mother is dead," I said, eyes on the magazine. "Extremely dead. Could not be more dead."

The real estate agent gawked at us. Her Lutheranism could not withstand reality.

"She's dead as shit. Crazy amount of dead."

Lars scrunched his face at his mother. Tom looked at his shoes.

"She's dead as hell," I said. "And Mr. Boris is a deadbeat. This rules. College!"

We unpacked the rest in silence.

AFTER HOURS OF Tom, Chris, and I lugging crap in trash bags while Boris muttered about his back and read Victor Frankl "for the laughs," my younger brothers were officially college students. Or at least seventeen-year olds who lived in a college dorm less than 24 hours after their mother died.

Nauseous and aching, I popped one of the two percs I'd salvaged from forgotten bottles and walked toward the truck. Tom and Chris followed, probably dreading this goodbye as much as Mom's actual death. I'd tried eating an apple around lunch but started sweating and gagging after the first bite. I may have crapped myself a little. Withdrawal, grief, whatever. There was a fentanyl patch or two under Mom's mattress, unless someone had stolen it (after I had stolen it), but I knew I'd have to either quit cold turkey soon or turn to street heroin, a decision, even for someone who daydreams chronically about practicing self-care by (trigger warning!) shooting himself in the head, I considered crossing the Rubicon. Or, given the impossibility of planning a funeral and socializing at said funeral without narcotics, solving the Rubik's cube. I couldn't even be a fucking drug addict without money hindering my goals.

I felt jealous of my mother.

I'd definitely crapped myself a little.

"Hey, dudes," the Obergruppenführer from earlier called out as the four Glicks stood around playing emotional chicken.

"What?" Boris and I said simultaneously.

"You fellas didn't amend your Student Informatics Puzzlebox!"

"What?" Tom and Chris said simultaneously.

"Your SIP?"

I stared this guy down for the first time. Crocs, mismatched socks, khaki shorts with more pockets than students at this *regionally prestigious* diploma-mill. Seemed Boris and I registered his nametag at the same time because he spat out his gum as I hooted and clapped. Rudy Hess.

"Scatter," I yelled as Boris hummed the *Benny Hill* theme song. Tom and Chris started sprinting around the Oldsmobile, chasing each other *Scooby-Doo* style until Rudy took flight for the check-in station.

"Messhugeneh," Boris said. "What, now we gotta sit shiva for your mom?"

Mom. Bible-literalist, down-playing that she married a Jew, she'd probably smack me the way I'd acted today, and, finally feeling high, I couldn't decide if I cared.

"Bubkes," I said. "We're goys and you know it."

The student affairs guy re-appeared. Sans polo. Only A-shirt and recovery tattoos.

We stopped riffing.

"Look, I hate this," he said. "You think I enjoy working forty hours a week peddling this bullshit? My gramps is a semi-homeless ex-heroin addict who raised me into a drunk myself. So you don't know me, buddy."

"We were just joking, dude," Tom said. "My brother is a comedian and—"

"I heard all about his *set* with Lars Kiffmeyer and his mom, Dr. Wilkens."

"Doctor Wil—"

"And, the joke is on you two, because I'm the Resident Assistant for your building."

I looked at my brothers. They glared at me. Victimized, per usual, by a wraith for a father and half-blind nihilist father figure.

"So, here, yes," Hess said, forearm veins popping, "take the SIP, or don't, but ask yourself: can you care about lives that look different than yours?"

He tossed his papers in the air and sloughed off. We looked at each other, scratched ourselves.

"We're gonna go smoke, I think," Tom said.

"Y'all should leave," Chris said.

"Don't get caught," I said.

Boris farted again.

The old man and I saluted the boys. No hugs were exchanged. I told them I'd text when I figured out the funeral. Classes at this barely accredited state school started Wednesday. I told Mom they should've just gone to community college, that when she died I'd be stuck either financing their education or screaming at some financial aid officer to finance their education.

Boris gave them each a Minnesota state quarter and limped to the van.

I SPENT THE rest of Labor Day weekend bolted to the upholstery, suckling from a fifth of Wild Turkey 101, reading up on get rich quick schemes and NA meetings. I even sent some standup clips to a reality TV show. *American Idyll*. A talent show meets obstacle course meets MKUltra. Still, the tears leaked with other fluids: A funeral to plan, an opioid habit to kick, and an iced-over mother, stiff in some morgue.

Things were looking up.

I did the noble thing and decided to quit drugs not because Mom died, not because Boris overdosed on cocaine my first day of kindergarten, but because I was left with one perc, zero mothers with cancer, and a national holiday to endure. Saturday night, indeed, happened as I remembered. The fentanyl had decamped, the pill bottles pilfered.

As I drifted in and out of consciousness, the doorbell rang. I ignored it. It chimed again. I vomited. My spine felt singed, my right knee—a knee I'd needed surgery on since high school—pulsed with heat. I hadn't felt like this since my jock days. Every movement like two tectonic plates grinding against each other. My muscles somehow had the spins. Three knocks now. This lacked the panache of Burroughs, the tragedy of Lou Reed. I'd simply been on the verge of diarrhea since Sunday evening. No novels or Sister Rays to show for it.

I shoved myself off the couch and wobbled toward the foyer. I yanked the door open.

"J.G.!" my aunt Lydia screamed. "Hi!"

I blinked at her, licked my lips. My grandad muttered something in Polish. Lydia's daughter Cassie muttered something in white trash.

"Can I come in?" Lydia said, coming in.

"Uh." I stepped aside, retched in my mouth, swallowed it, and yawned. Maybe I needed that last perc. Or I could buy smack from Nehemiah's old dealer, punt on life, let Lydia, Tom, and Chris plan two funerals at once.

My godmother, grandfather, and 23-year-old cousin plunked into kitchen chairs. I inched to the table, stiff-armed the wall, and leaned against a cabinet. My calves twitched in my shorts. I was not sure I could get up if I sat down.

"You look really good, J.G., all things considered."

A pee stain etched my left thigh. I sniffed, blew my nose into my elbow. I smelled like fart and ammonia.

"Yah," my gramps said, tickling his suspenders. "Not bad dere, Julian."

"Have you started work on your mom's funeral?" Cassie asked, scratching her crucifix. "My godmother's funeral?"

"Um," I said.

"Because maybe Pastor Phil could help? Or the bankruptcy lawyer? Do you need money, hon?" Lydia said, knowing I needed money.

Sunday night, running the numbers in a flood of sweat and dried puke, it seemed possible, but not probable, that I'd make it to November in this house, internet and basic cable intact, if I ratcheted down to one meal and no snacks per day. If it got real bad, or there were unexpected costs before I returned to work after my seven days of unpaid bereavement leave, I could always supplement my caloric intake with 12-step coffee and donuts. Could always supplement my $13.72/hour with selling blood.

"I've got everything under control, Lydia."

"You betcha. Of course you do. But, and don't take this the wrong way, is there a reason you're shivering? It's 85 and sunny and the A/C isn't—"

"I miss Mom," I said. "I have a cold, and just want someone to tell me it's gonna be okay and make some chicken noodle soup, and now nobody ever will."

"Right."

We all stared at each other, rubbed our faces.

"Look, Auntie, Gramps, this has been a rough couple days and I really—"

"We'll get goin' soon dere," my grandfather said. Mom's cat, Lou Grant, brushed around my leg. "But, da ting is J.G., is yer ma owed me a bit a money, ya know."

I fiddled in my flannel and popped the last painkiller.

"Meow," Lou Grant said.

"This is not a good time, Gramps," I said, hoisting the cat over my shoulder and trying not to drip sweat on his ears. My credit card had a $5,000 limit. I'd swallowed up most of that on Mom's utilities bills and groceries once she stopped working in April. Tom and Chris received almost no financial aid, and we all lacked health insurance. Lydia, at least, knew all this, lived off her dead husband's trucking company inheritance, and smirked at me anyway as she bolted from the chair.

Lou Grant leapt from my arms and scurried away.

"Of course," she said. "Not a good time. A good time for interest then. If Paula couldn't learn some fiscal responsibility, then maybe you can, even on a security guard's salary."

I shook my head at her, upturned a palm. Cassie, who never graduated high school but collected diplomas from all sorts of treatment programs, nose-laughed.

"Shame you can't be more like your friend, J.G.," she said. "I see Stephen Scheisskopf on TV all the—"

"Mmm."

"Around a grand, is all, Jude. I ain't sayin' ya gotta pay it today, but I'm fixin' ta have it, well, sooner than later, yah?" Gramps said. "Sorry for the timing and all. Just anudder ting, I know."

Everyone stood. Gramps looked spryer than I did.

"I'm lying down now," I said, digging fingernails into my palm. "Nice to see you guys. I'll let you know about the funeral, and the money."

Hugs exchanged, tongues held, they slammed the door and muttered obscenities outside.

I stumbled toward the couch and pried a photo of Mom's parents from the wall. Konrad and Yulia. Scowling in a suit and sundress respectively. Judging by the color in their hair and lack of liver spots on their hands, this was around the time they'd given Mom up for foster care.

I spiked it, glass confetti raining on the rug. Standing over the crinkled gloss, I stared at my grandparents. Barely literate, speaking English like elementary schoolers. Sixteen-hour days in the fields for him, black eyes and boiling oatmeal for her. Konrad only stopped working a few years ago at 75, not because he even needed the money anymore but because he had no hobbies outside of drinking.

Yulia died when I was in diapers.

I glanced to the only other photo on the wall: my high school commencement, minutes after I made 10,000 strangers laugh for fifteen minutes, Mom clenching back tears as I wrapped her in my big arms.

"Why couldn't you love her?" I said, chewing my lip.

No answer from Konrad and Yulia.

I finished the Wild Turkey, jackhammers pounding my skull. It was 11:06 a.m. when I chased booze with an entire bottle of ibuprofen PM and eased into another suicide attempt.

"YOU WANNA WATCH *Matlock,* honey?" Mom said, groping across IV tubes and blankets for the remote a few weeks before I graduated college. I sat bedside at the University of Minnesota oncology ward, picking at lukewarm hospital food—chicken tenders, smiley potatoes—and considered telling Mom I'd been suicidal since junior high.

"Sure, yes. *Matlock.*"

"And then maybe explain what happened the other day? With this Colorful Stubbies class?"

"Cultural Studies."

She inhaled with a wince, exhaled with gasps. She didn't deserve this, and she knew it, grinning through the bone pain and the morphine drip. I held her hand as she nodded off to Andy Griffith's twang, waiting for her to wake up and/or battle back chemo brain so we could discuss why a counselor from Health and Wellness had left "an urgent message concerning Jude's mental health."

It started in Dr. Nehemiah Weaver's class.

No, it started when I enrolled at a liberal arts college.

See, even with 95% off the sticker price because of financial need, I still couldn't afford school. That extra $3,000, multiplied across four years of rising tuition, was a year of Mom's wages (when she was healthy enough to work). I actually sent some of my work study payout her way so Chris and Tom could afford reduced-price lunch.

To eke out a degree that wasn't designed for me, I lived in an off-campus trap house without heat and ate seven to ten times a week. Ramen noodles, whiskey and cornflakes, whatever opiates I could skim. When folks questioned the necessity of going hungry while attending a liberal arts college, I asked what their parents did for a living and, undoubtedly the progeny of cultural anthropologists or corporate raiders, they would shut up and/or not invite me to parties.

I went to the rich kid school and not the state school because the former was cheaper for the handful of unfortunates they deigned to admit. And it bolstered the CV (especially when *who you know* is only construction workers and typists). I had a Jesus-in-the-Temple aversion to loans, so the cheapest option was the only option. Hunger, foolishness, grinding toward Phi Beta Kappa. A poor kid from Guatemala, a semi-depressed gal from Albania, and my first-year roommate, Ignacio—the child of Mexican migrants and the most compassionate person I've ever met—constituted my antisocial network.

I worked a flex-shift abating asbestos, lead, and mercury three nights a week. Spent my breaks wolfing down cognitive neuroscience textbooks, novels by sad-ish white men. I obsessed over maintaining a 4.0 not because I liked school but so I could prove my haters less right. At SureVac Systems, my coworkers—wife-bashers and heroin addicts, guys who didn't graduate high school and knew exactly one person who went to a four-year college (i.e., me, aka, "College Fuck")—rained shit-talk as we scraped floors, knocked out walls, loaded barrels, and developed mesothelioma. Combined with earning $8.00/hour copying and faxing grant proposals in the Psych department, I saw life after graduation as unskilled labor or, if I got lucky and postponed killing myself, unskilled office work supplemented by standup.

Things were looking down.

A few days before that night at Mom's bedside, the Monday morning after Spring Break, I got off at 2:00 a.m., sleep deprivation and nausea making the drive across the Mississippi almost impossible. I had three hours of class starting at 8:00, a sociology essay I hadn't started due in 48 hours, a mother who found it difficult to breathe on her own, and the senior thesis that none of the Wellness Center shrinks or Al-Anon steps could do anything for me. When I cobbled together Medicaid, or endured the sliding scale clinics, I'd bested citalopram, sertraline, fluoxetine, bupropion, venlafaxine, Omega-3 fish oil, Cognitive Behavioral Therapy, Mindfulness-Based Cognitive Behavioral Therapy, lithium, diazepam, doing pushups, Psychodynamic Therapy, Client-centered Therapy, Eye Movement Desensitization and Reprocessing, David Foster Wallace references, hiking with vegan lesbians and/or dudes who unironically celebrate 4-20, entertaining libertarianism, disavowing libertarianism, yoga,

Pilates, sleeping eighteen hours a day, sleeping eighteen minutes a day, captaining high school and college football teams, hating Reid, loving Addy, gabapentin, live comedy, live improv, daydreaming about Madeline Einstein, getting ejected from the financial aid office, and memorizing poems by poets who committed suicide. None of it worked, never even approached that numbing and emotional blunting your mild-to-moderate depressives lament when taking *happy pills*. My brain is a magma flow of self-harm every day and the only thing that's ever plugged the volcano is opiates. Ignacio and my fellow boarders at least understood suffering.

Sore and sad from loading portable showers onto pallets, I slouched toward our could-be condemned home to find a group of dudes buzzing from a bong. They hacked and spat and sucked from their forties. Another guy puked and then pissed in his vomit. I gagged and sighed. Someone offered me a joint as my phone pulsed. I waved him off.

"Yo, J.G., right?" said Ryan Yoder-Henley, the blond, bandana'd scion of a hedge fund billionaire. We sat next to each other in Nehemiah's class, Ignacio across the room; he'd been over to the house a million times, lived next door freshman year, and seemed to be boning and/or trying to bone Madeline Einstein despite a rumored girlfriend at another Minnesota liberal arts college. Per Reid, Addy had matched with him on Tinder during one of their break-ups, though Reid always looked for excuses to pork girls out East. "Is it true you know Stephen Scheisskopf? That Fox News contribu—"

"Is there a party upstairs?" I asked, glancing at my car and contemplating a night in the backseat.

"Raging like Pinochet at U Chicago," he said. This was my (unfunny/esoteric) punchline, disseminated at the Roast of Milton Friedman, an Econ department event I had headlined to zero fanfare before finals last semester. Madeline Einstein had captained the thing, only relented to my presence when nobody who wrote for the humor magazine, including co-editor-in-chief Nala Bashir, could produce more than three minutes of live comedy.

"Great." I pivoted, started for the street.

"Because Ignacio and Nala said you knew . . ."

My phone vibrated again. The University of Minnesota hospital. Every time a call rolled in, I assumed it was *the call*, that I'd have to flip from enduring conversation with hipster gentry to enduring conversation with medical oncologists and coroners.

"Hell—"

"Don't worry, but I fainted," Mom said. "Lydia couldn't get down in time, so Boris took me to the ER. I crawled to the phone. Neurology for now but probably Oncology later. My white blood cell count is dangerously low."

"Why would that be?"

"Well, either the last inpatient chemo sorta depleted me, or, uh, maybe it's spreading. Bone marrow, they think."

"Jesus Christ."

I felt it immediately. A jolt down the spine. This was not *the call*, but it was Mom's, my, demarcation line. If it *had* spread to the marrow—and an email from her oncologist a few hours later confirmed her fears—we were looking at no more than eighteen months. She'd be dead before my 24th birthday.

". . . and I was just wondering," Ryan slurred at me, tottering over as I paced in the front yard, "if you could maybe put me or my dad in touch with this Scheisskopf guy? Because—do you *know* Ignacio Martinez or Rosie Rafowitz-Fackelmann? We've got this project in Econometrics looking at media companies? So . . ."

"Jude?" my mom said. "You sound busy. I'm gonna let you go."

"But—"

She hung up as Ryan prattled on. I flipped him off, bounded across the grass, locked myself in the car, and wore myself out trying not to cry.

When I woke up late for Cultural Studies/Creative Writing/Creative Whining class—*Personal as Political, Self as Character: Artistic Meditations on the American Experiment*—my mood was apocalyptic. Back throbbing. Checking account stocked with tumbleweeds. Mother really going to die.

I'd packed pills and a loaded flask. We were discussing two books that made no sense as companions: *Racecraft*, a psychosocial debunking of race as either legitimate or immutable, and *The Great Gatsby*. James Baldwin, the poor bastard, was assigned as ancillary reading for our cohort of rich whites, D-III athletes, Ignacio, and me. Nehemiah—or, at that point, Dr. Weaver—had been combative lately, notebook-punting and blackboard-slashing his way through *Moby-Dick*, *I Love Dick*, and *Dick Van Dyke*. Like Ishmael, I felt the loomings of catastrophe.

I stepped into the empty room and kicked a desk into the corner; I always sit next to the exit. I pondered my unhappiness, wondered if it would ever get better. They'd said college would be the best time of my life, but it was eight semesters of watching people make friends, meet up for drinks, blow college radio show hosts, kvetch about Plan B, major in English, smoke spliffs, smirk at people from the Midwest even though we were in the fucking Midwest, stumble from house party to house party, sling nickel beers and dollar shots, fuck Phillips Academy field hockey players, fuck Marlborough School violinists, fuck responsibilities, and most of all shrug-off the ups-and-downs of years 18-22 because this was America and our president was nominally liberal and a veritable inspiration, and life was bad at times, sure, but we'd all find ourselves. As if there was anything worth finding.

Schmidt was right; it doesn't get better. Every stage of life simply gets worse in different ways. And the only kids who saw that were the ones like me, or like Nala and Ignacio, the ones who shouldn't have been there, who no one wanted there, who were tokens of economic or racial diversity, who knew higher ed—whether a B.A. or M.F.A. or M.B.A.—was not for us. Too skeptical, too beat-down by life, too concerned with our physical hunger and our financial foolishness to debate Foucault's panopticon or close-read Henry James. Instead, we muttered during lectures and wrote angry emails to college administrators who didn't give a fuck if we felt so socially isolated that we regretted every second of matriculation. As long as we ginned up tuition payments. Here, at my idyllic liberal arts college, I ossified my hate for rich people. And, to me, anyone with college educated parents or more than $60,000 dollars in yearly family income, anyone who has never been forced to seriously consider living in your fucking car or chose between tuition and eating, is rich. Fuck them.

I seethed and swigged as people giggled down the hall. Why am I so angry? So sad? Is it the eye? That any time two strangers giggle on the bus I assume it's about my appearance? Folks say it's fine, a super-lazy lazy eye. Nothing debilitating, freakish. But goddamn, I can't see a couple drunks whisper at Liquor Lyles without the shot of fear, the creep of self-consciousness chiseled by Scheisskopf and Madeline Einstein and even well-meaning adults asking what's wrong with my own scarlet letter. *Cyclops. Peter Falk. Beauty Is in the Eye of the Jude Glick.* My first impression is always the wrong one, always looking and feeling less than. Not like I sought this bile or crafted this misanthropy. How else could I survive? The only weapon that's ever defeated the stares, the talking about it behind my back, the horror of meeting new people is . . . irreverence. Jokes. This is what landed me on stage at Acme Comedy, at a network reality TV tryout, at the MAOI with Stephen Scheisskopf and the president-elect of the United States.

I flicked dandruff from my matted mop. Ryan Yoder-Henley staggered past.

"Sick party last night, Drew," he said, hitting a vape pen, "you shoulda rolled through. Nala Bashir and Belcalis Pulido got possession tickets, but other than that it whipped ass. Or maybe grass."

"Chortle," I said, chewing my lips. Hungover and high, he planted himself next to me, adjusted his bandana. Of course, Belcalis and Nala are both women of color.

"Seriously, man, you can be a bummer sometimes, y'know that? Even Ignacio Martinez thinks so. Do you know him?"

Unsure if he was patronizing me or honestly this stupid, I ignored him, fingered two roxis, smashed and sniffed them as Ryan scrolled Instagram. It was 7:52 a.m. Already drunk, and now drifting into a euphoric top coat with a suicidal base, I slipped into loathing and envy. The scuttlebutt was Yoder-Henley had spent four years jizzing his way from Snelling and Grand to downtown Minneapolis. What did Ryan, or any of these professional-class progeny, want other than to tell people they lived in New York or LA, where they continued to have bad sex and worse relationships? I sighed, scraped gunk from my eye. Why do the people with nothing to say receive the most encouragement to say it?

Ignacio entered, pouted at me. A phalanx of army jackets, skinny jeans, and backwards snapback hats soon followed. Gals from Brooklyn high-fived blokes who summer in Nice, their laceless boots and gluten-free bodies producing an orgy of status anxiety. Madeline Einstein—brown Doc Martens, ripped tights, wavy black hair and a scowl—glanced at Ryan, then a football player who had allegedly made her cum after a Geography majors party, then Ignacio, then not me.

That I cared about this shit—which legacy admit plowed which eco-poet, how the brinksmanship of 21st birthday invites reverberated across our liberal arts campus—glazed me in self-dissatisfaction. Christ, I had a mother with Stage IV cancer. Maybe that explains my own metastasizing rage.

I was open about only attending America's 24th best liberal arts college because I didn't get in anywhere better. I never visited, never owned a book stuffed with college profiles. Only took the ACT because we qualified for a fee waiver. I applied anywhere that would let me apply for free and landed in the top-25 of *U.S. News & World Report*. Since high school, anytime I needed a jolt of anger to endure another eighteen-hour day at the museum or helping Mom, I would think of my college classmates, or at least the white ones, sons and daughters of corporate litigators or neurologists or art historians, folks who joked about the "idiots" who subsist on ramen and Burger King.

Seven minutes after class should have started, bourbon and pills and suicidality humming through my marrow, Nehemiah limped to the lectern holding his head. He reeked of Wild Turkey 101. I had a hunch he was an opiate addict, but today would confirm it.

"In America," he slurred with bobbing cornrows, "you're either hooked on pills, hooked on phonics, or you grow bangs and head to a school like this. Guess where your faggy professor lands?"

Groans, shudders, mentions of safe spaces. I pictured Nehemiah's office, all books and specialty rugs, caked with weed clouds and what might've been opium, the two of us reading Burroughs on his white chaise longue and whisking each other's—

"Now, before you round up pitchforks and make a list of demands on some Tumblr, who wants to present on whatever I told you to present on?"

Most of us were five weeks from graduation and took this class to satisfy the multiculturalism requirement. Nehemiah was a visiting assistant professor—an adjunct (i.e., a well-educated babysitter)—and half the class had been Snapchatting through lectures while the other half, including Madeline Einstein, had the audacity to demand educational value in sternly worded letters to the Provost.

The football player who allegedly made her cum and only got in here because he could long-snap raised his hand and started reading from his iPhone.

"Well, um, first," said White Man Who Liked Fishing, "I'm thinking my two most important identities are that I like sports and that I'm a Republican."

"Bravo," Nehemiah said. "A case for Wisconsinite reparations. But what does that have to do with Barbara and Karen Fields, or F. Ska Fitzgerald?"

"Um."

"Insightful. Thank you for sharing. Who else then?"

Ryan Yoder-Henley raised his hand. Madeline swished her lips. Ignacio tapped his phone. We'd noshed cafeteria food together pretty much every day until this semester, but we hadn't seen much of each other lately. My *Junkie* cover might've explained this; the twice a week habit had transformed into twice a day, and the sicker Mom got, the more access I had to weapons-grade narcotics.

"I've got, like, a comment if that's cool," said Ryan.

"Sounds cool," Nehemiah said, swaying at the chalkboard.

"Cool. First, I think Derek has to check his privilege."

"Doooo-doooo-doooooooo," I screamed like an airhorn. "Ahhhh-oooooooga!"

"Second, if we can, like, tie this to the texts? I think it's really problematic of both Derek and, respectfully, you, Nehemiah, to even consider these things together, or in conjunction with ourselves. It's a really messed-up, like, provocation to insinuate that something as serious as systemic racial injustice can be considered alongside melancholic white people."

"Guessin' we're gonna have to agree to disagree on this," said White Dude Who Would Capitalize *bell hooks*. "I'm thinking you're too dumb to see how PC—"

Long-snapper and Ryan yelled over each other as Madeline Einstein nodded. I started screaming "Order! Order!" in a British accent while pounding a fake gavel on the table. The whole room laughed, and I knew I'd honk-off to this memory later. "Will the Right Honourable Gentleman refrain from Derek-shaming and recant his defamation of the, ah, Right Honourable Gentleman?"

"What?" they both said.

"Thank you," I said.

"This is really stupid," Ignacio said, jutting his head at me for support. "This juxtaposition of low-and-high stakes, no? I mean, Dr. Weaver, as a person of color, I am just really tired of white male pain being centered as universal while, at best, black and brown bodies are relegated to the academic margins. I know I'm not alone on this."

More nods. Even from me. Madeline Einstein scribbled something, passed it to Ryan.

"Agreed," she said. "And that women don't even factor into this? That they aren't even allowed to speak—"

"I am very bored," said Nehemiah, who until now had smiled and let us all parrot social justice talking points.

"Whoa," we all said.

He massaged his temples. "You just don't get it, huh?"

Eyes drifted to notebooks, hands rustled bags.

"There are two classes in this country, and, by dint of your social privilege, pretty much everyone here is in the oppressive one."

"I thought you were progressive, Dr. Weaver," Madeline said to snickers and nods. "You don't actually support Derek's—"

"Self-aggrandizement," he said. "Exactly what Fitzgerald and the Fieldses wrote about."

The NPR donors, the *Politico* readers hiked foreheads, upturned palms.

"Guilt without behavioral change is no better than ignorance."

This line earned applause. At least until Nehemiah shredded his lesson plan.

He was negative, y'know, he was a smart guy, but the anger as he stabbed chalk at the blackboard and drew two circles, not intersecting, labeled *So-called Interests* and *Lived Experience* made the room quiet.

"National SEIU will be endorsing a former Walmart board member for president come 2016, so what does progressive even mean? Like, what'd the first black president do for the ghetto except lecture kids to pull up their pants? What about all the women planning to vote for the wife of a rapist?"

Madeline turned burgundy. "Easy for you to say when nobody's policing your body."

"What are we even talking about?" Ignacio said.

"This is all the same problem," Nehemiah said as he chucked chalk at the board.

"It's not the same problem!" Ryan said once he confirmed Madeline was looking at him. "It's my responsibility as a privileged person to say that. What would you know about—"

"I am both of these books," Nehemiah said. This hushed us again. His thumbs traced his eyebrows. What looked like a syringe poked out of his khakis. "Both of my parents went to Morehouse, and I didn't grow up in the hood, which is what y'all expect of every black person, and I moved here for grad school and dropped out, and sold cocaine because I had an English degree from Carleton without job prospects, and got a woman pregnant, and kept moving blow—including to pregnant women—and then I got clean and stopped slinging, and moved in with my paralegal mother and police officer father back in Atlanta, and got a PhD from Emory and made my way back here, never knowing what happened. And that's the story of America, okay? Monstrous fictions that perpetrate monstrous crimes, and not a single one of you would know anything about that because you've lived charmed lives. Because no matter how well-cultivated a goddamn reading list I put together, you *can't* get it. Life will never force you to. So consider this mentorship: read Naomi Klein. Read Schopenhauer."

We were shocked. The DC-lifers who dry-tug to William F. Buckley would say our bubble had been breached, that we were snowflakes. Like high school, I was not popular, would never be popular, but my classmates knew I didn't give a shit what people thought about me (provided they were at least thinking about me). I was angry at Nehemiah for lumping me with these silver-spooned louses, and angry at myself for spending eight semesters obsessing over these people for a useless degree and three suicide attempts.

"This is hilarious," I said, sans inflection. Thirty-six eyes blazed toward me. A twitch of nausea. The buzz of both social anxiety and the spotlight. "Schopenhauer beat a woman unconscious on his stoop, dude. He was basically the first Men's Rights Activist. Take the red pill, Nehemiah: everything is stupid and nothing is sacred, including the distinction between comedy and tragedy."

"Hilarious?" Yoder-Henley said. "How is that funny, man? This guy just bared his soul without irony, and that's funny to you?"

"Yes."

"I find that really offensive and, like, unfair to Nehemiah, even if I disagree with some of his conclusion. Because—"

"It's funny to me that you don't see your complicity, is what's funny to me."

Nehemiah steadied himself on the lectern. "Would you like to expound, Jude? Or perhaps apologize for the incursion?"

"Nah."

"What?"

"I don't care," I said reflexively, a Skinner rat pressing a lever. Madeline whispered to her neighbor. Ignacio thumbed his iPhone; my antiquated slider buzzed. "You all feign compassion for the poor, or lament the state of healthcare in this country, and then you'll be making 100k within five years of graduation because your parents went to Harvard and hooked you up with some LinkedIn contact. You're all suffering tourists. So, no, I don't care."

"You have to care. The whole point of being here is to care."

"This is so goddamn stupid. Me. You. All of us."

"But our median ACT is 32, well above the national average!" said some Groton Academy louse who's now a famous memoirist (much like his famous memoirist father).

"I just don't understand how you people do it. The stories we tell ourselves. The divisions we create. We're hacks."

"Hacks?" Ryan said. "What's more hack than the sullen white guy in English class?"

"Certainly not the rich guy who treats women like cum receptacles," I said, officially becoming a Salinger protagonist. Madeline stared at me.

Ignacio mouthed: "Stop."

"That's a pretty bleak worldview," Madeline said.

"So it goes."

"I'd like to think there's more to life than that."

"You'd *like to* think so. That's my whole point."

Heads turned to each other. I overhead the words "Condescending" and "Columbine."

"Jude, am I gonna have to coax out whatever it is you're doing here like this is some Socratic dialogue?" Nehemiah said. "You can't be so cavalier with—"

"What are *we* doing here?"

"What are *you* doing here, Mr. Glick? If you don't wanna be here today, don't."

"Even your junky ramblings are missing the point, dude."

"Jude, buddy, you're the asshole who wrote a poem about black people getting killed by the cops," Yoder-Henley said to snaps. "You're the dipshit who wrote the short story about domestic abuse. If you don't wanna be here, then I'm not sure you're the one who should—"

"All the liberals in this room, other than Ignacio, go home on breaks and tell their parents they're making the world a better place while working people get poorer and my mom dies because we can't afford good healthcare. And don't even start me on diversity when—"

"Jude," Nehemiah said, wobbling toward me. The needle fell out of his pocket. I stood up at my desk.

"—got killed by the cops, you fucking asshole."

Nehemiah stared out the window.

"You have no idea what I've been through," I said.

"You don't either," he said.

Two campus security guards beelined across the Quad. I shook my head, looked at him then Yoder-Henley. "We can agree on one thing, Nee: we don't wanna be here. And I don't wanna sit in another classroom full of pompous liberal piety, listening as you all lament that 1-in-6 people in this country are hungry, or that 65,000 a year are dying of opiate overdoses and vote for politicians who've never gone to bed hungry. If this country isn't a joke then what is it?"

"J.G., look—"

"That you people can just smile and shrug and pick up a useless hobby like creative writing without wanting to burn yourselves alive is, like, the banality of evil."

I flipped my desk and beat my own face as the security guards burst into the classroom.

This was the last time Nehemiah would teach. And the last time I'd speak in class.

"Honey?" Mom said, yanking me back to her chemo room. "You're mumbling to yourself. Is there something you want to talk about?"

I looked at the IVs sprouting from her port, the hollowed features, the balding head. I pulled a Bible off Mom's tray and thought of Nehemiah getting fired as I argued with a school counselor. I saw Ignacio in New York, some dive bar in Bushwick, getting quiet as Madeline Einstein and Nala Bashir and Ryan Yoder-Henley gossiped about my meltdown at some alumni meetup.

"I'm fine, Mom," I said. "I'm just glad I can be here with you."

"You don't . . . you aren't thinking of hurting yourself? This call—"

"I have seen something else under the sun," I read. "The race is not to the swift or the battle to the strong, nor does food come to the wise or wealth to the brilliant or favor to the learned; but time and chance happen to them all."

"Jude," she said, spitting on herself as she squeezed my hand. "Promise me, okay? Promise me you'll never give up. Promise me you'll stay strong for me, and your brothers."

I squeezed back for a long time, until she started dozing again, whispering her grandma's name—Julia—as her hand went slack.

I closed the Bible and looked out the window, across the river, into the glimmering Minnesota slush.

I AWOKE GREGOR SAMSA-STYLE and found myself transformed into someone who'd kicked opiates.

Or at least someone able to pry himself from the couch. My shoulder throbbed, but anyone who doesn't prefer physical pain to emotional pain is either rich or stupid.

My phone pinged. An email from that reality TV show, *American Idyll.* They wanted more footage, teased a live tryout in a few weeks. Basically, this was *America's Got Talent* but performed in high-pressure situations: lips of volcanoes, NYC subway tracks during rush hour, Madison Square Garden while loaded with horse tranquilizers and koala penis. Million-dollar prize if you endured the indignities and the fact that a certain real estate mogul running for president was executive producer.

I tossed my phone under a pillow, stretched.

I was groggier than I'd been even coming out of eye surgeries, but the soft-suicide didn't take. So stiff upper lip or whatever. Deal with the immediate issues of funeral planning and poverty. I still hadn't found Mom's will.

At precisely 9:00 a.m., I made phone calls, faux calls: lawyers, doctors, accountants. Almost nobody answered. The pro bono housing rights attorney said Mom did not, in fact, file bankruptcy, but that the expedited foreclosure would, indeed, give us 90 days tops, well, nope, now 87, to vacate the premises. Boris and I had misinterpreted the papers; the bank, some suffering factory partially owned by Stephen Scheisskopf, Sr. and one B. Ryan Yoder-Henley, had alerted us to the sheriff sale, to be held in four weeks. Usually, according to what I gleaned from non-profit sites and Intro to Econ final projects, a defaulter had six months past the sale to live rent-free/stressed-out until the new owner kicked you out. A *redemption period,* they called it.

"So why do we have 90 days tops?" I asked. Lou Grant rubbed against my feet. He looked as nervous as I felt.

"87. 87 tops. Could be six weeks, too."

"Regardless, I—"

"For all intensive purposes, you—"

"Intents and purposes."

"Supposably, and undoutably, 87 is correct. Irregardless, the bank is claiming the home is abandoned."

I looked at Lou Grant, who looked up at me. I'd set food out for him Labor Day morning, but outside of my half-assed chin-stroke as Gramps asked for his money, he'd been slumped outside Mom's bedroom meowing. I winced into a crouch and rubbed his belly.

"Abandoned."

"Since your brothers are no longer minors as of September 6th, they chanced it. And lucked out when she died."

"Okay, but I live here."

"You aren't on the mortgage though. So four weeks until the sheriff sale, five until the redemption period is up, and you were gifted a sixth by the judge. All non-binding. The weird thing is that they're doing this at all. The bank. Most foreclosures in Minnesota aren't judicial. But they brought this to court to speed things up. If you live in a middle-class neighborhood, there's a lot of value to lose when a house down the block goes into foreclosure."

We went around like this for an hour. She apologized, said their firm had been busy because someone took maternity leave, and that the court filings, the judicial foreclosure process, had "slipped through the cracks." This is what pro-bono legal help got you, I guess. No fees for no service.

I invited the woman to the non-existent funeral anyway, fed the cat and spent a half-hour on the floor, rubbing his belly and sniffing back tears.

Then I called Mom's church, asked for this pastor, Phil, whom she had leaned on when her fellow soldiers in Christ (or whatever) were busy tending to their personal miseries. I'd never met the guy, but he'd been praying weekly with Mom for seven years. Any time God came up between us, I regurgitated some pablum gleaned from my Philosophy minor, banalities about attachment leading to suffering and how he who has fifty loves has fifty woes, or something else vaguely Buddhist that I read on a yoga t-shirt. Mom died genuinely believing I would rot in Hell.

The doorbell rang twenty minutes later and an old, snowman-shaped white guy in a black velour tracksuit stood outside.

"You must be Julian," he said. "I've heard a lot about you."

"Sorry. Come on in," I said.

We shook hands with false-starts, herks-and-jerks then creaked to living room, juked stray IV poles and boxes of medical tape. There was an oxygen machine I needed to return to some corporate or government entity, but I didn't know how. I missed my mother being there to tell me it'd work out, even if I was sure it wouldn't.

Phil sat in a folding chair. I plunked on the couch.

"It's nice to finally meet you," Phil said. "Your mother was a wonderful person."

"I know."

Silence.

"She sure did suffer a great deal. Did she go peacefully at least? I heard my colleague Pastor Lewis stopped—"

"I was told her last words were 'Why? Why?' but I'm not sure because I was busy overdosing on fentanyl. And I get to live with that the rest of my life." I scraped a forming tear from my good eye.

"Your mother died knowing with absolute certainty that the Lord has a special plan for you, Julian. He who trusts in the Lord—"

"Sure."

His stomach bubbled. I would've offered him something to eat if I had anything to offer him to eat.

"Well," he said, staring at the oxygen machine. We sat. Birds chirped. Someone needed to be up to this, and I wasn't. We hadn't made eye contact since the handshake.

"Uh," I said.

"What can I do ya for then?" he asked.

"I need help with the funeral."

"Well, sure. I can officiate it."

"No. I . . . how can we throw a funeral without using a funeral home? Can you just do it at your church?"

"Why wouldn't you use a funeral home?"

"What the hell did you two talk about?" I asked.

"I'm sorry, Julian. You're going to have to calm down and just lay it out for me," he said, leaning forward, elbows on knees. "Your mother said you were like this."

As much as I wanted to bark back at him and Turn This Into A Thing, I needed help, needed to get this done for her.

"We . . . I can't afford a normal funeral, Phil. Can't you just do it? I'll cut you a check. But that $5000 sh—. . . stuff? Impossible. I have like $2000 available in credit, maybe."

Phil rubbed the back of his head.

"Where is the body?"

"Getting butter-knifed by some half-stoned medical student."

"I take it your mother hadn't read First Corinthians 6:19."

"God has a plan, or so I'm told."

He sighed.

"Look," I said, ignoring his boredom, the patience draining from his eyes. "No casket. No soloists. No drunks to lock in a closet. I'll cobble together some eulogists, you give a sermon about mustard or turning water into Mad Dog 20/20, and we'll sing a hymn or two then eat turkey sandwiches. Isn't this a thing?"

"Sure, yes, we can do all that. It's not exactly cheap, however."

My legs started bouncing. "Okay?"

Phil sighed. "It'll run around $2500 dollars. And the officiant generally appreciates an honorarium."

I stared at him.

"It's, I mean, it's a lot of work on, ah, the end of the master of ceremonies. Takes me, him, away from his hot dish blessings and bouncy castle christenings."

"What is with you fucking people and money? My grandfather burst in yesterday and—"

"Son, I'm a busy guy, and this is America. Do you want me to do this or not?"

"Uhh," I said. "I—"

The doorbell rang.

"Lemme get that." Phil nodded. I looked back at him from the hallway and he was stretching his elastic waistband, staring at his dick.

Addy stood in the doorway, spaghetti-strapped and flushed. And then Reid popped out from behind her, polo-clad and smirking.

"Surprise!" he said.

"The hell are you two doing here?"

"Making sure you're okay," Addy said, administering a non-consensual hug. "I'm so sorry, Jude. It's gotta be awful here all alone and—"

"I'm actually ridiculously busy. Like, not even in a millennial way with eight pilates classes and some podcast club to join. I'm planning a—"

"We brought you a 24-pack and fried chicken," Reid said, sliding past me and hefting a soggy bag and case of Coors into the kitchen. "I'll even defrost some frozen vegetables. It's what Momma P would've wanted."

Momma P. Back in junior high, all my friends used to call her Momma P when Malik, Reid, and ten other future arts administrators would play *MarioKart* in the basement and compare masturbation habits. Mom'd order us all, sometimes 20-strong, pizza she could barely afford. She liked my friends and hangers-on more than I did.

I led Addy to the living room, let Reid fumble around with the Banquet Beer.

"Pastor Phil, Addison. Addison, Pastor Phil."

She and I crashed to the couch.

And then my phone buzzed beneath a pillow, *Benny Hill* theme song at full-blast.

"I gotta take this," I said, popping up and striding through the front door.

It was Tom. I'd never had a phone conversation with either younger brother. No exaggeration. Even in college, we exchanged emails only after Mom pleaded. We just didn't like each other. I was the vengeance-obsessed George Carlin cosplayer who tried to dominate any room I entered and often succeeded. Chris, Tom? They were B- students who liked drugs and bowling. Chris played varsity football, wore the same number as me, might have been better, too, but opted against playing in college, against scholarships, because it was "too much work." Tom experimented with facial hair (handlebar moustaches, Fu Manchus, Saddam-exiting-the-spider-holes) and ate edibles before dozens of middlebrow movies a year. Neither one showed any interest in intimacy. I'd tried talking about Life After Mom, but they'd shrug and keep GameCubing. Maybe it was them, not me. Or maybe I was indifferent. Maybe they were smarter than I thought.

"Everything okay?" I asked as clouds whisked past the sun.

"Mostly," Tom mumbled. "But Chris . . ."

"Chris what?" I heard Mr. Bonser, the neighbor, wobbling arpeggios with his theremin.

"Well, both of us, kinda, but more Chris—"

"Tom. Seriously."

"Okay, well we both got possession tickets."

"Again."

"Again."

"Jesus, man. What would your mom . . ."

I stopped myself. Not sure if it was for Tom's psyche or mine.

"Ah," he said as some dubstep gurgled in the background, "we're gonna come home today I think. As soon as Chris finishes up with the cops. His was bigger."

Done with his theremin, Mr. Bonser now plunked away on his

Hammond B-3 organ. He claimed to have been a session man for Prince, but every half-dead musician in Minneapolis says they jammed with The Revolution at First Ave, turned Bob Dylan electric, or mastered liver cirrhosis with The Replacements. This flyover provincialism, the clinging to your hometown as though you chose to be born there, as though your love of the Midwest or Rust Belt wasn't simply Stockholm Syndrome, made Stephen Scheisskopf and his animatronic fascist the Republican nominee. We needed to get out more. But we also needed to pay rent and student loans. Plus Amazon Prime kept raising prices and Netflix did, too. Every Millennial or Gen-Xer I knew was either overemployed or underemployed, either hungered for country club memberships or just wanted to endure a gig without a uniform.

"You get busted by that Hess guy?"

"Um, sort of," he said, a megaphone now blaring over the EDM. "My roommate, Lars? His brother is in Tau Kappa Epsilon? But we're minors, so—"

"Don't do anything stupid," I said, Reid still banging around the kitchen behind me. "Well, stupider. Like join a frat. Your birthday is Saturday."

Tom muttered some non-assurance as I hung up.

Mr. Bonser's garage lurched open. A fog machine rumbled at his pasty shins. Mom liked Bonser and he liked her; they traded zucchini recipes and ragged on Food Network contestants. He even offered his A/V equipment for Bingo at racist family BBQs.

I double-timed back to the living room.

". . . so that's how I ended up Triangle-player Emeritus for the Bemidji Association of Euphonium Enthusiasts *and* the Percussion-centric Ensemble of Sven and Ole Jokers," said Phil, a smile plastered across his face. Reid sat on the oxygen tank, forehead stitched as he glanced from his work Blackberry to his work iPhone.

"And we're back," I said, Addy exhaling, as I sunk into the couch.

"Great. I was just telling, ah——"

"Addison," she said.

"Madison, this lovely young woman, lovely city too, a real sweetheart, about the trials and tribulations in the North Country polka scene."

Addy started standing up. "I'm going to go smoke a cigarette with Reid, I think."

He looked up, smirked.

I clamped my teeth, inhaled.

"Just as soon as we finish up here," she said, plopping back down. Reid returned to defrauding the American middle class via Microsoft Office Suite. He looked Guantanamo Bay levels of sleep-deprived.

"Neat-o. Well, where were we?" Phil said, checking his watch.

"Dead and in Hell," I said. "Also known as Minnesota in 2016."

"You've got a mouth on you, young man."

"That is literally true," I said with my mouth.

Addy elbowed me in the ribs. I still had it. A dormant volcano. Until there was someone to impress. My mother found this the most frustrating thing about me, outside of being destined for eternal damnation: the inability to display genuine emotions without that veneer of banter, one-liners, or self-loathing, as if this commitment to deflecting my own discomfort with humor and shade-throwing wasn't a pathetic and transparent feature of my deformed personality.

"So," Phil continued, Addy, too, now typing on her Galaxy, "2500 dollars. You'll also need a bulletin, I presume. And you'll need to handle obituary stuff yourself."

"Can you fine folks do the bulletin?"

"For 250 extra dollars we can print and design 250 copies." I did not have $250, but I also did not have $2500, so the numbers struck me as theoretical, like Democrats with conviction or Republicans who weren't racists.

"Jesus."

"That is the business I'm in," Phil said. I was half-enjoying our repartee. We'd make a decent team. Abbott and Costello. Sonny and Cher. Books and Dumb.

"Fine. 2750, plus an honorarium. When do we do this?"

"You tell me."

"Saturday?"

"Wedding officiant at a bingo hall."

"Sunday?"

"That's the fifteenth anniversary of 9/11. And I'm pretty busy on Sundays."

"I thought you were semi-retired."

"I am. I referee LARPing every other weekend. I played in college. St. Olaf. Surprised your mother didn't mention that. She told me you were a pretty big sports fan, or used to be before you went to that Maclackluster—"

"Help me out here. Friday? Say 11:00 a.m."

"That should be fine," he stood up. I did too. Addy stayed seated. Reid mumbled numbers to himself, looked like undercooked steak. Dawned on me this was the closest I'd ever get to a corporate board-room: mildly hungover and wearing a groutfit while grieving. Reid cursed at something on one of his phones. "We'll need those names by 11:00 a.m. tomorrow. Who's speaking and the like. Guess we'll pick some hymns."

"'How Great Thou Art,'" Addy said, still fingerbanging her screen.

"You're too kind. But really, Hattie, this is my job. I appreciate it though."

"No," Reid said, looking up. "She's right. Momma P loved that song."

"She did?" I asked. The last time I attended church was Christmas Day last year, and I was rolling on MDMA from the night before. I couldn't differentiate the hymns, just as I couldn't differentiate what-ever the Cantors groaned about the few times I'd landed with Boris' relatives at a synagogue. I'd been baptized Catholic, but Tom and Chris hadn't. Too much domestic strife at the time. Still, Mom in-sisted we all get *confirmed*, but she'd so soured on Catholicism, and I was such an annoying adolescent atheist, that she let me do it at the Lutheran church a few blocks away, where both Scheisskopfs and I went to pre-school. The only hymn I knew, "Amazing Grace," had been stained by the sobbing version I'd endured at Malik's funeral.

"Yes!" Addy said, sniffling. "You don't remember? Senior year, you had a bunch of people over for a bonfire right before graduation, and when Reid and everyone went off to smoke and you were being pissy somewhere, your mom hung out with me and Val and some girls and—I don't think Nala would've been here?—but Paula played it on the piano for us. It was honestly weird, but so, so great, Jude. She was an incredible woman. You're both such passionate people."

I looked at the keyboard in the corner. Literally gathering dust. It was an electric piano, I guess, full 88 keys. Older than me. Mom and Boris had bought it when they were still dating. She'd strum a guitar and he'd plunk away and then they'd switch, filling their apartment with Neil Diamond or Simon and Garfunkel approximations to the delight of their fellow boring white friends. Before she died, Mom had played more frequently, but I'd never bothered to ask what she was playing. Or why.

"Well," I said, suddenly realizing all the memories I could never again discuss with my mother, these Madeleines I'd forget, had already forgotten and forever missed the opportunity to share with her, "let's do that one then."

Addy glanced up again, saw my eyes misting, returned to the phone with a sigh.

"Right-o," Phil said, shaking my hand, "you take care of yourself. May God bless you. And payment is expected upon delivery."

He patted me on the back, left.

I laid a hand across my face, battled grief with a scowl, and whipped my head like one of those inflatable car dealership dudes flapping in the wind.

Phil slammed the door on the way out.

"That was extremely fun and not awkward," Reid said, pocketing his phones and shuffling away. "I'm gonna avail myself of your toilet. Or, well, the bank's toilet."

"Why isn't Reid at work?" I whispered as he disappeared down the hall.

Addy upturned her palms and made a frown equal parts exasperation and scorn.

"Goddammit," I said. Tom was calling again.

Addy nodded, rolled her eyes. I didn't bother to leave the room.

"What's the deal, dude?"

"Do you know where I could get twelve hundred bucks?" It was Chris this time.

"Do I know where you could get twelve hundred bucks. No, no I don't. Why?"

"Because I'm gonna need a thousand for the car fine and like two hundred for—"

"Godfuckingdammit, Chris."

I kicked the oxygen machine. It toppled over. The backplate popped off and a pink accordion folder leaked out.

"Sorry," Chris said.

"We are poor, kid. What's so difficult about this?"

"Everything," he said, hanging up.

My foot throbbed, worse than my shoulder, but I was too angry to care. I stumbled over to the folder.

"What's going on with your brothers?" Addy asked.

"It's irrelevant."

She scrunched her face. "Oookay . . ."

I picked up the folder and started thumbing through it.

"I still wanna know why Reid is here. And I—"

"Jude, is it that hard to understand? We wanna be here for you. We are, like, literally here for you. Reid asked if he could stay back and—"

"Could've been addition by subtraction if—"

"Oh, he knows math now!" Reid said as he swooped in and replaced me on the couch. Addy twitched into a smile and dropped it when she noticed me noticing.

"Well, something doesn't add up with you taking a day off on short notice."

"I quit," he said.

"Is everybody a comedian today? If you quit your job, Stephen Scheisskopf is a DSA member. And I'm financially secure."

I plunked into the folding chair, but I was too anxious to sit. So I slid it across the laminate wood and pressed my face against the window. It was raining. I dropped the folder at my feet. Too many decisions to make already. I couldn't endure more, whether reading or thinking.

"How are you, Jude?" Addy asked. "I mean, really?"

"Adequate." I leaned harder into the glass. Across the street, as cars rolled through stop signs and blue yard signs shook in the wind, Mr. Bonser, orange Zubaz billowing, scampered from his riding mower and flapped his arms.

"Adequate?" said Reid.

"Adequate."

I heard a shift on the faux leather, a whisper. I kept staring at the drizzle.

"Have you been following this MAOI thing?" Reid said, voice straining with pseudo-friendliness. I wanted either pills or a home-cooked meal. "The FBI, the Sheriff's Office, MPD all agree that it was a political stunt and *not* a terrorist attack—they even had your buddy Nehemiah or whoever on Anderson Cooper—but, of course, the whole right wing ecosystem is claiming cover-up, conspiracy, ISIS, whatever. Classic Steve Scheisskopf, I guess. Saying when they win they'll rally 'to restore Western Values.' Pathetic."

"Though it was funny," Addy said as Bonser barrel-rolled into his garage, "that you stumbled across Nala Bashir—and Patty fucking Schmidt—on Saturday morning."

"The Strib interviewed Nala, about Schmidt," Reid laughed. "We all thought she was dead, or off-the-grid, or whatever, but I suppose we've been too busy to follow local radicals."

"Well, you aren't anymore," I said. "Now, you're unemployed. Even worse than underemployed like me."

"Why does that bother you so much?" Addy said.

"You *told me* to quit on Friday night, J.G. But, oh, right, you were under heavy manners."

"I was. I am."

"Well, I was too. Which is why I walked into the office yesterday, took all my remaining vacation time, and put in my two weeks."

"Ironic on Labor Day," I said, swinging around, head squeaking on the glass.

"No, that would be Tuesday. Y'know, yesterday."

"What are you talking about?" Addy's hand rested on Reid's. Thunder clapped a few miles off. My foot and shoulder pulsed along with the shake. "It's Tuesday." I saw on their faces it wasn't. I patted my jaw and felt a pubic beard, an eyebrow of a moustache. "Jesus Christ."

I let me and the chair crash to the hardwood like the blade of a guillotine.

"We called yesterday," Addy said. "If there's anything we can do—"

"Jesus Christ," I said, squeezing and yanking hair from my scalp. "Jesus H. Christ."

Less than 48 hours until showtime.

I lay there for a while, trying to conjure Mom's voice. Rain pounded the windows as my closest living friends whispered to each other. At some point, Reid picked up the folder and started shuffling papers.

"Hey, bud," he said. "There's some important stuff in here. Your mom's will."

"Great, I'm the official executor of this disaster," I craned my neck toward him. "Anything else?"

He bit a lip. "Well, actually, there's a document from the State of Minnesota outlining how much your mother owed. Obviously, your inheritance was zero but—"

"But you can't inherit medical debt. And the foreclosure won't tank my credit."

"Correct on credit," he said. Light burst outside. The sky cracked. "But Medical Assistance? Our version of Medicaid? Turns out the

Paula Glick estate is on the hook for $47,000 in hospice care costs."

"But there is no estate."

"Yeah. But she does have $3,800 in a checking account and owns the van that Tom and Chris drive."

I gnashed the inside of my mouth until I tasted blood.

"Look," Reid said as he stuffed the papers back in the folder, "from a policy perspective, it makes sense, man. Do you know how much end-of-life care costs? Not saying it wouldn't be easier under single-payer, but—"

"You're a fucking psychopath."

The neighborhood flashed and shook again. Lou Grant bounded down the stairs.

"Jude," Addy said, now squeezing Reid's arm, "I wanna help. Seriously. Just ask and—"

"Okay, I'll ask: why the fuck did I wake up half-dead in my car Saturday morning and not at Reid's place?"

"J.G., relax, I told you that I went to Addy's and—"

"But then why was Addy apparently prancing around some leftist circle-jerk with Patty Schmidt and Nala Bashir?"

Turning to each other, Reid knocked his (personal) iPhone to the floor. It slid to my blistered and calloused feet. I picked it up.

"Hey!" Reid said, now rising up.

I unlocked it, first try, Reid's birthday, and scrolled through his messages. Before he swiped it from me, I made out:

r u serious? reidsy don't tell him. . .he'll lose it. . .not THIS week at least.

"Tell me what?" I asked.

They touched eyes again.

"Jude," Addy said, swaying to her feet. "You know we can talk about anything. So—"

"You went up to Duluth with The Mogul and they talked you into working for the campaign? After what Steve did to Malik? Are you nuts?"

"Uh," Reid said.

"J.G., look, he isn't working for Stephen, okay? And, yeah, fine, his cousin invited him to meet the most famous man in America, but he isn't gonna vote for him. Right, Reid?"

"Right. Of course. He's an idiot and a fascist. And so is Steve."

"Jesus, I don't even care what you do, man," I said, sitting up. "But Addy? Someone who claims to want to do big things in life, whatever the hell that means, somebody who says nothing is more attractive than hunger? Somebody who not only has found a way to function as a capitalist automaton, but also donates her salary to liberal causes and, somehow, is the most mentally healthy and centered person I know? Addy, the most perceptive person ever, doesn't see this for what it is? The first step toward you going completely John Galt-psycho? The Capitalist at Rest, eh? Shacking up with people who ruined my mother's life, and Malik's life, and now are coming for mine? Fuck you, Addy. No dick in the world is worth that."

"I told you, you misogynistic jackass, I don't work for him, and I *won't* work for him," she said.

"Whatever. Ads, I hope you're enjoying the man Reid is becoming."

They stared at me. Stunned. Faces twisted in disgust. I'd pegged them. It was maybe a little harsh and loose, but I had pegged them and they knew it. Because everyone thinks they want to know the truth but runs away when confronted with it. To protect self-esteem. Again, who's the child here? Laugh at the world's foolishness, you will regret it; weep over it, you will regret that too; laugh at the world's foolishness or weep over it, you will regret both.

White light filled the room. A bang, a shake. The lights spasmed out. Rain punched at the siding as I started to giggle, rising in pitch, as the two of them stared at me. I knew they couldn't figure me out, that now they never would. I enjoyed their discomfort.

"It's like this time I was at the corner store on University at 3:00 a.m. Stomach rumbling, craving halal food, drunk, suicidal, coming off some useless showcase at ACME, and, while I'm standing and talking to Ulysses—yeah, judge him, that's where he ended up, I'm sure he says, 'Hi!'—these two masked bastards burst in with bats and start swinging at shelves and the register," I said as my yips and jerks turned into convulsive sobs, "and U.P., in one swoop, like he's a samurai unsheathing his sword, he brings up this gun and points it at the guys, waves it from side-to-side while the dudes knock stuff around right next to me. But they see the gun, as U.P. is screaming and thrusting it at them, at us, and he fires a round that whizzes into the ice cream counter and smashes the glass and, as it's bursting everywhere, the dudes, they drop the bats and sprint out. And I'm laughing. I'm laughing so hard I fall on my ass. I'm laughing in a pile of glass, my arms and neck bleeding, shards lodged in my coat and I'm laughing. Because who really gives a shit? You two are dating? Or Reid is a proto-fascist? Or Addy wants to be well-dressed and well-fucked and that's it? Or none-of-the-above, and I'm wrong about this like I'm wrong about everything? I'm just . . . I'm hurt that you even thought this was worth keeping from me. What other secrets are out there if you'll lie about something as meaningless as this?"

Reid put his hands on Addy's shoulders, peeked from behind her head. She was crying, too. Heavy gasps.

"Are you okay, dude?"

"I don't even know what that means anymore."

We lingered like that—Reid and Addy watching me unravel on the floor—as the rain pummeled the house, beating down so hard it could bruise the roof. But it wasn't my house much longer, never was, I guess. It was my problem, all of these were my problems, but it'd all be easier if a tree smashed into the living room and smushed me like a bug.

"Thanks for coming," I said, cries slashing through the thunder. "I love you both. You're all I have now and I love you."

5.

BORED TO DEPTH

I ALMOST TURNED him down.

I should have turned him down.

A buddy, Perry Slutsky, who works in booking, who mostly quit comedy because it exacerbated his risk of liver cirrhosis, called earlier that summer, frantic, because he needed an opener for a gig at First Avenue, a famous non-comedy club that had booked famous comedy, and didn't know a goddamn thing about comedy.

So I gave him names of people I didn't hate. Folks whose success would not lead me to jump off the Washington Avenue bridge.

"But why can't you just do it?" he asked. "You're cheaper and this is a great opportunity."

This is the sort of thing Addy would say. Always this assumption that faith in yourself, some foolish hunger to make things better, this Gatsbyish optimism, wouldn't most likely explode like a stink bomb, dousing everyone around you in filth.

I'd made tens of dollars doing comedy. Sorry to brag. Mostly biker bars in Onalaska, Wisconsin or the restaurants attached to Springhill Suites in Bismarck, North Dakota, three- or four-hour drives to do half an hour in front of ten people who didn't intend to see comedy, all for $50. Maybe $100 if it was a holiday weekend. I never enjoyed comedy, always viewed it as a life-ruining compulsion like extreme couponing or sticking your genitals in a VCR, yet I drunk-drove and opted into self-harm at ten-to-fifteen open mics a week for the last four years and, every once in a while, got thrown a half hour for a few beers and cut of the door at actual joke joints in Minneapolis and St. Paul.

But this was something else.

A critically acclaimed comic who can anonymously ride the bus might gross $5,000 a night. A comic you recognize from TV could swing $20,000 or more. Legitimately famous standups, and there are maybe five in America right now, could take home hundreds of thousands of dollars a night. Close to a million when they sold out arenas.

This was some guy in the middle. He'd bring his own opener, some fellow semen-crusted Angeleno who'd get a third of the net payout, throw me a couple hundred bucks, maybe, and likely berate me backstage and/or openly mock me on stage. They'd middle-act me, people paying almost no attention as they closed their tabs and hit last call. If you care, it's called a check spot. Also, if you care, you're a comic who already knows this shit.

Anyway, I said yes.

I didn't tell any of my friends though.

Mom wanted to drag her oxygen tank to First Ave and wheel around the standing room only pit while I got too drunk on stage and barfed up twenty minutes of my probably hack material. She never understood why I did standup or wrote tragicomic short stories that would never be published. Could not fathom my need to be seen. My hunger.

"Why would anyone do that?" she'd ask. "You have a college degree. You have real options, Jude. I just wish you'd find something, anything else to make you happy. Advertising?"

Although she screamed at me for reading too much, I suppose this counted as support.

On stage, the chosen opener of the guy who voiced an animated duck was bombing. So the opener cut his set short, but not before closing with how he and the headliner had outsourced the comedy to "autistic jack-o-lanterns with daddy issues and Marfan's syndrome. Ladies and gentlemen, give it up for a macro man with a micro penis, a future suicide, your next comic: Jude Glick."

"Thank you for killing," I said, adjusting the mic slowly, needing to do twice as much material because the headliner had insisted on drinking in his dressing room until 10 p.m. It occurred to me that once his set lost steam, the opener did this on purpose. "Let's have a round of applause for Turner, a man so charming he was encouraged by the Make-A-Wish Foundation to develop terminal cancer."

This played okay. I'd need more than okay to reach 10 p.m. and/or not GG Allin myself.

"How's everybody doing?" I asked to murmurs and shrugs. "Please don't answer; that's a rhetorical question. But me? I'm really happy to be here. Mostly because I'm on Prozac. Rare for a comic to be a miserable piece-of-shit, obviously, doubly so because this isn't an AA meeting, at least yet, but I wanna thank Turn, and our headliner, and First Avenue, and mostly Perry Slutsky, my dear friend, for this awesome opportunity to gather material for my suicide note. See, I don't get out much—I only get invited to parties at knifepoint . . ."

It went like this for a while. That is: decently. They preferred my hatred of everything to Turner's hatred of everything other than himself. I riffed. I did crowdwork. I pumped out my twenty, tried stretching it to twenty-five, and lost steam with fifteen minutes to go.

I glanced at the wings, saw Perry winding a fake crank, coaxing me to keep going.

"So, this is a fun little tidbit," I said, venturing into non-joke, punchline-less territory, a dangerous place for most comics, let alone a nihilist alcoholic who'd hoovered three beers on stage. "My mother is dying."

Nothing.

"Ha! ROFL! LMAO!" I said, gripping my beer tighter. "She's been at it for a while, this dying business—which isn't terribly lucrative—but the most annoying thing about her withering on the couch and slowly starving to death is that she thinks God has a plan. And maybe he does. But it should've been Plan B."

Outside of the smattering of New Atheists, this didn't do much. And it shouldn't have. It wasn't funny. Or insightful. It was hack. I can go twenty-eight minutes—tops—without devolving into another asshole who thinks they have something to say but most certainly doesn't.

"Did you know? Every job in America is either in Marketing, Finance, or Poverty."

"You aren't Bill Hicks!" someone yelled.

"I know. I'm funny," I said. "Funny looking!"

Thirteen minutes now from the red light above the soundbooth, my salvation, my ticket to almost no money and a lifetime of shame. "No joke: I'm out of jokes. The lack of jokes is on me."

"Kill yourself!" someone else yelled.

"A foolproof way to kill yourself is trying to achieve your professional goals, or develop meaningful relationships with people you like," I said to a few yucks. "But you people already knew that. You're hungry for that promotion to regional manager or ski-cation to Vail while I'm hungry for a fentanyl lollipop and a tube of Elmer's glue."

This was getting weird. Too weird. Had crossed some unknowable tonal border and changed the air. I knew it was about to get worse, that my hole would widen and deepen, that it would sprout teeth and gnash me to death if I didn't fight back right now. But on some level, I wanted it to deteriorate.

"Who here is married?" I asked. Hands shot up. There were hoots, claps. "And who here regrets getting married?" Some laughter. Some applause. Some assents. I could still save this. If I allowed myself to think this was worth saving.

"Pretty sure you're actually married to the idea that the world has something to offer you. But, trade secret, it doesn't!"

I looked back to the wings. Perry held up two fingers. Either he wanted to save me or he'd had enough. His face twisted. He whispered something sharp to someone else backstage.

"Adults know life is meaningless," I said. "It's, like, a secular rite of passage, a Bar Mitzvah without the grinding tweens and wasting of money. To not see it, or, even worse, argue that we should skip and lollygag through this hell anyway, means you're a child. Or a rich person. But I repeat myself."

The red light came on early. I glanced to the side of the stage again, saw the headliner holding up what was probably my check and snipping it in half with a scissors. I still don't know if that whole evening was a ruse, the universe carving another Jude Suffering Notch in the belt, more ammo for the conviction that some people are born to win and most of us are born to lose, but in that moment, I wasn't even angry or suicidal or concerned about how bad things were and how bad they would be. I was just tired. So tired of my life being my life. Tired of wishing I was somebody, anybody, else.

"So that's my time, folks. You've been a great crowd in the same way the crowd who crucified Christ was a great crowd and—"

"Encore!" someone shouted. It was unclear if this was sarcasm, but it's all I needed to flip into unrepentant misanthropy.

"Hang yourself, you will regret it; do not hang yourself, and you will regret that too; hang yourself or don't hang yourself, you'll regret it either way; whether you hang yourself or do not hang yourself, you will regret both. This, ladies and gents, is the essence of all comedy. Good night and fuck off."

I dropped the mic, hopped off the stage to light applause, waded through the crowd with a few smacks on the back and a few more beers poured on my head, drank behind the wheel, told Mom the show went great and then proceeded to spend the next 48 hours in bed, phone off, blinds drawn, pissing in bottles, certain I'd off myself if I left the room, slipping in and out of dreams in which I stood in front of a giant audience, a basketball arena, and told my life story, unleashed my true self while the crowd ignored me and played Candy Crush on their phones.

THREE HOURS BEFORE the funeral and Tom couldn't find his shoes.

I smiled, clutched Mom's rosary beads. Occam's razor suggested my life, wholesome and Midwestern and barbarous, would never relent into tolerability; indeed, I'd nicked my chin ten minutes ago, dripped blood on my tie. Addy wouldn't answer my calls or texts. Stephen Scheisskopf kept peppering CNN, Fox News, and NPR with rumors of Somali "no-go zones" in Minneapolis. And Lars Kiffmeyer's brother, Kayden, the recruitment chair of Tau Kappa Ep, had pilfered any residual patience my mother bequeathed Saturday night by turning my brothers into frat pledges.

Friday sunrise and I hadn't slept since coming unglued Wednesday afternoon, since my foray into recreational anesthesia Monday night. Too much to do. Obituaries submitted, credit cards maxed out, a GoFundMe monitored, a social network of nurse aides and diesel mechanics, pre-school teachers and stay-at-home evangelicals providing not even enough for one more mortgage payment, let alone the funeral and *Star Tribune* posting and Tom and Chris' legal liabilities to Winona County. My conscious uncoupling from opiate addiction butted in while I haggled with the church, or rang Boris: sweating on the toilet, losing fluids through both ends. I rewarded each completed, or more likely attempted, task with a swig of Wild Turkey.

Last winter, when Mom could still walk, we spent a Saturday

morning shopping for suits. Chris and Tom asked why we needed suits now if we'd lasted this long without them.

"Part of growing up," she said, holding onto my arm, "is knowing what you have, and what you don't. Because if something happens to a relative—"

"Like who?" one said.

"Yeah, what might happen?" the other said.

I looked at Mom, regretting we couldn't make knowing eye contact.

"Just trust me," she said. "You'll need these one day."

Back in Foreclosure House, we climbed into our suits. My hands shook as I held cheap silk to Tom's, then Chris's, neck. Pseudo-rich-people-clothes for the working poor, the Republican candidate for president's name emblazoned on every tag. Boris had never taught us anything stereotypically masculine—outside of substance abuse—and I hadn't worn a tie until my second year of college, but whatever grotesque half-Windsor I twisted together beat the coked-out flop-sweat look endemic to the Glick twins.

"So would that be okay? The car thing?" Chris said as we stood in the living room. Tom was uprooting his closet again. He'd assured us both the Kmart dress shoes existed, had not been transformed into a bong.

"What?" I said, my phone buzzing.

"If you take Mom's van? When we go back to school? It's just, well, they have our license plate number and it's such a small town I'm thinking the cops will—"

"Yeah, yeah, whatever."

Miserable enough in the present, I listened to a voicemail from Addy.

"Goddammit," Tom shouted from his bedroom.

Soon as Reid and Addy left the other day, I'd felt unsteady, like wearing someone else's prescription glasses. I missed Mom so much, I realized, sliding through my lockscreen, that it eclipsed grief. I hungered for one more conversation with her the way I wanted a second functioning eye. And this hurt was, like, hurtful. To Addy. Reid. Whoever. And myopic.

"Hey, it's me. Reid went off to get drunk and watch Tottenham play Everton, even though today is, well, today, and I was just . . . thinking. Thinking about how you really hurt me Wednesday and it isn't okay," the message said. Chris wandered off as I stared stroke-like at nothing in particular. "I understand that I can't understand what you're going through, Jude. And that I probably never will. But I've had days when I couldn't get out of bed, too, and it sucks. I haven't had a slice of your pain, maybe, but I have feelings. And the other day you hurt those feelings. If you view your friends with the same hate and cynicism as everyone else—even if I kinda know where it comes from—I don't know if you can call them friends. I hope you do. Or at least would call me a friend. Because maybe I like nice things and enjoy going to shows or a fancy dinner, but that doesn't make me some psychopathic bitch. Neither does hooking up with someone who makes me feel special. Even if he isn't, if we aren't, perfect, okay? You have to let people live. And let people in. Allow yourself that. Like, me? I'm allowing myself to see Reid, not exclusively, but to feel good about myself for once. And maybe it'll work this time? Because why not try it? That doesn't make me a bad person. It just makes me a person. There's a world outside your head. If I can get off, I'll see you at . . . well, y'know, I'll be there if I can. Bye."

"Found them," Tom said, waving Boris' bowling shoes.

"Those are . . . perfect," I said.

Something scratched at the front door. A raccoon flinging garbage, I figured, or maybe someone from the bank. Worst-case scenario, a door-to-door magazine salesman still reeking of crack pipe and boner pills.

It was actually a combination of all these things: Boris. As drunk as I'd seen him since NAFTA's infancy. Swaying in his Minnesota Vikings muumuu, he looked like Grimace on ketamine.

"I donut thing I'm in a way conducive to attending a funeral," he said, perp-walking into the foyer and toward the living room's excess medical equipment. Salinger's *Nine Stories* fell from his sweatpants.

"What way are you in?" I said.

"I'm in a bad way. With a bad crew."

I had planned for this actually. Had used some precious credit on a brown suit for Boris. I'd even hung it over the oxygen machine. If it didn't fit, I didn't care. He'd look insane, yeah, but acceptably insane as he popped the buttons off the slacks and sweat circles into the jacket. Much better than a beached whale dressed as the purple Teletubby. The suit ensured two hours of mild humiliation, and then he'd slither back into his hole and dissolve.

He looked around. Tom had opted for a bland, navy three-piece;

Chris, conservative pinstripes and a fedora. Me, I'd opted for a pink-and-gray combo, something befitting defiant congressional testimony or securities fraud, not ring-leading a funeral. I knew she wouldn't have approved if she could see, but chose it anyway.

"Lose the hat, Chris," I said. "This is a funeral. Not 4chan."

"I'll stay here and keep watch. Shit Sivva," Boris said.

I sighed, glanced at the smattering of rubber gloves and whiskey bottles. Photo albums caked the rug. Cousin Cassie, probably methed out and definitely blasting Breitbart Radio, had picked up some of the least-depressing captures, promised to mash together some nostalgia on particleboard.

"Put it on. Now," I said, pointing at the duds. $200 I didn't have, spent on something I didn't need, and shouldn't need to provide a theoretically grown man.

"I read a studly at the solarium, I, the library which says thieves often use funerals to—"

"Boris."

"I'm not slur I can mencken. Naked. Make it."

"If you don't want to come to the funeral of the mother of your children, the woman you married and could never quite shake off, fine. Fuck it. But you'll have to live with it, Boris, another regret, just like the ones I'm sure you have over treating her like shit the last fifteen years of her life. Regret you'll never admit to, Boris, because you're a fucking coward. You're a fucking coward and we're late. So either come or don't, but fuck off. Don't make an ass of my mother."

It took him twenty minutes, and multiple bowel movements, but Boris made his way into the suit. He looked like a *Red Asphalt* victim, wreaked of Wild Turkey 101, and, at best, resembled a Southern Senator with tertiary syphilis, but nobody would call the cops on him for leering. Probably.

So we climbed into my car, the Oldsmobile I had just agreed to lend Tom and Chris. The silence smothered me. All forlorn window glances and squeaking upholstery and absence. With no farts to proffer, Boris must have felt the same and flipped on NPR.

"It's called the bowling-ball test, do you know what that is?" the Republican nominee for president said. "That's where they take a bowling ball from twenty feet up in the air and they drop it on the hood of the car. And if the hood dents, then the car doesn't qualify. Well, guess what, the roof dented a little bit, and they said, nope, this car doesn't qualify. It's horrible, the way we're treated. It's horrible."

"Get a load of this crap," Boris said.

"Turn it off," I said.

"Why?"

"Boris, please."

He turned it up.

"Folks, Hitler? Bad guy, okay? Bad guy. But tough. Tough guy, believe me. Had some interesting ideas. Solutions."

As we pulled into the church, they cut away from the rally and into an interview with Scheisskopf. I punched the center console and jerked the car to a stop.

"Listen," I said, turning toward Boris then Tom and Chris in the back. "Mom didn't eat shit her whole life to get shown up by Lydia and Cassie and all these other tormentors from her past, okay? So don't give anyone any reason to think we are less than a fully functioning family, even if they know it's bullshit. Got it? Don't embarrass her. Not today."

I pulled Mom's rosary beads from my pocket and held them for a second. Tom gave a weak nod. Chris, too. Boris just sighed, lurched from the car, and unleashed an explosive fart.

"MAYBE MY FAVORITE memory of your Mom—and, really, you, Judy—is your high school graduation, when you gave the commencement speech?" said one of Mom's high school friends, a blonde and banged evangelical mother of five, clasping my hands around hers as my mood, already wavering an hour into the pre-service meet-and-greet, crept closer to oblivion, completely toppling over as we remembered what probably counts as the high-water mark of my small and pathetic life. "God, the way you hugged each other after! And then let go and did it again! Oh, you loved each other! All 10,000 people could feel it. I mean, she'd just been through another round of chemo, and she was so, so proud of you, Jude. It was never about her. Ever. And I just remember her looking up at you, and it's like she could see your face, you know, just all the life you've both lived in that smile of yours, and I just had to cover my own face with the program because I was crying so hard."

"Right. Of course," I said, tears twitching at the corners of my eyes, a wretched development as, despite all my bluster against rigid gender roles and all that liberal arts kid gobbledygook, I would not let myself cry in public, not in front of side-eyeing cousins leaking chew into coffee cups, not in front of my grandfather, bolo tie, jeans, workboots, steadying himself on the elbows of hunched great aunts before stealing off to Pastor Phil's office for another nip of Crown Royal.

I had decided to do this sober. Or at least what I considered sober. Having inherited Boris' chemical proclivities, I'd prided myself on never boozing or doing drugs in front of Mom, Tom, and Chris. I would be drunk and/or high, sure, but I wouldn't let them see the process. Not so much as a single beer, even in front of the extended family. The memories of Boris tooting cocaine at the breakfast table or swilling straight from the bottle in the school parking lot—horrified mothers gasping as he raised his eyebrows and swerved home—cemented my disgust for public drug use.

Still, I'd banged a few thousand milligrams of gabapentin to beat back any lingering junk sickness and to postpone the grief till post-funeral. Maybe 200 people already signing guest books and handing aunts flowers and sharing memories. Snippets of despair and pride I overheard as another old white woman tapped a shoulder, cradled an elbow, rubbed my back. Folks waiting for me to finish up with the smiling, forced hugging, and reminiscing before inching around like a clock to the next segment of playacting someone who wanted to be here. Where the fuck were these people when I was putting off school to help Mom shuffle around the U of M oncology ward, one arm wrapped around her thinning waist and the other steering the IV pole?

". . . and the house? Lydia was saying something—"

"We'll figure it out, I'm sure. Well, I'm not sure but—"

"Let go and let God."

"Right."

Someone tugged at my sleeve. Any time I finished one conversation, heads swung my way. Multiple people shouted my name. Tom and Chris were doing their best, I guess, stalking the decaf and donuts, trying to mimic my back-clapping and cheek-kissing, but I knew they wanted to sit with Boris on the church steps, eyes locked on parking lot (in)action until Pastor Phil rounded the family and closest friends out of this lobby and into his office for a pump-up prayer/briefing.

Forehead peck declaring the end of this conversation, I half-turned toward the tug and found myself embracing the walker-aided mother of another of Mom's high school friends. As she rasped something about their last phone call and, half-senile, tied it to when a preschool Stephen Scheisskopf threw scissors at my head, I squeezed her as tight as I dared and reverse-pivoted to a pocket of empty carpet.

And then, impossibly, I saw Nehemiah. In his work clothes.

"Hey," he said, wrapping me in a bear hug. "How you holding up?"

"Wish I could take bereavement forever," I said, removing myself from the hug and genuinely smiling for the first time all morning. We hadn't spoken since I balked out of work by voicemail. Even with Mom being prodded by some med-school scalpel, I'd endured the week with less anger than fifty hours at the MAOI.

Down the hall, toward the main entrance, a flurry of raised voices nicked my attention. But I realized I had missed Nehemiah. And it'd only been six days.

"Loss is a helluva thing, J.G."

"Thought both of your parents were alive." In fact, I knew this; I kept a signed copy of Nehemiah's well-reviewed—and, thus, hardly read—recovery memoir, *Queer and Loathing*, in the Oldsmobile trunk. His cop dad and paralegal mom, evangelicals who admired their son's creativity and felt compassion for his intersectional marginalization (or something), stole the few scenes he'd bothered to write. The most famous A-list black actor—yes, that one and not the pulpy, goofy one—had purchased the option rights for below-market rate. This infusion of cash, not junk, had probably kept Nehemiah clean. For now. A high-functioning atheist, he'd sworn off NA.

"You remember that story I told your senior year? My rock bottom?"

"Sure." The hubbub stage-left stole my attention again. Seemed Boris and his white hair had started stomping and hooting at some bloke in coveralls. Tom and Chris shuffled that direction.

"Used to sit in my car, rain bashing the windows, and pray that I could get sober enough, and hopeful enough, to stop selling drugs. And why? Because I'd fucked myself over, y'know? All this before I even knocked that poor girl up to before I moved back to—"

"Bullcrap," Chris shouted and flailed as Tom nodded. "No, no way. Take them back."

"—and, well, maybe now isn't the time, J.G., but there's something I've been meaning to—"

"You gotta hash that out, Jude," Boris slurred, huffing toward us. "Those flowers."

"What?"

He shot his hands up like a catcher corralling a wild pitch, stomped to the bathroom.

Just outside the foyer—Nehemiah palming my lower back—I found Principal Schmidt shrieking at a delivery guy, her athleisure the same pastel hues as the wreath.

"This lady is nuts," Tom said. Chris tugged a flask from his back pocket, and I knocked it from his hands.

"Fuck you, Jude," he said, following Tom back into the morass.

"What is going on?" Nehemiah asked. The lingering geriatrics shrugged, shook their heads, scattered down the hall.

"You'll never believe who sent these flowers," Principal Schmidt said.

"What are you doing here?" I asked. Nehemiah rubbed his head, teetered on his heels.

"This is comic opera. The audacity, the perniciousness of—"

"Ma'am, I'm just doing my job," said the working schmuck. He turned to me. "Sir, would you sign this? I need to get going."

"Um."

As I knuckled my temples, Nehemiah grabbed the man's clipboard, scribbled his signature, replaced the delivery guy beside the flowers.

"Stephen fucking Scheisskopf," Schmidt said.

"What?" I looked at Nehemiah.

"I'm . . . I'm gonna leave you two be," he said. "J.G., I lo— Uh, let's catch up later, okay? Nice to see you again, Patty."

"What the hell is going on?" I said as Nehemiah plucked a cigarette from his pack and burst through two sets of doors. Schmidt and I still stood just outside the foyer as I glared at the wreath. Flanneled nursing-homers and Lutheran mothers occasionally waddled past. Through the glass, I saw several friends—but no Addy or Reid—hitting a blunt in the parking lot.

"Your mother and I were very close in her later years, kid," she said. "I'd even visit her during chemo."

"You?"

"And to think that Stephen Scheisskopf would inflict himself on this legacy by ordering—"

"You'd sit with Mom? And yet I haven't seen you since the high school commencement speech."

Schmidt nodded, but she'd already mentally escaped cross-examination by snatching Scheisskopf's sympathy card.

"Dear Jude, Tom, and Chris," she read, adjusting her chained half-moon glasses, "I speak for my parents, my sister Gwendolyn, and my campaign associates in offering my deepest condolences. We've had our differences, you and I, but Paula Glick inspired all who knew her. The generosity, tenacity, and love that your mother modeled is something we should seek to incorporate into our lives. I am so, so sorry, Jude. Sincerely. Your family has suffered a great deal, and I think of you all often. Keep enduring, J.G. Yours is an inspirational story. With sympathy, Stephen Scheisskopf."

"I think I'm gonna puke," I said, swallowing hard.

"That is such a hack joke, Julian. I mean, really. And you consider yourself a comedian. Perhaps you've lost your edge."

My forehead pulsed with sweat. My chest sprung then snapped like a rubber band. I clamped my eyes shut and exhaled. And in the darkness, I saw my mother gritting through another blood transfusion, stealing a five-minute nap at work after a sleepless night with the twins, screaming at the school district superintendent for failing to protect her precocious and damaged oldest son from vultures who pecked at his insecurities. I saw this and, rather than faint or joke or upchuck, I rubbed my eyes open and sighed. Because she needed me to be strong today and I didn't know if I could do it without the usual crutches of booze, pills, jokes. Without her.

"I should get back in there," I said. The service started in an hour and there were still rounds to make. My friends had shifted inside now, but still no Reid or Addy.

Schmidt patted me on the cheek. I looked at my clump of bros. They shrugged shoulders, upturned palms, scrunched faces. I marched toward the old folks, arm cocked for a firm handshake and a distraction from how my hate for this life seemed to multiply every second. And as I forced another smile, secreted more G-rated banter, I saw Nehemiah slouch back to Schmidt, hoist the wreath and its easel, and carry it into the chapel.

AN HOUR LATER, sweat pooling on my ass, knees and back stinging with each step, Pastor Phil was leading me, my brothers, and Mom's side of the family down the center aisle of the sanctuary, some dirge rumbling from the organ. All the pews were filled. The 500-person capacity had been topped, even, as a few folks, including Boris, stood at the back of the chapel. Another pang of grief lanced the surreality. This was actually happening. We were here because Mom was dead and, no matter how badly I wanted her to pop up from behind the pulpit, to walk out from behind a curtain, to materialize and explain that this was all a big misunderstanding and that she just wanted to watch *Andy Griffith Show* reruns while the cat and I lay at the foot of her bed, the creep of reality burrowed deeper as we sat down.

She wasn't coming back.

I'd slapped together a funeral, brushed off the Glick-side weirdness and Schmidt's inexplicable appearance to hug so many people and share so many stories that my arms ached and my throat itched, and I'd done it all for her even though she'd never see it, never see how I'd thrown her a well-attended memorial service when all I wanted was to shrivel on the couch. To replay the voicemails I'd been saving all summer.

Flanked by two aunts, who led me to my feet when we were supposed to stand and sat me back down when we weren't, I wasn't present. I was anywhere but here. Pastor Phil wasn't prattling on between hymns, joking through his introductions, and calling me to the stage for the first eulogy. It wasn't that I was nervous. Just as Mom's high school friend had reminded me, I'm indifferent to crowd size, to stage fright, find a one-on-one conversation far more harrowing than riffing before thousands, but unlike the hours of standup or the thrill of a packed gymnasium roaring at your bits and making you feel wanted for the first time in your fucking life, I was here to wrap up my *mother's life* for these people, to send them off with a deeper understanding of my hero, to care so they don't have to, so they can move on, forget her, throw her in the memory incinerator with the rest of the corpses they've known and discarded. I wasn't here. She was here. She was here for the last time, and I knew it as I adjusted the mic, and took a panoramic view of the crowd and realized that after this moment, I'd be trudging through life alone and without her, yes, but alone with how worn down I am every day without her guidance, without any genuine warmth or care, no real interest in me or my brothers beyond the abstract knowledge that *it sure must be hard for those boys, huh,* alone in our inability to ever find ballast, alone and trapped in amber with our longing for her, an infinite loop of grief that's played, whether loud or soft, every second of every day since she's died. Alone, crying in a T-Mobile store after replacing my phone and losing her voicemails, alone when her rosary beads, beads

I don't pray with and never will, break and scatter just like my life did when she died, sobbing big, painful gasps of grief on the bus like some cautionary tale, some example of what happens when you miss someone so much it hurts. Alone in this shed. Alone. Alone. Alone.

"NICE SPEECH, FAGGOT," my cousin Cassie said as I sat down with Mom's family an hour later. This was halftime. A reception hall. Folks limped through the post-service lunchline, expecting me to rally for more handshakes and Bible verses over cold cuts and back pain. "Thanks for making us look stupid!"

Chris and Tom popped up and wandered toward another clump of congregating olds.

"Are you done?" I said. She crossed her legs. "Because I'm—"

"You're just like your father, is what you are."

"Mmm."

The service went fine, I guess. Embarrassing but fine. Once I started counting, there were no fewer than 86 mentions or allusions to Jesus in the other three eulogies, a torrent that almost certainly shocked my friends, their parents, and the more secular acquaintances Mom had picked up through me over the years. I was surprised myself. Unless we were yelling at each other about abortion or political correctness, we tried to avoid theology and faith.

"Great job, Jude!" someone called out. I low-waved in the voice's direction.

"So funny, too! Your mom would've been so proud!" another voice said.

"Pathetic," Cassie said. "It's all a joke to you, isn't it? Tradition. Family. This should've been about Paula."

Cassie was four years older than me and had two kids by two men, both of whom had moved on to creampie other rural dental hygienists and/or hoover Bud Light while complaining about manufacturing gigs (that never existed) disappearing under *That One.*

"A real knee-slapper. I need another meniscus surgery," I said.

My grandfather shook his head, muttered in Polish. Aunt Lydia helped him up and they inched toward the sandwiches and distant relatives. I blinked, thought of Marcus Aurelius. Then, realizing I knew almost nothing about Marcus Aurelius, meditated on David Letterman.

". . . I mean, Lord Almighty, if Paula wasn't too good for you kids. Asshole college fucks, all of you, either too stupid to do anything useful with yer fancy degree or too smart for the rest of us to see it, 'cause yer workin' the same shit jobs as the rest of us but have ta drop all your references and jokes in a freaking eulogy . . ."

As Cassie kept ripping into me, I looked around for Boris. He was leaning against a pillar toward the back of this reception hall, obscured from most of the round tables and casseroles, unlit cigarette bobbing from his mouth.

". . . the, what's the word yer tarbaby president would use? Audacity. The audacity to stand in front of all these good people and not mention the Lord? I mean, hallelujah if it wasn't like spitting on yer Mom's grave! But, oh yeah, you're too poor to afford one so—"

"I pity you, Cassie," I said, standing and shoving the chair into the table—too hard, people shot looks and whispers—and pivoting toward Boris' corner. "Go icefish for another racist drunk to fuck."

The aunts and uncles stared at me in horror; I grinned back. If they wouldn't drive Mom to her own mother's funeral—and they didn't, a high school friend of hers did when Boris was in prison— surely, they wouldn't give a shit when the house went under and I found myself blowing dogs for Rite Aid coupons.

"You alright, Boris?" I asked. He looked worse than usual: bags like two black eyes, face scraggly and prickly like a cactus, his lean against the pillar more like a firing squad victim sliding down the wall. Still, as much as I wanted to feel for him, I couldn't make the leap, couldn't do anything but loathe. I'd endured the last three hours for Mom. Now I just wanted to curl up with a book of matches and douse myself in gasoline.

"You know, Julian," he said, eyes on the parking lot, "no. Not really."

"Good." I considered slapping him. The stains on his suit, which I now couldn't return, suggested he'd been slugging whiskey. I couldn't locate Nehemiah or Schmidt to run interference.

"The house. It was the house."

Like Ahab alone on the deck, he watched Mom's friends and family—people who'd tried to love him because they loved her—hug and sniffle and crawl into their Suburbans.

I sidled closer to him, tried to make eye contact, but his gaze wouldn't budge. He took out his flip-phone and snapped it in half.

"What the hell are you talking about?" I asked. The only thing I ever seemed to ask anymore.

Someone belted my name. The somber stuff was over; now the

buzz and chatter of this basketball court-sized room felt more like an engagement party than post-mortem tuna salad and grief. Panic pricked my chest again. I'd seen dozens of high school friends, my only source of wealth, but still hadn't seen Reid. Or Addy.

"I tried, Julian. I did. It wasn't too good, maybe, but I tried."

I'd seen Boris despondent thousands of times, really every day of the marriage, but his distance, the twitching of his lips and the gaze into nothingness—just blowing leaves and condom wrappers—reminded me of the tranquilized psychotics we'd visited for a psych class field trip.

"Wh—"

"I'm a bad person, Julian. I guess you're right. Least three people came to my dad's funeral, but what'll I have? You don't come, I don't blame you. I never provided anything. I just took and took. Mom and me both, maybe. And now, it's not enough."

"Boris."

"I tried to buy the house, Jude. With VA benefits and leftover 401(k) scratch. Another mortgage, at least. Stall them, I thought. But nothing, Julian. The bank just called. There's not a motherfucking thing we can do."

Reid's parents, all jitters and smiles, just like their son when he sniffed the market equilibrium of coke and dilaudid, ambled over. In the parking lot, Pastor Phil held a green bill to the sun, pocketed it, and inspected another. I hadn't paid him. Or thanked him.

"Your parents left us a little something, right? That's what Mom always said. Few thousand you were holding onto, I thought."

Boris rubbed his neck, still wouldn't look at me.

"Nobody's gonna be living in their car," I said with a chuckle. "That's months from now anyway. Maybe I'll be famous by then. *American Idyll?* This reality TV show—"

"Beaker. Jesus, Beaker. There was never any money from your grandmother. From anyone. Either side. If there had been, you think I'd be what I am? You'd be what you are? Maybe it can't buy happiness, but it at least makes it an option. What's my life now but disability checks and this splintered family? But using a fentanyl patch like truth serum, so I can have a real conversation with you for once."

"Boris, c'mon, man. With comedy and the museum, I can figure something—"

"You either laugh it off or kill yourself. I should've been sorry sooner."

He flipped around, walked toward the plastic plates and silver-ware. I shook the dose of reality from my brain and opened wide for a group hug with Reid's parents. I didn't know it, but this would be the last time I'd see Boris until after New York. Jail. Tom and Chris grabbing life by the horniness and getting bucked to the pavement.

"Really beautiful service, Jude," Reid Scheisskopf, Sr. said.

"And all those flowers?" said Randi Scheisskopf. "We even heard, um, that—"

"It was very nice of Stephen," I said with a clenched jaw, scanning for an escape hatch. Nehemiah must have left. Schmidt must have been scared off by all the alums riffing and staring. "Please thank him if you get the chance."

"Of course," said Mr. Scheisskopf.

I smiled. My good eye hurt from lack of sleep and excessive brow-vaulting. I could not recall the last meal, or even snack, I kept down.

"Sorry about Reid and Addy," Mrs. Scheisskopf sputtered. She rubbed blonde hair between her fingers. "There was . . . something came up at Reid's work? And Addy—"

"I know they'd be here if they could," I said, patting one of her hands as Mr. Scheisskopf interrogated his shoes.

"You're a born performer, Julian," he said, still not looking up. "That eulogy, I mean, my God! Your mother would be so proud!"

"It was nothing," I said. Boris slumped into a folding chair and poked at some fruit. Cassie burped her daughter while Lydia bounced the son. Male cousins and uncles crossed their arms, tapped their boots. Grandpa Konrad tugged his suspenders, glared. My phalanx of high school friends debated politics in their blazers and took quick toots from a flask. Tom and Chris sunk into the room's periphery and sent Snaps of the thinning mourners. And, taped to an examination table in a medical school basement, Mom's frozen stare and open mouth gave me permission to cry for the first time all day. But I refused. Recycled the grief and the hurt into another hollow smile. "This was all a big nothing."

6.

WHITE LIGHT, WHITE HEAT

"ONLY 90S KIDS Will Get This," I shouted a month later, leaning against the stool as the red light above the stage flashed. "A hundred thousand dollars of college debt and a job that doesn't require an undergrad degree!"

"Encore!" the crowd wailed. My comic pseudo-friends—Brandi Bates, Perry Slutsky, the PeterPuff Girls—nodded and whispered in the back. If they'd endured the professional envy for ten whole minutes, I must have done okay.

"That's my time, folks. I'm Jude Glick and I'm already regretting everything that's happened in the month of October. Nonetheless, don't despair, but remember: when they go low, we go high. And when we go high, we lose elections. Thanks and goodnight."

I whipped out my phone, pressed the digital rap airhorn app repeatedly, slid the mic into the stand, and bowed. Maybe they liked it; maybe they didn't. Either way I'd be returning to work tomorrow. Failing to impress the suits and hockey-watchers and real-job-havers couldn't compound my other failures. Even a 10% chance of being seen on TV by Madeline Einstein, to say nothing of Stephen Scheisskopf, rationalized whatever shameful *audition task* came next.

I shook the rheumy hand of Gunnar Peuschold, my primary *American Idyll* competitor. Tossing the red curtain aside, I burst into the narrow chasm backstage, really just a brick hallway, and exhaled.

I hated Gunnar. He and the producers knew it, which increased the odds they'd cast two Midwestern comics and not just one. He

123

was an exurban cokehead. A wet-brained and weed-withered community college dropout who only joked about pheasant hunting and pussy yet had spun his misogyny and ironic racism into multiple appearances on *Conan*. We were the only comedians who made it to the last round—everyone else back here whisper-sang over nylon-stringed fingerpicking or hula-hooped to Kenny G while juggling buckets of fried chicken—and the idea of piggybacking to primetime television disgusted me. But this was my first legitimate chance at financial success, so fuck art. What a privilege to have taste. To have options. If Gunnar's borderline fame could drag me to New York, I'd do whatever these network ciphers asked.

Some VP of Development huddled with one of the producers. They mumbled my name as I de-pocketed my flask of Everclear 190 and slugged with a pant. I was about to force down one more—the prospect of another night nuking freezer-burned dino nuggets and sighing into Mom's cat had me considering suicide again—when the VP, Brandon or Troy or Chad, another Ivy League football dipshit with a screenwriter dad and JD/MBA from USC, a living-breathing-and-back-slapping piece of empirical evidence that the meritocracy had died (if it had ever existed . . . and it hadn't), trotted over, Tom Ford suit (he told me within thirty seconds of meeting three weeks back . . . even though I hadn't asked and didn't care and told him I didn't care) constricting his tanned and kale-dependent body, his straight and white smile, his family's ability to afford dental and orthodontic work, on full display.

"Drew!" he said, offering a handshake I coughed my way out of. "Such a—"

"Drew?"

"Jew?"

"Jude. My name is Jude."

"Of course. Yes. Who could forget that! June the Obscure!" He ran a hand through his slicked-back dome of blond hair.

"How can I help you?" I asked, looking for a clock, already losing interest.

"Help me help you is what you can do! Now, I don't want to jump ahead of the process, but would you be able to make it to New York in, say, a few days? Should our team decide that's optimal, of course."

"Sure."

"Great!" He looked around me, through me, thumbs-upped the

producer, who jotted notes on her notepad and adjusted her headset. "Should it get to that point we'll be in touch, yeah? And if not, you've been lovely throughout all three rounds."

His fist, asking to be bumped, jutted toward me. I bumped lightly, not wanting to catch whatever defect made someone so hideously optimistic they could update LinkedIn without stuffing a 12-gauge in their mouth. What a pathetic thing is confidence. As though this pre-programmed high achiever had anything to do with his own success. Son of a lawyer-doctor couple who grew up in a house full of French novels and Ornette Coleman records. Acela Corridor Brownstone, or even just a big and dumb house on Lake Minnetonka. Some dipshit who slid out of the womb destined for cello lessons and Talented Youth Writing Workshops and moviemaking seminars. An algorithm churned out to learn the patterns of fake laughter. Wine sipping. Name dropping. In their Terry Gross interviews or Emmy speeches, the only thing they should thank is being born a winner when their lifestyles wouldn't exist without losers.

"Thanks for the opportunity," I said. He nodded, skipped back to the producer.

I slouched past the green rooms and took my seat at the end of the bar. Pried Mom's rosary beads from under my flannel, kissed the crucifix, and tried to conjure her voice. Then, two fingers raised for a double Wild Turkey neat, I decided to utilize this decent mood and dial the old man.

Although Boris and I had never spoken on the phone before Mom died, at least since the divorce, our talking over each other and long pauses gave us both something to do and/or the delusion we had someone who cared about us. He and Mom had talked at least once a week until the very end, or so he said, and he'd apparently been driving her to appointments (out of guilt? boredom?) as we deteriorated over the summer. Our conversations hinged on my knowledge of sports and reading of the local newspaper, or the latest academic travails of Tom and Chris, the latter of whom had been drinking more and maybe selling weed. Their possession charges cleared up with something north of $2,000 in fines and a hundred hours of picking up trash along the St. Croix River, but I had to learn it from the mother of some friend of theirs, a lovely and boring woman who—rightfully—worried they'd end up like me (but stupid and lazy) without Mom's guidance.

Boris didn't answer, so I slammed my Wild Turkey in two

125

burning gulps and left for the bus stop. Every walk around the emptying house, every open mic disaster or stifled chat with Boris only made me miss her more. Pain striking me at random like the tingle of a phantom limb. I couldn't watch a Vikings game or microwave lasagna without quivering and trembling. Forget the fame or the revenge. All I wanted was to share one more *Matlock* rerun.

I HAD LOGGED a few shifts since the end of bereavement leave, but they were all private events—weddings, pagan sex rituals, pagan sex weddings—either before or after hours. Nehemiah, without ever mentioning it, had eased me back into the horrors of underemployment. But a call from Management put the kibosh on his charity.

This was my first day back in gen pop.

After signing out my radio and weaving through the bowels of the museum, I entered the locker room. And the first thing I saw was John Coogan's fat white ass. The ass, which jousted from John's little slice of hell, resembled a Jackson Pollock, or maybe tuna salad, with its grooves and splotches, streaks of red and blue and yellow. John, whose tenure had outlasted my Mom's entire life (and would probably outlast mine), presented as a human but reminded me more of the sputtering animal robots from Chuck E. Cheese.

He yanked up his whitey tighties with his hairy knuckles, somehow ignoring the skid marks plastered on the back.

"Excuse me, John," I said, trying to squeeze past him.

He spun around, almost clipped me with his belly.

"Are you an agent of the Disney Corporation?"

"Uh."

"Well, are you?"

I blinked at him. The rest of the locker room was empty.

"Because my sources, like Nehemiah, see, the black fellow, my boss, you know, well, don't you? Don't you know him? Because, he, well, I've been here awhile. I know everything. Ear to the ground and the like. In fact, I own a periscope *and* spelunking equipment. Irregardless, someone in this museum is working on behalf of the Disney Corporation."

"Nice to see you, too," I said just as his mini-corndog finger poked my chest.

"Wouldn't you like to know!"

"John."

"Where do you come down on the question of eternal return?"

he asked as I squished across the carpet. Yes, carpet.

"Like the Nietzschean concept or—"

"Many people are saying that a hot dog is not a sandwich. The agents of Disney are amongst the unbelievers. What I can tell you with utmost certainty, Jed, is that their foot will slip. And their day of calamity is forthcoming. Vengeance will be mine. All I need is the word."

"Right," I said, rifling through my stuff. Unlike every other male guard's locker, I hadn't decorated. Just as moving in with your boyfriend makes things serious, or whatever *When Harry Met Sally*-speak plays as normal human banality, taping a pair of tits to the aluminum and storing a lute would suggest this job wasn't a failure but my future. A comfortable, personalized future. So I refused to decorate.

I did keep two books—*Between the World and Me* and *The Conspiracy Against the Human Race*—and an emergency bottle of Bacardi 151 for run-ins with acquaintances. Beyond that: my black cardigan, blue cowboy shirt, stiff khakis, and thrift store black dress shoes. The underachiever's starter pack.

As I buttoned up the sweater and flicked on my radio, eager to get to Nehemiah's office (or, really, command nook) without any non-Coogan social contact, the Sicilian guy, Umberto, G-9 his call number, almost as high as Nehemiah's even though Umberto had been here longer, shuffled over and worked on his locker combo.

"Your mother," he said, avoiding my eyes, "terrible. Helluva thing, no?"

"Uh-huh," I said. Coogan continued to mutter.

"We, how you say it, missed you?"

"Yeah?"

"No," he said, snickering and flinging the locker open, "of course we didn't. Well, I didn't. But good to see you anyway, eh? Eight hours in your head will be good thing for you, I am sure."

I nodded. With job requirements like *Enduring Indignity* and *Other Duties As Assigned*, I'd learned, after a year of physical threats from patrons or calling ambulances on convulsing docents, that nodding was the only option.

Out in the hallway—we were far under the museum, a bunker essentially—Nehemiah mumbled to management. Dolores Fitzentraiger. Thor Nesterstinko. Bob Smith. Probably about me, as they tight-smiled and scrambled to their offices when I approached.

Nehemiah had only worked here four months longer than me,

but his desperation to out-earn adjunct wages via overtime (and service as one of our union reps) shot him through the ranks, and he now captained the 8:00 a.m. to 4:00 p.m. shift, Tuesday through Saturday, our busiest hours and busiest days. Mostly because the other chief guards, stammering Mormons and bipolar photographers, perma-tripping pony-tailed drummers and face-pierced urban farmers, had no interest in making the same $21.50/hour with the addition of actual responsibility. If we lost power or someone had a heart attack, Nehemiah coordinated the response. Otherwise, he designed floor plans on the whiteboard and trained new guards. It was an awful job, and he knew it. The Emory undergrad and the PhD in Cultural Studies made me skeptical he'd ever deign to stick around a humiliation factory like this, but I underestimated him. Academia inflamed his sadness; his sadness intensified the desire to bang heroin; and his career-destroying addiction and guilt over his life Out There made a working-poor life more appealing than a working-high one.

He was not the only guard with a PhD. After the Great Recession, several sadder cases than Nehemiah—himself a pathetic expert on modernist social novels—had crawled into uniforms and welcomed the plantar fasciitis and gallows humor endemic to collectively bargained poverty.

"Jude," he said, shifting his radio off because the museum hadn't opened yet and any calls he received would only sour his day. "Sorry, man. How you been?"

"I've been . . ."

Living on frozen food. Getting teary at random. Waiting for cops to defenestrate me from Mom's house. Banking everything on a reality TV show appearance that probably wouldn't change things anyway.

". . . fine. Been fine. Thanks for asking."

"You sure? Because I . . . well I know what loss is like and—"

"Officer, I didn't know I couldn't do that!" someone rasped. "And, y'know, Carol, I found that punchline one helluva frame for white racial resentment in 2016."

Just then Carol, a wide and tube-nosed sociologist who'd been forced into early retirement by her school's Personnel Optimization Quotient, clanked down the hall with Sandy, a grandmother of twenty who'd been here longer than John. She spent her shifts reading while everyone else indulged their mental illnesses or papered them over with substance use.

"What's the quote? That anxiety is the handmaiden of contemporary ambition," Carol said as they waddled toward the break room. "The Gallery Guard as cultural critic," Sandy chuckled. "You'd think it was Dr. Nehemiah Weaver limping down the hall. Or Jude the Absurd over there." I looked at Nehemiah, who looked at his shoes.

They kept shuffling and wheezing down the hall.

"Y'all didn't know that? Sandy, I've been here a year. Not by choice."

"Know what now?"

"That I used to teach American Studies and Sociology down at Carleton?"

"I thought you were kidding. These kids are so ironic all the time, I figured you—"

"Nope," Carol said with a pant and head yank, asking me to push her oxygen tank. I did. "No. I absolutely taught there. Jude here could tell ya. He probably knew some folk who came up here to talk nonsense with the other liberal arts kids. Ain't that right, Jude?"

"Sure thing."

They stopped for breath, oblivious to the filling hallway. People contorted around the two women to pat me on the back or offer a low wave, but mostly I stood there, always fascinated with the wisdom of two women who had every reason to be bitter and somehow weren't.

"So," Sandy said to me as Nehemiah muttered and walked away. "You went to college and you ended up here?"

"We both did!" Carol said. "Gotta pay for high-deductible health insurance somehow!"

"Not everybody can win the race! At least *you* led for a while!" Sandy said with a laugh. They heaved into the break room, me inching with the tank close behind, where Nehemiah would soon explain procedures for any senators' visits or Civil War re-enactments taking place in the galleries. I'd stand there, avoiding eye contact and hoping he wouldn't welcome me back, and after enduring dozens of unconvincing condolences, the day and foot pain would start. And that's exactly how it went. Until it didn't.

BEFORE THE BLOODBATH, before the shattered wrists and throat slits and near-death experiences, I was bored. I was always fucking bored. As demeaning as I found my MAOI gig, the humiliating parties and social landmines planted by events at least kept me occupied. With suicidality and shame, yes, but on a regular day this job was so under-stimulating I wondered if I slid into drug addiction simply because it helped salt away the hours.

Nehemiah had stationed me on the third floor. The quietest of the three. European Art, mostly. Impressionism. Expressionism. A couple Picassos. Nine hours of either pacing our assigned zones or slumping against a pillar. And, if you could tolerate the guards stationed adjacently, exhausting your charisma, your shared interests, your suicide jokes. But because we couldn't leave our sections unless relieved by another guard—and since the seniors or physically disabled folks snapped up the desk placements—if you hated your proximal colleagues or just found them worse than shuffling alone, you spent your shift walking past the same installations, wondering how your life became blisters and regret.

I was in Area 32, talking to Colin Ressler, when the fascists arrived. Good old 32. A football field of free-flowing galleries, basically an open floor plan stuffed with late Northern Renaissance-inspired installations. Two Dürer prints, several Peter Bruegel the Elders, some Bosch, and one of five surviving Fabritius' alone on a wall. All flowing into a dim alcove where we kept Vermeer's *Woman in Blue Reading a Letter*, a literally priceless oil-on-canvas on indefinite loan from the Rijksmuseum (not that I knew any of this, or cared, before working here . . . if you find this shit boring imagine what it's like to spend fifty hours a week with the detritus), when I heard chanting below me, somewhere on the second floor.

We were leaning against the rotunda railing where 32 and 33 meet, debating the hundreds of cons (and zero pros) of graduate school.

"Weird," said Ressler, peering down.

You will not replace us! You will not replace us!

I bit my nails, looked down. Carol was at the main entrance, working the doors that led to the second floor and screaming "10-19" into the radio as bodies stampeded past.

"10-19?" I said to Ressler.

"This early? Nehemiah's gonna be pissed," he said, turning up his radio.

We called a 10-19 when there was something we didn't want to, or couldn't, deal with: galloping drunks, prom pictures, fingerbanging near the ancient Confucian gong. Anything that required

Nehemiah's deft touch but didn't elevate to the level of immediately calling the police. That'd be a 10-60 and it hadn't been employed this decade. We had called a 10-55 when Scheisskopf's sister Gwendolyn smashed her skull in the lobby, but even medical emergencies were rare in the age of opiate abuse and WebMD.

"Guards in 32 and 33, you've got trouble coming up the grand staircase and the Otis!" Sandy, who must have been in 23 hollered over echoes and stomping feet. We heard the rumble bouncing down our galleries before we saw it: a group of skinheads and neo-Nazis, some wearing a red hat associated with the Republican nominee, others swastika armbands, marched up the steps and started coming toward us.

"Oh, crap," Ressler said, hand twisting his split ends.

"We can't do anything if they're just here to—oh, crap," I said.

Bats. Chains. Shimmering brass knuckles.

"Jude," Colin said, "what do we do?"

The fascists were here to fuck something, or someone, up.

I'd been focused on my untriumphant return, and maybe we all had because Nehemiah didn't mention anything, but today was also the two-month anniversary of that non-terrorist attack. The one the Scheisskopf and *Breitbart* still frothed about. The one that happened the morning Mom died. Those Yemeni activists hadn't been charged with any felonies, but this didn't stop Scheisskopf from decrying the "leftist conspiracy against American Rule of Law."

Oh, there was also a presidential election next Tuesday.

The doors to the Otis opened and we saw what was about to happen: a horde of black-clad anti-fascists—a black bloc—had shown up to counter the alt-right with violence, surrounded by billions in Medieval and Renaissance art.

"Was there a friggin' protest?" Ressler said as the black bloc streamed from the Otis, in his area, maybe thirty feet away. "What in the absolute hell is—"

"Dude," I said, watching Sandy and Carol look up at us. "We gotta go over there."

The black bloc strolled, ten-deep, toward the fascists. Across the length of 33, the other half of this long corridor. Meanwhile the fascists, twenty-deep but gaining strength with a trickle up the steps, pretended to interrogate the Holbeins and Schongauers.

"The Aryans," said Ressler, an art history major.

We zipped around the milling leftists and stood between the

groups when, a few hundred feet behind us, near the Vermeer (and two stories up from the lobby), a phalanx of all black turned a corner and started our way. Reinforcements.

"Jude, this is happening."

"Excuse me, ah, ah, Captain?" John Coogan said over the radio. "Yeah, ah, looks like we need a light bulb replaced in 29 here, in the ah, ah, the Qing Dynasty, or, I'm sorry, the Ming Dynasty—what is it? A brothel? Looks a bit like a brothel."

The white nationalists continued perusing the galleries near the other stairs. Maybe thirty or forty now. The radicals came to a stop ten feet away, unfurled a *Good Night White Pride* banner as the two dozen backups jogged over.

In the middle: me and Colin Ressler.

Nobody was touching the art or breaking any rules, so we just stood as Coogan rambled over the radio.

"Yeah, hey, ah, Captain? Anyone know who the Captain is today? Is it, ah, Calvin? No, no. He's nights. Isn't Calvin nights? Well, any-who, looks like some little girl left her, ah, it's not quite a glove, you know, perhaps a mitten makes more sense. Though none of this makes much sense. It really isn't too cold out. Even for late October, which, ah . . ."

The brinksmanship continued—Coogan providing commentary—until a guy with an SS logo tattooed on his face wandered to a painting.

"Get a load of this shit," he said, loud enough for everyone to hear. "*Portrait of a Wealthy African*, it says."

A bunch of the fascists laughed.

"Excuse me," I said, stepping forward. Nehemiah had just popped out of the Otis with a few of our burlier guards and broom-toting janitors, and started weaving through the black bloc. "Excuse me, but please don't crowd the art."

They ignored me. My heart thumped like I'd bolted from bed post-nightmare.

"*Although undeniably Flemish or Germanic in origin,*" the SS guy read to whoops and hollers, "*it is unclear if the artist himself originated in Africa. Although dated around the time of Phillis Wheatley and Olaudah Equiano, the painting*—ah, fuck it. It's the shittiest one in here, anyway. No shock."

"Shut the fuck up," yelled someone from the black bloc a few feet away. I caught Nehemiah's eyes as his peacekeepers squeezed into our no man's land. One of the janitors cracked his knuckles.

"Get the fuck out of here," another voice said.

"Why?" a new fascist said, voice caked in condescension, this one wearing a tailored suit, not too different from Tom's at the funeral, but coiffed with a Hitler haircut. "We're just here to enjoy the art. Make some friends. Take in the galleries. The same galleries you and your Muslim Brotherhood friends so desperately want to destroy, just like the rest of white culture. Because you don't have your own."

"Fuck off, fascist," a leftist said. The suited fascist looked kinda like Tom's roommate.

Both mobs were grumbling now as the alt-right leader, who spoke with the same polished smarm as Stephen Scheisskopf, strode into our demilitarized zone, thousand-dollar shoes gliding across the marble and standing two yards from the leftist banner.

"Would you look at these race traitors," the leader said, rocking back-and-forth and looking at me and Ressler. "Don't they know we're gonna win on the 8th? Scheisskopf has all but guaranteed it. And yet they cling to the losing team, the genetically inferior team."

"Fuck you," I said. He straightened.

"What?" he said. His poshness had disappeared. "What did you just say?"

"Fuck you, is what I said."

Ooohs! shot out like this was high school.

"Fuck me?" he said, not inches from my face.

"Yeah," a voice said. I turned and it was Principal Schmidt ripping off her mask and stepping toward the fascist. I dropped back as she slid in and towered over him. "Fuck you."

"Fuck me?"

"Fuck you."

"I know who you are, leftist lezzie. I'll doxx you. Wouldn't want 4chan looking into the company you keep. The immigration status or warrants."

"Kayden Kiffmeyer, right?" she said, cocking her head. "I love that idea. And I find your stunted masculinity ever so attractive right now."

"My what?"

"Your white supremacy really gets me going."

"Going where?" he said as his stormtroopers closed ranks.

"Here."

She kissed him on the lips.

Twice.

Wet and sloppy and cartoonish.

Nobody moved. One Mississippi. Two Mississippi.

Nehemiah raised the radio to his lips. "Carol," he said, "10-60."

The first punch cracked Schmidt straight in the jaw, sending her careening toward a janitor, who was protecting a gold sculpture. Then it all happened fast, both sides running at each other and screaming like *Braveheart*. Or a more primal Red Rover. Not sure of my role in all this, and not invested in protecting the art, I haymakered the first fascist I saw, crunching something as the guy staggered into a display case that didn't budge. He crumpled to the floor as I looked around. The action was mostly drifting down 33, where the fascist line had formed.

Blood splattering the marble. Shrieks and snaps. Schmidt unconscious. Ressler poking a broom at a chain-swinging white supremacist. An anti-fascist wobbling ass-up like a pigeon. The thought, fully-formed, flashed in my head.

I am scared.

Still, I clomped toward the kerfuffle, kicking some /pol/ dweeb in the ribs as he curled into the fetal position. The fascists were retreating—some had sprinted back down the staircase, another dove through the rotunda and landed with a thud and a scream—but then I saw the glint of steel and heard a mechanical click.

"Knife!" I heard.

"Help!" someone said.

Then a sheet of blood splashed a didactic and a figure in all black barrel-rolled away.

They didn't train us for this. They didn't train us for anything, really, other than how to deal with vegetative donors who shit their pants or school groups face-sitting on statues. The old hands had defused some fights, some domestic violence, but this was new.

Advancing, radio swinging from the antenna like nunchucks, I was bringing up the rear, I realized, too enthralled by some antifa beating on the stragglers, when I glanced at one of the bleeding and writhing leftists.

It was Nala

My *friend* Nala.

Schmidt was injured, something I'm sure had happened in her years of radical direct action, but Nala was President of the Peace Club in high school, had fixed a Eugene McCarthy button on her book bag. She weighed maybe a hundred pounds. She'd moved home for a CAIR internship. And some internet Nazi had shanked her.

"10-55," I called into the radio, now running into the scrum, "call an ambulance. Multiple 10-55s."

The melee had scattered now, small-group skirmishes radiating into separate galleries near the stairs, but a few good guys, including Nehemiah, were swinging bats at the thugs with knives. The suit guy lunged recklessly, blood dripping from the blade as I rushed to the front line.

It was clear Nehemiah's loyalties aligned with social justice, not SEIU 26, because he took two power-hops and launched an upper-cut that connected with the suit guy's right hand, snapping his wrist back with a stomach-turning pop and skipping the knife across the marble and into gallery 34. The momentum of the swing spun the fascist around almost two full revolutions and he landed at my feet just as another stormtrooper sucker punched me in the ear, bouncing my head off the marble.

I didn't lose consciousness but found my skull wet with blood and ringing. I touched fingers to my good eye—losing it is a never-ending source of anxiety—and realized instead I'd lost my glasses. I was trying to reorient myself when I heard the word Americans never want to hear in a public place:

"He's got a gun!" someone screamed, maybe into the radio, none of this made sense anymore and it all had the light dust of surreality I'd experienced after my only football concussion. I noticed the suit guy, right wrist hanging loosely at a 45-degree angle from his arm, reaching across his body to unholster a pistol with his left hand. He was a scooch of the ass away from me—I could almost kick his back—but as he fumbled with the gun, dropping it once, I didn't think of running or hiding or shrieking: I thought of Mom.

She thought I'd *make something of myself,* that trite white-person way of ignoring luck and privilege. And of course now she'd never see it. But since her death I'd been carrying around her rosary necklace in my back right pocket. I'd never used them, had no intention to. But just keeping them on me, when I knew how many nights she squeezed and whispered over them in the hospital or when she didn't know how we'd make it to the next month, pushed suicide out of mind for a few minutes, like an antidepressant that actually works.

So I dug them out and started untwisting as the fascist at my feet collected himself and his gun and, using one hand and his chest, tried cocking. The necklace had de-scrambled and his cock-and-safety-flip must have worked because someone screamed "Holy shit!" just as I lasso'd the rosary around his neck and pulled him toward me, hands crawling up the slack to yank harder and harder—his left hand, the gun hand, trying to reach back to my face, how funny would it be if someone other than me blasted my brains out, I thought on a loop, pulling harder, harder—and then, slapping me with his shattered wrist and starting to gasp, I saw the black muzzle of the gun directly in front of my left eye and I heard a bang and let go of my garrote because I assumed I was dead.

WITH MAJOR AMBIVALENCE, I learned I wasn't. The cops had arrived, a SWAT team, I guess, and someone had busted rubber bullets into suit guy's chest. If it weren't for all the dabbing vomit and mucous and infected tissue from Mom's abrasions and lesions, I probably would have passed out from the blood he coughed up.

Instead, I just closed my eyes and lay on the marble, still unsure what was real.

For a few minutes, I heard cops and medical personnel sprint and yell. I kept playing dead. But once the cuffed fascist stopped moaning at my feet, I pocketed the rosary and wobbled to my feet, watching Nala get triaged by some EMTs and, inexplicably, Sandy.

"Back away, sir," a cop said as I crowded the medical folks.

"Crud," Sandy said. "Crud. Crud. Crud."

Through snippets, I deduced that Nala was unconscious ("lotta blood on this here floor!") and that Sandy had been a trauma medic in Vietnam.

Guards and janitors tottered in circles, bumping into each other. Camera crews started setting up live shots as cops hollered about active crime scenes. I lay down, closed my eyes again. When I opened them, it was unclear how much time passed with all the radio-barking and stretcher-loading. Looking for Nehemiah, I found Ressler slumped at the base of a sculpture case in 33, panting.

"Dude," he said.

"How are we not dead?" I asked.

"Dude."

The cops kept zip-cuffing the fascists. They'd protested without a permit, we overheard a sergeant explain to one of our PR hacks, and security footage already showed conclusively they'd thrown the first punches.

"Jude," Ressler said, staring at his legs, "that dude with the gun? He's a fucking frat president at Winona State."

"What?" I said, already leaping ahead: that motherfucker looked familiar because he must have been Lars Kiffmeyer's older brother. Tom's roommate. My brothers had rushed a fascist fraternity. Of course. They didn't care about anything outside of edibles and nudes.

"Dude."

I stumbled around bodies and detectives and bodily fluids, still trying to find my friends. Nala had disappeared. Hopefully not in a body bag.

Then, down in 32, near the Vermeer, I saw Nehemiah's afro and hurdled over. Schmidt lay at his feet.

She was ecstatic, looking up glass-eyed and knuckle-scraped at the two of us.

"Good night white pride," she slurred into snores. "Good night, moon. Good night, stars."

"Nehe—"

"I'm gonna kill these motherfuckers," he said. "Godfucking-dammit, I'ma finish these motherfuckers off myself."

I reached out to rub his shoulder, y'know, some vague gesture of warmth, but he pulled away from me.

"Don't touch me, dude." He exhaled, sweat-covered and shaking. "I'm sick of fucking white people, man. Even the good ones. What even is a good one, at this point, when most of you unleashed fucking fascism?"

"Nee—"

"Even Schmidt. Class, class, class. You see who he was gonna shoot? Did you? Guess. Me. Black guy. Only black guy when he had white folk running around. Not that I'm gonna tell the fuckin' cops."

"I—"

"I'm just so tired, Jude," he said, slinking along the wall as they loaded another stretcher into the Otis. "What's changed in eight years, man?"

"Nee, c'mon," I said. "Look at how much better your life is since—"

"Since selling drugs to fucking pregnant women? Motherfucker, I still did that with a black president." He sighed. "You don't know what it's like, J.G. No matter how good a person I am anymore, or how clean, or how educated. I'm a black man, so I can get cut down anytime, dude. By cops. By white supremacists. By scared-ass regular folk who don't like the way I walk."

"I don't know what to—"

"No, you don't because there isn't anything to say, J.G. You can't be non, Jude. You gotta be anti."

"Anti?"

"Non-racist isn't good enough. Anti-racist is what I need. I'm done with liberal talk. That's non-racist. We need anti-racist white folks if this shit'll ever change. We need doers."

"Let's do it then. When Scheisskopf comes," I said, half-joking. Cops were milling around taking statements, my head still vibrated like a bell. Per usual, I had no idea what I was saying and just wanted him to feel better. Or to like me.

"When who—"

"They're gonna win, man. America's a farce. They have to. It makes too much sense. They're gonna win and rally here. Just like they promised."

He considered this. Longer than I expected, really.

"Would you be down? Theoretically, of course."

"Me?"

"Yeah. We'd need to know," he said, waving off a medic who was approaching with gloves and a kit. My head pulsed, not the side of the punch but the side of the bounce and whiplash, and a shot of fear iced through me when I realized I could probably use this to fetch pills. Total sobriety looked increasingly like the only way to a healthy or stable life. But that life sounded fucking awful. "When the time comes, Jude, you don't gotta show me."

I thought of Malik. Gasps. Fear. Loneliness. Born boxed-in.

I clapped Nehemiah's shoulder.

"I'm gonna go visit my friend in the hospital," I said.

Nehemiah just shook his head and watched the boots shuffle by.

AS I CRACKED my back in the trauma wing lobby, another would-be mourner flipped on CNN. Scheisskopf was introducing The Mogul in exurban Pittsburgh. Twenty thousand racist car dealers and abstinence-only-promoting school nurses hooted and snarled. The ticker scrolled with MAOI factoids and rumors.

"We are taking back what's ours, folks," Scheisskopf hollered. "And it starts with STANDING. UP. TO. AN-TEE-FUH!"

"Jesus H. Christ," I said. I'd been sitting with sobbing strangers— sober—for five hours. Nala had survived, at least, but only family could visit until the surgeon signed off.

I was not, uh, family.

This was already dominating Minnesota Public Radio. "Sign o' the times is more than just a Prince song," one broadcaster said on the ride over. A few acquaintances wandered the halls. High school activists. The performative liberals who'd solicited them for handjobs between class. More people I wanted nowhere near my life but who were now somewhere near my life. I had shed the uniform, but still hunkered behind a fish tank, scanned for anxiogenic faces. The occasional cop or local news dullard waddled through, took statements, asked if anyone had seen Julian Gladden Glick.

Thankfully, they hadn't. Under normal circumstances, I'd cultivate any attention and notoriety I could. But I didn't need cops digging through my shit, even if I'd done nothing wrong. Plus, I'd been on local news before for football, the commencement speech. Wouldn't sate my hunger anyway.

So whenever I recognized someone, I coughed into my shoulder, ducked into the bathroom. It was only 4:00 p.m., but Nehemiah's despair felt etched in the fossil record.

The museum, I had learned via all-staff email, would be closed indefinitely.

"Again and again," Scheisskopf said, cranking the dial to 11, "the so-called tolerant left—snowflakes, folks, snowflakes—they come charging at our patriots, our very fine people, but where is the guilt? Good Lord. And at the same museum as their radical Muslim terrorist allies! Where is the guilt for what they've done to this country's heritage? It's national pride? It's self-esteem? What's more violent, folks, the abortion-pimping cultural Marxists who want us to slaughter babies and impregnate out of wedlock until we're a diluted shade of brown, or the—"

I stood up, turned it off, lumbered toward the elevator. My bad shoulder throbbed, my head buzzed and tingled. Enough of this. I wasn't even close to Nala. A nod to her mother and brother, which I offered around noon, should have sufficed.

Who was the audience here? And did I always ask this question first?

As the elevator dinged and opened, out stepped Addy.

Maybe this was my answer.

"Oh my God," she said, wrapping me in a hug. And not letting go. "J.G., are you just getting out? Are you okay? I tried to call your brothers, but I couldn't get ahold of—"

"Nah, I came to visit Nala. I'm fine. Hardly involved. Did you . . . I mean has anyone—"

"Yeah, it's all over the news and Facebook. A certain someone has started twisting it into a fascist talking point, too."

"This certain someone is on CNN screeching in Pennsylvania right now, Ads. He's using it to introduce—"

"Jesus."

"Shame he isn't around, yes."

Someone bumped into my right shoulder. Pain rocketed down my arm as I turned and saw Lars Kiffmeyer—Tom's hockey-haired roommate—glare at me from the closing elevator. His hat was red with white letters.

"Did you know that guy?" Addy asked. "J.G.?"

"Nah," I said, clenching my jaw. "Thought I recognized him from standup or something."

"How's that going? You've been a ghost since—"

"I'm surprised you care."

"Jude, look—"

"If anyone's a fucking ghost, it's you and Reid."

Addy looked around. "Do we have to do this here? Now?"

I snorted. "You're right. Maybe we should do it at my mother's funeral."

"Here we go."

"His parents said he was at work, Addy, when 72 hours earlier you told me—"

"He was! Seriously. Yes, yes, no, let me finish. After you dressed him down and made him feel like total shit, he went back to work. And it's like they've been punishing him with these hundred-hour weeks."

"Really?"

"He hates it, Jude, but you were right. We took a break."

"Jesus, Addy, I didn't mean to—"

"Well, whatever you did mean, it isn't working for me. We were gonna go on our first date in weeks tonight, but when I heard Nala is half-dead, I . . . I dunno. How am I gonna sit through Surly and a movie tonight?"

I blinked at her.

"No, seriously, I'm asking," she said. "I miss you, J.G. But over the last six months you've been so angry. I tried explaining it to Nala, actually, but—"

"You've been talking with Nala about me?" I said, starting to blush.

"Good things! But, yeah, ever since that night at the museum, and then the rally that next morning, we've been seeing each other a lot. I should've kept up with her. *You* should've kept up with her. She's really helped me sort through what I want out of life, y'know? And whatever it is, it isn't what I've been doing. This PR crap. This consumerism. I actually took some time off, after she turned me onto—you'll get a kick out of this—Schopenhauer. Enlightened pessimism. Too pessimistic for me, but still. That's why I'm here. So why are you?"

"Because I'm a narcissist and loser? Because I have no prospects as a comedian, or a human being, and at least showing solidarity, or empathy, makes me marginally better than Scheisskopf? I don't know."

Addy squinted at me. My phone buzzed. A 212 number. New York City.

"Hello?" I said, as Addy crossed her arms.

"Juice, this is Cross Yoder-Henley. The SVP of Development at—"

"Lemme guess: you liked what I showed at the audition, but you feel that—"

"No. The opposite. We've been tryna get a hold of you. If you're game, you've got a spot on the first weekend of *American Idyll: Hunger Pains Edition.* That'd be next weekend. You're on the hook for your own airfare, fyi. And room, board, whatever."

"Holy shit."

"I don't even need a yes right now. But I'd like one."

"Holy shit."

"What?" Addy mouthed.

I covered the phone, mouthed a very famous three-letter network.

"Holy shit," Addy said.

"Say," Cross said, "sounds like you're awfully busy. And if you aren't, well, I certainly am. So make up your damn mind in, oh, ten minutes. And then call me back, 'kay? Seriously though. Ten minutes."

He hung up. I pocketed the phone.

"Jude," Addy said, "is this that reality show you posted about?

With the audition tape?"

I nodded. This was my break. My big, shameful, stupid break.

"So friggin' call him back, J.G."

So I did. I rang him thirty seconds later, committed to being in NYC six days after the fascist fracas. And if I'd known then what I knew now, I wouldn't have said yes. I would've dunked the phone, and my head, in the toilet. But I accepted the offer. I signed the papers. I faxed them. And, if I had the foresight to decline, if I could have swallowed my hunger, maybe I wouldn't be famous, and certainly I never would have seen the Manhattan skyline up close, but I wouldn't be the Most Wanted Man in America either.

7.

ROAD RULES/REAL WORLD CHALLENGE

"WHAT THE HELL are you talking about?" I asked a Hennepin County Sheriff. It was one week before the election and three days before my New York Hail Mary.

"Truck," said Lieutenant Joe Bob Donglefritz, thumbing an in-grown hair on his chin, "or curb?"

Two squad cars pimpled the driveway, deputies bouncing shot-guns on their knees. An eighteen-footer, the same sort I'd spent col-lege loading with asbestos and lead, idled down the block. Unfortu-nately, Tom and Chris had planned on spending fall break here this weekend.

"These papers, the pro bono attorneys? They said I should have till May if—"

"If the bank kept this a civil matter, which they didn't. Now, son, I ain't a social worker, okay? Do I look like Maury Povich to you?"

"Yes."

"I am the father . . . of this here law enforcement confrontation should it come to that, eh?"

I nodded. As he rubbed his crow's feet, I considered my options. I had sold anything of Mom's that didn't induce grief or guilt, and the twins hoarded their essentials (e.g., dab torches and erection sets) in Winona. Lou Grant and a Costco tub of Benadryl had shacked up with a neighbor. But 24 years of *my* life sat inside the house. And Boris was . . . somewhere. And all of Mom's relatives lived at least three hours away. And explaining to Reid, Addy, any of my friends or Mom's friends that I needed a place to live indefinitely required pride-swallowing that stuck in my throat.

The first snowflakes of the season hovered around Joe Bob's tan uniform. The sun sunk. We had an Alberta clipper blowing in Saturday morning, but I could endure in the van until NYC. Still, if I had to sell Mom's wedding ring, or her grandfather's Ortgies 7.65, she would've understood. Or maybe I could wrestle the sheriff's gun from the holster and commit suicide by cop.

"We've met, by the way," he said. I flared my nostrils, flexed my forearms.

"Is that right?"

"Couple times, even. Most recent was when ya got lit up and left in yer car a couple months back. Over Nordeast. If you recall, I let you off easy."

"Thank you for your service."

"Well, technically we ain't serviced this foreclosure until you make a decision."

I bit my lips, peeled off skin. Social mobility in America is either a truck or a curb.

"If it eases yer thinking on it, we charge for the eighteener. And storage is bonded."

"My mother left me $47,000 in medical debt. I make $13.72 an hour."

"Right," he said, holding some pink papers to his face, "that'll be a problem for you soon enough, but let's get this part over with, huh? Me and the boys got nine more of these today. So c'mon, bub, showtime."

"Aren't I entitled to an attorney or—"

"Not anymore. Curb it is."

He stuck two fingers in his mouth, whistled. His accomplices shot from their cars and double-timed toward the house. Donglefritz removed his nightstick. And cracked me across the jaw.

"That's for running yer fucking mouth," he said, brushing past. "Maury my ass."

They skittered the house like fascist roombas, smashing my great-grandmother's antique china, chucking picture frames out windows, macing my sheets and mattress because they could. Because I'd inconvenienced some pigs. And what was I gonna do? Call the ACLU? Videotape these random acts of cop-ness? Even if I'm white, I was still poor, and that summer, not ten miles away, a black St. Paul public school employee had been executed by the police on Facebook Live. The killer would never sniff jail-time, so, what, the justice system would take pity on my postmodernist paperbacks and poverty ethnographies? Maybe I had a liberal arts degree with an English minor, but I wasn't stupid. With the specter of debtors' prison already replacing the foreclosure anxiety, I didn't need another legal infraction or face bruise.

I massaged my neck. I exhaled into fists. I rolled my shoulders and watched them yank, pile, toss. My right molars throbbed.

To protect (capital) and serve (you foreclosure papers).

This was nothing new. My disgust for authority, and dick-swinging white men in particular, seemed as hardwired as my cancer. Before I was born, Boris once fractured Mom's eye socket. So she called the cops, they hauled a slurring B.G. to the drunk tank, and then Mom's landlord evicted her for causing a ruckus. You know the rest: Mom moved in with her abuser, got pregnant, got married and squeezed out the first of her trauma-stained children. As a five-year-old, I once called the cops on Boris when Mom was out of town for a funeral. We spent the night in a shelter for homeless youth, and when Mom picked us up with Aunt Lydia, she slapped me so hard I lost a tooth.

I massaged my welting jaw as a deputy pocketed my iPod.

"Cut that out," Donglefritz said.

His subordinate eyed him, me, him.

"Joe Bob, we—"

"Don't be a monster."

The officer tossed me the iPod, skulked away as movers manhandled my bookcase.

"Thanks for that," I said. It was a refurbished first gen that hadn't worked in years.

"Not like I enjoy doing this," he said, staring at his boots.

I knew how he'd rationalize it if pressed: kids to feed; nursing-homed mother-in-law; dog just had puppies. The same middle-class complicity that had us starving Yemeni children and shrugging at Flint's lead-poisoned water. Rich liberals were even worse than apolitical ciphers like Donglefritz. At least rich conservatives didn't even pretend to care.

"Why're ya muttering to yourself, son?" he asked.

"Because this doesn't need to be happening."

"You should maybe see a dentist."

"I haven't seen a dentist since Clinton was president."

"That seems irresponsible." He dug around his back pocket, produced his wallet, and waved a crumpled twenty-dollar bill.

"What's that for?" I said.

"Buy yourself something nice," he said, handing it to me. "Maybe a bottle of whiskey. Or some fucking manners. This system ain't fair to either of us."

He left. I unruffled the money and stood in my bedroom, squeezing Mom's rosary beads and wishing I believed in God.

I missed her. Even if she'd passed down her mistakes. Tried hard, too hard, to provide a comfortable life. To insulate us from her income, her high school education. She wanted the best for her three boys, and that was the fucking problem.

Eventually, Donglefritz returned. "Time to go, Hoss."

He led me through the bare house; I saw the salvage heaped on the curb. No more birthday cakes. No more *Jeopardy!* No more playing with the cat. No more peeling potatoes with Mom and making her laugh. No more beating Tom and Chris in *MarioKart*, or fingerpicking Springsteen songs in the bedroom. I'd sold our memories on craigslist for less than $1000.

Once outside, our neighbor, Mr. Bonser, the retired theremin player, waved at me as he cleaned his garage. I felt like crying but didn't want these men to see me break.

"Are you people done ruining my life yet?" I said once Donglefritz had sent his squad and the movers to the next house. We stood at the front door. Snow swirled as he slid a lock in the frame.

"Do I look like Judge Judy to you?"

"Ye—"

"I look more like Matlock, buddy. And you look like you're trespassing on bank-owned property."

"C'mon, man."

He sighed. I knuckled my temples.

"You want some advice, kid? Man-to-man?"

"Not exactly."

"Thank God. I don't really have any. My dad wasn't around neither. But, hell, you can't let 'em win, kid, eh? Keep going."

"Where?"

"Do I look like . . . ah, forget it. I'll leave you be, but between you and me, partner? This debt thing ain't gonna go away, y'know, so you gotta write the State er—"

"I wrote you people a letter. There is no estate. The estate is me, writing on goddamn cardstock, with glitter pens, that I am the executor of the estate."

"That's tough to hear."

"I agree. I think—"

"I mean, glitter pens? I oughta probe you with my service weapon, buddy. Glitter pens?"

"So . . . goodbye? Do we shake hands? Or are you gonna just, like, put a warrant out for my arrest at some point and—"

"Do I look like Miss Cleo?"

"Well . . ."

I blinked at him, feeling leaky. He stared somewhere above my left shoulder, rubbed his chin. My face still hurt.

"Hennepin County grant me the legal authority to accept the criminals I cannot change, the courage to change the derelicts I can, and the donuts to know the difference."

"What?"

"You seem like one heck of an asshole, but I kinda like you all the same. So, look, think on this: if you do not enter some sorta arrangement with the State, which requires either a court proceeding or a formally negotiated non-court proceeding, you will be in a bad way," he said, snapping into a smile and wink. He patted me on the back. "Take care, kiddo. Get yer paperwork done."

TWO HOURS AND one McDonald's shit later, I was shivering in a van I didn't own. If Tom and Chris hadn't been arrested their first day of college, I wouldn't even be driving it. Hypothermia seemed plausible, and neither Tom nor Chris had returned my voicemail. It had slipped into the upper single-digits. Mom bought the 1995 Chevy Astro with Boris pre-divorce. Per the decree, she got the whip, Boris got the solitude, we kids got the trauma, and everybody came out unhappy.

Since the electricity fizzled in the summer, the van had no heat. Since we lived in a neighborhood that had been victim to the opioid epidemic, it had no passenger-side window. Since my entire life cluttered the seats and trunk, it had no choice but to be my temporary home. I circled the block then rolled through snowdrifts to the park across from MAOI. Taking off a full two weeks when I only needed ten days now looked stupider than my Michelin Man jacket. At least I had my Grandpa Glick's gun in the glovebox.

I blew on my hands. When that didn't work, I shrugged into a third pair of gloves. This was fashion-forward; I soon applied a third set of socks to my booted feet. They kept playing a Scheisskopf interview on NPR that demanded more booze than I'd rationed for the evening, so I read Kafka by flashlight and debated crying.

Although I'd never been homeless—and, judging by the well-populated trashfire down East 25th Street, would never feel comfortable with the moniker—I *had* mastered running out the clock on life. Eight-hour jaunts to the library on college Friday nights. Playing catch with myself as Boris throttled Mom. Beers nursed between sets to avoid open-mikers and their tragically happy friends. Likewise, every job, maybe every human interaction, was a thing I endured until I could leave. Life is simply a joyless countdown.

So when I grew tired of *The Trial*, I whispered cuts from *The Sound of Music*. Mom had played Maria in high school.

Shrinks in white unis with Wellbutrin caches
Snowflakes that stay on my nose and eyelashes
Suicide winters that melt into springs
These are a few of my favorite things

A staggering man tapped on my window. I ignored him. He tapped again. I suckled my bottle of Old Crow and stared into the darkness. The fellow groaned, growled. Still, I refused to look. Maybe twenty minutes later, my liter of whiskey now backwash, I finally relented; I didn't want to open my emergency bottle.

He had built a snowman. He was fucking the snowman. I squinted as he changed positions. The guy looked familiar. Bearded. Leather jacket. Meth-carved. If I'd recognized him then, I would've apologized. Instead, I slugged the dregs and waited for sleep as the guy honked-off in the snow.

THE NEXT MORNING, hungover with nowhere to go until my Friday flight, I drove past the old house. The snow hadn't stuck. But the foreclosure had. As I approached the house from down the block, I saw a giant padlock on the front door. And chains. And then a padlock around the chains.

Across the street, Mr. Bonser was sweeping his garage again. He called out to me and, after pretending to ignore him, I surrendered, did not look both ways, crossed.

"Jude!" he said, ignoring the boozy stench. "How have you been buddy? Sorry to hear about your mom."

"No problem," I said. "Not your fault."

"Read on my Kindle that the house is in foreclosure," Mr. Bonser said, rubbing the back of his balding head.

"Sorry about that."

"No problem. Only kinda your fault."

"So."

"Yeah, y'know, cheaper to download sheriff sale listings than ebooks. Amazon has really decreased market competitiveness in a way that—"

"Look, Mr. Bonser, I've got—"

"Do you read much, Jude? You'd make one helluva shitty protagonist, but your life might be messed up enough for a self-published memoir that no one reads."

"I—"

"When I'd trade gardening tips with your mom, okra, rutabaga, back when she could walk and still had most of her face and could afford the Home Depot seeds, she always said your problem is that you gotta lighten the fuck up. Admit there are things about yourself and your life that you like, y'know? You've got one helluva exhausting personality."

"Thanks."

"Still, if you ever wanted to dumb yourself down and provide poverty porn for accountants and social workers, or frick, even just people whose only exposure to flyover country is *Fargo*, you could do a lot worse than writing about how much you and your life suck. *Sven and Ole Elegy*."

"Look, Gordon," I said, immediately doubting that Mr. Bonser's first name was Gordon.

"You know how I was in Bob Dylan's backing band? Jammed with Prince?"

Before this conversation, we had exclusively greeted each other or discussed his musical career.

"No," I said, "I don't think you've ever mentioned it."

"Ah, well, that's part of the reason I bloop and blip with the theremin still. In case the call comes, y'know? I still gig around town, play some corporate events and stuff, but mostly I just engineer live sound. Man, I can't believe we've never talked music."

"Right."

"But, oh! Here's the thing: it doesn't get better, y'know? I've seen brooding, artsy guys—frick, I kinda was one—and all they want to do is be more famous and have more people talking about 'em. But really they're just empty and broken people."

"I see."

"I mean, Prince died alone in an elevator. So your comedy career? Probably not worth it. Whatever you're trying to do with it, whatever you're trying to prove, the goalposts will keep shifting. Until your passion consumes the rest of your life. But, hey, whatcha gonna do?"

"Mr. Bonser, I—"

"You probably gotta get going to your homeless shelter or public library. I get it. I get it. I've got a big meeting—there's this giant, secret event my company is trying to land—so I should be getting ready anyway."

"Thanks for, um, the pep talk, Mr. Bonser," I said, sticking out a hand. He shook it, smiled.

"No problem!" Bonser said with a salute. "Nice to see you, Jude. Keep in touch when you're a total street person."

"Okay."

"Ah, right, one more thing: pretty fucked up you didn't pop over to tell us about the funeral, eh? Marcia was inconsolable. Staggering, really disgusting lack of empathy. Anyway, talk soon!"

Despite the warnings, and my fear, and having only my college roommate's couch as lodgings, Mr. Bonser had convinced me: I would show these fucking people. I would show them all. Life had tried to bludgeon me, to silence me, to grind me into blowing dust. But I endured. And I would endure. And I wouldn't let them win now.

8.

BRIGHT LIGHTS, BIG SHITTY

NEW YORK CITY is so boring it isn't even worth depicting, let alone skewering. There's nothing to it, nothing to say about it. Not because it's all been said. No, because it has no substance. No impression to leave. No flavor or memorable qualities. Real New York is like the taste of spit, the shape of water, the collected short stories of Raymond Carver. This metropolis-cum-cum-puddle, and all the people who live there by choice, are about as arresting as a Heritage Foundation think-tanker mansplaining reparations to a black woman. Or a nihilist older than seventeen.

Ahem.

Call time for Confessionals and promotional B-roll was 3:00 p.m. at Strivers Row—whatever the hell that means—and it was already 2:00. I refused to take a cab, and enjoyed performative liberalism too much to use a ride-sharing app, so I did what poor people do: something stupid. Like using public transit. Or being not from Manhattan. Thus, I found myself riding the AirTrain from JFK's terminal 4 to the Howard Beach station to the A station at 135th and St. Nicholas Avenue. Wow! The whole excursion would take almost two hours. But Real New Yorkers™ don't show up on time for things, I had read on *Vice*, because that would imply you aren't a psychopath. So, after whizzing through rarefied stops like Clinton-Washington and Port Authority Bus Terminal, I hopped off at 59th Street/Columbus Circle and climbed a bunch of stairs. Incredible!

Then I found myself on the street. A numbered one! I needed the bright lights, the big shitty to cultivate my philistine mind. My mom grew up on a farm; she'd sobbed when I floated moving to Brooklyn. Boris had grown up in Cleveland; he considered anywhere within six hours of the ocean elitist. And me? My desperation was Gatsbyian. I watched the Vikings every Sunday! I had muscular forearms! I owned several flannels! I was—shamefully—wearing one now! With the help of Midtown Manhattan, maybe I could overcome the manure of my childhood and understand why anyone ever liked Woody Allen films.

I looked up, around. The buildings were tall.

I walked a couple blocks, saw Central Park. The park was big. And central.

There were people on the sidewalks. Some were rich, poor.

They had food here, too. Some of it was sold from carts.

Couples laughed, kissed. A dog woofed, pooped.

Only in New York City, I thought to myself. Amazing.

Later, phone-in-hand, I wandered Martin Luther King, Jr. Boulevard, knowing that if I didn't come out of this famous, or at least notable enough to leverage a four-figure Kickstarter, this would be the biggest waste of time and money since I voted Democrat, or read John Updike.

"WELCOME TO DAY one of *American Idyll: Hunger Pains Edition*," said the spiky, tanned VP of Development I had met in Minneapolis. Fellow comic Gunnar Peuschold, my only acquaintance in this Harlem loft, raised his eyebrows at the unitarded dancers and pinstriped barber shop quartets milling in front of the stage. "My name is Cross Yoder-Henley, and since we have a lot of content to procure this afternoon, I need to make two things clear: First, just because you've made it this far does not mean you have any talent, potential, or guarantee of being seen on broadcast television. Remember, ten to sixty of you made it here from each of twelve audition districts, and come Wednesday when we go live and start the voting, there will only be three performing entities from each zone."

"Did you know that?" Gunnar whispered. I shrugged, scratched my forehead. Judging by the murmurs and shuffling—and the cameramen framing our confusion—none of us knew that.

"Two," said Cross, who I realized with horror looked like a slightly older Ryan Yoder-Henley, "you will have a couple chances today, and a couple chances tomorrow, to impress our team before you even sniff the judges. In other words, if you want the opportunity to eat literal shit while performing your talent for millions of Americans Wednesday night, you will have to eat figurative shit for me and my staff this weekend. Ergo, this is not the real thing but is instead another audition."

The other contestants groaned.

"Half of you will be gone by dinnertime. Any questions?"

"I got one, motherfucker," said a guy dressed like Jean-Paul Sartre. He was flanked by a cop, a construction worker, a Native American, and a dude in assless leather chaps. "Are you telling me that Hell Is Other Village People flew out here on our own dime from Charlottesville—right around midterms—to tryout for you suits a fourth, then a fifth, goddamn time?"

"You say you're from Charlottesville?" Yoder-Henley asked. Someone with a clipboard scurried up to Cross and mumbled something into his ear. "Ah, well I've been told we have 54 groups and individuals from District 12, so congratulations, Hell Is Other Village People, you've been eliminated. No exit? It's right there."

A SWAT team surrounded the boy band. Centurions rappelled down the walls. Zip-cuffs, assault weapons, and gladiuses prodded the five college professors through a door stage left. There was no fighting, or even spilled blood, but this seemed lucky.

"What the hell did we sign up for?" Gunnar muttered.

I glanced out the windows. Across the street, people waited for the bus. Newspapers skittered on the pavement.

"A way out," I said.

"C'MON, YOU GOTTA give us something," the production assistant said an hour later. We were in the basement cubicle now—a plot on the confession farm, per Yoder-Henley—and I felt my social capital correcting in real time. They'd festooned me with denim jackets, tight black t-shirts, a mime costume. I'd crossed my forearms, explained that I don't have tattoos or piercings. They'd screen-tested me; I'd patience-tested them. We'd discussed how I lost my virginity. How I lost the ability to talk about losing my best friend. *How I Met Your Mother.* None of it took; they were selling me off.

"I gave you my tragic backstory," I said.

"It's too dark," she said, twisting her blonde hair around a finger. "People want a reason to like you, not feel bad for you."

"I'm not asking anybody to feel bad for me. At least not yet. Not here. *I* feel plenty bad for me."

"Would you be willing to play the heel?"

"I have plantar fasciitis."

"See, you're too clever. That's gonna be a problem. It won't play in Peoria."

"I am a semi-professional comedian who beat out, like, 10,000 other applicants in the Upper Midwest, including Peoria. Because I am clever."

The production assistant face-palmed. She looked my age, sans the raccoon eyes and fear of smiling. She probably called her apartment a *flat* and knew how to pronounce quinoa. I met, or saw from the stage, hundreds of millennial white kids a year, but I felt like I'd seen this woman before.

"Hey," I said, "do I—"

She stuck her head outside the fabric box, yanked a walkie-talkie from her belt. I stared at the confessional camera. Ten minutes ago, her colleagues had insisted I was too ugly to make it to the quarter-finals but too useful—for marketing purposes—to not warrant a full two hours of interviewing and coverage. I wondered how Gunnar was doing. They guaranteed us only fifteen minutes of pre-fame. Which suggested I was close to surviving the day.

When the PA's full body re-appeared, she was tugging Cross Yoder-Henley into the cubicle.

"I understand you are compelling for all the wrong reasons," he said.

"I feel the same way," I said.

"What am I supposed to do with a Midwestern comic who *is* kinda talented but *isn't* very wholesome? This isn't a goddamn talent show."

"This is literally a talent show."

"This is a primetime reality TV show, okay?"

"I thought this was a meritocracy—"

"See, Mr. Yoder-Henley, he is quite funny," the PA said.

"And that is the goddamn problem, Miss Peaslee. If he weren't funny, but presented as mildly edgy, we could stick him on *SNL*, but what good does he do me here? Funny and edgy? Jesus, I need more than weird-looking incisive schizoids if I'm gonna sit in a chair like Eisner or Lack or even Lorne fucking Michaels one day."

"Well," I said, "why am I even here if you aren't interested in my comedy?"

"Because you're funny!" they said in unison.

We bit our cheeks, rubbed our faces.

"Isn't there anything that can set you apart?" Peaslee asked.

"Sources at this network suggest I am funny," I said. There was another thing that set me apart, of course, but I would've rather been executed with one of those gladiuses than mention his name on camera.

"What Lana is trying to say," Yoder-Henley said, "is that I have at least three comics from each district, and they're all funny. Or, if they aren't funny, like your buddy Gunnar from Indianapolis—"

"Minneapolis."

"Annapolis—"

"Minneapolis. One of the Twin Cities?"

"Necropolis. One of the Twin Peaks—"

"Where Prince is from? The Coen Brothers?"

"We know where you're from," Lana said. "Cross' younger brother went to school in St. Paul."

"Ryan Yoder-Henley?"

They looked at each other. Then at me.

"You know him," said Cross. "Why didn't you say anything?"

"Because I hate that motherfucker."

"Ryan Yoder-Henley is my boyfriend," Lana said.

"Sorry."

"It's okay. I—"

"No, I'm sorry he's your boyfriend."

"Look, Jewb," Cross said, cracking his neck. "I'll level with you: you're close to making it to tomorrow. Real close. Knowing Ryan? That doesn't hurt. Hell, Peaslee might've done you a solid, and greased the wheels for you in the early rounds. But I need—"

"I grew up with Stephen Scheisskopf," I said, immediately regretting it.

"Wait."

I nodded.

"That Stephen Scheisskopf? Like, his boss, his candidate, used to star on this network? *The Appre*—"

"That's the fascist," I said, staring at my shoes, breaking eye contact with either my interlocutors or the camera for the first time all afternoon.

"And would you be okay with, ah, synergizing this?" Lana said.

"For, say, content creation purposes?"

"I would have to think about it," I said, watching my knee bob.

"We would, too, of course," Cross said. "He's, um, a controversial figure. And, well, even gesturing at this connection could open up either legal or, God forbid, rating difficulties. But, I've heard enough, and the cameras have seen enough, to get you through the day, Jrue. I'll have to run this new thing up the chain, but congrats: you've made it to tomorrow—the Reaping."

As Yoder-Henley prattled on with the next steps, and weighed the pros and cons of exploiting my relationship to Scheisskopf, I finally gathered the resolve to look at Lana. She knew Ryan. Maybe she knew Madeline, or Ignacio. Maybe she knew of me. Maybe she already knew me. And now she knew Mom was dead, and I was working-poor and ashamed, and had developed an opiate habit, and drank too much, and lost my virginity on 4/20 of freshman year, and had fewer than ten sexual experiences since, and didn't get along with my extended family, and owed thousands of dollars to aunts and corporations and the State of Minnesota, and had a house that went kaput, and felt worse for mocking my brothers' RA back in September than yelling and shit-talking whenever they called, and had best friends who skipped my Mom's funeral to fuck in a church parking lot, and didn't blame them because all my other friends had cried since they loved Mom almost as much as I did.

And, also, I knew Stephen Scheisskopf.

I tried to glean this compounding disinterest, this devaluation of social currency, from her blushing face, but she wouldn't look up. At me or her boss. She just twisted her hair.

I SPENT THE next few hours pacing Harlem. Ignacio, the college roommate, wouldn't pick up.

It was a Friday night in New York City, and I had nowhere to be. Lana Peaslee had implored me to get the hell out before anyone changed their mind. We needed to show up by noon for more . . . whatever it is I was doing. This time we'd be inside a very famous building with an Atlas statue outside. Rand McNally would be proud.

Ignacio lived in Williamsburg with some combination of alumni I hated. Or hated me. These were the Marxist-Leninist slam poets and Adderall-addled Occupy Wall Streeters with enough talent, or unpaid internships, to work in arts administration or advertising. That none of them had majored in Arts Administration or

Advertising was perfectly logical, apparently. I guess I hadn't majored in Being Suicidal Around Art.

Honestly, I wasn't even sure who lived there.

As I lugged my backpack, laptop bag, and social anxiety around St. Nicholas Park again, my phone buzzed. The sun was setting, and the wind reminded me of Lake Superior. Not that I had ever been to Lake Superior.

"Salutations," I said to Ignacio.

"Bit of bad news," he said, voice muffled by laughter and wobble bass.

"There is an election Tuesday, yes."

"I'm on a party bus to Fire Island."

"That's still a thing that happens?" I wish I'd brought my coat. Or the gun.

"You can still crash at my place, but we're sort of having a—"

"C'mon, Ignacio."

"They know you're coming, baby, don't worry about it. My room is available. Like, if you wanna sleep there? Because they'll probably be having a party?"

"Who knows I'm coming? Iggy? Ig? Hello? I don't even know . . ."

The line went dead.

"Jesus H. Christ," I said.

I paced the park. Wandered across it and headed south toward Columbia. Got spooked by the Ivy League campus and kept walking: low-rises, honks, Harlem transforming from Black to White.

I walked and walked and walked.

Then I saw a water-balloon-shaped old man with big headphones and a belted walkman and no better option on this autumn Friday night than wheezing beside a dog. I saw this, and I stood on Morningside and 121st, and I cried. Heaves. Jerks. An ache in my face and throat. Eyes dripping like an IV bag and splashing my luggage and shoes.

Witnessing the loneliness of another person has always tanked my mood. What could I possibly say or do to make their lives not suck beyond the shallowest of smalltalk? And all it would do is make me feel better *about me*.

As a kid, for big occasions, and because we were gross, we'd go to buffets. And while I slurped unhealthy gobs at my one sit-down restaurant meal a quarter, I'd see the loners, almost always widowers, staring into their mashed potatoes and gravy while young families—blacks and whites and latinos and asians and indigenous folks, all poorish but beaming with the rare opportunity of indulgence and having choices—laughed over jello cubes or pork chops. And even though this was a family tradition all four of us seemed to cherish, I would always excuse myself to cry. This happened every time. Nobody ever questioned it (though you should never enter a buffet's bathroom under any circumstances), but it got to a point, later in my mother's life, where I would request restaurants we liked less. Because I just couldn't fucking handle another hour of imagining the untold frustrations and losses of these lives. Folks living in the most materially prosperous nation in human history, and all it gets you is a thousand-yard stare into lukewarm meatloaf.

A car zoomed past. Shouts of pussy, faggot, bitch.

At 125th and St. Nicholas, I pocketed my phone, stretched my already tightening hamstrings, and stood at the threshold of the subway station. I dug out the rosary beads and cradled them. "God, give me a lane. Give me a lane. Give me a lane, and I'll promise to change."

Didn't do the sign of the cross or say amen, but I felt a little better. So I plunged into the heart of whiteness: the A train then the L. Then Williamsburg.

EMERGING AROUND 8:00, just as the Bedford Avenue L stop swarmed with dudes in linen button-downs and the jean-jacket-clad yogis who fuck them, I felt genuine panic for the first time since Mom died. This seemed less than optimal. Not doing comedy horrified me more than doing comedy. Museum-based rage and shame were default settings (unless Nehemiah was calming me down). Even poverty—the indefinite grind of hating myself and my circumstances—jolted me from bed, maybe, caked me in sweat each night, pummeled my subconscious with threats of homelessness and failure, making sleep as attractive as Stephen Scheisskopf, but this fear and exhaustion doubled as hunger. I wouldn't have been watching dudes with unicycles fumble for their MTA cards without this desperation.

But *this*? Bedford Avenue on a Friday night? Without hydrocodone or fentanyl?

"Lord, give me strength," I said at the top of the steps.

I shambled south, clutching Mom's rosary beads so tightly they almost snapped. Past a sex shop called *a-DICKS*. A thrift store called *JUNKIES*. A bar called *The Needle and Spoon*.

Back home, we had friends who'd overdosed. A couple dozen times, Nehemiah had dragged me to Grace Trinity and Higher Ground Catholic Charities for after-work NA, but after a while I'd flaked and no-showed so I could hit more open mics. Feature spots. Emcee gigs. Chasing fame. Vengeance.

I thought of Malik. Ten years on Wednesday.

Median rent in Williamsburg was $3000/month. Mom had never made more than $2000. If I cracked $1500, I considered myself flush.

The Williamsburg Bridge loomed up ahead. Sonny Rollins, too. Malik told me the story, all those hours tooting at the sky. Malik, who wanted to play saxophone but never learned.

So sick of being nobody. Of being Jude Glick. Eldest son of Paula Lucille Glick and SSDI for the blind. A one-eyed grotesque with quick wit but slow progress.

The drunks waddled and slurred on Bedford. Designer sunglasses at night, holey jeans tight like a second epidermis. Chalkboard signs hawking $9 Happy Hour pints. Apartment buildings named The Dunlop, The Mendelsohn, 101 South. Smiling copywriters, wired graphic designers. They hoisted racks of Tecate. They sipped Rolling Rock 25s. They had forearm tattoos and beards, vinyl collections and Instagrams. They expressed derision or irony toward everything outside of their particular pet interests. They laughed at sports, class rage, and Schopenhauer. They listened to dial-up modem sounds in Bushwick warehouses. They shopped at a Whole Foods made of glass. They described their sense of humor as "dark but not too dark." They were probably taking an SSRI but needn't worry how to pay for it. Once, after a really bad breakup, they flirted with suicide, but had no plans to tie the knot.

I sideswiped a dude with my backpack. On the right. My blind side. He'd been entering a bar called the TRICKLE DOWN.

"Watch it, dipshit," he said. I weighed a retort, or a fight, opted-out. He huffed and puffed a bit more, but I just kept walking. Until I stopped at the end of the block. Through the window, he joined a group of guys at the bar, all of them wearing red hats with white letters. Jesus, how on the nose are these people? When I remember Mom, hunched over her computer with a back brace, disc-slipped and legs on fire, not even the cancer, just what it took to raise three fucked-up kids in a future foreclosure house, when I remember her hard swallow and trembling lips on the phone with my football coach, who had called to investigate why the captain of his team hadn't paid the $250 activity fee, when I think of her whisper and how she'd been praying for a waiver, I want to joke about these fucking idiots on farms and factory floors listening to neo-Nazi agitprop while unknowingly signing up for Laffer curve bullshit, but I can't.

I stomped to the bar, yanked their sandwich board from the sidewalk, and smashed it on the pavement.

If anyone noticed, they didn't care.

I considered calling Addy, decided against it.

Kept trudging. Kept glaring at the MFA students and social media managers as a hint of epiphany escorted me down S 5th Street. Maybe I didn't actually hate these people. Maybe I reserved the real hate for anyone who'd step foot in a Republican-themed bar. But maybe the hipsters had nothing wrong with them. Maybe I despised their lifestyles, their ability to win the game, not because I found it vapid and unjust and indicative of the helpless suffering Mom endured her whole life. No, maybe I didn't hate them.

I was just jealous.

Because I would never hold hands with a smart, beautiful young woman as we riffed through Brooklyn. Because I would never meet some mutual acquaintance at Union Pool, or Charlene's, or even Liquor Lyles back home and give them a hug. Because I was 24 years old and already brined in bitterness like Boris.

I closed my eyes, tried to will Mom's voice into my ears.

Nothing.

I tucked the beads under my flannel.

The gentrifying and gentrified ambled around me and/or bumped into psychotic homeless men. The bridge was across the street. After a few blocks in the wrong direction, I finally hovered outside a cum-colored four-story with moss growing on one side.

Deep breaths, Jude. Endure.

I'd ride couch until tomorrow night, hopefully avoiding Ignacio's roommates after these thirty seconds of social crucifixion. Then, if The Reaping went well and I actually had a shot at stealing scenes in network primetime, I'd eat the overdrafts, shvitz and worry at a Chinatown hostel.

I pressed 4B.

The door clicked and beeped, but I was too slow; it had re-locked before I shoved it. So I stood there. And stood some more. Not only imposing myself on people but too unsophisticated to open a fucking door. What the hell was wrong with me? What did I want to happen here? Use reality television to caulk my leaking self-esteem, just another man-child tantruming and lashing out until I received the attention I was convinced I deserved?

Yeah, pretty much.

Slumming it in the subway like a bona fide (i.e., oppressively poor) New Yorker appealed to my social anxiety, but Mom wouldn't want me to give up, even if it was unclear what I might be giving up on. So I tapped 4B again and launched myself on the bleep, blasting the door into the foyer and banging Madeline Einstein in the face.

"Oh, God. Sorry," I said, laptop bag swinging as she held her nose. No blood, I thought, please no blood.

She took her hands from her head, inspected the palms, sniffed, and rubbed her nose.

No blood.

"I don't think it's broken," she said, fingers brushing her sweater, liquor bouncing off her breath. "What are you doing here anyway?"

"In—"

"New York. Didn't I see you in Minneapolis in, like, September?"

"Seems plausible."

"Right."

"Ignacio didn't—"

"He said someone would be crashing here, but he didn't tell us who."

"Well."

"So," she said. More college acquaintances buzzed in. We inched down the vestibule, away from the door, near the stairs and next to a wall of mailboxes.

"Ohmigod, hi Mads!" a voice said.

"Ahhh!" someone else screamed.

"It's been so long, Tiny Steiny," some other person shrieked.

Hugs were exchanged, cheeks smooched. I coughed into an arm, hiding my face. The five newcomers, the cloud of bonhomie and Beefeater, stumbled down the grimy hallway and up the stairs.

"Nice to see you, Jude. Good talk," Madeline said, presenting a fist to bump. Anything to limit physical contact. She followed the horde, took steps two-at-a-time. I heard whispers and laughter. A door opened and people cheered.

TEN MINUTES AND ten dollars later, I stood across the street, under the bridge, sucking from a liter of Old Crow Kentucky Bourbon. If I got picked up for public intoxication, I'd at least have a place to sleep.

Williamsburg Bridge. Literal shadow. They lived close enough to peg a late-night jogger with a well-chucked whiskey bottle. South Fifth. Between Driggs and Bedford. Under the bridge, behind some fencing, it looked like a group of homeless men had circled around a trashcan fire.

The rosary necklace hung and swayed like a thurible, searing me with grief. I looked up at the apartment. Those people had a mother or a father. Maybe just a fuckbuddy. But somebody, somewhere, made them seen, heard, felt, missed. Allowed them to function at jobs or parties without experiencing every social interaction as a referendum on rational suicide.

Madeline must have known. And, if she didn't, Belcalis Pulido, or Rosie Rafowitz-Fackelmann, or whoever the fuck Ignacio lived with must have known. That I was here and broke and trying not to be broken any longer. He promised me.

We kept up, the two of us, so Ignacio wouldn't just bail. Not without a good reason or a premonition. The election was Tuesday. Maybe they'd outlaw being queer, sex outside of marriage, sex inside of marriage if it didn't seed a kid. People joked like this, regular millennials, not comics, the people at the party joked like this—I heard them over the panhandling and thump of Rihanna—and whether or not they had the same apocalyptic anticipation I did, they still lived their lives, cementing the decision to chemically alter mine. I couldn't go back in there. Not after that. Not drunk. Not shamed. Not me.

So I decided to un-become myself. I decided to get high.

Since my first open mic as a sophomore, I hadn't gone longer than two weeks without booze. I hit a few AA meetings. I considered 90 in 90. I got reported to Health and Wellness for outlining an alcohol overdose plan in my Positive Psychology class. And then hoovered a fifth of Karkov after the social worker referred me to inpatient treatment I could never afford.

Opiates had been different. Kinda. When Mom died, my Will to Percocet died with her. Talking a doctor into prescribing me something for chronic pain, when I was on record and self-described as a moderate-to-severe drunk, wasn't worth the risk of a $30 copay.

Thus, "sobriety." Besides, beating drugs made me a little proud. I missed them every day, yes, felt a tingle and giddiness like a cock springing into action whenever I thought of hydros or roxys or fentanyl lollipops, but I showed myself I could, like, still tick boxes, achieve goals. Maybe not like the old Jude, the football awards and commencement speeches and magna cum laude honors at a top-25 liberal arts college nobody has ever heard of, but the security guarding and scuttling standup sets in Fond Du Lac hadn't subsumed my ability to accomplish things, hadn't totally erased Mom's influence.

I hopped the fence and headed for the homeless encampment. Creeping into the darkness, I felt on the precipice of something catastrophic—a feeling that became homeostasis as the week, and the night, progressed—but a man in a beanie, sweatpants, and raincoat snapped me out of it.

Racistly, I jolted back. Entertained running away.

"What're you doing?" he asked. The bonfire was maybe ten yards deeper into the gloom.

"Uh, I'm new here and need some help," I said.

"You are not the type of guy who would be at a place like this at this time of the night."

"Can you . . . do you know where someone might, uh, look after me?"

"We don't run a daycare here."

"No, no sir." What the fuck was I doing? With my electronics and $200 in cash, I was extremely muggable. I felt guilty for having the thought and guiltier still for assuming I could find heroin, or that I needed heroin, from one of NYC's 60,000 most vulnerable.

"You a fucking mute now?" he said.

I shot my hands up like a cop halting traffic.

"I need pharms. Horse."

"You think we plant soybeans and ride ponies under the Williamsburg Bridge?"

"I think you might sell heroin."

He licked his lips. With his right thumb, he rubbed the knuckle of his left. The guys around the fire laughed at something. Traffic rumbled overhead. I could see the base of the train tracks.

"To take the edge off," I said. "Booze isn't, uh, it's not—"

"No need to tell me, man. I used to tie-off in the pews of St. Mark's church before readings."

"Mmm."

"If you're looking for something to take the edge off, and you've got one helluva a sharp edge, boy, there are options beyond street dope."

"Painkillers?"

"I'm talking sobriety, motherfucker. What kinda idiot tries to buy heroin from under a bridge in New York City? What if I didn't have an MFA in Poetry from Cornell? What if I was having a psychotic episode? What if I was a cop?"

"What's the difference?"

He chuckled, shook his head.

"We can get you some dope, kid, but goddamn." He continued the thumb-massage.

"I don't have any works but—"

"Is this *Naked Lunch*, motherfucker?"

"What?"

"Snort the shit. But don't kill yourself with my fucking drugs. I knew Jim Carroll."

The distant rattle of a train. Honking cars. The smell of dried puke and stale piss.

I glanced toward Ignacio's place: cars dropped people off in front of a side gate. Bicyclists de-mounted and chained their rides to an inner fence.

"Jackson for half a gram," he said. "Take it or leave it."

I had no idea if this was a reasonable price. Nehemiah, back before he got sober, asked me if I wanted a "toot" during office hours one day, but that was the closest I'd come to doing heroin. I knew some comics who used regularly and, sure, I knew how to shoot by osmosis, but using meant they were reliably passing out and not reliably showing up to gigs or open mics.

I handed him a crumpled twenty. He shook his head, jammed it in his back pocket, shuffled over to a gym bag, bent down, dug out a basketball shoe, and pried something from the toes. Still shaking his head, he went in for a handshake, smacking a baggie of smack in my palm. I knew immediately, given the weight, that this was enough to kill me.

"Do you—"

"Nah," the pusherman said, "I'm sober."

"Right," I said. The ground started to shake.

"Seriously. I work outreach for the BRC and it don't pay shit."

"So you sell—"

"Ain't nobody talking about how fucked up the recession was, or what it did to the young people. Still feeling it. Look at Tuesday. The choices. You'd be surprised how many kids like you turn to street dope."

"Sure." I wouldn't be, but I didn't want to explain this.

"Every day thousands of people say, 'I can't take it anymore!' But they do. Because they find a way. Some got the wood-carving hobby, some got their God, some got the real estate developer with a God complex. Me, I sell heroin so I can keep myself off the streets. And help those men around that fire."

The ground started to vibrate.

"That's right. Who do you think bought them coats? Who do you think gets them into a hostel or hotel if the shelters fill? And where do you think the money comes from? That blue Nike bag. But have you heard a single mention of poverty, let alone homelessness, in any of those debates or campaign propaganda? Please."

The ground shook harder. He produced American Spirits from his pocket, packed them. "You smoke? My sponsor recommended cigs in place of alcohol. Booze would have killed me."

"Mmm."

"Don't do some shit like this ever again. You got lucky."

"I know," I shouted.

He hollered something back, but I couldn't make it out. The train screeched and bounced overhead as I stuck the baggie in my cords, nodded at him, and slouched toward the fence.

AS I LANDED on the sidewalk, somebody called my name.

"J.G.!" Ryan Yoder-Henley shouted across the street.

I half-waved at him, crossed. He stood in front of a gate that led to a fire escape. Yuppie drunks were in various stages of rising up and down. Ryan wore a leather jacket and a wristwatch that shone in the moonlight.

"Didn't know you were in the city!"

"I am presently in the city," I said.

"That is really fucking cool, man."

"I'm actually a little warm here."

His arms flew wide for a hug. He clenched me. I saw no choice but to reciprocate.

"Did—oh, dang," he said, palming my shoulder, "I heard you're in town for that show!"

"Lana didn't tell you?"

"Lana?"

"Lana."

"Did you . . . are you—"

"This weekend is the final audition. I find out if I make it to live TV tomorrow afternoon. Regardless, pretty sure I met your girlfriend and your brother today."

"Lana went to Carleton, dude. There's no way you didn't meet her at an Ignacio party."

I let this hang without comment. We had reached the stage I always reach with people I find boring or scorn-worthy: awkwardness. I could Fake It Till You Make It for 30-90 seconds before molting the good cheer and generating bleak new one-liners and nihilistic riffs.

"So standup, yeah? You were always kinda funny," he said. From the winding stairs, someone called his name. A woman's voice.

"Thanks."

"I mean, no offense, you weren't, like, the president of the comedy club or a writer for the *Hegemonocle*. Like me and Mads and even Nala Bashir . . ."

To anyone with serious aspirations—and I don't know what else to call my obsession with external validation—the *Heg* was pathetic. Maybe malevolent. It would hurt your chances. Bad habits, unfunny writing sessions. Binge-drinking without the suicidality. Yawn. I didn't write for the *Hegemonocle* because learning someone wrote for it was like learning someone was a neo-Nazi; they were irredeemable.

"Right," I said.

Clomping down the steps. We looked up. Madeline Einstein. We were still just outside the gate.

"Ryan Yoder-Henley, would you—"

"Look who I found."

"Good lord," she said as Ryan drew her in and pecked her cheek.

"I *am* feeling a bit like Jesus," I said, staring her down.

"What?" Ryan Yoder-Henley said. "What did—"

"You're both welcome to come in, of course, and, J.G., sorry but the other door? With—"

"Don't worry about it," I said, fingering the heroin in my back pocket. I looked up at the apartment building, then the street, then Ryan's confusion and Madeline's fake smile, "alea iacta est."

A COUPLE HOURS later, I was lacquered against one of Ignacio's bedroom walls, listening to Rosie Rafowitz-Fackelmann's life story, and seriously considering suicide. Seriously. I had the means this time and nobody I cared about would find me. I'd been sucking directly from a pilfered water bottle of something strong and brown, now definitely too drunk to snort heroin without dying of respiratory depression. See, I had no opiate tolerance, and, judging by the misplaced Old Crow bottle, I was either dangerously drunk or so hypoglycemic that Kentucky bourbon happily replaced the meals I'd been missing. Either way, one small sniff for Jude, one meaningless death for mankind.

"Are you even listening to me?" Rosie said.

"What?" I said.

"I was telling you about, like, my childhood? How my dad was an associate art history professor who never made full professor, even though he was tenured? At U-Maryland, which, you know, it's amazing I survived Sidwell Friends with his income."

"Mmm." As Rosie prattled on, I googled the salaries of Maryland public employees.

Just outside the door, the NGOers and gallery assistants were rubbing their genitals on each other in a big sweaty clump. Thankfully, the door was open and we were not alone.

This was my longest conversation of the night, but not the one I wanted to be having. After Madeline got a few in her, I made a point of making her laugh so hard she puked. And I succeeded. Vengeance was mine. A riff about how the last time I felt close to another human being was when I jerked off on the obituary page. Mary Frances McInnerney was, technically, my most recent sexual partner. She hadn't been STD-tested because she wouldn't be caught dead in a Planned Parenthood. Until I brought the wad to the one on Vandalia Street. Her final resting place was a trashcan in the lobby. Me, I came up clean, save for the nurse telling me I was a dirty young man. In lieu of flowers, please don't masturbate on the obituary pages.

Something like that.

You had to be there.

". . . I mean, because you seem pretty creative," Rosie said, placing two fingers on my forearm and stroking the wrist.

"Um." I hadn't seen Yoder-Henley for an hour. By now, his partner should've finished her shift at the content mill. Ryan sucked, but it beat Rafowitz-Fackelmann's designs.

Wait, maybe, it was the bit about the time I got so stoned on edibles I literally forgot my own name and, when confronted by Mom the next day, told her I'd been method acting. Whatever.

"Did I tell you I'm a creative writer?" Rosie said, nestling into my twitching shoulder.

"A creative writer?" My status radar flared. Lurking professional envy.

"Yeah, it's amazing. Working with brands, devising commercials. My partner Cara and I went to, like, Sundance last year? Did you know we had a Super Bowl ad that—"

"I'm sorry, what sort of writer are you?"

"A creative writer."

"So, you write thirty seconds of ad copy for multinationals, most of which are either degrading the environment or lobbying congress to loosen consumer protections, or both, and this ad copy is focus-grouped and story-boarded ahead of time, yet you consider yourself a creative writer?"

She blinked at me.

Dr. Isaac Rafowitz-Fackelmann made $89,555 in 2009. He made $98,056 in 2015.

"I gotta get going, Rosie," I said, bailing out of the room before she had time to dump a drink on my head or slap me.

As I thrashed to the door like drowning sailors toward a raft, I heard several people yell: "No fucking way." Bursting into the loft proper, I almost toppled Ryan Yoder-Henley.

"Hey, dude," he said, adjusting his manbun. He looked like a surfer despite growing up on the Upper West Side and his dad own-ing a controlling interest in a Midwestern NBA team.

Open floor plan. Few places to hide. Bartender on one end of this big space—set-up on the kitchen island—and a DJ on the other. In the middle, writhing millennials who had stopped shaking their asses and started shaking their heads.

"Hey, Ryan," I said. A group of dudes in pink mesh downed sev-eral shots in succession. A fully naked woman, bodypaint sliding down her breasts and legs, stopped hopping and started blowing "Taps" into a kazoo of dubious origin. "What's going on here?"

"Come this way," he said, yanking me across the dancefloor to the windows overlooking the Williamsburg Bridge. A five-bedroom loft. The entire top floor of this apartment building. Private access via the fire escape right outside Madeline's bedroom. It made no sense that Ignacio lived here.

He didn't. He'd fallen behind on rent and they kicked him out. Ergo, a weekend getaway at Fire Island where he could fuck out the shame, Ryan explained.

"But that's not even the worst of it," he said. "You see those three black Suburbans?"

"I do, in fact, see those three black Suburbans." I don't know why I was being such an asshole; Ryan had been friendly all night. It had been almost two years. People change. Maybe.

"Guess who's in one of those three black Suburbans."

I didn't need to guess. I saw his thinning hair from fifty feet up.

I checked my phone to text Ignacio, but he'd already texted me.

> *sry about 2nite, bb. long story that i'll explain later. . .but check out this messed up text i got from belcalis pulido. you might wanna stay away from her 2nite. js.*

> *<Subject: NoSubject> weird way to end up taking your room, i know, but what's weirder is that I'm at a party with Jude Fucking Glick and he's lurking in the corner pretending this is totally normal and that people might even want to talk to him. . .wtf. . .*

> *lol thought i'd pass it along babe. sry again. watch out for special guests too* 👀

I pocketed my phone then punched the wall. This should have gotten me kicked out, but my luck had changed, I guess.

He was here.

Stephen Scheisskopf walked in with my high school football buddy, Ulysses "U.P." Patterson—all 5'6", 350 of him—and two dudes, as tall and thick as pillars. Shaved heads. Shoulders like steel pipes.

The music cut out. The dancers plucked themselves off each other's groins. That naked lady was still blowing the fucking kazoo. I crossed my arms and pictured Nala Bashir clutching her throat and bleeding on the MAOI tile.

Flashes. Snapchats. Boos. The dudes in pink mesh spiked their

169

shot glasses with a crash and stormed to the alternate exit. Mostly, people just stood in the giant loft, listening to the air conditioner whoosh. It was unclear who'd invited him. Until it wasn't.

Like a V-J Day kiss, Scheisskopf cradled Madeline Einstein and kissed her. The black waves of her hair looked like a mirage against his pallor.

The music faded in. Guess we were just rolling with this.

"Like a dog licking its asshole," I said to no one in particular.

"Please," Yoder-Henley said, "neither of them are mammals."

"A barnacle sucking off a whale."

"What's that make you, J.G.?"

I looked at Ryan. Rosie Rafowitz-Fackelmann staggered in our direction.

"A lobster being boiled alive."

The party grinded back into, well, grinding. Presumably, the cocaine sold by Scheisskopf's guys served as a moral lubricant. Once Ryan left me, and I finished hiding behind a plant when Rosie slurred within earshot, I set up next to a speaker, pretending to rub my temples but actually covering my ears.

No eye contact, though I couldn't stop staring at him. But the room was so big, and the music so loud, and the kazoo lady so nude, that we could avoid each other's orbits. Until I ran out of booze and had to decide between slithering through the hedonism to the bar, or remaining alone and deaf.

Maybe this made sense. The queer folks and minorities had scattered, or at least escalated their drunkenness in response to Scheisskopf's arrival, but most revelers considered him a clown. And not a class clown like me. Or a pathetic, hacky clown like Gunnar Peuschold. A honking, sweating, dog-whistling, prematurely balding fascist who piled into his car with all the Western chauvinists and Julius Evola readers and Stormfront mods, latching themselves onto a rapist game show host, the biggest clown of all. What were privileged white people good for but normalizing oppression?

Someone splashed me with wine, steadied themselves against my chest.

Lana Peaslee.

"Sorry, sorry," she said, just now looking up, "I—ohmigod."

"How was work?" I said, whisking the slosh from my arms and hands. If anything, the dancefloor had grown more packed in the last twenty minutes. Stephen didn't chase the liberalish Brooklynites to Union Pool; he drew them here.

"Ah, yeah, right," she said, eyes flitting from me to the mass. I squinted, could not locate Ryan either.

"Sorry about earlier," I said. "Ryan isn't such a bad guy, actually. Or, well, maybe he is, but he could be worse. Not richer, but worse."

"That naked kazoo girl bumped into me." She pointed, as though I wouldn't know which one. "I didn't mean to, like, run into you."

"Really, not a big deal."

We listened to the thump and bloops. Both of us were pinned. No sign of Scheisskopf or Ryan. It occurred to me, just as Lana opened her mouth again, that Ryan must have been kibitzing with him.

"I'm . . . I'm sorry, Jude, but I have some bad news."

"Bad news?" I slipped a hand in my pocket, pinched the heroin baggie.

"My bosses? They . . . look, we really like your—"

"Lana, I'm not friends with Scheisskopf. I've seen him once since high school. I had nothing to do with him showing up here, and he had nothing to do with me. Is it a crime to—"

"Cross says that the flower thing? And something about a guy called Marfan? Marvel?"

"Malik."

"Well, both Standards and Practices and the General Counsel agree that we'll open up the show to controversy."

"This is a talent competition held on the lips of volcanoes. Live sniper fire. Climbing the Empire State Building without a harness."

"Jude."

"I flew out here for fucking nothing? Debased and humiliated myself on camera for two hours, on my own goddamn dime, because you all didn't do your research? Why? Why?"

"I picked your name out of the stack. Ryan never really liked you, but people said you were smart and driven and there was this class of his I sat in on? I was on spring break and it was the night after this party at your college house, or whatever? When the professor was, like, fumbling around on drugs? You're an interesting thinker, J.G. Interesting voice. And, well, Ryan had mentioned that you kinda knew Stephen, but I thought he was—"

"Why does this keep happening?"

"J.G., I—"

"I need a motherfucking drink."

I wriggled past her, banged into a guy with horn-rimmed glasses. When he started to protest, I stiff-armed him into the wall and pounded toward the bar, indifferent to obstacles physical and social.

And, still swim-moving and body-checking, I saw dreadlocks. But by the time I realized they belonged to Ulysses, and that I was too close and trapped against bodies to escape his smile, I inched through the crowd and offered a bro hug.

"My man," he said. "We heard you was here from some dude-ass called Ryan."

"Been too long, Ulysses," I said, glancing for Scheisskopf. The twin towers stood an arms-length from Ulysses; Stephen couldn't be far away. "What have you been up to?"

I gestured to the bartender, but U.P. knocked my hand down. "Fuck that, J.G. Drink this."

He handed me a fifth of Hennessy. I swigged, scanned.

"I been doing all sorts of stuff, bruh bruh," U.P. said, screwing on the cap. "Been driving Steve since last summer though."

"How is that going?" The dancing crowd shoved us closer together. U.P. was pressed against his goons. The music pulsed and pummeled. I appraised the ceiling. It seemed to breathe, bulge, recede.

"It's a job, man. Y'know how it is. I heard you work at the MAOI? Ran into Leon Walters, or something once?"

"Yeah."

"Ran into Stephen, too, huh?"

"He mentioned that?"

"He's changed, bruh. I know you wasn't friends or nothing in high school, but Stevie is a complicated dude. I know he be sayin' all this crazy shit on TV, and between you and me I don't exactly support his boss, y'know, but it isn't easy being in the spotlight. Mostly an act anyway. Like, see what happened when he walked in? How weird it got? He can't go grocery shopping, or turn up with his girlfriend without—"

"Girlfriend?"

"Madeline, bruh bruh. Didn't you know her in—"

"Hey, Ulysses," a voice said behind the parting giants, "did you—"

"Stephen," I said as he wriggled shoulder to shoulder with U.P. A lightning bolt through the crowd. He'd been hidden behind his mass of men.

"Julian," he said, offering a hand, which I shook, "the scuttlebutt was that you'd departed for the evening."

"You've got sources on the ground, eh?" U.P. chuckled at this. Scheisskopf smirked. I'd never noticed the allure of his eyes. Powder blue. And sad.

"I've got a hand in every cookie jar and a fly on every wall, J.G. Don't you forget it."

U.P. averted his gaze. Behind the twin towers stood two more twin towers. I might have seen Madeline's hair between a gap of black t-shirts and muscle.

"Look, Stephen, I'd love to catch up but—"

"So let's catch up, Julian."

I blinked at him. Someone kept hollering about their Instagram story. The Hennessy stung my throat and eyes, but I just stared at Stephen. Blank, pitiless. I could not decide if I wanted Lana and Ryan to see this or not.

"Seriously," he said, clapping my shoulder. The pinstripes of his suit matched a perfectly folded pocket square. I was wearing one white sock and one black one. My boots had holes in both arches.

"Steve, this is maybe not the place to—"

"We'll go to Madeline's room. No worries."

I side-eyed Ulysses. I could read a room, or a person, with X-Acto knife precision, but this situation curdled my stomach. The panic of Bedford Avenue returned.

My knees shook. The heroin shifted.

"Madeline's room," I said.

"Just you, me, and Ulysses," he said. "I've got something I want to show you."

U.P. nodded at me. Scheisskopf snapped twice and one of his men pivoted toward bedrooms on the perimeter of the dancefloor. As he led us through the morass, a fullback bursting through the hole, the flashes and Snapchat narrations gave me vertigo.

YOU COULD SEE the Williamsburg Bridge from Madeline's floor-to-ceiling window. Over the red girders and hurtling trains, a building that looked like a miniature US Capitol shimmered green.

"The Weylin," Stephen said, pacing. Ulysses leaned against the door. The goons stood outside. Madeline had slugged a G&T when she saw our cavalcade of stunted masculinity beeline for the bedroom. "I've got it rented out for a party next Friday, but when we win, there'll be too much to do."

"And we'll be back home," U.P. said.

"That's right, U.P. We'll be at the MAOI Saturday afternoon. Permits already approved for the rally. Secret Service and our people have started scouting the park and neighborhood. I'll open for the president-elect. Hopefully, you'll be there, too."

The angle was too steep to see under the bridge.

"I'm serious, Julian. This is going to happen. And that's why I wanted to talk. Hell, that's why I came to the fucking party."

I turned around. Guitars tuned in the main room. A famous Brooklyn dance-rock band had shown up uninvited for an impromptu set.

"You know what Wednesday is," he said, staring at me.

"Ten years."

"Big of you to send a thank you card, Jules. My parents really appreciated it. Paula was a helluva woman."

"Beautiful bouquet."

"I hear you've had some financial troubles."

"I consider my troubles existential, but you aren't wrong."

"Ten years. And that was the same house he—"

"What is this about, Steve?"

U.P. tapped a thumb on his belt.

"I just wanted to talk," Scheisskopf said, still not blinking.

"You have never, in your whole life, just wanted to talk."

"Can't slide anything past Jude Glick. At least not much. No one ever has."

The drums were going out front.

"I had an interview a few weeks back," I said. "I'm trying to leave this museum gig because it pays like shit, I'm allegedly a smart and talented guy, and the State of Minnesota is teabagging me."

Stephen blinked.

"And, look, Steve, the HR lady asked where I saw myself in five years. And I told her. I did. Dead, in jail, or famous. And that's why I'm in New York."

"I know."

"And because of you, even if I never wanted to appear on this *America's Got Talent* meets *Lord of the Flies* nightmare, I can't. Because you're toxic. Unless you're a shrieking Facebook mom, or a neo-Nazi, even being seen with you is dangerous. I dunno how the fuck Madeline is doing it."

"She isn't who you think she is."

"Clearly."

"What *do* you want, Julian? Because, well, I am lately in a position to help. The flowers were a test-run. See, this new station in life has caused me to reflect on certain painful memories. People I've hurt. People who have hurt me."

"All I ever wanted was a lane." I glanced at the ceiling. "God, give me a lane."

"Come here," he said. "I have something for you."

Ten years. I didn't think of Malik every day, but I couldn't shake his face now.

"Look at this," he said, handing me a phone.

It was a picture of an MAOI security guard. Clip-on tie, blue shirt, black cardigan with khakis. The guard stared at a woman's ass in yoga pants. Mesmerized. This twentysomething, clad in all-black, had bent over and popped her booty because a fascist had her in a headlock. And the guard just stared at the butt.

The guard was me. It was a meme of me. Someone's blood, probably Nala's, oozed in the background.

"I don't get it," I said. There were these random people who became memes, of course. Even I'd encountered some of them on social media. A sweaty and stoned guy accompanied by rubbish like "Marilize Legaljuana." A dreadlocked college white girl used mostly for hippie-punching. An anthropomorphized cat who one might call grumpy. I knew the internet neo-Nazis stole cartoons or comic strips and reconstituted them as white nationalist propaganda, too, but the idea of that being me seemed impossible. "Are you fucking with me?"

"I am deciding how to spin it," he said, stuffing the phone in his suit. "Whether the focus should be that you are a Deplorable, or a Social-Justice Sex Wanter."

"Steve—"

"Don't make me use it, Julian. There's another way."

"What are you—"

"You have an interesting story, J.G. Your mother, the cancer, the house. Doing all the right things and yet never getting ahead. Debt and tragedy. And then the Malik angle."

"C'mon."

"What I'm proposing, Julian, is that you come work for me. For us. We have a rally in Minnesota on Sunday. A hangar in St. Paul.

175

Once we win, and we will, you become sort of a symbol of American Carnage."

"American Carnage."

"Factories closing. Drug overdoses. Shrinking life expectancies. Whole swaths of the Midwest and South and inner cities living lives of voiceless desperation. Deaths of despair. So I want you to tell your story. If you do, you'll be compensated handsomely. You'll be famous. You'll show up on Bill Maher. MSNBC. Fox News if you want. You don't even have to say you're a Republican. You can keep doing comedy. You just have to say you feel seen. Because so many people, for the first time in their adult lives, feel seen, Jude. We are losing our culture. We are becoming a country without ballast. Without values. What the fuck is multiculturalism but dilution and disintegration. All these degenerates outside that door are gonna bed some racially ambiguous, gender-bending freak tonight while hard working people, like your mother, lose their houses and savings and fucking hope. And for what? Why? Because some trust fund liberal arts student feels offended? It's bullshit. What is a society without rules? Without order? Without a narrative. We don't have a goddamn narrative anymore, Jude, and it's my job to crank the rhetoric. And I want you to help me."

I bit my lip. U.P. sighed into his fist. The keyboards and rhythm section slinked into a groove. People cheered as Scheisskopf offered his hand.

"I'm serious, Jude. I want to do this together."

"What did you call it?"

"American Carnage."

"And how much money are we talking?"

"Whatever you want. I can buy back the house through a shell company, put it in your name. I can set you up with the right people. Agents, producers. A memoir, a cable contract. Voice of the working man. Like Joe the Plumber, but funny and charismatic. Staying power. Only I will know my involvement level."

I touched eyes with Ulysses. He immediately looked away.

The hand hovered. Scheisskopf held my gaze. Powder blue.

"I am removing barriers to entry. You are simply providing a human face for our policy goals," he said.

"Carnage, huh?"

"American Carnage."

I pivoted, looked out the window. The Weylin flared red.

"I don't need you to agree with me. All we are is partners."

Perhaps Scheisskopf was a fascist and a psychopath, but it clearly hadn't hurt his social standing. He'd be back in this room once the party petered out, shtupping my college crush. And, other than the smattering of minorities and LGBTQ folks and immigrants who found his ascent terrifying and threatening—to their activism, to their bodies, to their continued existence—nobody else here seemed to care.

I already knew Reid and Addy wouldn't give a shit. Hell, my lack of careerism had always humiliated them. And Mom's family, though too focused on mortgages and children and hockey to follow politics, still carried enough white rage to support Scheisskopf's game show fascist. So, maybe, they'd finally support me.

"I know that hunger, J.G.," Stephen said as the drummer bashed cymbals and a synth riff burst into climax. "And I know that foolishness. So come with me. If not for yourself, or your mom, then for Malik."

Ten years on Wednesday.

Thirteen years old.

Eighth grade.

I turned around. Smiled at Stephen. Pulled my hand from my side. Stepped toward his outstretched arm. And held his head as I made-out with him.

Sloppy, tonguey, ironic forced kissing.

"Hey," U.P. shouted as Steve leapt back.

"The hell is going wrong with you?" said Scheisskopf, retreating to a corner.

"You called me cyclops every day for ten fucking years. You destroyed my best friend's life. I find everything about you, and your politics, a white supremacist circle-jerk, buddy, so don't invoke my blind single mother or my black best friend ever again, you neo-Nazi dweeb."

"Giving voice to the carnage all around us makes me a—"

"Shut the fuck up, you fascist fucking clown," I said, now crowding him. "American Carnage is spending your life hunched over a keyboard, or in a coal mine, or in a classroom for shit healthcare and no benefits. American Carnage is twenty-six dead at Sandy Hook and three hundred murders on the South Side of Chicago. American Carnage is growing up in the projects like Malik with no way out from the start because of racist cowards like you."

"Julian," U.P. hollered, "back the fuck up."

"Because white men like Steve can't police their imaginations, black men are dying."

"J.G.! Step off."

"Go to hell, Ulysses," I said as he reached for something in his waistband. "I said no to Scheisskopf and you could, too."

"Julian, step away or I'm finna drop you," U.P. said, pointing a gun at me. I had Stephen pushed against the wall like he'd been pushed against my locker in high school.

"Do it, U.P. Shoot me. What's another death when—"

A splash of something on my face. Blood? No, it stung. Like my eyes were sunburnt. Like I'd snorted a habanero.

Pepper spray. Scheisskopf had pepper sprayed me.

And, as I banged around the room screaming and blinking, he kicked me in the knee, which cut me to the ground with a bounce of the head.

I rolled around, clutching my face. The door opened. Shuffling. Noise from the dancefloor. I still couldn't see, but now felt hands around my collar and belt, hoisting me into the air, smashing my skull against nightstands and walls, and next thing I knew I was being swung through the door and crashing to the floor.

I opened my eyes. Looked up. Scheisskopf staring down at me.

"This was your chance, you prideful idiot," he said. "And you blew it."

Then, like a frat bro stomping an empty beer can, he ground my dick and nuts into the floor and, through the side door near Madeline's, left with his thugs.

I shrieked and slobbered and wailed. I slumped in the sweat and the blood and the plaster.

The band played on.

Nobody came to my rescue. Nobody said a thing. Whoever had seen it either lost interest or lost empathy in a haze of sweat and coke and EDM. Drunken revelry in the background, hoots and hollers, inevitable sex, every twentysomething in America feeling the fear and drinking anyway.

So I sat, suffering in the hallway, rubbing my eyes, closing them, prying them open, sniffling, crying, replaying whatever the hell had just happened while, twenty feet away, a hundred Brooklyn creatives writhed and hoovered and sniffed to actual Brooklyn creatives.

Against the wall, folks coming and going, I probably looked like a passed-out jabroni who'd slurped too many Mike's Hard Lemonades.

Then, after half an hour of thumps and cheers, it flashed before me like Paul on the road to Damascus.

The heroin.

MADELINE HAD A private bathroom, and since Scheisskopf and his stormtroopers escaped to Argentina, or whatever—and since I hadn't seen Madeline or her friends after the Blitzkrieg (not that I'd seen much of anything other than shoes or my tears staining the hardwood floors)—I clambered into the bedroom, which somehow remained both unlocked and unoccupied.

Simply being inside it alone, the place where she undressed and masturbated, made me horny and disgusted with myself. And even more resolved to huff heroin.

I flushed my eyes and face with cold water. I couldn't tell if this made me feel better or worse, but I rallied regardless. Mace, bear repellent, pixie dust, whatever Scheisskopf hit me with had worn off. I once pepper sprayed myself as a bit, so I could endure the physical discomfort. Now, the pain referred from somewhere deeper, somewhere ancient and humiliated and confused.

Sitting on the toilet, playing with the baggie, the shame increased with my falling blood alcohol content. I'd treated Lana like a therapist. Seen Rosie as a boring audiobook and she knew it. Lacked the maturity to reciprocate Ryan's kindness, even if he probably wanted something from me. Been castigated by a good Samaritan drug dealer. Loathed and shit-talked by Belcalis Pulido, whom I hadn't spoken to but alienated with my existence. At what, I realized suddenly, must have been her housewarming party.

And, of course, Scheisskopf.

Here I was, in his bangbuddy's bathroom, twinged with sexual desire for once, or maybe just a residual crush, hungry for a conversation with someone who, other than laughing at my schtick, never gave any indication I was a human being.

Sick of being Jude Glick.

I pulled out a credit card, emptied the H on the countertop, and cut lines. A murmur through the floorboards; the music had not faded but had evaporated. The heroin taunted me.

The party had gone totally silent, which massaged me with a little hope, but then I heard the pop and crescendo of a police siren. And understood this was not, in fact, good.

My heart bounced against my sternum like a basketball speed dribble.

Boots on the landing. A walkie-talkie crackled.

And, then, my phone rang.

507 number. Rural Minnesota. Where Tom and Chris went to school. I'd already missed two calls.

Outside, bangs on the front door.

"Police," a low voice said.

Other voices calling for Madeline, where's Mads, did she leave? Who even lives here anymore? Not Ignacio? Really? Well, fine, get Rosie.

Knock, knock, knock.

507 number. Didn't recognize it. Tugged Mom's rosary beads from under my flannel and accepted the call.

"Hello," I said. A voice that might have been Rosie's trilled outside.

"Is this Mr. Glick?"

"This is Julian Glick. Can I ask who's—"

"So you are not the father of Tom and Chris Glick."

"No, I'm the older brother." The front door creaked. I stared at the lines of heroin.

"Well, we don't have a Student Informatics Puzzlebox on file so—"

"Is everything—"

"There's been a major incident involving your younger brothers and Tom's roommate."

"Is . . . wait, what are you saying?"

"Mr. Glick, I can't go into specifics over the phone due to HIPAA regulations, but Lars Kiffmeyer has been expelled pending review. Your brothers, meanwhile, are in both legal and medical trouble."

Yelling now. The woman was crying and pleading while another woman's voice barked something I couldn't catch.

More sirens. Stomps and radio static. The heroin jumped out against the black marble.

"Mr. Glick?"

"Look, could you contact the father? I mean provided this isn't an emergency? Because I'm in New York City. I'm in show business which—"

"Sir, Mr. Hess, the RA-on-duty this evening, alerted us to some peculiarities regarding Boris Glick. And we couldn't reach him anyway so—"

"Okay but I'm just not sure I can—"

"Personally, my recommendation is that you get to Winona as soon as possible. Because the longer you wait, sir, the harder this is going to be to unravel."

Men's voices. Getting closer. Pounding I could both hear and feel. Christ. The cops were outside Madeline's bedroom. Which I hadn't locked.

"Can you call Lydia Olerud? She'll be listed in the Dawson, Minnesota—"

"Yes, but she won't be able to do much. The only names we have on file, given the lack of the Student Informatics Puzzlebox, are Paula, Boris, and Julian Glick. And unless Paula is available, or Boris is contacted, we can't move forward in any substantive way without—"

"Fine," I whispered as footsteps brushed outside the bathroom, "I'll be there as soon as I can, but—"

"Is there anybody in here?" a man's voice called. "Hello? Anyone."

"Mr. Glick," the phone said as the door handle jiggled. "Mr. Glick, we—"

I turned the phone off. Exhaled.

Two lines of heroin.

Banging on the bathroom door now. I brushed the dope into my palm, stood up, threw the bag in the toilet and rubbed the powder from my hands.

"Hello?" a cop said, angrier this time. "If someone is in there, better come on out, pal, before I come on in."

The heroin wouldn't flush. I flipped the handle, removed the top piece, kicked the bowl. Nothing. Just circling and circling.

"We hear you in there, motherfucker." A shoulder into the door now. It bulged and receded.

I jiggled the handle again and the baggie started to disappear. As it sank into the hole, I slammed the seat and cut the lights. Just as the door burst open.

"Where is he?" one asked, a Sgt. Francesa, I made out through the flashlight beam. His partner, Ofc. Russo, crossed his arms.

"Come out of your cave," he said.

"We in *Batman* now?" I said.

"Where?"

"Wanna know how I got these scars?" I said.

"Julian?" Russo asked as he flipped the lightswitch. "The Jokester, eh?"

"Why so serious?"

"We heard about you from our referral, buddy."

"You a nut, huh, kid?" Francesa said, opening a cabinet.

"Sure," I said. "You're a professional racist, but I'm the nut. Sure."

They both puffed out some nose laughter. Francesa turned me around, facing the toilet.

"What the hell is he talking 'bout, eh, Franny?" Russo said, starting to pat me down.

"He's drunk. Depressed. Another one of these born-on-third-base losers who don't know how the real world works," said Francesa.

"You got me!" I said, throwing my arms up in mock guilt.

"He ain't one of them uppity things from earlier, at least. Privilege and crap. Like there was any advantages ta bein' born on Cianci Street in Paterson fuggin' New Jersey," Russo said. "No dad. No prospects. Still send Ma money."

They were elbow-deep in my cords, searching for vindication. Outside, I heard the partiers bang down the steps, a couple other cops shepherding and/or threatening their drunken flock.

"Yah, yah. Build a wall, caterpalt 'em all over the middle of it till they learn some friggin' respect, eh, Russy? Them black lives in the wagon? Don't matter. The yellows? The browns? Don't matter."

"So whatser story, Jude? Kid like you hangin' round these snow-flakes."

"Long story," I said. "I—"

"Russy, Mr. S was wrong," Francesa said, squeezing my biceps, inspecting my nose. I noticed both wore black boots with red laces. "He ain't a fairy. He's one of us. Reason he left the monkeys to throw shit at each other."

"Right on tha money, Sarge," Russo said. "Mr. S had bad info for once. Guy's clean. Well, maybe, if ya catch my drift. Rosie, cute little thing, huh?" Russo elbowed me in the ribs too hard to be taken as only playful. "You musta hit that tight little ass and ticked her right off 'cause she, she—"

"Pump 'n' dump, yeah, Jude?" Francesa said with a grin. I returned it. "Ya move on her like a bitch, eh? He's muggin' for us, see? Jude here grabs 'em by the pussy!"

"Gotta do something, partner, 'cause she didn't have *nothing* good to say about you. All sorts a names and made clear you don't live here, and won't be back."

"Me, I'm partial to that Belcalis cunt. Thick ass on her, eh? Wouldn't mind pounding that from the back."

"How's that for oppressive."

"Jude here's got the *privilege* to stick it in whatever twat he wants."

"Towel-heads? Wetbacks? Kikes, even? Proud Boy like you, ya gotta be drownin' in it."

"Jus' make sure ya come up for air!"

They both laughed and, knowing my role but hating it, I did, too. The pat-down stopped. Russo clapped a big authoritarian paw on my trapezius. The ability to cycle from social justice warrior to aggrieved leftist to sports-playing blue collar white guy to the pseudo-nihilist comic we all know and loathe might be my one true talent. Not sure if this means I'm a hollow human being, a sociopath, or too socially anxious for public conviction, but I nodded and pounded fists with them.

"Jude," Russo said.

"Yeah?" I turned around. They both crossed their arms.

"You ever come back to *our* women, *our* people—and yer young, but I recommend it—get in touch. And use yer head. Don't look for solidarity where there ain't none."

"We're dispossessed," Francesa said. "You know it's true, too. Why you think we've stuck around on the coast, Jude? Because soon, when we win this election, we're gonna start takin' back what our people built."

"*What's ours*, Mr. S calls it."

The clomping down the steps continued. More radio chatter. But I couldn't see any cops as I poked out of Madeline's bedroom.

Teeth crushing my inner cheek, I offered a tiny nod to *what's ours* and, hands shaking, crept into the hallway. Empty. I was halfway down when I heard it.

"White Lives Matter, Jude."

I turned back toward her room. High five. Laughter.

"Whassup, Jude?" Francesa said. "No blood and soil for you?"

"Yeah, you okay, kid? Too drunk? We can get ya home if ya

want," Russo said.

"I forgot to say something, is all," I said, exhaling, booze-breath lingering in my face.

"Yeah?" they said together. We stood in the doorway where Scheisskopf's muscle had kicked my ass an hour ago.

"You're fascists. And cowards."

"What?"

"The only thing more worthless than white people are white cops."

Francesa tapped two fingers on his holster. Russo sniffed.

"And, whatever, fuck it: Black Lives Matter."

I WAS LUCKY I didn't lose my eye.

The darkness came quick.

I assumed I was fainting.

But nah.

Courtesy.

Professionalism.

Respect.

Nightsticks.

Fists to the nose, boots to the balls, thwacks to my ribs and stomach as I tried to roll over. And then a heel to the spine.

Coughing, already lying in my own blood, one of them grabbed me by the hair and smashed a bottle on my head, while the other prodded my anus with what felt like a finger.

The guy up top, done with my scalp, jammed a knee toward my brainstem and rubbed my face in the shards of glass.

A kick to the temple, another to my liver. I started throwing up and, now slipping in bile, trying to get to my knees to take a deep breath, they ripped something from their duty belts, shot it at my face, and left.

Hacking, throat swelling, the sensation of choking—to say nothing of the burn radiating from my open face to lacerated back—I heard them lumber down the hall.

There were voices. Rosie, Belcalis, a few other stragglers shouted at them, but then a baton smacked something hard, maybe a computer, and the voices stopped.

"All you fucking faggots with yer cunty presidential candidate, don't fuhget who runs this town. And whose gonna run you people out of it come November 9th," Russo yelled.

"We can always come back for more," Francesa said. "Don't test us."

"You kids make me fuckin' sick."

"Nazi scum," Ryan Yoder-Henley said. It hurt to blink. It hurt to breathe.

Another whoosh through the air. Then a thud, a snap, this time accompanied by a scream.

"You broke my goddamn leg," he shouted, hopping in agony.

"Yeah, and if ya report this, the blow you sniffed with them cultural Marxists in the wagon'll put you in jail till both yer parents are dead, you coke-eyed soy boy," Francesa said. "Your pal here crossed the wrong people, the wrong person, so—"

"Scheisskopf sold the fucking coke," Belcalis said.

"Say that again sweetie," Francesa said. "I like a big-titted angry beaner."

People were crying now. Ryan kept screaming as boots kicked furniture, maybe a shin or two. It sounded like Russo pulled Belcalis, over slaps of dissent, in for a kiss.

"We know the type of crap yer up to," Francesa said. "And, if ya really wanna know what'll happen next time, if ya really wanna see what'll go down if you throw another multi-colored fag fiesta—"

"We got fourteen words for you," Russo snickered.

"Eighty-eight if ya ain't careful."

They clunked out the interior exit, but Russo must have popped back in.

"If Deplorable Dave is conscious up there," he said, "tell that cuck Stephen Scheisskopf appreciates everything he's done for the Force."

With that, he slammed the door and returned to the beat.

My eyes watering, totally soaked in most body fluids, I pushed myself off the ground with a stinging face, puffy everything, limped back to Madeline's bathroom, rinsed my eyes with water, and stripped down to my boxers. I could deal with the cuts and bruises and any broken bones; I've been walking around with a shredded AC joint and no cartilage in my right knee for years. But the pulsing of my eyes, the sensitivity to light, the seething pores required something to be done. So I threw the flannel and cords I'd been wearing out the window, packed up all my stuff, and limped down the hall, walking past the puddle of me seeping into the parquet.

In the main room, I ignored the whimpers and whispers and

shuffled to Ignacio's room. Or what was his room.

I grabbed my stuff, slipped into my only other clothes—sweatpants and a Vikings hoodie—and massaged my swelling head.

Back in the kitchen, Ryan sobbing on the ground while Lana stroked his hair, I limped to the fridge, opened it.

These clichés had soy milk, almond milk, rice milk and, not a single animal product. Not even a Temple Grandin magnet on the goddamn door. But after knocking things around and blocking out whatever these people were shouting at me, I bogarted a single school-sized carton of 2%, lifted my face to the vaulted ceiling, and showered in pasteurized liquid. Eyes, cuts, and scrapes at least a little bit cooled, I picked up my two bags. With the entire room staring at me like this was a Bigfoot sighting, I dragged myself toward the door.

"Jude," Belcalis said, "are . . . are you okay?"

Right index finger to my bad eye, which I gathered had almost completely swollen shut, I shot a thumbs-up with my left hand. Milk dripping, I looked around for Rosie and when I made her out—mouth open, staring through me, almost drooling on the kitchen island—I squared my shoulders to her and exhaled.

"Now you have something to write about," I said. "Creatively."

Blinks. Laughter down the street. Chants of U-S-A. Frat bros gearing up for premeditated assault.

"Jude," Rosie said.

"Yeah."

"Thanks."

"Say hi to Ignacio," I said. "Oh, and Rosie? Ryan? Lana?"

"Yeah," they said.

"I'm gonna get that motherfucker back. I promise."

"Wait," Lana said. "Stephen—"

"I'll kill him if I have to, but he'll pay for this."

Then, heaving my battered body toward the side door, I ignored the weirdness and winked.

9.

IN THE PENIS COLONY

"YOU'VE REACHED THE voicemail of Boris Glick. The date is July 21, 2003. Please hang up," Boris' voicemail said.

I tottered into the MSP terminal, considered trying Lydia again. Maybe even Principal Schmidt. Tom and Chris, per the half-Polish ramblings of my grandfather, were not dead but did need their legal guardian to get them out of jail and/or rural Minnesota's corn maze of a hospital system. Something about DUIs and blood on the brain.

Only I wasn't their legal guardian. And Boris had been AWOL since the funeral.

I *was*, I realized while firing up Mom's van in the long-term ramp, too drunk to drive. Even on a Saturday morning. In the rearview mirror, my right eye looked like a Bulbasaur. We'd idled over Minneapolis for a couple hours, granting me the audacity to slug my entire fifth of duty free Cîroc Coconut before the pilot muttered something about inoperable light-rail conditions. My alcohol tolerance, although not where I wanted it, was certainly pre-cirrhotic. It took me about ten shots to feel a buzz. Five hours total to finish that much booze rendered this my least horrific option.

Like any heartland suicide-risk, I'd driven drunk weekly since college. Brisses. Funerals. AA meetings. So with the extended family closer to South Dakota or Iowa than Minneapolis, and Boris still not picking up, I crept onto the 494 service road. Sleet battered the trashbag window. Even on this Saturday morning, the entrance ramp looked like a used car dealership. I alternated which hand I sat on.

Wintry mix. Same slop pounded Malik as he gasped in a St. Paul ditch. Ten years on Wednesday.

I flicked on NPR, flicked it off. It wasn't too cold, but the threat of Scheisskopf's voice had me shivering. I accelerated to 10 mph, merged. The trash bag swelled in the wind like the head of a hard-on. My forearms ached as I squeezed the wheel.

Back in New York, they'd be starting orientation at 30 Robber Baron Plaza. Some unpaid intern, even lower than Lana, an NYU Tisch kid whose dad roomed with Lorne Michaels or negotiated a harassment claim for the *Today* show, would ring me soon, frantic— all coke drips and breached contract legalese—until I implored them to escape the entertainment industry and hung up/hung myself.

Booze fumes wafted from my breath fog. I slapped myself, half to stay awake and half for having taken creative writing in college. The legal owner of this vehicle was now a science classroom's skel-eton, or maybe a rogue morgue employee's taxidermized RealDoll. I slapped myself again. Mom probably hadn't been paying insurance for this van, which could pose problems for me as I continued to live in it this winter. Or drunk drove it this fall.

I didn't even like Cîroc. Or drinking.

A semi flashed lights and screeched toward the shoulder as I passed him on the left. If Tom and Chris hadn't lost much executive functioning, or wouldn't need long-term care, getting kicked out of school would be good for everyone: they could move into Boris' one-bedroom, and we could all avoid more familial debt.

Deep enough into the exurbs to see aborted fetus billboards, I turned on a polka station and did not check my buzzing phone. Too risky. Myron Floren wheezed away on his accordion as I drummed along on the dash. How Mom had enjoyed these hooting Germano-Slavic clunks, yet had lived in St. Louis and Little Rock in her twen-ties, mystified me.

Still, I turned it up as another car drifted for the shoulder. I didn't see anything up ahead, but eased off the gas. Boris, paranoid about black ice and/or interactions with the "fuzz," recommended never driving above ten in a snowstorm.

I glanced at the odometer: 20.

"Ah, shit."

I started sliding around.

Roll out the barrel!

The van listed left a bit, so I tapped the brakes and shifted toward the right lane. My front end made it, but my back end seemed to shimmy across the center line.

We'll have a barrel of fun!

I torqued right, then left, then right again as the van careened toward the shoulder.

Roll out the barrel!

I cranked left this time, trying to flow with the fishtail, which I should've been doing as soon as I felt the wobble. Too late. The van started swinging around like a shotputter.

We've got our blues on the . . .

I whipped clockwise, and with my glasses dangling, the backside yanked right again, flinging my skull against the headrest, a tilt-a-whirl, but, no, we weren't done because the car kept spinning until it banged into the retaining wall, catapulting my face into a splash of driver-side window and center console.

Run.

As I slapped around for my glasses with one hand and pressed my head gash with the other, the airbag blasted me like a straight-right to the nose. The van beeped hysterically. I found my glasses, somehow intact, and then interrogated my bleeding face.

Just a trickle. More purple than Grimace, but I wouldn't need a doctor. This would be fine, provided the state troopers didn't get involved.

I cradled my dome, a basketball player in a triple-threat position.

But the van wouldn't start.

"What now?" I said.

I removed the key, blew on it like a Super Nintendo cartridge. Tried again.

"Please. Please start."

A siren wailed in the distance. Nothing.

"Shit. Shit. Shit."

Still nothing. I pounded the steering wheel.

"C'mon, motherfucker. Start."

No luck.

If I ran, I'd be hitchhiking to Winona. In a blizzard. But I'd avoid the DUI. Though bailing would leave all of my books and clothes roadside in unincorporated Rice County. In a blizzard. And with civil asset forfeiture funding most rural towns in America, I might never see my stuff again. And they'd probably seize the van, too. In a blizzard.

"Goddammit."

The engine revved this time but wouldn't turn over. Sirens closer. Not sure where, though, because I was perpendicular to the road.

"I'm begging you. Why? Why won't you just start?"

Jail scared me. Boris—who called himself "prison strong" pre-divorce—avoided discussing his year in the clink. Sure, he avoided discussing everything outside of microwaveable burritos and Howard Zinn, but any time I brought it up, he would get paternal, the idea of his eldest son locked up making even him fatherly.

"I'll fetch you from a party. I'll get you a lawyer. I'll take the heat for you, J.G., but don't ever go to fucking jail. Just don't."

There was the gun. I hadn't sold the gun.

Boris's father had nicked the Ortgies 7.65 from a Nazi officer at Buchenwald. A family heirloom, it served with distinction in various domestic disputes, culminating in Boris using a broken TV for target practice one drunken afternoon in the 1990s.

But I'd never fired a gun. And didn't plan to start. I was the only male relative on either side who hadn't at least hunted. Even Tom and Chris got covertly baked and helped Konrad slaughter pheasants once a year. I refused. Liberal piety, toxic masculinity aversion, etc. Killing myself, or a trooper, seemed optimistic. And the only thing I liked about myself was my pessimism.

I could do movie-villain intimidation. Or try. But I had no interest in murder. Yet.

The squad car shrilled, now loud enough to hurt my ears. I cranked the key again.

Nothing.

I pulled the Ortiges from the compartment, cocked it. Felt the careening cop through the floorpads as I set the gun on a passenger seat stack of books.

"Mr. State Trooper, please don't stop me. Please don't stop me. Please don't stop me."

I exhaled. If Stephen Scheisskopf could address millions of pilled-out proto-fascists each week, I could bluff my way out of a felony. Deserted highway in a snowstorm, enigmatic growling, threatened wife and kids. Swerve toward Winona and find out how badly the brothers messed up.

Seatbelt tugged aside, I unlocked the door, tucked Mom's rosary under my sweatshirt, and wondered about the nearest backup.

Then the cop blew past me.

Didn't even slow down.

I shoved the gun back into the compartment, tried the ignition again. She turned over, but I was still stuck to the retaining wall. Drive. The goddamn thing was in Drive. I pressed the brake, pulled the lever into park, turned her off, then on, then found myself reversing onto the shoulder and scooting down I-35.

Don't think and drive, kids.

I inched south for several minutes. No cop in sight. Snow skipped across the four lanes. Visibility was glaucoma-ish. A thousand feet up, a car idled in a turnaround. Possibly the cop. Jimmy Sturr beeped through the "Clarinet Polka." I removed my foot from the gas and let the van drift down the Interstate. I needed to call Gramps, so, phone fished from my cords, I committed another traffic violation.

To my surprise, he picked up.

"How's dat now?" he said, answering on the first ring. I had pulled almost even with the turned-around sedan. It looked like a Crown Vic.

A shriek, a WHOOP-WHOOP!

"Gramps, it's J.G. Real quick: I wanted an update on—"

"Where'n a hell ya been, eh? Tot you was in New Yerk?"

"Well, I rushed back once—"

"Why'n the hell'd ya do that, huh? This was yer shot at makin' some money, people was tellin' me."

"Yeah, Gramps, but—"

"Dey's gonna be fine, we're thinking here, okay?"

"I still don't even know what happened. I got a message from Chris and voicemail from you, in the middle of the night, and then everybody just—"

"Hold yer horses, dere. Jussa second."

He covered the phone, hollered something barely English, barely language. In the rearview mirror, through the blowing drifts, the cop flashed his high-beams, then his emergency lights.

"You still dere, son?"

The cop crept closer. Sirens again.

"Not much longer," I said, not pulling over.

"Yah, well, might be better that way. If ya cut town, I mean."

"What does—"

"Nevermind. Couple things I heard through da grapevine. At the Legion. Scheisskopf. Jus' get down to the hopsittle quick, yah? De twins is gonna be okay, but they got some legal issues with the school, with some drugs. Roommate problems, or something. Fellow name of Hess sayin' yer brothers boxed his ears pretty good. Dey should be outta the medically induced codas by Monday morning. So don't hurry, or nothing, but get the fuck down here."

As he hung up, the cop started tailing me. Anxiety and anger had sobered me enough to think I could beat a field sobriety test. I'd feel certain with a little more liquid courage, but this level of drunkenness could probably beat a DUI.

So I pulled over, gripped Mom's beads. Slid the van into Park.

The squad moseyed within ten feet of my bumper, angled left. I could see the trooper scribble, hold something—a radio? a vape pen?—to his mouth.

The cop lurched from the car, tugged his ten-gallon-hat over his face. The trash-bag flapped. Snowflakes leaked through my shitty tape job and the newly broken window, landing on me and lubing up the dry-ish blood. I stared at the ceiling. The trooper knocked on my roof.

"I saw you earlier, sir, and you aren't fooling anyone. So we can do this the easy way or the hard way," the lady cop said, tipping her hat. "I don't much care which."

"Good morning to you, too," I said. Sgt. Westerberg. Aviators, buzzed head. Built like a junior high lineman.

"State Patrol." She thumbed her badge. "Do you know why I pulled you over?"

"I was driving too well?"

"You're being pulled over for a busted taillight and reckless driving, sir."

I fake-sneezed, massaged my tailbone. "Oy gevalt!" In custody hearings or halfway house altercations, Boris had modeled schlepping in the same way Mom had modeled hard work and discipline. It was not lost on me who I'd been taking after since her death. "I just dislocated my lumbar."

"License and registration, please."

"Can I ask why—"

"You have a broken taillight, and I have probable cause to suspect you just got in an accident. So, please, let's make this easy on me before I radio for backup in a blizzard."

I stared at the glove compartment. We were the only visible cars in either direction. Everyone else had pulled off the road. She'd maybe entered Mom's license plate into a database, but it wasn't illegal to drive someone else's car. Even a dead person's. Possibly.

"Sir, I'll count down from five."

I fidgeted. I could smell myself, all booze and body odor.

"Five."

My legs bounced. My feet tapped. The gun promised either an escalation or elimination of my short-term problems.

"Four."

But murdering a cop could hurt my Klout score.

"Three."

Though a Johnny Cash-like live album, from a state penitentiary, might land me in *THR*. Especially if I Carlinized my act and openly antagonized Scheisskopf.

"Two."

Ted Kaczynski went viral. But so did Sirhan Sirhan. Lee Harvey Oswald. Why kill a cop when I could kill Scheisskopf? But why kill at all? NYC might've been a bluff. There was still time to join him.

"O—"

"Here," I said, handing over my license with a tremor. "Sorry. I'm under a lot of stress."

"This is America, man. Who isn't?"

"Mmm."

"Insurance?"

"Uh."

"You wanna maybe dig around that compartment for me?"

"Not really."

"Is there a reason why?" She interrogated my license. The snow was coming down in clumps. I gnawed my cheek and stared at the glove box.

"Not really."

"Fine," she said, then waddled toward her car.

I expelled air like a horse, swayed my head from side to side as I crushed the steering wheel in my palms.

The fuck was wrong with me? With us? If only my family wasn't my family. From Gramps on down. Would Tom and Chris be okay? Would I ever even know? Not unless I made it to Winona. But could I ever forgive myself, regardless? Entrenched poverty, soon-to-be college dropouts, no role models outside of some fratty creeper and whatever they gleaned from Dale Carnegie. *How to Lose Money and Isolate People*. What if I'd cobbled together an extra month in the house? One last mortgage payment. Two thousand dollars I didn't have, sure, but maybe wave it off like the other $50,000 I didn't have. I'd stopped answering Lydia's texts about money. Me and my sadness might've annihilated Tom and Chris, too, but a long frat weekend ensured bludgeonings of chance, or alcohol poisoning. And, Christ, I could never forgive them if they traumatized some girl. We were raised by a single mother. We watched *Roseanne*. None of us had ever downloaded Bumble, let alone Tinder. My brothers as goddamn frat boys. Even associating with those walking erections felt like a personal slight, but if Boris-leaden PTSD hadn't chastened their cock-first thinking, why had I even bothered with father-figure counter-programming?

Behind me, the trooper futzed with a computer. I bashed my forehead with the thick of my palms. Left hand for fucking up. Right hand for reverting to rhetorical questions.

Sgt. Westerberg made a radio call. The wind gusted. The trash bag bulged, receded.

Watching the non-window swell and settle, I thought of Tuesday night. Brandi Bates had offered a co-headlining spot at an election night showcase. My non-foray into reality TV had superseded the offer, but I could talk my way back onto the bill. Enduring the election alone, or even with friends, placed the spotlight on suicide. Scheisskopf and The Mogul winning made too much sense.

I slapped myself, trying to stay lucid. Westerberg was now on the phone. She nodded. She laughed. Stepped out of the cruiser, hand on holster. Zipped her coat as she approached.

"Mr. Glick," the cop said, "are you aware that this vehicle is not tagged to you but is instead titled to a Paula Glick?"

"You betcha." Sirens. Lightbar in the distance. It occurred to me I had not eaten in 48 hours. I needed to either burp or puke or disembowel myself.

"And are you aware that there is a warrant out for your arrest in Hennepin County?"

"You betcha," I said, "as of five seconds ago."

Two more cops strolled toward my car.

"Before I ask you to step away from the vehicle, Mr. Glick, is there anything you want me to know about either your van or personal status? Just so we avoid problems."

I looked over my shoulder: an acoustic guitar (sans case), three copies of *The Great Gatsby*, one hundred paperbacks worse than *The Great Gatsby*, two dozen comedy albums, two football trophies, a bottle of Aveeno, a box of tissues, a mattress and bedding, several flannels and sweaters, four pairs of pants, one suit, Mom's jewelry box, and two funeral bulletins. A gun in the glovebox. A fifth of Wild Turkey 101 under my seat.

"Mr. Glick?"

"Y'know, the insurance info is probably beneath my chair here if I can reach it."

She nodded but stepped away. The other officers now surrounded the van. *Little Chicago, MN*, I read in the rearview. After laughing and rummaging, I found the neck of the booze. So I popped the cap, opened my mouth, and doused myself.

Next thing I knew, I was face-first on the asphalt with a bloody nose and a knee prodding my spine.

"The fuck was that?" Westerberg said.

"A sudden movement."

"Okay, smartass, anything else?"

"I've got a jockey full of bourbon."

WITH NO REAL income to garnish, no assets other than a car in Winona and some Tom Waits' references to brutalize, and no family to vouch for my character, Minnesota decided to hold me in contempt of court. I had ignored their manila envelopes and assumed a blue state wouldn't lock up a grieving, underemployed depressive for his debt to bureaucracy.

I was wrong.

Maybe you thought debtor's prison was twee, like the electric chair. Or quaint, like a living wage. Or barbarous, like a humanities degree. Or just, like, illegal. Well, you'd be correct, at least technically speaking. But, as Officer Donglefritz explained from his cruiser, after about six hours of untreated wounds and hematomas in the Rice County Detention Center, America got more Dickensian than Truck or Curb. Or even Boris' parole-mandated 12-stepping.

See, the state jailed people who owed civil debt all the time, not for an inability to pay but for refusing to follow a court order (i.e., to pay).

"Therefore," he said through the separator, "not a debtor's prison."

"But I'm under arrest because I am indebted to the state," I said, "in violation of some civil statutes. So I am being imprisoned over debt."

"No, no, no. You don't get it. You're being imprisoned because it is illegal to ignore a court order."

"What am I supposed to do when the court is ordering me to do something I can't do?"

"That's not my problem," he said.

"I never said it was."

He turned around as he sped a stoplight somewhere around Lakeville.

"Do I look like Atticus Finch to you?"

"Actually," I said, squinting at him. "Yeah. I'm serious this time."

He stomped the brakes, sending my handcuffed and un-belted body hurtling into the plexiglass divider. I felt the welt above my good eye form as soon as we started moving again. Cars honked, swerved. Joe Bob punished the accelerator.

"Watch yer fuckin' mouth or we'll charge you with resisting arrest. Again."

"But I'm already under arrest. For not paying my debt."

"For the final time, bud," he yelled, glaring at me through the rearview mirror as blood trickled down my face for the fourth time in 24 hours. "This has nothing to do with your inherited debt, okay? This is about ignoring various mandatory summons to either develop a debt repayment plan with the State of Minnesota *or* to reach a plea deal over your mother's debt. The debt is irrelevant here."

"Fuck you," I said, tongue and lips glossed in my forehead's run-off.

"You should have that laceration looked at," he said, whipping a sharp left that flung me rib-first into the right door. "You'll have to, actually, at the detention clinic. Hope you brought your insurance card. And that you're in-network."

I wiggled back to a seated position, right shoulder firing geysers of pain with each inhale.

"How long am I being detained?" I asked with a pant.

"Ya got a Monday morning court hearing. At that time, should ya not demonstrate an ability to facilitate some sorta arrangement with Minnesota's collections agencies, you'll probably be locked up till ya can."

"How is this legal?"

"Do I look like someone who gives a shit to you?"

"No, sir. No, you don't."

ONE OF MY earliest memories is the farewell party Konrad threw himself before moving to a trailer park and selling the family farm. I remember a sister saying something to Mom that made her cry, Boris rubbing her back with one hand and squeezing a fist with the other as we stomped across gravel to the station wagon. He told Mom the sisters were jealous, had always been jealous, because she "got out of this shithole and raised a son who'll not only go to fucking college but go to goddamn Harvard, Paula."

I did not go to Harvard.

I did go to jail.

"Wait here," Donglefritz said, handcuffing me to a bench in the county detention center.

"Yessir."

This was a big, carpeted vestibule that smelled of scalded rubber and fish sticks. Two picnic tables, plastic and inked with everything from veiny dicks to veiny dicks with swastikas, constituted the only other seating options. The only other civilians here were two old queens in assless leather chaps playing Connect Four. I nodded at them, no idea why. One snorted while the other adjusted his leather vest. I glimpsed a nipple pierced with a Nazi-ish eagle. Log Cabin Fascists, I guess.

Ten years on Wednesday. Famous, in jail, or dead. And, for Tom and Chris, another decade of medical-industrial complex oppression. At least I didn't expect things to work out, which is why I'd never joined a frat or cultivated my credit score. As Donglefritz returned with a smirk, I wondered if the central difference between me and my brothers, or maybe even me and Boris, or me and Mom, was that I knew I was a mess while they refused to see it.

"Your problem, Julian, is you refuse to see that you're a mess."

"Oh."

"So, here's what happens next. Do you wanna know what happens next?"

"Do I?"

"Well, hell. Do I look like—"

"Could you stop doing that? It hasn't been funny for a while."

"Sorry."

One of the queens burped. Donglefritz and I looked over, looked away when they caught us looking.

"What happens next," Donglefritz said, "is you go to gen pop."

"Cool. More trauma."

"But because, well, frankly, kiddo, you ain't exactly jailbird material, I've got a proposition."

I upturned my palms, scraped the cuffs on my wrist.

"We have this pilot program goin' where we release non-violent offenders. And, even though you're a smartass, you are a non-violent offender."

"Wait," I said, "why are we doing this in the lobby if I'm gonna be released in—"

"Thing is, you need a permanent address for us to do this. Because, unlike a hospital, we will not release an inmate to the streets. At least not between October 15th and March 15th."

Incredible. My prospects were so bleak the authorities thought I was safer in custody.

"But if you want, I could fudge for ya, is what I'm sayin'."

"But why?" I whispered. The queens' asses squeaked.

He looked at his skin. Then my skin.

"Oh, for fuckssake, Donglefritz, you racist-ass—"

"I'm doing you a favor kid. I just need an address."

I did not have an address to give. I hadn't been to Boris' in years. Addy had just moved. Reid's traphouse, which had multiple addresses due to the clerical error of his stoner landlord, could not receive mail.

I shrugged. My right shoulder burnt. Dislocated again, I realized.

"Well then best I can do is put you in the medical unit," Donglefritz said, "but it's solitary confinement."

"So is the rest of my life."

AFTER TEN SALTINES, two turkey and mayo sandwiches, an unsuccessful call to my high-school-principal-turned-legal-and-or-spiritual adviser, and a reread of Hennepin County Adult Correctional Facility's *Crime and Punishment* paperback, I spent Monday morning clad in an orange jumpsuit, head pulsing like a volcano because of antidepressant withdrawal.

The medical unit was neither medical nor a unit. Ten cells the size of small bathrooms, and I didn't see a doctor despite Donglefritz's guarantee that each inmate received a screening upon admission.

"Sorry about that. Weekend, bud," he said, escorting me through the innards of Hennepin County Government Center. My headache felt like a power drill to the ear. I could barely hear him. My rotator cuff seared with every sharp movement or breath. And this, I kept reminding myself, was the better option. As my, uh, colleagues flung shit and howled, I thought of Mom gritting through another round of chemo. "Between you and me, the only reason we even have medical staff is to make sure we ain't civilly liable in case one of you jokers croaks."

"How do you live with yourself, man? You seem like a decent dude."

Donglefritz cracked his neck, jerked me into a wall.

"Jails and prisons provide most of the psych care in this country. Rank-and-file are basically social workers. Triagin' domestic violence, kiddie diddlers. Overdoses and shit, okay? On toppa the other crap. You think that cops or COs doin' health and human services is the mark of a functioning fucking society?"

I didn't answer him. We inched the halls in silence until we reached a holding chamber.

"This is Gary Linnihan," Donglefritz said as he opened the door. "Yer public defender."

"Great."

"I bumped you up to priority, buckaroo, okay? Said you're having a medical emergency and are non-violent. At least half that is true. Unclear which half."

"Why are you doing this?" I asked as he placed me in a rolling chair.

"If you knew," he said, "you'd probably hate me."

I glanced at the lawyer. He shuffled some papers, didn't look up.

"I'll be waiting outside," Donglefritz said. "Your hearing is in fifteen minutes."

"That's it?"

"Sometimes it's less than that."

I shook my head as he left.

"You ever seen *Better Call Saul?*" Gary asked.

"Never got around to it," I said.

"Ah, me neither. Guy's a public defender in the first season, I think."

"Reassuring."

After some smalltalk, I soon gathered that my public defender—a bloke from some third-tier law school despite Princeton undergrad—had a disappointing CV and even spottier beard. Nice hair though. A longer undercut, you might call it, so not fascist.

Resistance, etc.

"I'll get you out of this," he said. "I know Patricia Schmidt, by the way. Which is why I wanted your case. She got your messages and texted me. Don't worry about bail. Worry about Schmidt."

"Yeah?"

"She's a bit, uh, busy lately. What with this ICE case in the news."

"What ICE case?"

"Ah, heck, get a load of this."

He placed the *Star Tribune* in my lap. Scheisskopf, The Mogul, and their St. Paul rally on the front page. He flipped to the Local section, where I saw a picture of Nala Bashir being escorted from this very building by two US Marshals.

"That's my friend," I said, as he took the papers back.

"Figured. Schmidt mentioned something about knowing her from the ol' principal days."

"I don't understand."

"You know how she got sliced by some fascist? The Battle for Western Civ, or whatever the alt-right's been calling it? Well, she goes in to ID the suspect—some frat guy named Kiffmeyer—but then, lo and behold, ICE is waiting in the goddamn parking lot and arrests her."

"But she's lived here for like twenty fucking years. She had a green card."

"Yep. And I guess she got a marijuana possession ticket after some spring break party her senior year, and they've decided to deport her."

I stared at him and his crooked tie, before the buzz and snap of overhead lights forced my eyes closed. I couldn't concentrate. This couldn't be real. My stomach roiled.

"Look," he said, "we've got a case to win and—"

"They're gonna fucking deport her? But the fascists haven't even won yet."

"The 44th President is the Deporter-in-Chief. Of course they have."

A bunch of dumb shit happened next, I reckon, but 72 hours without the psycho-pharmaceuticals I'd been taking for five years (despite their not working) and days of ass-beatings rendered me half-awake through the legalese. Gary yanked me up by the sleeves once or twice, maybe, but mostly some judge rubber stamped my release. Or at least that's what the paperwork said as I came to outside the courthouse holding a plastic bag of my belongings. I rubbed my accidentally bearded face and confirmed they'd just postponed my first delinquency payment, and thus subsequent hearing when I could not pay, for thirty days.

"Have a good one," Gary said, bro-hugging. "Don't be a stranger. I chair the DSA social justice working group if you're interested."

"I'd prefer a gulag, comrade."

"Suit yourself. But really. You look like shit. Here's a Men's Wearhouse coupon. Oh, and you should really call Schmidt. She might know more about your brothers."

"Do *you* know anything?"

"Of course not. I was a legacy admit."

"No, about my brothers."

"You're in the frat, too? Jesus, Schmidt didn't say—"

"No, Gary, about my biological brothers."

"Ah. *City Pages* reported that a bunch of rapey Proud Boys got into a DUI accident in downtown Winona, but they weren't disclosing names. Other than Kayden Kiffmeyer."

"So, these guys keep winning, huh."

"The punchline is tomorrow night, Julian. Everything else is just set-up."

"I don't like the way this looks. I guarantee it."

He shrugged. I took his low-end haberdashery coupon. We shook hands. He swiveled, strolled. And left me in downtown Minneapolis, as snow began to fall, with only one place to turn.

Boris.

I HOPPED OFF a bus and started roaming the couple square miles I remembered as close-ish to his place. And, a few hours later, I was still wandering. And it was still snowing. My legs, years removed from failing to propel me from working poor to alum of an East Coast school with strong brand position, now spasmed, a sharp pain that overwhelmed the creep of my headache, the throb of my shoulder. I walked another block or two then planted myself on a curb.

Why me? feels whiny and melodramatic. What a retired theater kid says when he can't afford to dye his hair like Neapolitan ice cream, or pierce his asscrack shut. So instead I ask: why *not* me? If I had either succumbed to cancer as an infant or taken a neuroblastoma blast to the dome in junior high, we'd all be better off. You too. I would've written a tragic blog, appeared on Oprah. I'd get a deathbed book deal and the royalties could have covered whatever happened after I tweeted out my last words and became an inspiration to boring white people everywhere. We could have kept up with the Joneses. Or at least made enough money to meet them, if I could endure the radiation fog and fatigue. Instead, I was the last man standing, or, I guess, sitting. Me and Boris.

Then I remembered his Say Yes to Certain Drugs talk from the day after Mom died. He'd said something about living and farting near a McDonald's.

I was down the block from a McDonald's.

A few minutes later, I was dry heaving in his parking lot.

The van, its rust rings and the duct-taped dashboard whipped with the first heavy snowfall of Winter 2016, indicated that Boris was home. And that he somehow acquired, or reacquired, some of my possessions. I found an empty beer can rolling across the lot, remembered the number 304 for some reason, and calculated which window belonged to him. So I tossed the tall-but-unfilled-boy at his apartment. Dead phone, no buzzer, no way to contact the bastard meant for the first time ever I wanted Boris under the influence of beer. Or, I suppose, a beer can.

"Who's there?" he said, giraffing out the window.

"It's Jude," I said.

"Who?" he said, staring at me and making eye contact.

"Your prodigal son."

"I'm not interested."

"Boris—"

The window clenched shut. The shutters drew. I assumed this was a bit.

So I waited, waited, waited, wind whacking the freezing sweat on my forearms.

"Boris!" I yelled, chucking the can at the window. It nicked the frame, flopped to the grass, and pinged with whipping slush.

A shadow moved behind his blinds. He was either coming to get me or going to get drunk, so I crunched to the front entrance and sat on a stoop.

When he finally limped out in sweatpants and red Chuck Taylors, bifocals fogged and shave uneven, I didn't hear him call my name; I was too occupied coming up with an apology, an explanation, for, well, everything. But when I felt his waddle on the cement and caught him in my peripheral vision, I didn't need to say anything, realized there was nothing to say.

Boris wrapped both arms around my back. He hoisted me to my feet, and laid his head on my chest, squeezing my shoulders against his wide gut. I stood limp until I looked at him and saw the wincing, the quivering cheeks, the eye circles. So I squeezed back. Hard. Firm. My facade, my pseudo-masculinity punctured again, blubbering, heaving on my dad, a man I hated, wanted to kill, as recently as Labor Day weekend. But now we were two men, two generations of misery, holding each other in the cold as sleet slapped our faces.

AFTER A SHOWER and microwaved Campbell's, Boris told me everything. Which, for Boris, meant he was almost silent.

"Van? Got a call from a Donglefritz. Cut a deal. Said he recognized me."

"From what?"

I blinked through my throbbing head, administered a self-massage. But this just irritated my swollen face. Boris knuckled his neck as my right shoulder crackled like popcorn. Maybe tomorrow I'd wheedle some psycho-pharmaceuticals from a shrink resident. Or halfway-houser. I still needed to call Brandi Bates about standup, too. I was so stressed and sore it almost amused me. Almost.

"Boris, just tell me."

"From when I beat up Mom. Maybe some other crap. I dunno, J.G."

Boris owned one kitchen chair—stolen after the divorce—so I sat on his leather couch, also stolen after the divorce, and craned my neck to hear him over the blare of CNN pre-election coverage. He was maybe a yard away.

"I threw your stuff in my locker," he said, scanning the parking lot, the white swirls. "Your booze. Your books. Clothes. Not much else."

"Right."

"Got a padlock combo. We'll check it out later." He chomped a fingernail, could tell I didn't believe him. I read the *New Yorker*. I filtered ACLU emails into my spam folder. Poor people, even poor white people, didn't get out of jail free.

"You sure, Boris?" On top of his other faults, he lied like a shy toddler.

"Actually," he said, mouth squishing (and still not looking at me), "they took everything. Books, clothes. Money, booze. Donglefritz saved the van because it's Mom's."

I picked at a scab. The room teetered.

Civil asset forfeiture. If you get arrested, they take your shit. Guilty, innocent, charged? Irrelevant. In progressive places, they might let you buy it back. A few hundred dollars and your stuff is . . . yours. In the sticks, where Mom grew up, they funded social services—entire governments—with seized property auctions. In minority communities, they'd pull you over, beat you then shoot you. And, when an uncle or cousin scraped up the courage to confront the occupying force, they exhausted your bureaucratic patience and financial wiggle room, demanded payment for the trauma of picking through your deceased relative's trunk. If they hadn't pawned your car.

"So, uh, there's some forms or whatever. Top of the fridge," he said. "We oughta go tomorrow morning."

The pain bulged through my temples, receded. I was wearing a tracksuit. Black and orange, the official pregame attire of my shitty alma mater's shitty Division 3 football team. The only clothing in this apartment that wasn't covered in a suicide attempt or Boris' psoriasis. My NYC clothes (i.e., the bloody clothes I'd worn to and from jail), were soaking in Boris' tub (i.e., his washing machine). At least I had Mom's rosary beads.

"And the twins?" I said. Boris pressed his forehead to the glass.

"Don't you wanna talk about New York?" he said, still not looking at me.

"Not till you talk about the twins."

"Mistakes were made."

"Boris."

On TV, the CNN anchor was predicting a rout for the Democrats. Tonight in Philadelphia, their candidate would appear with the president who had deported Nala, shout platitudes at 40,000 people in between Bruce Springsteen songs. Inspiring stuff. Half the people who can vote don't.

"Are you sitting down for this?" Boris said, as I remained sitting down.

"Are *you* sitting down for this?"

"Yeah."

I continued to sit. He continued to stand.

"Just fucking tell me, man."

He exhaled. My stomach lurched, diarrhea or vomit imminent.

"Fine," he said, plopping into the kitchen chair with a groan, "but promise you won't be mad."

"I don't promise."

"Great. Well, they're conscious now. Should regain most of their motor skills but language is iffy. Them doctors in Winona. I don't trust that rural shit, Mayo-affiliated or not."

A surge in my throat. I choked it down.

"Boris, wait, I—"

"That goddamn fraternity. Lars. Kayden, the older brother. One who took BBs to the gut? At your museum? Anyway, they messed up real bad, the four of 'em. Not that I was all that helpful. I could've maybe done something but—"

I burst from the couch, shot my hands to Boris' collar before he could block the blow. I yanked and shook as Anderson Cooper cut to commercial.

"You better tell me right fucking now what the hell you did, or I swear on Mom's grave I'll fucking kill you like I should've years ago."

"Jude."

"Talk, motherfucker."

He looked away, smelled like shaving cream and Schlitz.

"An accident. Some hazing thing. Your car. Wrapped it around a streetlamp. Heads skipped off a bench or a parking meter. Like torpedoes through that windshield, y'know? Driving drunk from some pledge thing gone nutty, right, like *Animal House*. Or like I was saying to Konrad, which he didn't get because he's a goddamn moron, all those people, Mom's, more like *Animal Farm*, this story is so fucked. Beastlike."

"They totaled the car. And you were there."

"Their fall break" —voice monotone and soft, eyes somewhere else— "Lars kid, that hockey one? Well, he'd taken leave or something. Moved his stuff out and everything. Friday afternoon. Saw that mom on the way out. Tom said Lars'd pinned some girl behind a frat party. Rape. Attempted, at least. These rich white boys, just like Steve Scheisskopf, maybe even your friend Reid, using girls up, wringing people out like towels. Because they can. Nobody stops them. Nobody stopped him."

My throat filled with stomach acid. I clamped my jaw as it leaked through my teeth and I jammed it down again.

"So the roommate got kicked out," I said, "and you—"

"Okay, so, Lars is gone. But it's hazing weekend, or whatever. They don't listen to me none, but I told Tom not to go through, to drop the frat crap. Didn't matter. Extraordinary rendition. Middle of that night. While you were globetrotting. So this wakes me up and I get drunk. Too drunk, and for that I really am sorry. But so . . . I dunno. Christ, Jude. It boggles the mind."

I exhaled. Shallow and quick. Anything else and I'd puke. "Finish."

"Lars, he's still gonna pledge. His brother was the recruitment chair, and I guess the sicko brother was a big influence. Even though he was arrested in that melee or whatever. The frat, it's one of them off-campus ones, according to what the cops said at the hospital, so to prove their loyalty, the brothers, I mean your brothers and all the wannabe brothers, they gotta sneak into a sorority with bags over their heads, and tiptoe into some girls' rooms or whatever and"—a whisper now— "grab 'em by the pussy."

I felt dizzy. My stomach sloshed and heaved. "They were encouraged to commit rape."

"That brother is a piece of work, J.G. Had 'em on *Hannity* yesterday with Scheisskopf."

"Jesus."

"Talking about political correctness. Can't make it up. And, look, I wasn't good to your Mom, y'know, with . . . well, that's part of why Donglefritz is tryna take care of you, is because I never could. But your brothers? That night they refuse. They won't do it. Get into a fight and everything. Chris throws a guy into a bathroom mirror. Though this Lars likes 'em, says they'll need a getaway car anyway. And if they won't grab 'em, then they can at least drive, is his reasoning. After the Patrón. And that's how Tom and Chris leaked their brains all over Huff Street."

"And you were there?" I asked as the vomit percolated. "And you let this happen?"

"Sorry, Jude, sorry. I didn't know what they wanted with the booze. I mean, I—"

My fist cut him off, a right hook he deflected as he kicked me in the bad knee. I launched backwards into a bookcase. A wastebasket toppled in the process.

He covered up. I dropped my hands. We stared at each other.

"They're gonna survive," he said. "Really."

I nodded at this, but my stomach lost interest in decorum. I dropped to my knees, pawed for the trashcan.

Bile, cracker remnants. Coughs and sweats and groans. Face

pulsing, shoulder smoldering, I didn't hear Boris rock to his feet and fetch the ice pack, which he placed on my neck as I spat.

"When were you gonna tell me?"

"I'm not good at this stuff," he said. An erection medication commercial blasted on-screen. Boris turned it up. A middle-aged couple rode horses, played volleyball, danced tango as a saxophone wailed. "People. Saying the right thing."

"That's not good enough."

"You have every right to be angry with me. Everyone is angry all the time and that's not even angry enough, honestly."

A low voice rumbled about night time, the right time. The voice said to be wary if the right time lasted longer than four hours.

"So what about healthcare?" I said, prying my head from the can.

"Well, I rummaged through the van and found them Medicaid forms under my old man's gun." With a limp, Boris took two steps toward the TV, flipped on MSNBC. Just as the couple squirted mustard on their hotdogs. "The 7.65 might be the best insurance plan of all, frankly."

"Oh, Jesus."

"I bet he has healthcare."

"So it was never sent in."

"Fascinating use of the—whaddya call it—passive voice there."

I'd failed again. Actively. The promises to Mom, the desire to spare my brothers from institutional indifference. Couldn't mail two forms yet I always found time for standup. For delusions. Maybe the biggest fantasy was that I'd been a good son and brother.

Boris saw this in my quivering face. Or the DTs crept into his brain and liver. Because he produced a flask from his sweatpants, suckled.

"What?" he said.

"Nothing."

"Look, J.G., what if you started a podcast or something? Y'know, like a Twitter? Ashleigh Banfield was talkin' about that. Maybe it would—"

"Boris, the advent of podcasting has destroyed more lives than US foreign policy."

He nodded. "Never knew that."

I groaned to my feet, steadied myself on the bookcase, plunked to the couch.

"I might recommend getting famous though," Boris said. "Now

might be the time."

"Duly noted."

The TV cut to black. A familiar voice, his Queens accent bright and barking *approved this message.*

"Boris, could you—"

"Shh," he said, turning it up. "I get a kick out of this shit, y'know? I was reading some fuckin' book—like one of them textbooks of yours? Sociology or some crap?—and this guy says that 'anxiety is the handmaiden of contemporary ambition.' Or something."

"Heard that somewhere. Felt that everywhere."

Boris freefell beside me, offered the booze. I waved him off.

We watched the commercial:

A screaming comes across the sky. A jetliner soaring above and zipping through some clouds, dipping below them to reveal a giant prairie. The camera capturing barns and lakes and main streets from 10,000 feet. The plane dives. The landing gears shoot out. A football stadium appears, packed with thousands of clamoring white people, many in red hats when, finally, the jet skids across the turf and rolls to a stop. In the crowd, people scream, cry, spill beer. Scheisskopf in a three-piece suit, hair gelled to one side, springing, snapping, and screaming like an NFL coach arguing a call. "This country," he says as people rush from their seats to the plane, jumping over security guards and fencing, wanting to get close to Him, "is not what it used to be! But our people—OUR PEOPLE!—are as strong as ever! And we won't allow globalists, bomb-throwing radicals, and men wearing dresses to STOP. THIS. MOVEMENT. No, no! No more snow-flakes crying for safe spaces! No more radical Islamists destroying our culture! No more antifa supersoldiers suppressing freedom of speech! No more carnage in the streets! No more. No more. No more. There's only one way to avoid it, folks. And here he comes. We must, and he will, make America great—"

I clicked it off. Then puked down my shirt.

"Hey," Boris said.

"Lemme get a hit of that," I said, wiping my mouth and pointing at the flask.

Boris handed it over.

Wild Turkey 101. I gulped the whole thing. Burped. Stumbled to the bathroom, slipped out of the tracksuit, dunked it in the sink, and avoided eye contact with myself in the mirror.

An election tomorrow night. Maybe a gig. Ten years on

Wednesday. And Mom's birthday.

Boris materialized in the doorway.

"Jude," he said, rocking from foot to foot. "You probably need these."

My antidepressants. Salvaged from the van. He tossed the three bottles. But when I interrogated the label, it said Boris Julian Glick.

"Boris, what—"

"Don't worry about it."

I didn't. Same pills. Same dose.

I spent the next few hours half-asleep on his couch, using the pistol as a pillow.

10.

HYSTERICAL NIHILISM

THE WORST NIGHT of my life, Election Night 2016, the night I almost got murdered inside an ER lobby, started out as one of the best. After 34 minutes of a 30-minute feature set, I had assailed Minneapolis' hipster gentry with every symptom of my severe-and-recurrent major depressive disorder, of my social anxiety disorder, of my post-traumatic stress disorder, of my being an obnoxious white man who can reel off long passages of anti-natalist philosophy while non-suicidal millennials, or even just liberal arts grads who don't live in their cars, laugh their fucking complicity away.

This was a gig at the CC Club. I was killing.

From the stage (i.e., several warehouse pallets covered with drywall), I was on top of the world. Or, more accurately, on top of the building materials Nehemiah and I had poached from the MAOI loading dock.

Everything was beautiful and nothing, outside of my childhood cancer scars, hurt.

Except that the headliner, Brandi Bates, still hadn't shown up. And I was almost out of jokes. Falling on a grenade to protect a bar and my fledgling goodwill was, like, not ideal.

"When exposed to the BUSINESS MAJOR STONE, Guys Who Use Homophobic Slurs in High School evolve into Dudes Who Wear Khakis And Like Money," I golf-whispered at the mic, three-hundred yuppies yucking and hollering from Surly-splattered carpet and red vinyl booths. Over the years Road Dogs had muttered, in between double-fisting cigarettes and/or railing against 12-step programs while vacuuming rail whiskey, that election night gigs, especially a showcase jammed with regulars and IMDB-Pro-havers like tonight, could generate lots of buzz for younger comics. The penal colony aspect of election results, the beer-shot combos, the CNN interstitials, the subtext that we were riffing while Rome burned, all of it made urine-caked dives like the CC Club tolerable for bookers and promoters and, hell, even agents or producers. That The Replacements drank themselves to death here, wrote songs about drinking themselves to death here, only further lubricated my artistic resolve. If Westerberg and Stinson, those dilaudid-deformed derelicts, could make the Midwest seem tolerable to a bunch of neurochemically functioning Gen-Xers, then I could conjure a few more laughs for millennials.

Still, no Brandi. And no battle-tested act.

"Hahahaha!" I shrieked into the mic, to confused stares and nervous laughter. "I am definitely not now laughing at my lack of material!"

The last time this happened, at First Avenue, with my buddy Perry Slutsky playing The Cool And Good Friend Who Implores Me To Keep Filling Time, I quit after 35 minutes, leapt from the stage, rolled an ankle, and stomped out of First Ave under sheets of booing and Leinenkugels.

I had now been on stage 35 minutes.

But, again, I was slaying. Or had been. And although this country was a festering abscess of inequality and suffering, I was gonna get mine, goddammit, I finally felt it. My own festering abscesses of inequality and suffering would be worth it, would ooze fascinating Terry Gross conversation fodder, if I could just stretch my act until Brandi and her moderately long Wikipedia page fluttered through the front door. As soon as she showed up, I'd skip across the parquet and linger over a glass of Wild Turkey 101 while admiring copywriters filmed Snapchat stories of my alcoholism, and then casting directors, managers, scouts for TV and film elbow-tapped "the weird-looking feature with political material that slayed" and handed me their business cards, asked if I had a pilot or spec script.

Just a few more minutes, J.G. A few more minutes.

"And I don't know who created . . . Pokémon GO," I said with a pinched nose and a waddle, "but I'm trying to figure out how we get them to have Pokémon GO to hell, you neoliberal shills."

Behind the soundboard, stage left, next to the antique jukebox and popcorn machine, Slutsky vaulted his eyebrows and pretended to churn butter. The message, unlike the Democratic candidate for president, was clear: I just needed to keep killing, keep killing time. We'd soon return to watching the grim, dazzling returns. We'd soon see Stephen Scheisskopf commit seppuku once the Associated Press declared the highest, hardest glass bong shattered. We'd soon ironically pour one out for Andrew Breitbart's bloated corpse. But I needed one more roll to cement my Having Murdered, a final flurry to cap off the only stretch of unmedicated pleasure I'd found in the worst two-year-stretch of my life. Get to Brandi; get to feel good about myself; then get to drink brandy until I no longer cared about feeling good about myself.

"Perry! Perry!" I screamed, the crowd tittering and looking around the pool table, the skee-ball, feeling unconsciously the extinguishing momentum I consciously needed to reignite. "Just do it, do it, do it, do it!"

This was Glick's Last Stand. The beat dropped and I started grinding my ass on the stool, shouts of "WOO!" and "AY!" almost drowning out my rapping:

Do it now
Lick it good
Fuck this country just like you should,

Right now
It's no good
Antarctica is melting just like you should,
my neck, my back
Lick my suicide ideation and my crack

My neck, my back
Lick my pussy and my crack
My neck, my back
The Democrats voted to invade Iraq

My neck, my back
Lick my pussy and my crack
My neck, my back
Only Russ Feingold voted against the Patriot Act, uh!

As I crumped and rapped a verse about U.S. Imperialism and appropriated black culture, I made out two suits whispering and nodding to each other at the bar. As the second-to-last act, my only compensation for the evening was unlimited drinks, unless Bates threw me some charity, but I'd spent four-plus years enduring open mics and driving to the Fond Du Lac Chuckle Hut and not killing myself for this moment. Three-hundred-plus strangers would be telling everybody they knew about some Area Man who pseudo-stripped and spit leftist agitprop to Khia.

The beat faded. The crowd groaned. Still no Brandi. On a giant flatscreen above the bar, maybe a hundred feet from the stage, Wolf Blitzer and Scheisskopf, his male pattern baldness and fascist sneer intoxicating even then, even while muted, were discussing The Magnate's overperformance in the Midwest. He was, per Stephen's smirk, within striking distance of winning Minnesota, flyover country's most reliably Blue state. I glanced at the ceiling. It seemed to breathe. The call light was still green, and it was now past midnight, what would have been Mom's 52nd birthday.

I shrugged at Perry. Perry shrugged at me. I shrugged back at Perry. Rule-of-three poisoning even non-comic behaviors. Ending the evening with crowdwork would deflate the good vibes, and I did not want to workshop material with bookers or producers or even just men in Italian wool in the house.

The audience, perhaps alerted by their news apps or simply bored with the few seconds of my dead air, started whispering, scrolling Twitter, watching Scheisskopf talk Truman-Dewey.

And still no Brandi Bates.

But we did have the PeterPuff Girls. Blonde triplets. Poppy and Prudence and Piper. They had agreed to split a fifth of Tito's for every swing-state the Democratic Nominee lost to Scheisskopf's Real Estate Dullard. Prevailing political punditry suggested they'd spend the night sober. So we'd been eyeing the coverage gapemouthed as She lost Ohio, then Florida, then North Carolina. The former Secretary of State was down everywhere; it appeared the PeterPuff Girls would be down facefirst in vomit and political despair before bar close.

On CNN, an electoral map flashed mostly red. Near the exit, back of the bar, Poppy Peterson swayed. Prudence and Piper, shaking neurodegeneratively, toasted to the country being toast. A barkeep creased his forehead, removed another fifth from a high shelf.

"A group of white people that isn't funny or interesting is called an office," I non-sequitered to scattered laughs and claps. A bandage. I licked my chapping lips. "The German word for 'Unspeakable Horror at the Vapid Agony of Contemporary Living' is POD-CAST."

As I ransacked my brain for a tight, or even just amusing, riff, CNN cut to a picture of our high school, then a picture of the MAOI, then three mugshots of those truck-driving Somali dudes, then the Battle of Area 32/33. I couldn't read the subtitles, but Scheisskopf was now pointing at the camera and laughing. A chyron declared that Republicans would maintain control of the Senate. This ensured, at best, nothing positive would happen to any non-white and/or non-middle-class Americans for the next two years. I'd probably have less access to healthcare, more access to debt. Tom and Chris, if I ever mustered the courage to see them again, would have more brain functioning than the entire legislative branch.

Goddammit.

And still no Brandi.

Christ.

Perry swung his arms in big circles, a third-base coach waving me into a home-plate collision. I blinked. Then a thud. Poppy Peterson's head swishing across oak. Another thud. Down goes Prudence. Piper rubbed her nose, tipped back a shot, palmed her face, stayed mostly upright. This had been going on since the openers at 10:00 p.m., political positivity trickling like Mom's good old doxorubicin drip. Pockets of crying leaked from the audience.

I exhaled and, after what might have been ten seconds or ten decades of silence, fiddled with the mic stand.

"What's the deal with observational comedy?" I said.

Chairs scuffed carpet. A non-ignorable group of drinkers sighed, checked their phones, stood up. A man in lederhosen yanked an organ grinder out of a barrel and dusted it off. WHAT WOULD LETTERMAN DO? flashed like electroshock therapy in my brain.

"Don't leave!" I said, peripheral vision catching Perry crouch and dial a number. "I'm just about to make comedic observations about comedy. It's meta! By glossing over the fact that it's stupid, or maybe even mentioning it outright, I'll be able to lampshade the problem!"

"That time Brandi rolled a joint on *Broad City* was high art," someone shouted. "A conceptual masterpiece! She's not a downer like you!"

"Yeah, where is she?" another voice barked.

"You'll have to wait and see," I said. Perry was now massaging his temples. "Just like you'll have to wait and see if tonight goes down as the last night of the American Empire."

"More like of your career!" someone else yelled.

"LMAO," I screamed, ass still intact.

"Really funny," the guy said back.

"ROFL!" I screeched, standing completely still.

This was happening again. Just like First Avenue. I patted my back pocket for the secret stash of Everclear 195, remembered I'd left it in my glove compartment/living room in favor of MD 20/20. Hobo Wine.

What Letterman Would Do is walk off the fucking stage and move to Los Feliz. Quit on the Midwest, or maybe life. Sit in the garage with the car running. Start an unethical relationship with a production assistant.

"You wanna hear my unironic thoughts on our political situation? Surely, a white man explaining politics to you is an interesting use of your time?" I said.

This earned a few chuckles, but the atmosphere felt pre-tornadic. Seemed we had all realized, instantaneously, that America was about to irrevocably change.

"Politics are, like, totally boring," a pretty blonde white woman almost certainly named Berit or Greta complained to her hulking, SS-officer-looking date. "She's gonna win anyway, so."

I stuck a thumb in my mouth, bit down on the nail.

Minneapolis is a very liberal city, and comics/comic-adjacent people skew left, but it occurred to me that, until the last ten minutes or so, most everybody here, including the PeterPuff Girls, saw the biggest political night of our lives as a joke. A sitcom. A one-act piece of experimental theater. Politics hadn't fucked up their lives, their mother's life, their best friend's life. My psychic stick of dynamite, lit by Brandi's tardiness, accelerated by Scheisskopf's camera mugging, was running out of fuse. A 24-year-old college-educated leftist with plenty of talent and opportunities and privileges and yet even I couldn't get ahead without money, or connections, or a different class. Couldn't escape myself or wintering in my fucking car in the coldest city in North America.

I stiff-armed the mic with one hand and cupped my mouth with the other, prepared to heckle myself. Time to explode.

"Yeah, you fucked-up, sweater-wearing asshole, which you bought from Goodwill today, by the way, tell us what you think of politics," I said. "Because they might be boring, and we might be too financially and racially comfortable to give a shit about the New Gilded Age, but it isn't as boring as you transparently killing time before Brandi shows up, right? I mean, she was on the show with the underemployed millennials experiencing hi-jinks in a global metropolis! No, not *2 Broke Girls*, Jude, the almost identical but somehow cool one! Poverty is funny when the characters smoke pot!"

More sighs. Light booing.

I paced the stage, Converse tapping a section of particle board. The blonde and her date, a man I now recognized as a professional hockey player, shrugged into their North Face coats. In my brainstem, I felt Scheisskopf smiling from some gold-plated conference room, shaking hands with The Mogul and his family, whispering to the literal fascist who since August had chaired the campaign, looking down on New York City, feeling in his own lizard cognition what must have been felt around October, 1922 in Rome, or January, 1933 in Berlin.

"Okay," I responded to myself, voice cracking, "sure thing, J.G.! Thanks for the feedback! Just one second." I procured the fifth of dragon fruit fortified wine—blood red—and slurped half the bottle.

Was I self-destructing?

Hmm . . .

It appeared I was self-destructing.

Perry was literally tearing his hair out and examining it. The suits at the bar shook their heads, gestured to the barkeep for their bills. Like vultures, certain memorized passages of philosophy circled my death-rattling Will to Humor.

"Obviously, my time is short—our time is short—so I wanted to leave you with this: the stakes are high," I started, absolutely no fucking idea where I was going. The Scheisskopf interview wrapped up because the Associated Press had now predicted, with 98% certainty, the Democrats would lose Pennsylvania. He fist-pumped as they smash-cut to Anderson Cooper toddling around some suburban Pittsburgh precinct. I slammed the rest of the Mad Dog, pocketed it. "The stakes are higher than me on a fentanyl patch. See, on one side, you have a party of psychotic fascists, and on the other, you have sycophants to capital who are culturally liberal and nothing more. On one side, you have a party of kleptocratic vultures who honk-off to starving grandmothers, who dream of a future with even less access to healthcare, with even more poverty and suffering, and on the other, you have a party of kleptocratic vultures who honk-off to starving grandmothers, who dream of a future with even less access to healthcare, with even more poverty and suffering, but have seen *The Wire*. On one side, you have a white supremacist organization, and on the other, you have the architects of mass incarceration, of drone warfare, of mass deportation, of the genocide in Yemen, of reading literary novels and pretending this is somehow a useful hobby in a country where one-sixth of children go to bed hungry each night, of racism masked as colorblindness, of podcasts, of sexism covered in performative wokeness by shithead men like me, of more inequality than the Jazz Age, of George Carlin knock-offs who live in their cars. And of my friend who lived here on a green card for twenty years getting deported. So the choice is yours, people. My choice today was not the former, but the latter; I took a dump in a ballot box. I voted for the Democrats. So, if you're feeling down, remember that America is great because America is good. For nothing."

I took an exaggerated step from the mic. One glance at the audience and I knew I couldn't leave on this. Any goodwill I'd conjured in forty minutes had just evaporated in forty seconds.

Fuck.

It hit me again that it was my mother's birthday.

J.G., you fucking loser, you coward. Jesus H. Christ. Still the scared kindergartner blubbering in the kitchen as Boris choked on his own vomit and you debated whether it was better to call the cops OR better to let the old man die.

It is curious that while good people go to great lengths to spare their children from suffering, few of them seem to notice that the one (and only) guaranteed way to prevent all the suffering of their children is not to bring those children into existence in the first place.

Of course Brandi wasn't going to show up. Of course He was going to win.

In early youth, as we contemplate our coming life, we are like children in a theater before the curtain is raised, sitting there in high spirits and eagerly waiting for the play to begin. It is a blessing that we do not know what is really going to happen.

Just like Addy's fundraiser. Just like First Avenue. What to say? How to fucking close?

A smattering of giggles at something I hadn't said. Glasses clinked. Ice rustled. I'd overdosed these tragically happy people on realism, these cubicle-farm allies, these salaried soon-to-be Tesla owners, these kale salad eaters, these careerists who confused self-esteem with existential significance, these ingrates who took their good health and financial security and adequate neurochemistry and wasted it on bourgeois delusions like romance, or failed romance, or kvetching about failed romance, the Midwesterners who considered optimism, concealment, ignoring problems as the one true religion, or else became coastal flotsam who took handouts from their parents to live in Brooklyn and chased shallow fuckbuddies who worked in graphic design and wrote poems, and considered accessing pleasure, whether intellectual or sexual or interpersonal or artistic, a valuable pursuit while pretty much anyone without an office job found themselves crowdfunding medical bills or stealing fish antibiotics from Petco. And I could see it as the mumble, this mainlining of the agony and the accuracy, ramped into an uneasy roar that I had to salvage what, until quite recently, had been a great set. My best ever set.

Had I changed? Can people change? Could I choke-down my impulse—my destiny?—to shoot myself in the dick? The audience downed mugs, applied scarves, ordered Lyfts. Was it even worth impressing these useful idiots, these television and film psychopaths, these ciphers who confused appreciating or consuming art with having a personality?

Politics is boring. God, I despised these people. I knew their game. Here I was, one shrug from killing myself every single day for the last fifteen years, one upturned palm from stepping in front of the Green Line, or sticking my head in the snowblower, or finishing myself off with Mom's chemo pills and a spoon of fucking black tar, and they had the audacity, the hubris, to pretend they understood. *We all feel like this,* they whispered to each other while administering goodbye hugs. *It's not like we're happy either,* they muttered with eye-rolls as I self-immolated at the silent mic. *We're all in the same boat, man,* they lied while nibbling the last cool onion ring.

Well, fuck them. They who had hobbies or interests or orifices which brought them joy, which segmented life into the pleasurable and the endurable instead of one unremitting suicidal slog. They who did not relive the rapes, the shrieks, the smashed Wild Turkey bottles and battered women shelters, the belted necks in college, the pangs of Mom's funeral, of Malik's funeral, of the suspicion that despite my uneasiness with masculinity, with men, with anything Boris and I might share, I was just another fragile male ego to be massaged, another mad at the world white guy tantruming because things had gone somewhat differently than my preferred outcome. They who were not motherfucking children like J. Gladden Glick, toddler-esquire.

The suits both checked their watches. Perry stuck palms over his eyes.

Why is it that, in spite of all the mirrors in the world, no one really knows what he looks like?

I scanned the crowd, as it back-cracked and yawned and arm-stretched like students before the dismissal bell. No Addy and Reid. I never invited friends to gigs, but made an exception tonight. Maybe I knew I was going to kill. Maybe I knew I was going to implode. Maybe I just forgot what it felt like, two months after Mom died, to have someone rooting for you. That it might be okay to love, and be loved.

The real meaning of persona is a mask, such as actors were accustomed to wear on the ancient stage; and it is quite true that no one shows himself as he is, but wears his mask and plays his part. Indeed, the whole of our social arrangements may be likened to a perpetual comedy; and this is why a man who is worth anything finds society so insipid, while a blockhead is quite at home in it.

The audience scooched chairs and applied scarves. The ceiling, again, was breathing. It bulged and receded. It seethed and settled. Perry's hands hovered, expression blank, ready to cut the mic and raise the house lights.

This was it.

Mom fought. Mom endured. Mom went fifteen rounds every goddamn day. I did too, for a while. Persist, motherfucker, persist. No more throwing in the goddamn towel.

I turned my back to the crowd, fished her rosary necklace from under my thrift store sweater, and pivoted to the mic.

"Before you get the wrong idea about my political and philosophical views," I said, the adrenaline pulsing so hard the CC Club looked like a Kandinsky, Perry's thumbs-up evoking Dali, ten one-liners torching my synapses at once, "and before you report me to the police for not being funny or making sense, I wanted to share a few reasons you should disregard anything I ever say. Here are Ten Things I Hate About Me:

1. That my Myers-Briggs personality type is C.U.C.K.
2. That what doesn't kill me can only make me disappointed.
3. That I'm gonna start a LARPing league where me and my friends pretend we all didn't peak in high school.
4. There is no four.
5. That there is no four.
6. That all my friends are into, like, post-shoegaze and fucking people who own Fjallraven and all I'm into is making suicide jokes in job interviews.
7. That I'm starting a paleo diet where I live for 29 malnourished years and get murdered with a spear.
8. That you either die an alcoholic or live long enough to see yourself become an alcoholic.
9. That the nuclear holocaust would be an improvement for me and everyone I know.
10. That y'all have been a great audience and I almost fucked it up because I'm a grief-spackled, treatment-resistant depressive whose only hobby is self-sabotage. Thanks, folks, let's give it up for your host, Perry Slutsky!

They must have erupted, interpreted the last five minutes as some Andy Kaufman-esque pseudo-meltdown, but I was woozy with endorphins and the overhead lights were sighing with relief. When I no longer felt faint, I clapped, shook Perry's hand, realized Brandi still wasn't here, but that I no longer cared about being a good sport. If the CC Club never booked me again, fuck it. Slutsky wiped his brow, smiled, exhaled. I did too, noticed my hands were shaking as the almost-victims of my Holden-Caulfield-without-the-charm-or-hat misanthropy deflated into an orgy of shoulder rubs and ass-pats and external validation. Before Mom died, I never cried, I papered over my tears with classroom outbursts, and Scheisskopf or football violence. But lately, I'd sobbed several times a day. In my car before work. On the marble at work. As Nehemiah tried to cheer me up on the marble at work. Cheeks scalding, tear ducts twitching, I bumped and wandered to the bar for my liquid salvation, half-listening to Perry explain that headliner Brandi Bates could not make it (i.e., addict/comic code for some sort of relapse), and that she wanted us to double-down on drunken revelry before the U.S. collapse! I tucked my chin and pulled the sweater over my head.

Then I started bawling.

Because I was the feature—because Brandi, who I hardly knew but, unlike most comics, did not despise, hand-selected me as the final feature on a 12-bill showcase, and because none of us had agents but all three of us had signed a contract with the CC Club's "promoter," an ex-lawyer (and now sous-chef) named Big Al who'd flamed out of both the punk scene and open mic circuit (but knew how to and liked organizing shows)—Brandi not showing up meant two things:

First, the 85/15 door split, on $10 cover, belonged to me.

Second, even if those suits or agents or whoever had come to see Brandi, I had murdered, then almost bombed, then re-murdered. Meaning I was, as absurd as it may be, the headliner, the biggest name here; exchanging cards, or at least chatting me up, the only way to salvage a sub-freezing election night spent in flyover country.

Since starting, when you subtracted gas money and motel rooms and non-comped drug/alcohol consumption, I'd made maybe $1,000 doing standup. Tonight, I'd be walking away with at least $2,550 in cash.

This was more money than I'd ever made in a month, let alone a night.

I still owed the State of Minnesota $47,000 for Mom's Medicaid debt; I still had an upcoming court date related fiduciary delinquency; and I still lived in my car in the coldest metro area in the United States (or, even worse, with Boris). But $2,550, on top of the museum and coupled with the exposure tonight might bring, would give me a chance to redo NYC and climb out of this financial crater. A chance. All I'd ever wanted was a fucking chance.

God, give me a lane.

I blew three big breaths and lowered my collar. The bartender had placed a glass of 101 in front of me. Two strangers in Italian wool stood on either side of my stool.

"Mr. Glick," one of them said, "that was some really thrilling anti-comedy at the end there."

"We thought you'd lost the thread," the other said, clapping a hand on my shoulder, "but you seemed too smart, too skilled for that. Though Mad Dog 20/20? That shit'll kill ya."

"E. Horton Munkelhorton," the first said, extending a hand.

"Senior VP of original programming at Comedy Cen—"

"And I'm Ferris Finklefunk," the second said, "the showrunner and EP of—"

"*The Afternoon-ly Show* with, uh . . .*"

I mouthed the famous syllables, unable to name aloud a guy who had postered my room since elementary school, whose standup specials had laughed me out of countless acts of self-harm. "I know who you guys are. Nice to meet both of you."

"Great," Munkelhorton hooted, "well, look, ah, J.G., I'll cut to the chase: we're here to see Brandi. Kinda. Our flight from LA had to emergency-land at MSP is why we're here at all, but I was prepared to ask Brandi to audition for a half-hour tonight, so—but you, you really, ah—"

"You blew us away, man," Finklefunk said as I downed my Kentucky bourbon in one gulp. "Look, I'm in dire need of a warm-up act who can do political and topical stuff, and do anti-comedy like you did at the end there, and appear on camera as a correspondent. And Horty—"

"Well, I have a lot of specials I need to air, and a lot of tape I don't want to watch," Munkelhorton said, scratching his stubbled chin, "so—"

"And you'd need to submit a packet to become a full-time cast member?" Ferris said, now squeezing my rhomboids. "But Horty would film that set you did tonight, like, whenever you can? No questions asked. And we could do it from Minneapolis, which is actually helpful to me, because it looks like there's gonna be demand for a flyover country correspondent, judging by these early election returns, and we'd—"

"What is happening right now?" I asked.

"I'm proposing a talent holding deal. There's a surprising amount of talent in this igloo dump," he continued. "I mean, even if Gunnar Peuschold gets rammed by the 6 train tomorrow. Tight five at Grand Central during rush hour is the challenge. *American Idyll* can sniff my jock. I'm glad you bailed. Between you and me, Cross Yoder-Henley is a real asshole."

"Would any of this interest you?" Munkelhorton asked, eyes drifting to the TV above us, Wolf Blitzer paced before a CGI coal mine superimposed with twenty mesothelioma-havers representing Pennsylvania's twenty Electoral College votes. "It is, of course, a paid opportunity. And while we make up our mind, I'd discuss keeping you on retainer with your agent—"

"My agent?"

Finklefunk's eyes narrowed. "You do have an agent?"

"Of course," I said. "Addison Bockenhauer? She works for a boutique firm in town. Works with musicians a lot—the Minnesota Orchestra?—but she does TV and comedy, too, obviously."

"Grand," the men said in unison.

"So," I started, "would I sign something to—"

"Is Addison available?" Munkelhorton asked. "Because, that would make things a lot easier on me and—"

"Plus," Ferris whispered, winked, "we could escape the goyim and red-eye back to The City."

I rubbed a hand through the hair I could not afford to have cut, happy for the first time that both Boris and I could grow Jewfros when poor or unkempt (i.e., always).

"Addison should be here somewhere," I said, looking around the slumped Sisters, the self-medicating comics, the DJ setting up his equipment, the audience I wanted to find me sexually alluring for reasons I could neither explain nor act on.

Ferris checked his watch. They both looked like a young Jeff Goldblum without sex appeal. "I mean if she isn't, we could always meet in New York the next time you—"

"I'm sure she's here," I said, certain she wasn't here.

The suits shared eyebrow vaults, chewed their gum. I clutched the rosary beads to my chest, begging a God in whom I did not believe to deliver me from awkwardness.

Then Addy, flushed and struggling with her scarf, blasted through the door.

"Ah, there she is."

I weaved through drunken sways and backpats, took her by the elbow as I waved off the bouncer.

"You need to bail me out here," I whispered.

"Nice to see you, too," she said. "Reid said Stephen's been all over CNN and—"

"I might have told two very powerful comedy dudes that you're my agent, and that we'd love to get something in writing before—"

"Well, here she is," Ferris said, slouching over. Munkelhorton was counting bills and sticking them in a non-Kmart wallet.

"So," Munkelhorton said once the handshakes and introductions dissipated, "the question I have for you is a numbers one."

"Perfect," said Addy. "I failed high school Pre-Calc and didn't take math in college."

"Funny," Munkelhorton said. "But, look, if we're talking a week-to-week retainer for J.G. here, y'know, until he's met the writing staff and seen some production meetings, and feels ready to tape his half-hour?"

Addy removed her hat. "Is that a question?"

"Look," Ferris said, radiating hate with his smile as he snuggled into his topcoat, "if this is not the appropriate environment, perhaps you two could fly out this week. Assuming this is something you're interested in for your client?"

We stared at her. She bit a hangnail, watched us watching her bite the hangnail. What I loved about Addy, and what people found either frustrating or magnetic, was that she loved toying with power. With men. She was a beautiful millennial who put up with sexual harassment all day so she could eventually torch every Minneapolis industry that orbited the PR firm she was determined to own.

We were emotionally intimate, discussing everything from sex with Reid to my lack of sex with anyone. And, until this moment, as she allowed the three most powerful men in the room to squirm and download this finger-licking image for future fap-fodder, I assumed we were absolutely platonic. Never even honked to her. When, New Year's Eve 2013, both brown-out drunk (and me having recently snorted Vicodin), we made out at midnight, then after midnight, then after one or two more midnights in distant time zones, and she invited me into Reid's bedroom—he was abroad with the whole Scheisskopf clan—to fuck, or at least see her brown curls drape down her naked tits and back dimples and yoga-instructor-ass, or whatever a white male novelist would say, I declined. And she'd been mad, sure, but I'd mumbled something about Not Wanting To Lose What We Had, whatever that meant, and, when she undressed and straddled me and offered to do mouth stuff, I still declined, and she was still mad, and I explained what it's like to watch your father rape your mother, and how undoing *that* mental image requires years of therapy I could never afford. So we'd never hooked up again. But, at the CC Club, drunk and dizzy, hoping for a breakthrough Finkle-funk and Munkelhorton and I all thought, for some reason, she could make official, I felt jealous of Reid.

Maybe I didn't love Addy. Maybe I was in love with Addy.

"Here's my card," she said, plucking something from the neckline of her dress. She bit her bottom lip. Munkelhorton coughed and twitched. "Conference call Friday? You know, just so Jude and I can slow things down and think about our options? He's lately had a lot of interest from other networks. I'm sure you heard about *American Idyll.*"

Finklefunk nodded. Addison removed her parka, handed it to me. Strapless. Black. Tight. A cocktail sort of thing. Toned and tanned arms. Munkelhorton seemed catatonic. Jesus H. Christ. When even sexless schmucks like me will objectify you, being a woman must be impossible.

"So," she said, flitting her eyes at a bartender, who dropped what he was doing to bring over two G&Ts, "if we're all done for the evening, I was hoping that Jude and I might—"

"I, uh, have a lot of cocaine in my hotel room," Munkelhorton said.

Heads swung our way. Addy blinked at me and swished her lips. "Mmm," I said.

"We have an early flight," Finklefunk said, yanking his partner's arm away from our crowded spot at the bar. Before he left, though, he rummaged around his back pocket, produced several crisp green rectangles and stuffed them in my hand. "Just to be clear, any sort of contract arrangement with Yoder-Henley should be null-and-void by now, but if it isn't we'll pry you out of it. And for this courtesy, we'd hope you don't pursue other options."

U.S. Grants and Benjamin Franklins.

"Something to remember us by," he called over his shoulder, guiding Munkelhorton toward the exit. "My secretary will reach out. Looking forward to Friday."

We both smiled at them until they were out the door and hailing a cab.

I was holding $1,500. And, as Addy sipped her drink, Perry Slutsky waddled over with around $2,500, or at least he planned to, until Addy's smile faded and she slammed her gin and tonic on the bar.

"What the fuck is wrong with you?" she said. There must've been two hundred people left in a room built for fifty, and I felt glances graze us. We were escapism now. Maybe all I'd ever been for other people was escapism. Maybe I failed at this, too, and that's why I'd be public enemy number one by Saturday night.

I slugged my bourbon. Then my cocktail. Perry squinted at me, saw subtext I was too self-absorbed to consider, crept back to a booth of comics and comedy-adjacent depressives. The bartender scurried over with another Wild Turkey. I pounded that too, ignoring Addy, letting her simmer and stare like Munkelhorton and Finklefunk.

When I finished drinking, when the thirty seconds crossed over into cruelty, I broke my silence.

"Look, I'm gonna be famous, Addy," I said, granting myself a smile. "Finally. The salad days are just beginning, is what's wrong with me. What's right with me. I'm finally gonna get inside the TV and show everyone—from pre-school to the food pantries to the Meadowbrook recess, from North Junior High and the lonely Friday nights, from people calling me a goddamn retard, a goddamn faggot, because of the way I look and not going to prom and not respecting me no matter how many passes I deflected or jaws I cracked—that they were wrong about me. I did it, Ads. I did it. We did it. Couple more meetings and my life finally fucking starts."

I was, I realized, almost yelling, almost shrieking with watery eyes at her. She just stared into the cases of liquor, head lolling, a teetering bowling pin.

"Maybe this was all worth it, Ads. Maybe this moment, this night, is why I didn't kill myself, y'know? Why I didn't give up on—"

"Are you fucking nuts?" she said, backhanding me from left to right. "Again, Julian Glick, what the fuck is wrong with you?"

Just then, the TV smashed through a commercial break. Everybody looked up, even the bartenders. The DJ stopped tinkering with aux cords and computers, leaving a mist of feedback thrumming beneath the clinks of glass and coughs. Addy glanced above the bar, too.

"With Florida now in Republican hands, and over-performance in the Midwestern states of Michigan, Wisconsin, and Pennsylvania, our model now projects with 98% certainty that the next President of the United States will be—"

"Oh my God," someone shouted. "Ohmigod, ohmigod, ohmigod."

"He did it," I said, holding a cold hand to my still-bruised face.

"No," someone else shouted. "No way. No way."

All three PeterPuff Girls fell out of their stools and thumped against the beer-soaked, slushy tile.

"He really fucking did it," I said. Addy rubbed her wrist.

I looked around. Even if my audience cranked their hogs to Excel for six figures, or ran SOCIALS! for yoga-pant-brands that increased dividends through sweatshop labor, we voted Blue, whether we read Thomas Friedman or Noam Chomsky or exclusively Instagram comments.

We the people who had *inherited* a melting Antarctica. The *legacy admissions* to trillion-dollar-grift. Middle school sick days spent watching F-15s smart-bomb Arabs into (not-) supporting crony capitalism and democracy. We didn't want a wall between Mexico, or a Yemeni genocide, or a perma-burning West Coast. Or at least most of the people sobbing in this bar didn't. Hell, if I had money, if I were famous, I'd drive a Prius! Addy already did. Even Reid, whose cock throbbed to S&P Futures, conceded that—maybe!—the market wouldn't solve climate change, or the alt-right, or why Mom died with negative money. And, okay, perhaps we were too busy updating our fantasy football rosters and watching *The Bachelor* to stop these trends from destroying the post-WWII order, or whatever college professors (who mocked me for using "ain't" un-ironically) called it, but I was tired of excavating loose change from my friends' couches, and Addy was exhausted from enduring hundred-hour weeks of wage slavery and misogyny, and Reid was so sick of his life he'd spent two years getting blackout drunk on Schlitz after work, okay, but this? A rapist game show host as the 45th President? Even the people who had it figured out hadn't figured out how deeply and painfully we were being fucked.

Until right now.

Nearly every US politician and institution is and was reviled, but in a popularity contest you don't choose the class clown over the student government chair.

Unless you do.

WEEPING ACROSS THE bar. Head shaking. Rail whiskey shots. It wasn't official yet, wouldn't be for a little while, but this was happening. Climate change would be irreversible now. We'd probably start another war in the Middle East. White supremacy and Christian dogma would, once again, erase the fledgling gains of the last fifty years.

It got quiet and introspective and sad.

So I started laughing. First a chuckle, then a high-pitched giggle, then a heave, shoulders twitching and stomach tightening.

People looked at me like I'd just microwaved a cat. A deluge of "shut the fuck ups." A couple beers, too. Some onion rings. But I couldn't help it. Politics isn't boring; it's a joke. The Midwest is a joke. America is a joke. If it isn't a joke, what is it?

"This isn't a joke," someone screamed, tossing a hotdog at my head. Addy, who continued watching as the chattering classes bleated about the Blue Wall crumbling and a Red Wall rising, finally turned to me as I calmed down.

"So are you going to fucking apologize?" she asked, massaging her forearm and glaring.

"You're the one who just slapped me."

"Unbelievable," she said, ripping her coat from my arms. She jerked into it with a wince.

"You'll get a cut of whatever I make, of course. I don't want money; I want comfort, Ads. Pay-off some debts, give a lot to charity, get Tom and Chris placed into assisted living and not a group home. Maybe even—"

"Jude."

"—endow a scholarship for working-class kids and students of color if—"

"Julian."

"—this takes off like I—"

The gin and tonic and ice doused me first. Then the follow-through. The tumbler, like a helmet-to-helmet hit, crunched my nose and then shattered at my feet. I clutched my face.

"I'm done with you," she said, slouching toward the exit, stepping over PeterPuff limbs.

"Oh, fuck you," I said, squeezing my nose. "You just—"

"Is this all I am to you? All any of us are? What the hell happened? To the sweet, funny class clown who loved underdogs like Malik?"

"Addy, c'mon." We were yelling at each other in the vestibule. A bouncer rolled his eyes, rolled a joint.

"Did your mom dying fuck you up *that* bad? I don't even recognize you, Jude. Do *you* recognize you? What about me? Or am I just some fucking instrument for whatever psycho fantasy you're roleplaying? Plug me in, or Reid in, or your brothers, or even Stephen if it means you end up famous? Was this all we ever were to you?"

"I"—my nose dribbled onto my sweater and Mom's rosary beads— "my life has been very, very hard, Addison. You'd think my closest friend would—"

"Would allow some casting couch creep to ogle me for a little money and a handshake agreement? I'm surprised you didn't introduce me as your goddamn hooker, with the way Munkelwhatever kept eye-raping me."

We stepped into the cold. Swirling snow. Arctic blasts. My coat, and the rest of my money, was inside with Slutsky.

"You don't have to tell me about sexual assault when—"

"You walked in on it as a kindergartner. Yes, Jude, we all understand your artist's pain. But here's what I don't understand."

"What?"

"How could someone with a mother so selfless grow up to be such a sociopath?"

Two vaguely familiar homeless guys started stumbling toward us with outstretched palms. They turned around as I wiped red from my lips.

"I'm not gonna stand here, dripping blood on fucking Lyndale, and take this abuse from some rich, pampered—"

"Are you any different than Scheisskopf? I mean, really?"

Boris would've hit her. Reid would have shaken her. Instead, I punched my left palm so hard I felt a divot form.

"Macho, macho man," Addy sang. "Jude wants to be a macho man."

"Jesus Christ. Y'know what, lady? You are a fucking cunt."

"Excuse me?" Addy said. Groups of smokers, interested at first, inched away from us, toward 27th, but the women side-eyed me, ready to interfere or call the cops.

Was I any better than Reid, than Boris, than any of the men I knew—all the men I knew outside of possibly gay Nehemiah—who treated women, with actions or words or grabs, as cum dumpsters? As emotional Bozo Dolls?

"You don't get it, okay?" I said, arms flapping. "If you lived my life, with my history, with my neurochemistry, with my freakish-fucking-cancer-eye, you would—"

"No, *you* clearly don't get it, Beaker."

Beaker. I didn't even know if Addy knew the family nickname. She'd never called me Beaker. Nobody did. Not anymore. No one could.

"It's my mother's fucking birthday, Addy, and you have the *temerity* to call me—"

"You're insane," she said. "It really is all about you. Paula's death. Her life. Your fake empathy for poor people, for fucked people. It's all about you. The depression and the Schopenhauer and the nihilistic garbage. The WOKE! comedy and the voice for the voiceless bullshit. And, oh, God, the way you pretend to view women as real people and not some fuck-and-forget rag like every other guy! Always about you. Everything. You really, truly, don't care about other people. I can't believe it took me this long to see it."

"Addy."

"You just launder your white male bullshit with buzzwords, Jude. But the world isn't the problem. And your life isn't the problem. You are the problem. Only you, Jude. All we've ever been is . . . is some demon to exorcise, some pool to gaze at. It's only you. You aren't deep. You aren't smart—"

"Addison."

"You're a cipher. You're fake. You're nothing."

"It's not—"

"No, no," she said, backing away from me as the smoking women trudged our direction. "Everything you've ever said to me, everything you've ever done to me, every choice and bitch-fest, every time you've checked me out, or stormed off when I made out with Reid, or shared a bit of gossip? It was nothing. You need people to fill you up, to make you feel important, because you're nothing. One eye on fame, one eye on making yourself feel famous until you burnt enough people to make it happen. This is all some origin story, right? The mystery beaker. The tortured artist with the traumatic childhood and interesting biography, who overcame the odds and defeated his past, and his cancer. But no. Because you are the cancer, Julian Glick. You are the fucking cancer. The beaker is empty."

I dropped my hands, stared skyward.

"I'm sorry, Ads. I am. Tonight was stressful. MD 20/20. Lots of booze. I'm still not used to functioning without drugs, and I guess I—"

"Get the fuck away from me," she said, tears lurking in her eyes, her voice.

"Addy, I said—"

"Please, Jude, if you ever cared about anyone, if you ever loved your mother for any reason other than fucking standup or memoir material, go into that bar, and clean-up, and get your money, and never talk to me again."

"Addy, c'mon, I—"

"I'm serious, Jude. Leave me alone. I don't want you in my life."

She was crying now. We both were.

"What did I . . . how did—"

"Get away from me." She shoved me in the chest, but I just stood there.

"I spent the weekend in jail, Addy. My brothers are half-dead. Scheisskopf had my ass kicked in New York and you haven't even dropped a text to—"

"We aren't friends, J.G. We never were. People might like you. They might admire your talent. Or your charisma. But you'll never have a real relationship with another human being. Because you don't want one. You bring all this suffering on yourself. Because if you aren't a joke, J.G., what the fuck are you?"

Nothing to say. No charm offensive could counteract the truth. She was right.

I considered a shoulder rub. Even a knee-drop and plea. But instead I left her shivering in a parka, smoking a cigarette she didn't want as she sobbed in a stranger's arms.

Padding my face with one hand, I brushed backwash and fried appetizers off my sweater with the other, and, rather than relitigating, stumbled through the dispersing crowd. My nose had stopped bleeding. Perry tried to get my attention, but I waved him off en route to the bathroom. Where I found Reid, purse slung over his shoulders, washing his hands.

"What?" I said when he looked up. "You too?"

"He's gonna win," Reid said, turning off the sink.

"Yeah, and I bet you voted for His deportation squads and Muslim bans."

My oldest living friend ripped a swatch of paper towels, dried off, and shrugged.

"Are you fucking kidding me?" I said. He smirked.

"The U.S. corporate tax rate is higher than any other OECD country."

I massaged my nose, noticed a pimple sprouting from the grease in real time.

"Reid."

"Look, it's a binary choice we're given, okay? Even if my cousin is a fucking fascist, their economic policy is going to do a lot more for the long-term health of this country than throwing healthcare at everybody and telling people it's free."

"Really?" I laughed. "Why am I even surprised?"

"You aren't gonna make me feel guilty with your simplistic lefty bullshit, bud." He reached for the door, swung it open, lowered a shoulder and stepped toward the hallway. But, halfway gone, he turned back, one final flanking maneuver, a last stab at hurting me. "Besides, didn't your fucking mom vote for Him anyway? Get off your high horse. Or are you popping pills again because it's the only way to deal with your economic anxiety or whatever bull—"

He cut himself off when my spit splattered his face.

For a second, maybe even sixty, Reid just stared at me, calibrating, a frozen computer program, wheel spinning. Outside: groans, curses, shot glasses slamming against oak. Outside further, Addison Bockenhauer feeling as lost personally as our generation now did politically.

"We don't need you anymore," Reid said eventually. "We don't need you, and you know it. So how different are you, really, from guys like my cousin? Your mother, you, him, you all fetishize the same things, even if you don't see it. I hope Addy finally said as much. All you've ever wanted is to matter, but guess what? You never will."

Like a windshield wiper, he flicked the saliva drip with an index finger.

"So is this it?" I asked. "Twenty years, and we—"

"Horseshoe theory," he said, shooting sputum at my face, splashing above my right eye. The puddle slid toward my swollen schnozz. "And—here's a word you can look up if it's too elitist for you, Mr. Blue-Collar Security Guard—I'm the farrier."

What would a left hook do, an uppercut? This bout predated the bathroom, the election, the old clapboard neighborhood, us. Physical violence more pointless than ever, only metaphysics could touch me.

Apparently, Reid disagreed, as he popped my good eye with an overhand right, snapping plastic splinters—my former glasses—toward the sink, the mirror, the end. I blocked the looping left with an elbow, launched a jab toward his nose, but he had slipped into the hallway; my hand caught door, immediately throbbed.

Masculinity is fucking pathetic.

For a second, maybe less, I was back in my childhood kitchen and Boris was slamming Mom's head against a wall while Chris hid behind a blanket in the corner. Tom's eyes grew like inflating balloons. Poverty, cancer, men who see the world, their tiny lives, as zero-sum. God, I was so very tired of the things I inherited.

But I whipped my head, exhaled, fluttered my lips like a horse, and patted Mom's rosary beads against my chest.

In the mirror, blood trickled from my crow's feet and shards of polycarbonate tangled in my hair. Another ass kicking. Literal. Figurative. It all feels the same. The biggest was yet to come, but I didn't know it. I blinked my left eye, held it shut, squeezed, re-opened, and blinked again, the spectre of going blind another family heirloom.

Sufficiently convinced I'd be bruised but not bilaterally broken, I trudged across the sticky floor and, from the hallway, watched Reid burst outside and scamper to Addy. His upturned palms, the hopping like a whiny kindergartner, the pointing toward the bar, his shaking right hand stopped only when some drunks swayed in front of the window, their mugs eclipsing my former friends arguing outside the pane glass. Rubbing my face, scraping out the biggest splinters, dapping my bloody head with a paper towel, I limped through the souring crowd, ignored their looks and questions.

Outside, Addy stomped across the powdered sidewalk, jumped into a cab as Reid howled at her, yanking on the door through the wind. The snow fell in clumps. The cab squished forward, Reid sliding alongside it and not quitting on the handle.

"Reid," I shouted, "give it a rest, man."

His head crept over a shoulder, and he spat at me again, then tugged like firemen pulling a body from a flaming wreck.

The window inched down. "Reid, stop it! Stop!"

But he didn't. Instead, he squatted, the tires barely rotating, quads and ass bouncing, jerking the door, and with one final heave he flung himself backwards, landing on his spine and skull with a crack and immediate groan. I palmed my aching face, dragged fingertips down from forehead to ears to chin and held the beads.

The cab stopped, fourway flashers casting an orange pall over Reid's choking breaths and spasms. I stepped over him, made it to Addy's door just as it inched open, and held it ajar.

"Hey," she said, "is he . . . are you—"

"We're a rotten crowd, Addy," I said, nudging the door closed, "you're worth the whole damn bunch put together."

Some stammers and false starts leaked from the window, but I just shook my head, and the cab drove off. Though I'd see Addy again, this was the last time we ever spoke, and even if I'm not proud of what happened in the hours after, I'm glad I went out with that line. Because, as I walked back into the CC Club, hopped the bar, stole a half-savaged liter of rail whiskey, and guzzled it outside, I figured something out: maybe she isn't worth the whole damn lot— I'm certain she isn't—but living with yourself necessitates lying to yourself. And if you can convince your friends, you can convince your family. Then your coworkers. Then strangers in Italian wool. And if you lie to yourself well enough—if, against all evidence, you believe you are the exception to the rule, and don't rely on other people to prove your thesis—only then can you become a successful comic, a wealthy PR executive, the philistine reality TV host who is elected President of the United States. So maybe it's here, kneading my temple as fluid leaked from my best friend's skull, that I finally started living the lie. That I first entertained the truth about myself and, paradoxically, started living at all.

THE EMERGENCY ROOM was quiet, and I was drunk. In my unprofessional opinion, as some homeless guys and I lugged him down 26th Street to the hospital in which my mother had once experienced post-surgery brain death, Reid seemed healthy, alive, and traumatically concussed. Outside of the sternal-rub-induced groaning, my chatter and panic had produced nothing but snores.

So maybe he was fine.

Regardless, the blood-caked scalp, the ambulance expenditures associated with even good health insurance prompted action and/or yelling for strangers to take action. Which, of course, did not happen. Nothing but drunks skittering from bar to bar and sobbing Democrats pre-grieving what would be coming soon. So, too far from the halfway house I'd relied on months ago, I scoured transit shelters for homeless men and/or alcoholics I might bribe to help me carry Reid.

We had succeeded. I settled on the two drunks who'd watched my meltdown with Addy. They didn't give their names, but they did give a trackmarked hand. $50 for the lug, $50 to keep me company. So they sat in the corner of the lobby playing Go Fish. Leaving me plastered in front of the TV, huffing the dregs of my pilfered whiskey bottle, half of which had lathered Reid's head to disinfect the wound.

It was almost 1:30 a.m., and I couldn't unpack the night's personal failures yet. Scheisskopf reaching the pinnacle of American public life. Addy muttering and crying and over-tipping on her ride home. My right thumb unable to bend, specks of matte black plastic and pseudo-glass smushed into my skin.

My shoulder ached. Maybe everything else did, too.

A third drunk tumbled in the lobby as I stretched my hand into a turkey. The odor preceded him. Swaying in an army jacket, beard-splotched, reeking of Mad Dog 20/20. Dragon fruit. The same shit I'd self-prescribed on stage.

"Android charger," he said, pointing at me.

The drunks looked up.

"Hess," one of them said, "where you been, man? Thought you got clean and then—"

"He did it. Commercial Fiction." Hess smashed a bottle on a chair, waved it. "It wasn't weed, it was fucking opium."

"Hey," a nurse shouted from behind the plexiglass alcove, "no drinking in here unless you're twenty-one, okay?"

"All you fuckin' Glicks are the same," he said, swinging the bottle around his head like a lasso. I realized it was the old man from outside the halfway house, from selling him what I had assumed was oregano the morning my Mom died, but I was too slow. He had recognized me first, frayed synapses immediately sensing on some unconscious level that I was the dude who'd traded good will for what would re-ruin his life. I raised my fists to block the spear of glass, but the jagged shank smashed into my throat, breaking skin before exploding on the tile.

"Quiet hours," the nurse muttered, turning away.

"Clean and serene," Hess said as he left. "Clean and serene."

I whisked blood from my throat, pressed on the gash as it spurt, gave up when Wolf Blitzer materialized before a map of the United States as the crawl screamed: BREAKING NEWS.

"The Associated Press has declared the 45th President of the United States will be—"

"Holy ass!" both of my street acquaintances shouted. "He really fuckin' done it!" There was a lot more bodily fluid on my hands and sweater than I could afford to lose.

Face smeared red, Reid with a traumatic brain injury, looking at a night shivering in my car, and now this, I have never wanted opiates, wanted to bang fucking heroin, more than I did in that moment. And things would continue to deteriorate.

The television cut to a ballroom, campaign signs and hats and only white people crowding the screen. The scrolling ticker confirmed it. America had elected a latent fascist as president. A guy who rose to fame and billionaire status through chintzy hotels and racism.

Stephen Scheisskopf, with a post-coital grin, an orgasmic glow reddening his bald-ass head, strutted from stage left and waved at the cameras. Chants of U-S-A interrupted him several times as he tried to start a speech. Finally, after a few minutes, my own head feverish and throbbing, my stare tunneling through the screen, through the walls and snow and all of the Midwest like some battle-weary soldier aghast in the trenches of Verdun, they quieted down enough for Scheisskopf to begin. All was quiet on the Midwestern front.

"The American Carnage is over!" he said to explosive applause as my undershirt now soaked to the skin with blood. "And we couldn't have done it without you, the real Americans, the forgotten people of this country.

"But before I introduce the 45th President of the United States, I want to tell a personal story that really speaks to how we did what we did, and how flyover country—my country—has finally taken back what's ours from these coastal elites."

Woozy now. Thoughts of Joe the Plumber and Ken Bone tickled my peripheral nervous system. My homeless compatriots looked concerned. Or maybe just horrified at the beginning of the end. I pulled Mom's rosary beads away from my throat and held them as Scheisskopf continued.

"My family worked hard, very hard, to make themselves wealthy. My father started as a lowly analyst and eventually pulled himself up to executive vice president of a Fortune 100 company. My mother, with no background in politics but a desire to make the world a freer and more Christ-like place, became the first female state senator to ever represent district 44A.

"But it's two friends from my childhood, two young men—one white and one black—who really exemplify how our side has dis-mantled a status quo which obliterates working class, righteous peo-ple."

Seemed I was bleeding a great deal. Seemed this was not, like, a good thing.

"After much prayer, when I was twelve, my family adopted a young man with a crackhead mother and no ties to his father. Or so we thought at the time. Malik became my best friend, a lighthouse in the storms of adolescence. Malik was not perfect—only one person has ever been perfect—but he was tenacious and charismatic and indomitable. I still think of him daily.

"But Malik fell in with the wrong crowd, marshalled by a boy I knew from early childhood we'll call J.G. Now, this young man, too, came from a troubled home: a blind mother with chronic health issues, an abusive and alcoholic heathen father, two younger brothers who struggled in school, infant cancer which left him scarred and victimized by bullies despite my best efforts to stop it. But this J.G. has a secret, a secret he holds to this day. And this does not excuse his behavior but does explain what happened to my dear departed Malik."

I blinked insanely, scraped my tongue across the roof of my mouth, chomped my cheek—tricks I learned from Mom in our hungriest years, when she needed to stay awake to hit some typing deadline as unpaid mortgage bills piled up and we couldn't afford the $70 calculator required for my advanced math class. My attention flagged as Scheisskopf droned about the election, about our shared history. I knew on some level he was slandering me to millions of people, but I just wanted to stay awake at this point. One of the chief anxieties of having no money, of having no family, is that you can't permit a trip to the hospital, a life-saving procedure, a followup for your childhood cancer without consciously allowing it. The stakes are too high, the life after medical care too daunting to not deliberate. I couldn't let myself pass out, even if drunk and bleeding profusely, because if I did, whatever life I might have would turn unmanageable, unlivable, if I ended up in a hospital, or God forbid, needed surgery. What if they found a tumor or performed an unnecessary x-ray? When I spent nights scraping asbestos off lead plates and stucco walls with puke-inducing migraines, I never told anyone, refused to even cut out of work because I was paid by the hour. Passing out now would doom me, and Boris, and maybe even whatever remnants of Mom's family could still tolerate me, could still be hunted down by debt collectors and cops.

". . . so I don't know if J.G. planted this heinous idea in young Malik's mind, or if Malik himself had been too corrupted by his inner-city upbringing, his hip-hop and gang role models, but he got it in his head that he should strike up a relationship with my younger sister, Gwendolyn. Him at thirteen and she only ten. Now, as much as we loved our Malik, my parents believe in family values and couldn't stand for this cruel act. But I guess the broken home of J.G., God bless him, could, because Malik moved into J.G's cramped bedroom for several months before something changed . . ."

I sniffed, touched my throat. Gash slowing down, maybe. But Scheisskopf speeding up, dangling me over my third rail on national television.

Listen. Malik moved in with us after Scheisskopf's family kicked him out for selling oregano to Gwendolyn and calling it weed. He used the money to buy new basketball shoes. I know because I was there. I suggested cayenne pepper flakes might add verisimilitude. When Mr. Scheisskopf found out that Malik charged his daughter $100 and seven minutes in the sauna, he yanked a clock from the wall and bashed Malik's face until teeth dangled. I know because I staggered with him to Nala Bashir's place. Even if the American Medical Association disagreed, the rest of us considered her dad a doctor.

"Oh my god," a female voice said back in the waiting room as Scheisskopf mugged and finger-pistoled through an applause line. "Oh my god! Becky! Becky! Page Dr. Bashir stat!"

"Okay, Google," I said as my head bobbed and Stephen smiled on TV, "call Mom."

"Becky!" the female voice said, "what the heck happened here? Becky? He's bleeding to death! He's bleeding to death in our lobby!"

"Ass," my street acquaintances kept chanting. "Holy ass, holy ass, holy ass. Holy fucking ass."

"Oh my God," the female voice said. I remembered, as Stephen adjusted the lectern microphone and cleared his throat, that I had deleted MOM from my contacts because she was dead.

"Okay, Google," I said. "Call Addy Bockenhauer. Pat Schmidt. Boris Glick."

Cold waves burst down my throat to my chest. Or maybe someone opened a window.

My left eye listed to port, but it caught a woman skittering between me and the TV, between the world and Stephen. She carried something puffy and white and looked ready to pounce on my neck.

"Don't call Boris Glick," I slurred, fumbling my phone. "Whatever you do with that Galaxy, you should for sure not call Boris Glick. Maybe Schmidt. Maybe Pat Schmidt. She'll know, right? Maybe not care, but will know. And she'll have an android charger."

"As Deuteronomy 9:11 suggests," Stephen restarted, my good eye rolling like a tumbleweed, clanking and shouting fading away as the nurse pressed something to my upper body. "What are we in life but vessels of opportunity? Foot soldiers in the battle of good and evil on the frontline of the Almighty's plan? So it was for me when I decided to marry myself to this yeoman's service, this yeoman's campaign, to end American Carnage. And so it was for my friends Julian and Malik when they, without even knowing it, chose the wrong side. For the race is not to the swift, nor the battle to the strong . . ."

As a foster kid, my mom had endured the clock-in-the-face trick just like Malik. Even though we didn't have much, we had more than he did, so we let him move into my bedroom, posted in a sleeping bag, while we figured out the next steps. I felt horrible, worse than usual, about the whole situation. I'd long given up on the parties he and Reid, and sometimes even Stephen, attended that summer and into the fall—had concluded I would never be more than a good friend and funny character to girls—but it still gnawed at me that Mal would slink home after finger-banging Laurel Gilbert or Erin McDonnell, stinking of cheap booze and cigarettes like Boris, only to crawl around the floor, knocking shit over, in the middle of the night. I envied his ease with girls, with boys, and though we were thirteen and I couldn't quite square my stunted sexuality, my Boris-infected anxiety around intimacy, it bothered me that he wouldn't so much as acknowledge that I was left out, ignored, maybe even used by him to nut on a sweater, to roll up with Reid and play naked Truth-or-Dare at Addison Bockenhauer's.

One night Malik tumbled into the bag and woke me up.

"The hell is wrong with you?" I asked. I had an Algebra 2 test in the morning and didn't have a graphing calculator that could do the long-hand work for me.

"J.G., dude, chill out," he said in the darkness.

"You do this shit when you lived with Stephen?"

"No, never. Why?"

I sat up. Images of hookups, of not even being gifted the opportunity of FOMO, swirled in my head. I slammed my eyes shut, tried to inhale a sob. I was thirteen years old, sometimes nicknamed Old Man Julian, carried a Frito-Lay-warehouse-sized chip on my shoulder and already knew an Ivy League degree was my only chance of escaping the Midwest, and maybe—if I worked hard and vanquished my social anxiety and whiteknuckled through interviews or networking events with people who assumed anyone from Minnesota was dirt—allowing Mom to retire. Miserable and envious and hardening into a misanthrope before I could grow a beard, I saw what my life projected to if I didn't get rich or famous: a penal colony. Involuntary celibacy. Eccentric and alone and drinking myself to death. Boris Glick.

"Julian, c'mon. I love you, man. What is it?"

"Nothing."

"You're a brother to me, Jude. More than that."

I felt him shift in the gloom. Was he standing up? The party stench seemed to drift with renewed vengeance.

"My ma always thought my dad was gay, bro. It's okay. You can always—"

"Malik," I said, feeling his eyes on me from the foot of the bed, an articulate stream, a provocative riff, spilling forth like it eventually would on stage. "This has nothing to do with that. I'm lonely, okay? I'm jealous. I'm lonely and jealous. I'm a punchline. I wish I was someone else. You or Reid. Maybe even Stephen. Someone self-assured and at least normal looking. Someone who isn't scarred inside and out."

"You are beautiful," he said, hopping into bed and wriggling up toward me. "You are one of a kind, Jude."

"Malik."

He had slipped under my blanket. His hand groped for my boxered lower half. I was barely pubescent and confused and had never even reached first base without the artifice of some hormone-infused game, and maybe I gave off some vibe, some desperation, or maybe I was—am?—still terrorized by the violence of sex and what humans do to each other in the name of love and pleasure, but horny enough to banter—flirt?—suggestively, with anybody who bolstered my self-esteem, I guess, whether laughs or hugs or just eye contact with my shitty face, but when Malik started kissing me and I kissed back, or let my lips hang on his lips, at first before his kisses drifted from my face, then to my chest, then to my stomach, I was uncomfortable, maybe triggered, flashes of Boris naked and Mom screaming, and so I wrapped Malik in an embrace right as he started stroking me, right as Little J.G. started motoring into Big J.G., gripped Malik right as he seemed intent on using his lips on another part of my body, and this bearhug became a medicine-ball-toss as I swung him to the carpet, his upper-right quadrant caroming off our dresser.

"Fuck," he shrieked, certainly waking up my family, "the fuck was that about?" Papers and coins and my math textbook plunked to the carpet. I switched on my bedside lamp, blinked until I made out his hand rubbing his ear.

"How'm I finna make the 'A' team with one ear and one shoulder?" Clomping in circles, his right shoulder bent chicken wingishly as he now hopped and dripped blood.

"You started it!" I said.

"Fuck, fuck, fuck!"

"You started it!"

"What the hell is going on up there?" Mom's voice roared from the basement. She must have been working.

"Who is gonna take me in if I can't lift my arm above my head, you fucking psycho?"

"What are you two *doing?*" Mom yelled. A metallic reverb bounced up the stairs. Mom would often bang into the aluminum bannister.

"Mal? Judy?" Chris said in a small voice from outside the door. "Can you quiet down?"

"Fuck!" Malik screamed again. "I am so, so fucked."

"Mal?" Chris said again.

I was finding it harder to breathe, as though bench-pressing while ball-gagged.

"You ruin everything you touch, you fucking faggot!" Malik said. I stared at the ceiling, which seemed to bulge and recede with the pulse of my accelerating heart. No stranger to trauma, obviously, and already shielded by ironic detachment, I giggled.

"Are you laughing?" Malik asked with a football coach's lack of mirth.

"No," I said, laughing.

"What are you laughing at?"

"Nothing," I said, eyes on the ceiling as Malik rifled his backpack for something.

I see now, from this shed, why I was laughing. If only I had seen it then, or in the waiting room, or before the MAOI rally. If only I had considered it possible as Malik produced a pocket knife and lunged at my head.

As the knife tumbled into a grounded teddy bear's eye and my mom whipped through the door and we all screamed and cried and made no sense.

As Malik yanked his basketball shoes into his backpack and sprinted past my wobbling mother and journeyed into the October frost.

As he spent several homeless weeks not returning my calls.

As his half-brother and cousins transformed him into an eighth-grade drop out.

As the confusion over what had happened that night led me to attempt suicide with Advil.

As life concluded logically: cocaine-dealing and drug debts and a sawed-off shotgun holding-up a gas station. Thirteen years old. Panicking when the getaway car didn't show up. Ditching the Mossberg but getting capped by the police anyway. Bleeding to death alone in a snowy ditch while I tried to flirt with Nala Bashir in Math class.

As Stephen refused to attend his funeral, and Reid and I got blackout drunk for the first time to endure it, and I cried so much that Malik's half-brother Martell—who'd got him hooked on coke and supplied him with baggies to sniff and sell—offered me two tiny white pills of Demerol.

As the last ten years led to me standing up in the waiting room on Election Night, and shoving the nurse trying to tourniquet my jugular, and saluting Scheisskopf and telling the guys rushing over with a stretcher that I intended to murder that man on the television. If only I had considered, as I wandered toward the door, intent on bleeding to death alone in a ditch, what Scheisskopf was explaining on TV:

"There are only the punching and the punched, folks. For too long, our people have been the punched—by the Washington Swamp, by the coastal elites, by the big city liberals handing out freebies to these lazy urban jungle baby-makers, to folks like my friends J.G. and especially Malik, who may have made terrible decisions, but still ended up dying alone in a county road drainage trench because liberals don't care about good Christian people, y'know—Malik punched to death, shot to death, in one of the most progressive cities in America, ten years ago. The punching and the punched like Poor Old J.G., folks, whose sexual promiscuity and wayward values and unholy upbringing do not change the fact that he and his mother were neglected by the career politicians in the Swamp and Minnesota, folks, were punched over and over and over again until J.G. is so deformed, so bruised and battered, that the only way to remake him is with an invitation from the 45th President of the United States. Yes. To accept an apology for the American Carnage wrought by people who had no interest in Making America Great. We are sorry,

J.G. But you will not suffer in vain. So, Julian Glick, J.G., Jude the Obscure, if you're out there back home, if you're listening in flyover country, this victory was for you, okay? You aren't Jude anymore. No. You're one of us. You're Deplorable Dave now. We won for you and all the punched people out there, okay? Because finally, for the first time in thirty years, we have a President and an administration who is going to punch back!"

Scheisskopf's face contorted into triumph as he shook the president-elect's hand and introduced him as 45. I stumbled into the freezing and flurried night. I felt every clapping hand in Middle America. Downtown Minneapolis narrow, the streets empty, the shouts of medical personnel shallow, 45 taking the lectern next to his VP and young son, and me dripping blood across the white street into a plowed snowbank. Dialing Boris and laying down, calling my dad who seemed drunk and just laughing into the phone, laughing my life away like I'd laughed since birth, laughing because the alternative was facing the truth about myself: that I was scarred by abuse; that I had chased everyone away; that I was an empty beaker; that Addy was right; that Stephen was right.

I had killed Malik.

My cowardice, my self-absorption, my laughter had killed Malik. I continued to bleed in the snow.

Ten years. Malik died because I either couldn't wrestle with my sexual trauma or couldn't accept there was a reason I'd been hooking up with men for years, a reason I had sex dreams about Nehemiah. After all the drugs and booze and hunger, I don't even remember what happened in my bedroom that night, but it doesn't matter. I know I killed him. I know because I carry it every day.

I clutched my throat. Blood spurted with my chuckles.

Somewhere, Boris mumbled about 911. But I just cackled and closed my eyes and accepted that I would die either tonight or on stage with Stephen Scheisskopf.

If this country isn't a joke, what is it?

If my life isn't a joke, what is it?

What is it?

What is it?

What is it?

11.

A FAN'S NOTES

MOM USED TO tell me this story we both tried to repress. Maybe she mentioned it after Malik died, one last time, though this feels like fabrication. Too easy, too comforting. Life isn't like that. But on the rickety porch swing, when no one else was around, and I could still fit on her lap, and we didn't have enough money and I didn't have a father and bullying made me sob on the bus both ways, she shared.

I'd tease it to Tom and Chris, prodding them toward revelation, an acknowledgment of how much our mother had suffered, but they never picked up the scent.

So she'd never told them. Or, like everybody else, they didn't care.

You know that Mom grew up on a farm and got shipped to a foster home soon after going blind. She never quite forgave her family but came closer than I did.

The foster parents beat her, molested her, starved her. Basic stuff. Mom survived chronic taunts of suicide, and even a few attempts, by gripping the same rosary beads I've been squeezing since she died. She would repeat this phrase, what I later learned is a Bible verse, over and over like a mantra: "And in His anguish, He prayed more earnestly, and His sweat became like drops of blood falling to the ground."

Not some novel about dating Brooklynites. Not some fantastic escapism with dragons and tits. She survived because others survived. She survived because enduring when you shouldn't is more valuable than lucking into a yacht on Lake Minnetonka or an Ivy

League degree. And I don't believe in God, but I do believe in Mom. That's why I haven't ended it yet.

She never explained it like this, of course, though it became the prologue to every decision she made.

When it got really bad, the state intervened, placed her with a family that beat her, molested her, and starved her slightly less. This pattern continued like a conveyor belt until she winced into junior year, when her best friend's family offered their guest room. The move would go down Saturday morning.

Because Mom was blind, intermittently homeless, and chronically abused, the high school nurse—the sort of person I wish I'd had in my life growing up—emptied a supply closet in the infirmary so Mom could store clothes and braille books. The only safe space in her life.

Mom had already been selected homecoming queen but wanted to audition for *The Sound of Music*. Saturday morning. So after the basketball game, rather than go out with her friends, or beg for a ride back to school by 9:00 a.m., she decided to sleep in the closet.

As she inched through administrative offices, bumping into desks and pillars, a muffled voice eked down the hallway, near her sanctuary.

She flipped the rosary from under her sweatshirt and cradled the beads.

Step, step, listen. Step, step, listen. The noise grew louder.

Mom had nowhere else to stay. Cellphones didn't exist. Nobody was supposed to be back here; only she and the nurse had a key.

Step, step, listen. Step, step, listen. Mom's fingers slid along the wall, her necklace bouncing as something crashed and then the sound stopped.

Outside the door, Mom prayed. Turned the lock. Pushed the handle. Leaned in. The door creaked. Her heart thumped. The closet was small. Just long enough for a petite young woman to lie down. The door floated, floated, floated until it banged into something thick and heavy. Like a sandbag? Mom inhaled, exhaled, crept into the closet. Groped the unknown. Nothing. Nothing. And then she screamed. Screamed so loud and long that a custodian across campus and the basketball coach reviewing film heard something primal and murderous and dropped what they were doing. Mom stepped back, still screaming, or maybe crying, stepped forward again and felt the scarred forearm of a hanging human being. Braille dots. Mom had taught her best friend braille. There wasn't blood. Just welts and missing chunks of skin. Her fingertips crawled across the flesh as she mumbled along.

Paula: How do you do it? So strong. I can't be. Too much. See ya.

Her friend survived. She'd even hugged me at the funeral. Mom still moved to the guest room, and after a hospital stay, everything returned to normal. But Mom stopped using the closet. Stopped gripping the beads for a while. Stopped muttering her mantra for years, until it got bad with Boris and she couldn't endure it alone.

"Why?" I would ask.

"I got scared," she'd say.

"Of what."

"You won't understand, honey."

"I wanna know."

The swing would stop rocking.

"I don't want to scare you, Beaker."

"I'm not. I wanna know."

"Okay," she said, "I got scared because what if we can only hurt other people? What if surviving isn't enough? What if that's a problem, too."

On the night Malik died, I remembered the doubt. And in her bedroom as she froze forever. And as I skulked through New York City. And as I watched the election results.

I considered the question, but I never considered the answer.

Because I hoped she wasn't right.

THE CEILING WAS breathing. It bulged and receded. It swelled and settled. It oozed a vague and esoteric pop-cultural literacy I could not quite place.

Pretty sure I was dead. Pretty sure this was not a hospital.

"You are alive. This is a hospital," a voice whispered over beeps and puffs.

Principal Schmidt. She sat in a chair at the end of my bed. Next to Boris. On my right: pulsing screens and dripping IVs.

I opened my mouth, but stretching my throat stung. I felt nauseous, the air thin and sepia-stained like drinking Mountain Dew on an empty stomach. That or—it jolted me with raised neck hairs, a wave of keys-locked-in-the-car panic—I'd been dosed with Demerol, fentanyl, opiates, relapse.

"What this is," she said, "is another stop on your magical misery tour."

"Least he isn't that, uh, Peuschold idiot," Boris said, eyes locked on the entertainment section. "Legs sawed off by a 6 train. Pride of Lino Lakes. Reality TV. Could've been you, Jude. I went to New York once. Kicked out of CBGB. Did you know Lou Reed was, whaddatheycallit, queer?"

So it was sometime after Thursday night. *American Idyll*'s first challenge. I twisted left, slid higher on my stack of pillows, and located the television. My skin boiled with every inhale, a flamethrower ripping from my neck and upper back with every exhale. Jugular wrapped in tape. The taste of battery lacquering my mouth. Still couldn't speak.

On TV Wolf Blitzer, parka-clad and hunched, stood outside the MAOI's six neo-Roman columns and hundred-step grand entrance as men in black pressed earpieces and laughed at some joke Nehemiah had cracked maybe ten feet away.

I gasped like a vapor-huffing Victorian and clutched at my neck. The chyron said it was 78 degrees in Minneapolis.

"... nicknamed 'Old Main' according to a professor-turned-security-captain named Nehemiah Weaver, who has asked to remain anonymous, this grand outdoor staircase stands maybe a hundred feet above Third Avenue, Anderson, and will provide stunning sightlines for the president-elect's first public appearance since Wednesday morning," Wolf Blitzer said, gesturing at the museum. "According to sources with direct access to the Office of Presidential Transition, the Minneapolis Police Department, Homeland Security, and Secret Service are expecting 20,000-plus people to settle along Third Avenue and Washburn Fair Oaks Park directly across the street, making this the largest outdoor event in Minneapolis since an impromptu concert for Prince, perhaps the only Minnesotan worth knowing, who died of a fentanyl overdose on April 21, 2016."

The rosary was gone. I checked under the blankets and pillows.

"Wolf, do we know the itinerary for tomorrow afternoon?" said Anderson Cooper.

"We do, A.C. More or less. After Minneapolis native and soon-to-be White House Senior Policy Adviser Stephen Scheisskopf provides his opening remarks, and introduces folk hero Jude Glick, the president-elect himself, Mr. Do—"

"Is it confirmed that Mr. Glick will appear? There were some health or financial issues if—"

"Sources close to Mr. Glick have guaranteed he'll be in attendance. Indeed, Anderson, according to Mr. Scheisskopf, J.G., or as the campaign is calling him, in a nod to figures like Joe the Plumber, 'Deplorable Dave' will play a central role in the proceedings—alongside other victims of American Carnage—before the President-elect's remarks. The new regime has even offered to pay for Deplorable Dave's medical expenses and various family debts if he obliges."

"For listeners who've struggled to keep up with a whirlwind week of news, who exactly is this guy, Wolf?"

"Anderson, as Stephen Scheisskopf outlined in his remarks Wednesday morning, Glick, er, Deplorable Dave is in many ways a victim of the circumstances which led to this improbable presidential victory. Or, if you believe the cynics, he is a victim of the economic division advanced by persons like chief speechwriter Stephen Scheisskopf. He's also become an internet meme in which he stares at a woman's rear. The bottom is in yoga pants, and as chaos swirls around him, Deplorable Dave locks eyes with two buttcheeks. Either way, A.C., he is a man we expect to hear a lot more from, and about, in the coming weeks."

"We'll leave it at that, Wolf. Stay warm and safe. Who knows what else lurks in flyover country."

Schmidt lit some incense sticks, dropped them in a bell jar, consciously avoiding my frenzied blinks. Boris kept reading the paper as my heart-rate monitor accelerated and CNN cut to commercial.

NOT SURE HOW long I slept. But since I was no longer bleeding from my slashed throat, the hospital had apparently asked me to leave. Dinnertime on Friday, no remaining PTO, presumably working at 9:45 a.m., so I needed to get on with it. Or at least remove the breathing tube long enough for someone to explain what my life had become.

"Um," Boris said to a nurse as Schmidt dozed, "the doctor? Wednesday? Bashir? Week of observation is what he recommended."

"We called the insurer," she responded, checking her AppleWatch. "They don't want to cover it. Just like they wouldn't cover the painkillers or exploratory surgery. He's stable enough. Probably."

"I've got two other sons facing long-term disability, and you're telling me that they'd rather release this one to my couch than . . . than, like, make sure he's safe in the short-term? All I do is watch football and drink and read Marx. The kids are basically orphans."

"Yep."

I shrugged at my dad. The nurse smacked her gum. Boris dug around his sweatpants for a pill bottle.

"What?"

I arched my eyebrows. Schmidt snored. This was my safety net, I guess. Holey. Unemployed. Wearing athleisure. When your mother dies young, nobody else is required to care about you. Instead, you're at the mercy of guilt and convenience.

Still: Boris called Accounts Receivable, who called my collectively bargained health insurance customer service hotline, which really meant the hospital's Accounts Receivable three-wayed a call with Boris to a third-party vendor who handled claim disputes on behalf of my insurer's customer service hotline, and settled my case in the coverage affirmative; but soon after the manager on-duty of my health insurance's customer service hotline called Boris directly to inform him, and the Wrigley's-popping nurse-on-duty, that, although the third-party vendor who handled claim disputes on behalf of my insurer confirmed, with gusto, that I was covered for a 72-hour Traumatic Injury or Near-Death Emergency Resuscitation (i.e., a TINDER)—assuming I would fork over the $6,000 remaining on my $7,000 deductible—I was not, actually, in the coverage affirmative, as the MAOI, who provided (i.e., negotiated and subsidized per the CBA of 2013) the insurance plan considered this specific floor of the University of Minnesota hospital system "out-of-network," because the U of M used a separate "medical informatics" system than the rest of the building, a "medical informatics" system supplier with whom the Museum was contractually obligated, per their agreement with the health insurance provider and SEIU 26, to consider a "bad actor" and worthy of "care disincentivization" due to "abnormalities" with respect to "prior accounts payable arrangements" predating the most recent CBA addendum of June 2015; and since the hospital wasn't sure they'd get paid, even though Minnesota statute 145C.07 insisted that emergency room trauma survivors spend 72 hours under direct observation unless a doctor such as one Ishmail Bashir, M.D., MPH, granted a waiver, the senior attending Trauma Physician could, in consultation with the Associate Vice President of Remuneration Management, countermand this legal statute with a signature and once-over from a member of the hospital's General Counsel office, even if the patient (i.e., me) did not display demonstrably sufficient symptomatology abatement because, and I quote, the "logistical care imperatives of the Inpatient Intensive Care Unit may necessitate actuarial overrides and/or treatment temperance should the coverage affirmative reveal itself as coverage ambiguous or coverage negative."

"Okay," Boris said.

They removed my breathing tube and IVs and stuck me in a wheelchair.

"If you wanna chance it, Mr. Boris," the nurse said, "you could try and count on your son's, like, celebrity bailout. From the campaign?"

"Eh," Boris said, rousing Schmidt, "we're too big not to fail."

HERE'S WHAT HAD happened:

My mentions, my DMs, my Facebook friend requests were clogged with DEPLORABLES 4 DAVE. A legitimate Political Action Committee had been founded to "Bring Deplorable Dave to Washington." A blimp, dragging an IDS-sized banner, had been making slow loops of Minneapolis ever since "Deplorable Dave had been found half-assassinated by a radical homeless libtard."

Nobody seemed to care that my name was not Dave.

An Instagram and Snapchat had been started in my non-name by Scheisskopf's lackeys. Various RNC delegates added me on LinkedIn. I had 101,647 followers on my verified Twitter. Sean Hannity's booker had left three separate voicemails. The Secret Service wanted to meet me before work.

And, per the front page of the *Star Tribune*, Finklefunk and Munkelhorton had disowned ever meeting me. Too deplorable. Scheisskopf's plan, pitched in New York, had not only been executed without my permission but the fucking thing worked: I was something between a meme and a celebrity. And all I had to do for the house back and our medical debts wiped-out was whatever Scheisskopf wanted. On national television.

"Where are you taking us?" Boris asked from the passenger seat of the hollowed-out van. The trashbag window inflated as Schmidt careened through Dinkytown. I lay across the back like a discarded couch. I'd been dragged into the ER, spurting blood, and placed into a medically induced coma to which nobody consented, but Schmidt's mania was more disorienting than my near-death experience.

"People," she started, lighting a cigarette and shaking her head, "are very uncomfortable with the idea that a nobody—like you, like me, like Gavrilo Princip, like Lee Harvey Oswald—could overcome his station, his nothingness, and his moment to do something that changes all of our lives."

"My apartment is the opposite direction," Boris said, producing a flask and hitting it. I felt dizzy, dehydrated, possibly drugged. Nehemiah lived around here somewhere. Schmidt probably roamed from commune to commune.

"Playing this how Scheisskopf wants is not without advantages. Your brothers are expected to make a full recovery after a few months of PT and adequate care. You might be able to subvert the fledgling drift toward fascism from inside the White House, or in between Fox News reverse mortgage commercials."

"Mmm," I said. My throat pulsed with each breath. We'd recovered my bloody undershirt, my snow-soaked cords, and my sticky sweater, but they said I hadn't come in with the rosary beads.

"But if the cup swings your way, drink from it, no? Because it might not come back around. So what if you want to leave your mark on society, on history, on your terms? So what if you conceptualize yourself as important, as inspirational to the suffering masses, the real ones, not Stephen's? Is that so bad? A justice-oriented Wikipedia page? Where is the harm in this?"

"Were you always this crazy?" Boris slurred. We passed Reid's flophouse, then Boris' old halfway house, and careened onto University going 60 in a 35.

"Who says I want this," I rattled. "Who says I'm not planning to burn Scheisskopf anyway."

"This is the first you're speaking of it."

"This is the first I'm speaking, Schmidt. I should be dead. I wish I was dead. I'm still not even sure what the fuck is going on. I wake up and everything is different."

"Welcome to America after November 8, 2016. All I am suggesting is that you contemplate what you want to do with this opportunity. You want the house back, your brothers to be taken care of, your debts eliminated? Fine. Selfish but fine. Get sandwiched between psychological torture and crippling debt on network TV. I don't give a shit."

Boris turned around. "Is this lady deaf, J.G.? I only called her Wednesday because I'd knocked out a 30-rack of Hamm's and she was in the phonebook. And at the funeral, right? I wasn't gonna try Grandpa Konrad or some shit."

"The harm in this wait-and-see approach," Schmidt continued as we motored toward St. Paul, incurring the honks and middle-fingers of rush hour drivers, "is that you are a pawn for America's id. Do you want to be a pawn for America's id? For Scheisskopf to win once and for all? Is the money worth it? The disrespect to the memory of your mother and Malik?"

Of course not, I thought, but what other option did I have? After the museum beatdown, Nehemiah had pitched the binary of being either non-racist or anti-racist, but what if action required death? What if it required walking away from financial security? From the fame I'd craved since childhood? From a lane out?

Schmidt must have seen this in the rearview mirror.

"What do *you* want, Julian?" she said with a smoky sigh. "Because, perhaps, perhaps, even your narcissism is of a shallow variety, no? This isn't a commencement speech. This isn't some esoteric and ineffable comedy success, some vague opportunity to exorcise the demons of recess bullying. This is real now, okay? The most incomprehensible thing since 9/11 happened on Election Night 2016, yes? And all I'm asking of you is to not let Scheisskopf win. You do what you're comfortable with; I'll handle my people."

"Is that the Fitzgerald House up there?" Boris said, as we screamed down the Summit Avenue shoulder.

Schmidt gripped the wheel, stomped the gas. 70. 80. 90. 100.

Then she smashed the brake. I flew into the bucket seats. Boris banged his head on the dashboard. My upper body imploded with pain.

Schmidt just kept smoking her cigarette.

After a few minutes, the van either filling with exhaust or Schmidt's Pall Malls or both, I looked up. The Fitzgerald House. Where he'd written *This Side of Paradise*.

Schmidt dug around the glovebox, stuffed the Ortgies 7.65 in her waistband. Boris moaned, suckled his flask. I scooched closer to Schmidt and cleared my throat.

"Is this really happening?" I whispered. We both glanced at the mansion. "He's really President? Schmidt, really? And Scheisskopf? What if I opt-out? What if I just don't show up? What can he do to me?"

Schmidt plucked the cigarette from her mouth and rotated it. The gun butt poked from her tracksuit. She jammed the lit end into her left palm.

"Father Berrigan, the Jesuit. When you'd act out, your mother was prone to discussing him. Perhaps you remember. She was, of course, haunted by the question of human suffering. As was Berrigan. Well, Father once said that we're all going to die in a world that is worse than when we entered it. Do you believe that?"

"My mom did."

"Your mother was a brilliant woman, Jude. And she raised a brilliant son. But more than anything, your mother was courageous. Are you courageous? Are you *non*, J.G., or are you *anti*?"

Schmidt ground the cigarette deeper into her skin. Then she stamped it out.

"Because your mother, for all her faults, was anti. She had a peculiar way of showing it, but she helped Malik. She ordered a hundred times as many syringes as she needed through Medicaid and gave them all to the biology department. Some of that debt you've inherited is mine, Jude."

Even Boris was rapt now.

"Beaker, listen. My whole life I've wanted to leave the world a better place than I found it, and I've largely failed. I've been blessed with a helluva lot more opportunities and privileges than your mother. Or maybe even you. But what have I done with it? Some antifa actions, some barking at Scheisskopf on the radio. A big nothing."

Schmidt winced and sniffled.

"Your pal Reid? He was on NPR this morning. Yes, he's fine. Sort of branding himself as a Scheisskopf and Glick whisperer. And he said that America is a demonstrably better place than it's ever been because people have the internet in their pocket, okay? Permanent War is a fact of global life, and the glaciers are melting, and income inequality has superseded the Gilded Age, and you have tens of thousands in debt for no reason other than some politician somewhere decided that this is how America should be. Well, if politics is how we disperse human suffering, I'm tired of not sharing the lack of wealth. There might be nobility in poverty, but there isn't much nobility in bench-warming. Are you on the field or in the stands? I've made my decision, and we're going to land at least a symbolic victory Saturday night with or without you, even if it kills me. Because maybe the fucking internet is in my pocket and GDP keeps rising, but suicides are too and we have neo-Nazis in the White House."

I looked to the Fitzgerald House. "The pursued, the pursuing, the busy, the tired," I said.

Schmidt nodded, stuck her hand in a back pocket. The rosary beads. She dropped them in my cupped hands as Boris started to giggle.

"That Stephen kid has been a punk since pre-school. Remember?" he said.

"Boris."

"And do you find it ironic that, uh, what's his name? Malik? That Malik was murdered for trying to survive? For stealing gas station hotdogs?"

"Dad."

"Victim of a victimless crime, kinda. Like them Somali guys, or even that girl Schmidt said was at your college. Criminal unluckiness."

I glanced from Boris to Schmidt. She plucked dandruff from her scalp. It occurred to me that my father—who for two decades had abstained from all substance use beyond life-destroying alcoholism—was high for the first time since the divorce.

"Boris, are you using again?"

Schmidt sighed, palmed her neck. "I'll see you tomorrow, J.G."

"Wait, Patty, shouldn't we—"

"The gun is an interwar German item. We'll handle all arrangements sans the moment of reckoning. Using it should not be your first option. But the less you know, the better. That said, you may want to clear the air with Nehemiah."

"This is all happening so fast, Patty, that I think—"

"There will be plenty of time for thinking after tomorrow. These people respond to one thing: humiliation. The threat of violence is simply our Trojan Horse. When the opportunity presents itself, Jude, I recommend a ballsy move." With that, she nodded at Boris, jammed a beanie low over her eyes, and started walking toward downtown St. Paul.

I gripped the rosary beads as Boris massaged his eye bags. He adjusted his waistband, excess sweatpants pooled and frayed at his feet. Sweat sprouted on my forehead as I grunted and contorted into the driver's seat.

ENOUGH FUCKING SPEECHES. Enough rhetoric and

meditation.

Maybe this story is simply biological.

The hunger. When Mom died, all I had left was the hunger.

I didn't sleep Friday night.

Burbling stomach.

12:00. 1:00. 2:00. 3:00. 4:00.

Some blocked number kept calling on the third minute of each hour. When I finally answered, a robotic voice asked me to bring my birth certificate, my mother's death certificate, and my Social Security card. Before I realized it was something federal, they had hung up.

And then it was time for work.

My last supper.

In green rooms, in locker rooms, in holding rooms, in comedy clubs and staging areas and arena tunnels, in pastors' offices and interrogation cells and the MAOI security station, whether drunk, or sober, or soberly ruminating on my drunkenness, the only thing that kept me inching forward was the promise that, if I endured long enough, I wouldn't be hungry anymore. I'd be somebody. I would finally fucking eat. I needed to be somebody who could finally fucking eat. Because Mom never had that chance as we skipped across Winnetka to food pantries. Because Boris never had that chance as his father pulled a German pistol on his mother. Because Malik never had that chance as he taught himself to read in the projects. But if I could grind out this Saturday, the final chase-down block on Scheisskopf's fastbreak, we could sit down and eat. I could taste it. I was tired of going to bed hungry. Give me a nominal jail sentence and a lifetime of fame and fortune. Easy call. I didn't even need to kill him. Vengeance is sweeter when both parties have to live with it.

So I waltzed through the Secret Service's metal detectors, and let them cup my ass, and finger my thighs, and reported for duty.

Addy was wrong. This wasn't always about me. But now it would be.

The MAOI had been officially shuttered since the fight with fascists. Once the press and the City of Minneapolis established that Scheisskopf had been serious about throwing the rally here, the advance team, DHS, and a phalanx of crew-cut/aviators/Bluetooth types had invaded the museum, run background checks on anyone the campaign wanted to use for PR purposes, and closed off the entire Whittier neighborhood to through-traffic. From Franklin to

Lyndale to Lake Street to 35W. Last Sunday, while my brothers' brains bled and I read *Crime and Punishment* in jail, The Mogul visited to rant about the No-Go-Zones that supposedly existed near Boris' place, and now he'd created his own.

"They's lookin' for you, J.G.," Sandy wheezed as she wheeled her oxygen tank past the break room. Some public entity owns the MAOI, and for insurance purposes, even when the building is closed because of possible political violence or a PEOTUS circle-jerk, state law mandates that security staff is always present. The Delacroix exhibit, where all of this had ignited, required guards in every gallery. And before I could be exploited for political capital, I'd be exploited by regular old economic capital.

"And Nehemiah?" I said, palms dripping sweat on my cummerbund. Usually, we wore the black cardigan, the cowboy shirt, the tan slacks, but for *Strategically Prudent And/Or Publicly Facing Deployment Opportunities* like today, we rocked maroon blazers with black pants and bowties. Malnourished and psychologically palsied Hugh Hefners making $13.72/hour.

"Yeah, him. You're s'posed to train some newbie on perimeter duty."

"They hired someone to—"

"Stupid as hell, I agree. Leva Bronstein. Tall and icy. Pink hair. Nose ring."

"Ah, John Coogan."

"Coogan is losing it. All last week he was muttering about the end times and how Walt Disney was a Nazi. But whatever. How you doin'? You had quite the week already."

"The guy who slashed my throat? Case of mistaken identity. He thought I was someone who wanted to be alive."

"You are bleak boy, y'know that?"

"Insurance kicked me to the curb prematurely. They shoulda just let me bleed there Wednesday night."

"There's some scarecrow with a Hitler-Youth vibe wants to talk to ya, too," Sandy said, puffing toward the freight elevator that would hoist her to Old Main. Several years ago, an armed rando with a criminal record had muscled into a lift with the 44th President. I'd looked it up as I thrashed on Boris' worn leather last night. The model proved aspirational. A public art museum was a terrible place for political theater, with the contractually obligated gallery guards hanging around. Schmidt had obviously intuited this after the Thrilla with Vanillas.

"Carol here today?" I asked. "All the other regulars are on the board."

Sandy shook her head. "She said she'd rather die than be seen with the next president."

"Little does she know, that might be an option."

"Still got it, J.G.," Sandy cackled, shuffling out of view.

A few minutes of crosswords later, as I waited to swipe in at 9:45, my phone buzzed. 212 number. Finally. Maybe Addy had negotiated the talent holding deal. If I could talk Finklefunk into helping me, I wouldn't commit televised assault.

I sprung from my plastic chair and bounded for the handicap bathroom.

"Hell—"

"This isn't gonna happen, Jude. Obviously," Ferris said.

I rubbed crust from my eyes, realized I skipped breakfast. "I saw that in the paper, actually. You and Morton seemed to—"

"Pretty damn clear that you aren't what you say you are. That wasn't anti-comedy on election night; it was your genuine worldview. You might think you're telling truth to power, but you're little more than an alt-right sympathizer. Who are you helping? Who are you hurting? No, no. Don't answer. I don't care what you think, especially if you're gonna meet with some fascist and lie about your representation."

"So this is about—"

"You know who this is about, okay? I'm extremely busy—and you are, too, according to CNN and your propaganda minister buddy—but thought I owed you a phone call, at least. Seems you aren't getting career advice from anyone sane."

"Did you hear about my . . . my backstory? I mean, I'm not exactly a fan of—"

"An email from Cross Yoder-Henley's assistant cleared all that up. Maybe the administration hasn't done their due diligence, but we certainly have."

"And?"

"And Addison told me everything about you, too. She isn't much better though. So before you do anything stupid this evening, listen. I've seen your type."

My heart bashed against my sternum. I've been replaying these next words over and over in this shed.

"There was a blind man visiting his friend one night," Ferris said. "Or picture your mom if you'd like. So Blind Guy goes to his friend's house and when it's time to head home, his friend insists he takes a lantern. And Blind Guy is like, 'Why do I need a lantern? I'm blind. Darkness and light are the same to me.' And his friend presses it on him anyway. Are you listening? Okay, so he presses it on him and says he knows that darkness and light don't matter to Blind Guy, but someone *else* might run into Blind Guy. So Blind Guy takes the lantern and leaves and, sure enough, someone bumps into him. And so Blind Guy, he goes: 'Watch where you're going, dipshit. Didn't you see this lantern?' And the guy who bumped into him just giggles and claps his back and says, 'Brother, your candle has burned out.'"

"Ferris, I wanna make this right. What can I do?" I asked, dragging my left hand down my face and kneading my cheek like Play-Doh.

"Stop clawing, Jude. Maybe your candle has burned out."

He hung up. I slammed the toilet cover, sat on it, and wondered if the Blind Guy was Scheisskopf or Jude Glick.

NEHEMIAH HAD BEEN avoiding me all morning. As we huddled around him in the break room, he refused eye contact. And at 9:44, as he reiterated to eight of us—not including Sandy, Coogan, and Leva Bronstein—that the campaign would be using this select group for photo opportunities at the site of the non-terrorist-attack and on stage, and that I would obviously become a prop, my mind wandered to Reid and Addy.

When had her candle burned out?

She had wanted, and probably still wanted (but since September I hadn't asked), to be a long-form journalist. Write big, influential pieces for the *New Yorker*. Sign a talking-head contract. Leverage her talent and charm and work ethic into a tell-all about growing up around Stephen Scheisskopf. What Reid was doing without the hard work.

The board of trustees and executive staff shuffled into our bunker. I'd never even seen the Director up close. They handed out the guest list, which we were to crosscheck once upstairs.

But, no, this wasn't happening. Mom was alive, and Nala was in America, and I was sitting around a bonfire with friends. I still had friends.

Addy's father was an anesthesiologist; her mother a drunk.

They'd divorced in junior high, when I knew her as someone Reid and Malik wanted to shtup. Not a person forced into impossible choices like the rest of us.

Maybe I'd never known her as that until half-listening to Nehemiah. The Museum Director demanded we treat this like a normal day unless specifically asked not to by the campaign or Secret Service.

"This is extremely normal," Nehemiah deadpanned. "The Cargill Family Commemorative Grand Entrance at East 24th Street, or whatever they're calling Old Main nowadays, has been converted into the stage, as you probably all know, and Sandy will be stationed at the desk throughout the duration of our evening. I'll eventually accompany a party of journalists and museum-higher-ups and fascists to the *Passionately in Love with Passion* exhibit, and J.G., in particular, but also whoever else is on duty in sections 24.1 through 24.8 are supposed to, like, ignore the press and the Propaganda Minister and just look suicidal like any other Saturday. As for any guards not onstage, well, your job is easy. Once the interior closes, people like Coogan are allowed to wander the TestosterZone—yes, I'm serious, that's what this paper says——which is *on* East 24th Street. Sort of a food truck lineup mixed in with Secret Service decoy vehicles and cameras. A moat of photo ops with working people. Or something. I am told there will be frankfurters and other treats. Obviously, the Old Main steps are like a hundred-foot incline from the street, and then the electric fencing will separate the TestosterZone from the rabble and media and soundboard, so that's a top-notch place to hang out if you want to be on TV. The idea is to create a party atmosphere, according to this other piece of paper, so I'd like everyone to stay as glum as possible. Any questions? If not, please feel sad all day. I have a PhD in Cultural Studies, and won't be making overtime this week, so I know I will."

At the bottom of the sheet, under the heading SPECIAL GUESTS OF **CAA/BIGLY PRODUCTIONS, LLC** —DO NOT ENGAGE THE FOLLOWING WITHOUT MAOI PR STAFF PRESENT:

Belcalis Pulido
Rosie Rafowitz-Fackelmann
Madeline Einstein
Ryan Yoder-Henley

Addison Bockenhauer*
Reid Scheisskopf*
Cassie and Lydia Olerud
Conrad Szymans
Gwendolyn Scheisskopf
Lars Kiffmeyer
Kayden Kiffmeyer
Joe Bob Donglefritz
*Denotes campaign employees

"Dude," Colin Ressler said as the paper twitched, "what the fuck is this?"

I grimaced, or maybe smiled. I touched his lower back.

"Saturday, Colin."

I trudged upstairs to my post with a metallic clanging in my ears.

"MY RECONNAISSANCE SUGGESTS shenanigans are afoot," Coogan said a few minutes later, sputum sprinkling the Formica desk. My brain swished inside my skull like an aquarium fish. The press, mostly national but some local, lollygagged in the lobby, sipping coffee and tweeting pictures of the Chihuly sunburst overhead. Secret Service agents patrolled the perimeter. Men toting large guns flirted with Marketing and PR staff, occasionally rubbing the barrels on non-consenting pencil skirts. My colleagues said nothing. They made more than me, but it still didn't cover their student loans. The 45th President would approve of this. Perhaps he'd even partake in the American frottage. Something about Dignity and Responsibility of the Office. At least the 44th President took the endorsements of rapists with decorum.

Cranial reverb. Roles to play. The idea, I guess, was to present our museum as functioning and apolitical and *not* prone to leftwing agitators or Radical Islamic Terrorism. To counteract the narrative sown by Scheisskopf so that we might . . . not have a narrative sown by Scheisskopf. Public arts funding the carrot, which perhaps made me and my fellow First Responders in the Fight for Western Culture the stick. We were all invited to political theater tonight—*Our American Cousin*—and nobody knew I was John Wilkes Booth.

"See," Coogan continued, "I was here when the actor/president visited, and I was here when the wrestler/governor attended a screening of *Being John Malkovich*."

"You're always here, John."

"Exactly, Jethro, now you are seeing the light! Did you know that the man who devised said film was a former gallery guard, just like you and me? This, of course, long before he transformed into an agent of Disney. This new president, you know, the large real estate fellow given to fits of racial animus and spray-tanning, this man, too, is an agent of Disney."

"That doesn't mean anything."

"It means that I am one sandwich away from blowing this place to smithereens," Coogan said. "A single sandwich. All I need is the word, the sign, and vengeance is mine."

"Mmm." My stomach rumbled.

"Two or more slices of bread, some sort of filling, and I shall unleash the indigenous American Berserk."

I scanned for Schmidt or Nehemiah, glanced at Coogan's instructions. Addy and Reid taunted me from his sheet.

Self-presentation. Marketing and Branding. Addison Valerie Bockenhauer. Mom loved Addy. Probably more than I did. Probably because she didn't actually know Addison Valerie Bockenhauer, only knew she was polite and would listen to farm stories and hymns and that we had bonded over Reid's callousness. Whereas I dreamt of notoriety, Mom dreamt of stability, and so she'd said more than once that I should marry Addy. Only she could fill the empty beaker.

She spent a year at Middlebury while he shot piss and puke and cum all over Dartmouth's frat row. He cheated there, and then back here on Thanksgiving break, winter break, spring break. Addy was miserable out East, but we weren't best friends until she'd transferred to the University of Minnesota and cried over how hurt and embarrassed she was for investing so much in a man, a man with the last name Scheisskopf.

As the Secret Service patted down the journalists and handlers—and the advance team explained that Nehemiah, various curators and I would be accompanying Stephen and the press on a tour of Delacroix one hour before the rally, before he trotted us all out for the firing line and/or stump speech—I remembered that Addy described sex with Reid as a sort of symphony. An addictive crescendo. This before he was alcohol-dependent and I was a junky.

I shuddered. I missed my friends. My fucked-up, pathetic friends. None of us were special. Reid flirted with everybody. Orgasms and money his only interests. Your standard libertarian, I guess, except he bucked the trend by having sex. May-to-August fuckfests while he was home, and then back to Hanover where he dated some Phillips-Exeter-educated sorority sweetheart who *summered* between Paris, Malibu, and the Upper East Side, who knew Rosie Rafowitz-Fackelmann from creative writing camps and Madeline Einstein from unpaid internships. American Aristocracy not so different from the Hapsburgs maybe. How poor and disenfranchised could I be if I at least knew these people, knew enough to repudiate them?

Denotes campaign employee. Jesus fucking Christ. You already know I hate the rich, but I hate people who admire them even more. My supposed allies didn't seek retribution; they sought assimilation. **Denotes campaign employee.** Reid had never worked for anything in his life and carried condescension like a fucking merit badge. Still he was too stupid to see his luck, and how little non-psychopaths cared about money. He had no perspective or principles and never did. So maybe I was the stupid one. Everything is will-to-power.

Addy, too. The more intimate we got, the less I understood her. Joan Didion posters in her apartment. Nonfiction workshops squeezed into her schedule. A minor in English, and yet she took the first job offer that wandered through her inbox, this Public Relations gig from a firm co-founded by her aunt. She graduated early. She'd had options. Rich-enough parents and a flock of Tinder matches. The rare combination of empathy and ambition. This is why Mom loved the idea of Mrs. Addy Glick even when everyone else in my life, Addy included, took me for asexual or gay or Frankenstein's monster.

When had her fucking candle burned out? She wanted to try and fail in New York. She wanted vengeance over the Tom and Daisy Buchanans of Middlebury and Dartmouth. She wanted to show Reid—and the women Reid had fucked and forgotten, and the popular girls who never quite admitted her to the in-group, and probably even me—that she had more to give than sex. More than some vessel for male adoration, some future housewife of Lake Minnetonka who fantasizes about murdering her husband, some stay-at-home vixen who pumps out 2.5 and self-medicates with Ativan and waits around for irreconcilable differences to sprout or else surrenders to Tupperware parties and boxed wine.

They were at the MAOI. I saw her black curls. And Reid's fauxhawk. This was real.

So I hopped the desk as Coogan called out, and trampled through media folks and PR handlers and people telling me to stop, and when I'd sufficiently ignored the shouts and the memorandum instructions and was almost close enough to touch her back as they shuffled around on some lobby group tour, a very strong hand clasped my outstretched forearm and pulled me away before they saw me and led me up a staircase I'd never noticed and threw me into a chair. And before I had registered what was happening, I was in a room with a bunch of soldiers and cops and Finkelfunk and Munklehorton and Cross Yoder-Henley and my old neighbor Mr. Bonser and Stephen Scheisskopf.

"SORRY ABOUT WEDNESDAY morning," Stephen said as I finished signing release forms at gunpoint.

"Thanks," I said, eyeing the mace on Ulysses' duty-belt. "I didn't care for her policies, but I didn't want your guy to win."

"Cut the cute shit, Jude. I'm sorry about your injury. We didn't want it to come to that, but we got tipped off."

"What are you talking about?" Ulysses crossed his arms, didn't lose eye contact. "How could you possibly be behind that?"

"The cup swung my way," Scheisskopf said, strolling under a single light bulb. I felt the presence of everyone else, but they'd faded into the walls. Maybe all the cruelty I'd ever endured, and certainly all the cruelty I was about to endure, came from straight white men. From Boris on down.

"Very funny."

"Cross had been monitoring your social media presence. We learned you had a gig. He called Finkelfunk and Munklehorton for something unrelated, you came up, Cross and I were already trying to produce this rally, and we figured a survival narrative would ice the cake."

"Sure, Steve."

"You know I'm acting, Jude, right?"

"No, I don't."

"You will be too."

"Whatever."

"Whether I believe this stuff or not is irrelevant. We've always wanted the same things, Glick."

I tensed in the chair. If I moved on Steve, they could probably murder me without consequence.

"You are under contract with the network for a reality television show, so there was no way we were gonna let you pivot left. No matter what Ferris wanted. So we all decided to work together. At least until I'm through with you. Just as I promised in Williamsburg."

"Stephen, what are you trying to do here? I don't give a shit what—"

"Oh, you'll be giving a shit shortly," Cross Yoder-Henley said, though I couldn't see him. "You're my property for one live event at least. That's today."

"And I'm at the mixing board!" Mr. Bonser hooted. "Can ya believe it, Julian? We linked up after all! It's like the opposite of your mother's funeral!"

"Lotta surprises in store," Stephen said. I was sweating so much my felt blazer was damp. "Here's the first one."

Someone shoved Lt. Donglefritz under the light. The butt of a rifle poked from the shadows.

"Talk," someone said, jabbing Joe Bob's back.

"Or what?" he said. "I voted for yer guy anyway. We're building a wall and Mexico is gonna—"

"Talk motherfucker," Ulysses said. "Tell his ass what you told me on Thursday."

"Ulysses, look, I said I was a rookie cop with a—"

"Tell J.G. what you did to my cousin. Why we was sitting next to each other at the funeral ten years ago today."

Donglefritz gulped. "You know how I've been, ah, kinda, ah—"

"Don't make me mace you, bitch. We federal now."

"Okay. Fine. I shot Malik. It was me. He was running away and I shot him, and I don't know why. But I did it. I shot your friend and he was muttering Beaker as he died."

I stood up, ignored the shouts to sit down.

"Fuck you," I said. "None of this is true. Stephen makes his own fucking reality and I'm not gonna fall for it. So use me all you want, but I gotta get back to work."

I started in the direction they'd thrown me from. The lights flipped back on. Ulysses cut me off before I got to the door.

"That's real, J.G. And that's just an appetizer. Tic-tac-toe, bruh bruh."

I looked back at Donglefritz. He was covering his face. Stephen shot me with finger guns.

"If you wanna be famous, I can make you famous. With staying

264

power. Real, lasting wealth and celebrity. You'll never have to worry about money again."

"Are you even a person, Steve?"

He laughed at this. Smirked.

"It's gonna be a long four years, Beaker. And an even longer four hours."

AS I STUMBLED down the staircase, shaking my head, Nehemiah and a stable of handlers, police officers, and M-16-carriers slid through the interior doors of our lobby entrance. The throngs hushed. I looked out to Third Avenue, the turnaround where busses usually dumped school groups. A tank idled near the Eros statue as Ressler argued with dudes in military fatigues, imploring them to keep the tank at least arms-length from the art.

I didn't see Addy or Reid. No sign of Leva Bronstein. I took my seat next to Coogan as photographers jostled and snapped. I did not feel like Jude Glick; I was watching a doppelganger on closed-circuit TV.

"I am off before the big show," Coogan said. "I am simply warning you."

"You aren't gonna ask what the fuck just happened to me?"

"I know every raindrop by its name. Yours is Julian and you have been warned."

I gnawed a fingernail, rubbed my face. The election was not only a national tragedy but millions of personal ones, too. Coogan had lost it. Stephen now had the power to play psychosis-inducing mind games on whoever he pleased. My liberalish friends had seen the iceberg up ahead and lowered a fascist lifeboat already.

I flexed a fist, watched my forearms ripple under my sleeves, thought of Mom and waited.

I DON'T KNOW how much time passed, but eventually the press recognized me and started volleying questions. PR staff tried to box them out. Coogan muttered about the Second Coming. Through the mics in my face and shouting police, I kept making out the phrase "Hollywood Squares." This, like everything that had happened since election night, meant nothing to me.

"OKAY, FOLKS, HELLO, my name is Nehemiah Weaver, and I am the security captain overseeing museum operations this afternoon.

I'll be handing you off to our Chief Curator, Dr. Moon, here momentarily, but then we'll all meet up right before the festivities start so you can take your places outside, and those of us participating in the event can find a seat onstage. There are already about ten-thousand people lingering at Washburn Fair Oaks Park, which is, for those who don't know, the Audience Staging Area directly across from the platform on The Cargill Family Commemorative Grand Entrance at Old Main/East 24th Street, or whatever. Ergo, before Mr. Stephen Scheisskopf gives his opening remarks and then the president-elect shares his, um, views on Western Civilization, Minneapolis' multiculturalism, and, I guess, poor people like me and my friend—"

"Jude," Lana Peaslee whispered in my ear as Cross Yoder-Henley, Finklefunk, and Munkelhorton shuffled across the lobby. "Once they get over here there's no turning back. You can still run if you —"

"Deplorable Dave," a pant-suited woman yelled, "you'll be coming with me. Your partner will man the desk until showtime."

I didn't stand up. A flurry of flashes and ripple of giddiness suggested Scheisskopf had just entered the room.

"Run," Lana said as her boss, various MAOI staff, and a Secret Service agent reached the desk. A panic attack percolated in my chest.

"Up," Cross said. "Let's go."

"What if I don't?"

"We'll sue you. And we won't settle. And who knows what Stephen will—"

Somebody bumped into Cross, slamming his knees into the desk. More commotion. Coogan yelling. People pushing, shoving, cursing. Either network security or Homeland Security hooked my elbows and jerked me upright. Two hands in the back sent me toward the pant-suited woman calling me Deplorable Dave. Behind me somewhere, Cross was still arguing.

I turned around: Leva Bronstein.

She didn't look much like Schmidt. Pink pompadour, septum piercing, eyeliner and clear skin. I'd never seen Schmidt with makeup. Same uniform as the rest of us.

"But I'm supposed to train with him! State law!"

"Jesus fucking Christ," Yoder-Henley said. I swam against the crowd as staffers grasped after me. Schmidt and a Secret Service agent were up in each other's faces.

"Scheisskopf? I don't know who that is. It's not my fucking fault this is my first day. I'm a goddamn temp guard. Gimme a break. Just let me train! I'm off at 3:00 like that guy at the desk."

A stiff-arm redirected me. The press shuffled in one group with Nehemiah. The campaign staff—Addy's head? Reid's watch?— moved in another with the Chief Curator and Director. And then the rest of us. The propaganda dregs: MAOI PR, producers and gaffers and writers and Cross and Ferris and E. Horton Munkelhorton and, finally, Leva Bronstein, the new girl.

"Where are they taking us?" I asked, gripping her forearm. We were making our way through the museum like a giant, roving mosh pit.

Schmidt might've answered, but we got separated. A cop's belly rear-ended me.

And as we passed the classrooms that line the first level, on our way to the Otis elevator, I thought I saw Tom and Chris reclining in wheelchairs, but I'll never be sure.

"SO THE SITE of near-unspeakable American Carnage was over here," Scheisskopf hollered to the press pool an hour later. We were standing in the final gallery and the adjoining Delacroix gift shop, directly above where the truck had crashed two months ago. While Scheisskopf spouted his propaganda, and the free press normalized it, I just stared at my favorite painting: Hamlet watching as the Gravedigger exhumed Yorick. Trying to stay buried myself. Keep it all underground. But I'd failed at that, too. I'd been repeatedly photographed lurking behind pillars while future cabinet members and famous politicos pretended to give a shit about the Pietà that inspired Van Gogh. "Just below us, Radical Islamic Terrorists tried to destroy a bastion of Western Values. But as you'll see in about fifteen minutes, and the president-elect's remarks soon after, the real tragedy was not under our feet, but under our noses all along: sandwiched between globalist Democrats and Republicans on the one side, and the disintegration of our heritage and very fine people on the other. And the man who represents our coming resurgence is right there!"

He pointed at me. Cameras flashed. Oohs and aahs. I looked for Addy, for Schmidt, for anyone who might offer counterprogramming to suicide ideation. Reporters and photographers trampled toward me and Mom's rosary beads, boom microphones and shouted questions and static electricity down all of our spines because they weren't excited to see me, there would be plenty of me later, they were convulsing because the president-elect had poked his head in, on cue, and then slouched toward some militarized holding pen.

Nehemiah, then the pantsuit woman, then a Secret Service agent shouted directions over the clamor. As the crowd jostled closer to the president-elect, who was absolutely long gone until he would appear on stage, a guy with a *New York Times* podcast smushed me into a wall, pinning my right shoulder to a fire extinguisher while various important white people throttled and hammered my left.

Just as the fat cop fired a blank into the ceiling, and everybody shut up, someone banged against my free shoulder, fell in front of me, and stuffed something in my right sock.

I gulped. Dry mouth. Sandpaper. Cheeks tasted like biting into wax.

No sign of Schmidt. She had disappeared. I feigned normalcy, pretended my heart wasn't beating like a meth-smoking metronome, but my shirts were sweat-drenched and squishy. The press hubbub dying down as their gaggle turned orderly and severe, my thoughts floated, peripheral, a lava lamp as the Secret Service arranged us like furniture. A SWAT team materialized to lead me, Nehemiah, and the rest of Terror Defeating Gallery Guards stageward. This was happening fast. Too fast. Which is what they wanted, needed, so if shenanigans were afoot, any inside actors would need to audible.

Where was Schmidt? Had they found her out?

The eight of us who were supposed to be on duty the morning Mom died, including me, followed a man in tactical gear. Single file. At rifle-point. Out of 24.8, the gift shop, up through 24, then over through 23 where they keep the Islamic art, and finally to the Oedipus Rex statue just outside Old Main's external doors.

"Which one is Jude Glick?" the leader barked.

My throat was too sore, my back too spasmy, to answer.

"The anthem starts in sixty seconds. The guests are already in their squares. So where is Scheisskopf's toy?"

U-S-A chants rumbled beyond the giant oak doors. Nehemiah yelled something about being the Shift Captain, and needing to quickly talk to Sandy, the legally stationed exit guard. I glanced to the third-level, where we'd fought the fascists. The ceiling was breathing.

It bulged and receded.

The military guys mumbled into radios, shouted code-numbers, then waved Nehemiah toward Sandy and the entrance. I was in the middle of the line, Damone Heffelfinger ahead and Colin Ressler behind. I closed my eyes, finally understanding what *sensory overload* means. As I opened them, Nehemiah brushed by us, SWAT guy at his elbow, and either mouthed or whispered the word, "Braille."

Mom never taught me braille. This never bothered me. I never taught her nihilism (though of course I tried). But now, I saw the selfishness. I never tried; she always did. So, in the last few weeks, I'd worked on the alphabet, had grinded my way toward comprehension. Read some Bible verses, stumbled through the Dr. Seuss books she'd had dictated to her by friends and then subtitled with bumps on the page.

I squatted as though stretching my thighs and back, rubbed two fingers along the quarter-cut silk sock sprouting from my right Kmart dress shoe.

Through the fabric, I made out the letters, muttered the sequence, assembled the message, and popped back up before the security forces could raise hell.

"I'm Jude Glick," I called out. The chanting transformed to a roar.

Two syllables now. A bass drum pounding the rhythm.

SCHEISS-KOPF! SCHEISS-KOPF! SCHEISS-KOPF!

"Glick?" the head honcho hollered. "Over here, guy."

Two men ushered me past Heffelfinger and the others. Then they yanked Nehemiah to the back of the line. Sandy looked no more present than the Oedipus statue.

"What's in your sock?" the soldier yelled.

I shrugged. Mr. Bonser's voice came over the PA, asked folks to remove their hats.

"What's in the fucking sock?"

"Pez dispenser."

"Pez dispenser?"

"A special WW2 version. German, if you catch my drift." I winked at his shiny head.

"We gotta go, Reinhold!" shouted another jackboot.

"Whatever. Showtime, fuckhead," the commander bellowed as the crowd stomped and clapped. Men in black suits tugged at the two-story doors. They lurched open with a groan. Just as the unseasonably warm air puffed me backwards, just as the flash of cameras and stage lights blinded me, just as the leader shoved me toward the blast of noise and nerves outside, I swung my head back toward Nehemiah, and mouthed the braille:

"Luke 22:44."

As they escorted me to my seat—a bar stool maybe ten feet from the lectern to the left, and a yard from Scheisskopf's La-Z-Boy to my right—I shut my eyes through the anthem and imagined I wasn't there. I thought of Mom and our tiny backyard and the wood-splintered swinging bench, and her voice, that beautiful voice I'd never hear again, the voice she used only in church or when one of her boys was crying. I saw her with a scraped face and a black eye, bills littering the kitchen, swaying back and forth softly as I lay across her lap.

But as the locked-out orchestra swelled and the off-key singing crescendoed, I opened my eyes, certain I was now on television and needing to appear composed. So as thousands of people mumbled or screeched the last stanza, I leaned on something of my own.

And in His anguish, He prayed more earnestly, and His sweat became like drops of blood falling to the ground.

MR. BONSER, WHO had done voiceover work for video games and maybe fucked Sheila E, asked us to please be seated. I plopped into the stool, my bad right knee at Scheisskopf's nipple-level. His hand fluttered above my thigh, crashed down, and clamped me. I looked at him. Mr. Bonser kept talking. Scheisskopf smiled with a blood-soaked dentist's serenity. The hand moseyed to my kneecap. He squeezed harder, wiggled it. This hurt a great deal. He had placed me to his left because I could not see out of my right eye. I understood this as he let go with a tut-tut.

Stage-left, far end of the platform, the seven other guards melted into an L-shaped sectional. Behind that, a large box or cage was covered with a tarp. Below us, on East 24th Street, hundreds of people— sandwiched between barbed-wire fencing, between the museum/stage and the thousands in the park—teetered from food truck to food truck. The TestosterZone. A Wienermobile sat at the east end of the street, to my far-right, below a speaker-stack and a probable video-screen. Thin crowd over there. So much for photo ops; with few MAOI employees, the true believers in this freak show would have to do.

I squinted with my non-prescription glasses through the blaring sun and lights. I thought I saw John Coogan, hanging back next to MPD officers near press row. I wondered if Donglefritz was still here. Same with the Oscar Meyer guy whose Wienermobile got toppled the day Mom died.

I knew there was an emergency exit somewhere behind me. Scheisskopf must've used it. Maybe the president-elect. The scene reminded me of Woodstock. Except, here, you could make out snipers in the trees.

I rebooted when Scheisskopf called out: "Hello Minneapolis!" I'd never done a full arena show, but I had opened or featured for big-draw comics. First Avenue the biggest, but a few-hundred pretty standard. There's that trite bullshit about picturing everybody in their underwear, or pretending it's just you and a friend, but that's impossible. Something this big is out-of-body. All lizard-brain and muscle-memory.

Scheisskopf would be too disoriented to defend himself.

Sweat lathered my right ankle and the Ortgies 7.65. I opted for no show of emotion and, instead, wondered if they knew we'd fought in high school.

"We are fighting a battle for Western Civilization against those who wish to tear this Christian nation apart. So say it with me now: *THE AMERICAN CARNAGE IS OVER!*"

Shades of Nuremberg. Lots of red hats and Confederate Flags. I looked for Addy and Reid as Scheisskopf droned about how Our Way of Life Is Under Attack! and how America Is Going To Be Great Again! We had all heard this speech before, and still the crowd whooped-and-hollered, each line a new buzzer-beater to celebrate.

I did not know what to do with my hands, or where to look. The sun dimmed a bit. I realized my trouble making out details had less to do with my uncorrected vision and more to do with bulletproof glass rimming the stage.

". . . which leads me to the reason we are here today, Minnesota! You are not forgotten, just as the brave folks who stood strong in the face of terror will never be forgotten! Give it up for the seven people who are passionately in love with . . . America!"

Scheisskopf gestured to his left, to Nehemiah and the gang. Between outbursts of the Rebel Yell, he listed their names. More captives set for execution than special guests of the president-elect.

I rubbed my throat and tried not to gawk at the crowd. Behind the waving gallery guards, the tarp covering that big blob billowed. The overhead lights faded. A spotlight swooped onto me. Stephen grinned from the lectern.

"We thank these patriots for courageously fighting Radical Islamists. But maybe the more *pressing* matter tonight is someone who is a recent addition to our movement. A gallery guard, yes, but also a soldier in the trenches of our War on Globalism, Elitism, and Washington Swampism! Some may know him as Deplorable Dave, but ladies and gentlemen, please join me in welcoming my dear friend, Jude Glick!"

Explosive applause. A shiver down my arms. My face on network TV, cable news, public broadcasting, and clip shows. The *Famous Alumni* Wikipedia page for our high school updated with a new name.

They kept clapping and screaming. Toward the edge of the stage, I saw myself smiling on a monitor. In the far corner of the screen, Yoder-Henley and Finkelfunk and Munklehorton whispered to each other.

"But as I first mentioned on our historic Wednesday morning, J.G. has a number of secrets. Would you like to explore some of them with me?"

YES they screamed in unison.

"Are you sure?"

YES. YES. YES.

"So, Jude," Scheisskopf said, looking at me, "would you allow us to learn a little about you, and a little about America, and maybe even make some money in the process? In the name of restoration?"

I felt 20,000 people hitch like a bad knee. Millions of television sets fell on my head. I gulped, glanced to the wings for someone, anyone, to give me direction. The Ortgies slid down my sock. This is what Lana Peaslee had warned me about.

On the monitor, Yoder-Henley started arguing with Ferris and Horton.

"Jude?" Stephen said. The crowd tittered. "Will you help *us* help *you*? Will you use this platform to not only benefit yourself, but to benefit our Blood and Soil?"

I nodded.

Whoops, chants, waving flags.

"Perfect," said Scheisskopf, "for the sake of our country and movement, let's get started. Many of you learned of Deplorable

Dave from our campaign, or, more likely, the internet—our great democratizer! But what you may not know about Deplorable Dave, and thus might not know about Jude Glick, is that he isn't a victim of American Carnage so much as a selfish, stupid liberal snowflake. So let's teach him a lesson, shall we?"

Twenty thousand people booed me. I felt it through the barstool. Tomatoes smashed into the plexiglass, which wasn't up for Scheisskopf, or maybe even the president-elect. It was up for me.

I offered a low-wave, gnashed my teeth together. The booing rumbled with a freight train's indifference. Scheisskopf, after either seconds or eons, asked them to stop.

But they wouldn't. He'd set them off.

Fuck your feelings! Fuck your feelings!
Lock him up! Lock him up!

I couldn't make out the individual voices, but it was clear enough: they hated anyone who didn't look like them and think like them. Whether they were plumbers or used car dealers or opiate addicts or my relatives didn't matter. They were here because they weren't non-progressive or non-multicultural; they—like their candidate and the moral ciphers who pimped him on TV—were anti. Anti-progress. Anti-diversity. Antediluvian.

"J.G. is not like his fellow guards. He was on the schedule, but spent the morning heroically feeding his painkiller addiction while his mother died. So please, once again, give it up for a man who is not a friend of the people, but who is in fact an enemy of the state, Mr. Julian 'J.G.' Glick."

They lit into me again. The pistol grip felt hot against my skin. Spotlight still burning, Scheisskopf produced a conducting baton and started waving it toward the couch on our left.

"And since the liberals and Democrats and other cowards with whom J.G. associates viewed this election as a game, and viewed us as a Basket of Deplorables, I say we give them what they want! Are you with me?"

As they cheered, some stagehands yanked the tarp off the blob. Beneath it was a giant square, 3x3, each unit the size of a living room with couches and recliners and desks. And inside these three-sided rooms?

Special guests.

In the center, the free space, Reid and Addy bowed. Cameras panning over the board, I turned around and puked, making eye

273

contact with Cross Yoder-Henley.

He shot me two exaggerated thumbs-up. Because the board looked like this:

Belcalis Pulido Rosie Rafowitz- Fackelmann	Madeline Einstein	Ryan Yoder-Henley
Lars Kiffmeyer Kayden Kiffmeyer	Reid Scheisskopf Addison Bockenhauer	Pastor Phil
Aunt Lydia Cousin Cassie	Gwendolyn Scheisskopf	Dr. Nehemiah Weaver

Mom loved *Hollywood Squares*. She'd been a contestant. Sometime pre-Boris, she'd won a sailboat but couldn't afford the taxes so never claimed it.

Stephen outlined the rules for the audience, but I didn't need to listen. Not that I could over the splashing fruit and hate.

Tic-tac-toe. Contestants take turns and select a square. Then Stephen lobs questions to my friends or relatives in the corresponding space. Answer provided by the friends/relatives, the contestants (i.e., me if it was my turn, or my opponent if theirs) can either agree or disagree with the supplied answer. Correctly agreeing or disagreeing with an answer captured the square. If the contestant failed to agree or disagree correctly, the square went to his/her opponent.

White people loved this shit.

The crowd would play the X, and I would play the O. Scheisskopf, as if it needed to be explained, made sure I knew the woman historically played the O (and that the first black president's last named had started with it). First to three-in-a-row won. I'd go first. Audience participation would decide if an answer was correct or not.

"If the Chosen People, the folks who rose up against everything Glick and his liberal ilk believe in, are again victorious, we will prosecute J.G. on day one of our administration for providing material support to terrorist organizations—We have video footage of him at two separate Black Lives Matter rallies!—and we'll make it so he can't show his scummy, disfigured face on another comedy stage as long as he lives," Scheisskopf said as the hordes nearly drowned him out. "But if J.G. wins, if for the first time in his life he does something right and noble? If he beats his nature and isn't a loser? Well, we'll compromise. He'll still be prosecuted and he'll still be *persona non grata*, because we are both a nation of laws and a nation of values, but the president-elect will indeed take care of his ill brothers and the debts his mother incurred. Even Jude, in his despicable way, is a victim, too. Almost."

I upchucked again.

Suicides keep rising, I thought as the gun hugged my ankle. Maybe a public self-execution would be enough. What, other than some face-saving commitment to Mom's strength, had kept me alive this long anyway? If Stephen really had tried to murder me because of what I did to Halfway House Hess, I didn't owe him an assassination; I owed him another thank you note.

As he babbled and the spotlight hung on the square, Lana Peaslee and a stagehand dashed over with a Lav mic.

"I prefer standup mics," I said as they clipped it on my lapel. "This is just another indignity."

"I tried to help you," she whispered, jamming an in-ear monitor at my head. "You can't say we didn't try to help you."

"Why have you been so nice to me?" I craned my neck, forced eye contact with her boyfriend. He was wearing a cast on his right leg. Reid rocked a neckbrace.

"Sometimes people are just nice, Jude. If you hadn't been such an asshole to Ryan, he might not be up there right now. Believe me, I tried to talk him out of it. So did your old friend Ignacio."

"I didn't snap Ryan's shin. Scheisskopf's cops did."

"Yeah, whatever."

"What does it say about you if you work for fascists?"

"You're the one onstage. You're a literal opener for someone who's endorsed immigrant concentration camps. 'They bring drugs, they bring crime, they're rapists.' Remember?"

"What's about to happen?"

Her assistant tapped his watch. They checked the levels on some device, radioed someone—maybe Mr. Bonser—and tugged at the lavalier one more time. Meme-me (i.e., Deplorable Dave staring at an antifa ass) lit up the monitor. Then they showed my mugshot. "Don't do anything, Jude. Endure the next hour. The questions and answers are mostly bullshit. He wrote them ahead of time. It's all a stunt and everyone up there was paid to do it, okay? He's just trying to provoke you. Opinion will turn."

"Wait, Lana, what are you saying?"

Raised eyebrows, cocked head. "The less you know, the better. Cross and Ferris and Horton and Stephen are fucking psychopaths. That's why they're rich and powerful."

I WHITE-KNUCKLED through most of it. Literally. Fists so tight my hands are still sore.

It started with the rallygoers, based on Applause-O-Meter, selecting the top left corner: Belcalis and Rosie. Scheisskopf, strutting and preening with his conducting baton, started the onslaught:

"Folks, say hello to these lovely ladies. Rosie Rafowitz-Fackelmann and Belcalis Pulido!"

Hi, Rosie. Hi, Cialis.

"Rosie, how do you know Public Enemy Number One?"

"We went to college together," she snarled, looking in my direction, "where he was a mopey little creep."

"How so, dear?"

"He thinks everything is a joke. He's only happy if other people are miserable. He's such a cynical a-hole that I can't even look at him."

Cheers. Boos. More tomatoes. Vaudeville. The hook? An antique pistol waiting for Scheisskopf to step within assassination range.

"And you, Belcalis?"

She glanced at notes on the desk. Below me, John Coogan, the only guard left in the TestosterZone, ordered a hotdog from the Wienermobile. The photo op had failed; none of my coworkers wanted anything to do with Making Fascism Look Fun Again. Only cops, cameras, and Coogan remained.

"Over here, Stephen," I mumbled as he drifted closer to the squares. "Over here so I can kill you." No sound through the in-ear monitor. They must have planned for my disobedience.

"I, like, kinda knew him from college?" Belcalis said. "But only because he wouldn't shut the F up in his classes and always made everything about him. With his dumb politics and his self-righteous attitude. And, like, more than anything?" She glanced my direction then stared at the desk. "His friggin' elitism. He was always, like, so obsessed with being from the Midwest or working class or whatever, but I never saw him care about . . .whatever it is this crowd here cares about."

"What should happen to him, girls?"

My neck hurt from straining, but they definitely looked at each other.

"Um."

"Well, that's fine," Stephen blurted, fumbling his notecards. "Leave that to me. Are you ready for your question? Yes? Okay. Rosie and Belcalis: Did J.G.—like so many liberals and Democrats and antifa terrorists—become an indoctrinated stooge in college? Bear in mind that his mother voted for Law and Order, Blood and Soil, and that he tried, and failed, to move to New York City."

They bit lips, twirled hair.

"Indoctrinated?" Rosie said, with a wobble in her voice. "No, not really."

The crowd hushed. Stephen drifted closer to the squares.

"I'm sorry?" he said.

"He wasn't indoctrinated. False."

Discomfort. No cheers, just talking. My eyebrows hurdled in fake astonishment. I turned my head to and fro for the cameras, hands clutching the sides of my head like *The Scream*.

"Folks, before we test their answer with the Applause-O-Meter, bear in mind that Rosie is a creative writer who—"

"No, I'm not. I'm a copywriter."

"Well, I—"

"Jude considers himself some tortured genius and he's a crappy listener, but he isn't a bad guy. He's an independent thinker. He's on the right side of stuff."

"He isn't like you," Belcalis said.

Twenty thousand white supremacists and soccer moms devolved into awkward silence. I stared at Stephen. He grimaced for a half-second. I don't think I'd seen him rattled since I roasted him in high school.

"The lady doth protest too much, methinks," he blathered, "or maybe meme-thinks. Get it? Get it, folks? Because J.G. is a meme? Not, um, a meme for our movement, of course, but a meme for everything our movement is not. So . . . so, right, the girls have answered 'No' and now, ladies and gents, it's your turn to vote on whether they're being honest or not. True or false?"

The screens must have lit up, but my monitor went blank.

True! True! True!

"Correct, folks, Jude was, in fact, indoctrinated into liberal authoritarianism."

Lock him up! Lock him up!

"We *will* lock him up, folks, on January 20th, but he's still got a chance to save his brothers, as we mentioned. After their drunk driving accident, they have extensive medical bills. Thanks, O-BongoCare! Unless, Julian, you are too cowardly to help your family?"

I flashed my hands in confusion and peeked at the microphone on my sweat-soaked jacket. My ass hurt from sitting on the stool.

"Boo-hoo," Scheisskopf said to a mix of laughter and tomato smashes, "the standup comedian is too afraid to talk. Or to help. Story of his life. What are we going to—"

"I'll take the bottom right corner," I said to millions of people. "With Nehemiah. The only black guy on the far-right in the whole country."

Eruption. Beer bottles, water balloons, rotten fruit. A moldy banana made it over the plexiglass and landed between me and Scheisskopf.

"Please refrain from throwing objects at the stage," Mr. Bonser said over the PA as the booing and lobbing increased. Much of it bounced off the barriers or fell short, pelting the TestosterZone.

"C'mon, folks. Behave! Let's get on with the rally! Don't you wanna see the president-elect?" Scheisskopf pleaded.

I shook my head. This was, perhaps, unwise. Several chicken nuggets skipped toward my stool. More near misses. A real violence in the air now. Confederate flags whipped like wind-torn sails. Some eggs splattered onstage. This continued until the cops and Secret Service started ejecting people. After more hectoring from Scheisskopf and Mr. Bonser, and a few seconds of the *Jeopardy!* theme song, they regained control.

"On with the show," Scheisskopf said. "J.G. has selected the bottom right corner. He has always been a bottom."

"For those playing at home," I said, "Stephen just made a gay joke in 2016. I guess he's stuck in the 90s. He hasn't grown since then either. Physically or emotionally."

Too loud and I could hardly see, but I thought Nehemiah chuckled.

Scheisskopf didn't. "Cut his microphone. We don't need the Fake News media running soundbites from a brainless sociopath."

"Don't talk about your candidate that way," I said.

This was poorly received. Someone shot a flare toward the stage. Now the Secret Service made an announcement, but I couldn't hear it. Below, in the TestosterZone, Coogan was wearing a hotdog costume. He was covered in fruit and beer.

For the first time, I wondered if Scheisskopf was bluffing. Could they actually have me arrested? For what? Being . . . somewhere politically controversial? Staring at someone's ass? Choking out a guy with an AirSoft gun? I'd been funny so far. Maybe Peaslee had a point. Who needs terrorism when I could out-charm him.

I started riffing. But they'd cut my mic.

Stephen strutted to the cubes, pointed at Nehemiah.

"What's your name, sir, and how do you know our loudmouthed liberal caricature?"

"My name is Dr. Nehemiah Weaver. I taught J.G. in college and, as you can see from my absence on the casting couch, I also work at the museum."

"And so you know that, like so many phony, lazy progressives who voted against this movement, J.G. missed his shift on the day this museum was attacked by Muslim Terrorists *and* that he is an Anti-American leftist? As the meme—which caught the internet by storm, mind you—proves?"

Nehemiah sighed. "Is that my question, or are you just Projecting Your Fears Again?"

"I'll take that as a yes."

"But—"

"Okay, so would you care to explain what brings you here today?"

"Other than the fact that Jude is under contract with a network and you're exploiting him? Well, you're also paying each person in these cubes ten thousand dollars to aid-and-abet your propaganda campaign."

Bananas smashed against the glass. Nehemiah dug in his back pocket, produced an afro pick, and jammed it in his hair.

Stephen turned to the crowd. "A bit uppity, isn't he?"

"Racist-ass, Nazi-loving motherfucker," Nehemiah said.

"Now, no need for that sort of—"

"You wanna know why I'm here, Stephen? Really? Because I love J.G. and didn't want him to suffer alone. Like you and your family did to his buddy Malik."

"Malik?" To my far right, I noticed Ulysses for the first time. He stood with the soldiers and agents who'd ushered us onstage. He muttered something to a man in black, who nodded and raised his lips to a walkie-talkie.

"Don't play dumb, Steve-O. It was your parents who threw Malik's ass to the wolves when they were done playing White Savior. For your mom's state senate run. Jude and his mom took him in and he messed up a bit, maybe, or didn't know what he wanted, but it was you and your parents who made Malik homeless. And that's why he died. Not Jude. You, Stephen. You and your white supremacist bullshit. And you wanna know how I know all this? Huh? Because I'm pretty sure I was Malik's absentee father."

My jaw dropped. No aversion to cliché could prevent this.

Nehemiah stood up and flipped his desk. Ulysses and the muscle stepped a bit closer.

"Please ignore the ravings of what is clearly another brainwashed Black Lives Matter—"

"Because white men can't police their imagination, black men are dying, Stephen. And y'all are complicit. Every white person in the whole fucking country is. And maybe I had drug issues and problems accepting myself for who I am, and maybe I fucked around too much and even sold coke to pregnant women or took sex for payment, or all sorts of shit I don't even remember doing in the early 1990s, but I never rode with a fascist. And Jude didn't either, and I'm glad he didn't. I'm glad we got up on this stage to—"

"Ladies and gentleman," Stephen said, turning his back to Nehemiah, "I'm sorry but because of non-compliance—a real shocker from a *homie* like Nehemiah—we are going to cancel this portion of the program. But before we do, I have some closing thoughts."

Nehemiah kept yelling, but they'd cut his mic.

Stephen was distracted. The goons were still twenty feet away from me. This was it.

"This game show was a nice idea," Stephen started, tossing his notecards back at Nehemiah and walking toward the lectern. Toward me. "But the real reason we wanted Jude the Obscure to show his face today is because we pity him, don't we, folks? Don't we pity him? I thought so. I thought so. Jude is a victim of what Democrats and multiculturalism will get you. Of choices someone in The Swamp made for him, but mostly choices he made for himself. The secret to my friend here, the secret to the crime and the gangs and the drugs that have stolen too many lives and robbed our country of so much unrealized potential, like my friend Malik, is that Jude is a coward. And a faggot."

My left knee started bobbing. I felt the gun stick to my skin. Boos rained. The setting sun breathed and receded. Behind me, Secret Service agents shouted across the stage. I cocked my head, looked left as Stephen reached the podium and turned off his lav mic. Addy, Reid, and Madeline Einstein stood gapemouthed as cops and soldiers wrestled Nehemiah to the ground. Gwendolyn Scheisskopf was crying. Someone tomahawked Colin Ressler with a nightstick, launching blood and brains to the yellow sectional. Reid said either "What the fuck?" or "Why the fuck?" over and over again like a malfunctioning pull-toy.

"People like Jude are the reason Malik Fleming became American Carnage. And the reason Jude's brothers became a skidmark on Mainstreet. And the reason deranged homeless slit throats in the snow. But the worst part, folks, is that he appropriates hard-working but left-behind people like you! And he gives you a bad name while his mother wasted away and died without a proper burial or funeral! But can we blame Jude? Can we really?"

YES WE CAN! YES WE CAN! YES WE CAN!

He was just a few feet away from me. I could get a couple shots off.

"I thought so," he said, pulling something from his suitcoat. "And you know why we can blame him? Because he didn't vote for the soon-to-be 45th President of the United States. But you know who did? His mother."

The crowd exploded in ecstasy. My internal monologue was a radio with weak reception.

"It's true. Yes," Scheisskopf shouted. "That's the real reason Jude is here today. While he threw his culture and history under the bus, his mother voted for the one man brave enough to put a stop to the illegals streaming over the border! Brave enough to stop the senseless genocide of our values and families! Brave enough to secure the existence of our people and a future for our children! His mother voted for the one man who opposes American Carnage!"

He tossed crumpled paper at me. An envelope. The foreclosed house's address. Mom's name. Inside an absentee ballot. Signed by her. And a notary public:

Reid Scheisskopf.

She'd voted for *Him*. She really had. My mother had voted for the avatar of everything wrong with America. Everything antithetical to the rosary she prayed over and the love she gave me and my brothers. She'd endorsed a man who hated everything about Nala and Malik and Nehemiah and even me. She'd been a hypocrite and a fraud just like the game show host psychopath who earned her vote.

My heart para-diddled. My lungs filled with grime. My throat and stomach overflowed with wet leaves. I found my right hand trembling over my soaking right sock.

This was it.

"We will close this chapter of American life and welcome in the next one, one authored by the 45th President of the United States. A man who will not stand for blaming the system when you, yourself, allow the system to punch you. We punch back, folks. We. Don't. Get. Punched. Because . . . Because . . ."

Scheisskopf let the thought linger as my fingers quivered, trying to secure the pistol. A grinding sound quaked both behind me and in front of me. My hands shook like a suspensionless pickup truck. The stage felt loose. My thoughts churned inside a snow globe.

LOCK HIM UP! LOCK HIM UP!

"Because . . . because they are all liars and vagrants, and we're cleaning house," Scheisskopf screamed. "Because we need to be less like Jude and his orgy of queers and leftists and freaks, and more like his loving Christian mother."

I finally pried the pistol from my sock and wriggled to a half-crouch, leaning against the stool. The crowd shrieked with energy. Scheisskopf swung his arm toward Old Main where I assumed the president-elect was making a grand entrance.

"No more suffering like his dear departed mother suffered. And there is one man to thank for this, folks. One man with the audacity to say 'Nope!' One man with the intelligence and compassion to be a voice for the voiceless Silent Majority. So without further ado, please welcome the President-elect of the United States!"

The gun was at my side. I glanced toward Ulysses one last time.

He and the goons were distracted by 45's entrance. I slipped my finger around the trigger and started to raise the gun toward Scheisskopf's head when he lurched toward the crowd, suddenly, like a hunting dog.

Sprouting from the Old Main steps, just above the street, a purple tube the size of a canoe appeared. I lowered the gun because I knew this feeling. The moments before a fight, or before a car wreck, when you sensed everything before it happened.

Like a clown car, several figures dressed in all black tumbled out of the purple structure. I was still standing with the gun in my hand. Scheisskopf's right arm still stretched like *Citizen Kane*. The heavy doors moaned, and in my peripheral vision I could see the president-elect's shadow, his orange head. In slow-motion, I squinted at Addy, who was now pointing toward the street. And I looked there next, just as the antifascists cocked their weapons.

Schmidt produced a megaphone and screeched: "Sic semper tyrannis."

Then total chaos. Squirts of lube, slingshots of dental dams, catapulted Fleshlights. The fucking and the fucked. Anal beads whipped like nunchucks. A downpour of sex toys. They cascaded like rubber snowflakes.

A break in the pattern stage-right, toward the amps and screens and Wienermobile, snapped me back into my body. The dildos kept pelting the glass, a few made it over and fell near me and Scheisskopf, maybe even the president-elect, but it was something else, something cylindrical, something somehow weirder in the seconds before machine-gun fire mowed down Schmidt and her martyrs that changed my mind about who to kill.

In a big, lazy loop, just like the pop-ups Boris would throw when we still lived together, something small and sienna and even more phallic floated toward Stephen. We followed the arc. End-over-end it kept rising and flipping forever until it deployed a parachute and drifted. Swaying and rocking and gliding until it slipped over the plexiglass and came right for us and bonked Scheisskopf on the lips.

I heard radio chatter. A pressure change. Guns drawn. I turned toward Old Main with a stutter-step as Stephen dabbed at his face and leaned into the microphone.

"Was that . . . was that a hotdog?"

It *was* a hotdog. The bun plunked to Scheisskopf's shoe; the wiener rolled to a rest between us. I remember we made eye contact. I remember blinking. I remember my stomach growling. And I remember the screams and gunfire as I felt agency for the first time in my life.

Tear gas. Flashbangs. Muffled fighting for the soundboard. Multi-pronged attack. Distractions. A mass of soldiers and cops descended on Schmidt and her cronies.

The fucking and the fucked.

So fuck Stephen Scheisskopf. Mom hadn't voted for Stephen Scheisskopf, I thought, turning toward the president-elect. Stephen Scheisskopf was nothing without the man stepping onstage. Fuck Scheisskopf and Addy and Reid and anyone else who gave these fascists cover. Fuck suburban voters and white moderates and All Lives Matter dullards. Fuck the market. Fuck civility. Fuck *a rising tide lifts all boats* when black men get murdered by cops and I buy my prescription drugs from Canada. Fuck the Acela corridor and graduate school and well-educated liberals who don't know any poor people or how shitty this country has always been. Fuck 'em. Fuck 'em. Fuck the War in Iraq and the last five presidents and anyone who's ever enjoyed *The West Wing*. Fuck me and fuck you and fuck the tribalism and confidence of the human race. If we couldn't beat the most venal and corrupt people in America, then maybe we're getting the apocalypse we deserve. Maybe white people fucked over minorities again because the only thing white people are good for is fucking over minorities. Maybe we were asking the wrong questions and providing the wrong answers. Maybe we're all fucked from the start. So fuck 'em. Fuck 'em. If we weren't going to fight stupid with solidarity, then maybe we needed to fight stupid with stupid. Maybe we should've fought jokes with jokes. Maybe Mom was as backwards and hopeless as the entire white working class because she was cut from the same white supremacist cloth. Maybe if you're only nonracist, you're just racist. Maybe we'd been amused to death and complicity. And maybe the only thing that could trump this reality TV show of suffering was my radicalized nutsack.

Here we go. I dropped-trou like a toddler at a urinal, pants billowing at my ankles, ass to the audience, testicles swaying in the white light and white heat, and I ripped the pistol from my side and raised my right arm while the sex toys and bullets jousted in the air—Scheisskopf shielding himself from the dildo onslaught—and I took a breath and swung my package forward and bounded once, twice, a third time for the president-elect's yellow hair, gun trained on his jowls, scrotum flapping in the breeze for my Teabag Party. And just as I left my feet and the skin of my balls grazed his mouth then his nose, time froze and my genitalia hung on the 45th President's face, and I heard a voice, baritone and angry.

"A hotdog," John Coogan boomed over the public address system, "is a sandwich."

And then the bomb went off.

12.

THE LOSER

"WHAT SHALL WE use," I slurred from the podium at Malik's funeral, "to fill the empty spaces, where waves of hunger roar? Shall we set out across the sea of faces, in search of more and more applause?"

The parishioners scratched themselves and whispered.

"Malik would want us to . . . enjoy this day as best we could. He wouldn't want us to feel empty," I said, my face exploding into a hot and snotty mess. "God, I feel so empty. I miss you every second. I'm sorry, Malik. I love you."

Someone helped me back to the pew where I ripped Wild Turkey from Reid's flask.

The objective was to die. We already couldn't stand. Stephen absent, Mom too devastated to either notice or counter the echoes of Boris, Malik's half-brother Martell weaved through the mourners and volunteered two 50mg Demerol pills.

"To straighten out," he said.

I'd been hysterical since we got the news. Alternating bouts of sobbing and giggling. Even if everybody insisted it wasn't my fault, I knew they were wrong. I knew I'd never forgive myself. I knew the guilt would gnaw at me forever, and that I'd waste a lifetime scavenging for scraps of relief. The hole had been dug with childhood cancer, deepened through Boris and bullying and poverty, but Malik's death stripped me of the tools and strength that might have covered up the void.

And, once Mom died, I'd been kicked into the pit. And I never stopped falling.

But there might've been hope in that church. A way to pour concrete into the gashes and caverns and bring me back to level ground. Life didn't need to be so hollow, maybe. I didn't need to be so hollow.

Old ladies shook their heads at us. Tom and Chris, sitting with Mom, mouthed "What gives?" while Addy, who I hardly knew, rubbed my back. Reid kept drinking. I thought of my dead friend and how hard his life had been, and how hard my life had been. Per usual, I wished I were someone else.

I took both pills. My first experience with hard drugs. As more eulogists took the stand, a warmth and fullness caressed me, wrapped me in a hug. A flicker of a different world. Less vacant. More loving. Poor people, rich people, middle-class people of every color packed the church. Malik had Sikh friends and Muslim friends and Jewish friends and friends of every Christian denomination. We were atheists and nihilists and optimists and drunks. The facts remained sketchy; they still remain sketchy. But we knew that—even in robbing a gas station, in possibly firing his shotgun and cutting through residential neighborhoods with police choppers overhead, in dying alone because of hopelessness, or need, or simply being a teenager who considered himself invincible—Malik had done his best. Everyone in this church, despite failing the beautiful boy in the closed casket, had tried to do their best. We'd tried our whole lives, just like Malik and just like my mother, and we'd mostly failed anyway. But everyone in that church kept going. Kept doing their best. Kept trying.

As guilty and complicit and exploitative as I felt at that funeral, it was the last time I didn't feel empty.

THE PRESIDENT-ELECT SLID across the marble as I somersaulted into Sandy's desk.

Outside, more gunfire and screaming. Franks and buns skittered across the floor. I scrambled to my feet, yanked my pants up then squatted. I needed to hide the gun in my sock. Except I wasn't holding the gun. And I didn't see it in the foyer or down the hall where the Secret Service and campaign staff were helping 45 to his feet.

"Get him outta here," the next-president barked with his Queens accent. He pointed at me, dusted himself off. "I told Scheisskopf, didn't I? Disgusting. Absolutely disgusting. Weak deal, I said. Too soon after the election. Bad hombres. And the liberals? Don't start me. I told you people. When am I wrong? Have I ever been wrong? I beat Crooked H and I beat—what's that look you're giving me—sixteen from the establishment and my own people don't even listen to me. Do they? Tell me if they do. What? Stop talking. Christ, this goddamn dump of a state. The fuck do I care about French art anyway. The EU has been very, very unfair to me. Not that crowd, okay? They're sick of Mexicans and drugs and bleeding in the streets. I told that bald dope. The kid's mom didn't vote for French art, she voted because we can't say 'Merry Christmas.' Terrible, just terrible. Stephen can stick with the Muslim Ban and we'll get him working on the Wall and arresting the drugs and crime. Enough of this other garbage. No more TV for him. Too big for his britches, okay? Because the towelheads from those shithole crackstacks you made me see? Like they'd vote for me. They didn't even blow up this failing museum, okay? Believe me. It's nothing like the Met. I only did this because Rupert liked the idea. I told him, I did, I did tell Rupert that I'm so famous—that this was all just a big fucking game show anyway—why not try it out. And did you like it? Because I did. Until that hotdog. And what were those things they threw? Very unfair. Very unfair. What? Don't touch me. No. Yes. But that's the one. He didn't save me. The funny guy right there. He assaulted me. I might as well be the president, so go ahead and shoot him."

"Ah, Mr. President-elect, sir," an agent said, interrogating his shoes. "Your pants, sir, are . . . might I recommend we triage the situation and get you somewhere safe and dry?"

"What?" We all inspected 45's lower half. It was wet. Something leaked from his trousers and pooled at his feet.

He'd peed himself.

Assault rifles drawn, a camouflage group sprinted toward us from the left. Ready for countermeasures. For this. Another group, covering the president-elect with a blanket, scurried the opposite direction.

I backed away from the suits and soldiers, crept toward Sandy.

"What the fuck just happened?" A military unit stamped down the empty corridor, yelling into radios.

She shook her head. "You tell me what the heck just happened, J.G."

"I didn't have anything to do with—"

"Don't wanna know if you did." She adjusted her oxygen tube. I whipped around the desk and plunked into an empty swivel chair. I sensed these would be my last moments of freedom for . . . awhile. "Minneapolis PD said that the stage kinda collapsed, but it's mostly just a mess out there. People flopping around with hotdogs and other phalluses. This'll be another thing, though, won't it? Prolly have to close the museum for who knows how long. And Coogan might be toast."

More campaign staff sprinted away. Sirens wailed in the distance. The Director of the Minneapolis FBI thundered over the PA, telling people to disperse. One of the Old Main doors was half-open, and I saw the tank from out front rumble across the smoky stairs.

"You better get your story straight right quick," Sandy said. "But don't tell me anything."

"What do you mean?" Around the corner, two voices called for Julian Glick.

"Well, you just stuck your private parts on the president-elect of the United States while a buncha kooks failed to blow up his rally. Saw the whole thing through them doors. And the rest of the country saw it through their TV."

The shouts and stampeding drew closer.

"Sandy, do you think Nehemiah was telling the truth?" I asked. My hands continued to quake. My knees knocked into the desk. The Ortgies pistol would be covered with my fingerprints, and we'd have nothing to show for our civil disobedience but federal prison and some *SNL* parodies. If Schmidt had even survived.

"He's been using. Since the election. Everyone's off their rocker."

"Wait, he's using? Oh, Jesus—"

"I'll tell you what I told him," she said, clasping my hands and warming them. "I wrote my dissertation on Nietzsche, who posited this: 'Whoever fights with monsters should see to it that he does not become a monster in the process. And when you gaze long into an abyss the abyss also gazes into you.' Someone should've told both of y'all long ago. If he was really your friend's father, it would surprise me. And if that was a terrorist attack out there and not a big ol' practical joke, it would surprise me. But I suppose all of 2016 has been one big fucking surprise."

"There he is," a US Marshal shouted. The soldiers burst past us through Old Main.

"You, get up," his partner said. They were both white men with Tom Selleck moustaches and Pillsbury Doughboy bodies. "Up."

"She's an old woman," I said. "She can't stand."

"Do you know Patricia Schmidt?" Thing One said. "Or Nala Bashir?"

"Nala Bashir?"

"We know who you know and what you did," said Thing Two. "We wanna know why you know them and what you didn't do."

"What? I didn't do anything."

"Exactly," they said.

"I'm not going anywhere. You can talk to my lawyer. Gary Linnihan."

"Already did. He's at the federal courthouse. We pieced this together ten minutes too late," said Thing One.

"We have a warrant for your arrest. This isn't the tiddlywink Minnesota crap either," Thing Two offered. "That lawyer ran his mouth, just like you. He didn't have much to say."

"I'm not going anywhere," I said. Sandy blinked at me meaningfully, but I couldn't discern the meaning.

"That's right," said Thing One, "you're coming with us."

"Shouldn't you be with the explosions and victims? I just got embarrassed on cable news and you wanna indict me because I'm in a 2011 high school directory."

"Calm down. It's chaos out there."

I popped up and stepped around the desk.

"Whoa, take it easy. Sit down."

"Why'd you bring up Nala Bashir?" I asked, inching closer.

"We didn't bring her up," said Thing Two, flicking handcuffs open, "we brought her down."

"Well, ICE did that mostly, but we *did* transport her to the airport, yes," said his partner.

My hands started trembling again. They started cornering me. "You what?"

"Look, we're a nation of laws, okay? If someone has been ordered out by an immigration court, he or she must be sent home. Even if the country doesn't have a government, and the lady had a green card."

"And you're tying me to her? To Patricia Schmidt?"

"We can show you the warrant in the van, but there's reason to believe your colleagues out there? With the little dildo stunt and wannabe Symbionese Liberation bombing? That you at least aided and abetted a buncha felonies."

"I don't understand. You're arresting me?"

"More than that, bubba. You are in a whole lotta trouble soon as we motor from Third Avenue," said Thing One, pulling back his blazer and stroking his holster. "Funny thing is, information from your buddy Scheisskopf turned us onto your, dare we say, radical inclinations, but he had no idea there was a leftist plot in the works."

"Quite the show, eh?" Handcuffs guy said. "That was some twist with your mother."

"And you two seriously helped deport Nala Bashir?" I asked.

They continued to crowd me.

"Part of the gig, kid."

"Deporting green card holders who don't even remember Somalia."

"Deport is a bit strong but—"

I kicked the gun guy in the groin. Handcuffs guy lunged at me, but I slipped his tackle and tossed his head into the corner of the desk. Sandy shrieked as I stomped my dress shoe on his neck and ripped the gun from his holster. Thing One rolled around howling. I pulled the trigger three times; he shut up after the second shot. Thing Two, gurgling and bleeding already, probably didn't need to go, but neither did Nala. I shot him in the temple. By the time I realized what I'd done, they were dead and I was fucked.

Sandy kept screaming.

"Sandy, Sandy? Listen to me," I said. "Tell Nehemiah I love him. And that I'm sorry."

She blubbered and wailed. I worried she might hyperventilate and pass out. My chest beat like a pneumatic drill. I thought I might be having a heart attack.

"Sandy, please," I said, taking her head in my hands and bringing our noses together. She kept crying but stopped making noise. "If Nehemiah is okay, tell him that I just wanted a lane. I wanted the shame to go away, and it didn't, and whether what he said tonight was for my sake or his, or just because he was high, I want him to know that I wasn't brave like him. I needed a lane."

With that, I let go. I fished in the bleeding Marshals' pockets for keys, found a lanyard in Thing Two's slacks, flipped the safety on the gun, tucked it into my waistband, and took hidden doors and card entry passages to Third Avenue. I found their van and crawled into it and fired it up. Full tank of gas. I looked at the museum and the Minneapolis skyline one last time then headed north.

I haven't looked back since.

I TOOK I-35W, trundling across black ice, listening to nothing but my chattering teeth. If they were coming, and they surely were, I didn't want to know. I planned on ditching the van as far north as I could go without refueling, and this plan avoided St. Cloud, via 169 North, then US-2 East. As the fuel light flicked red, and the sun flirted with rising, I ditched the van north of Bemidji, vacuumed two granola bars and half a liter of water I found in the glove compartment, and trotted alongside 72 toward the border. That whole first day, I walked for twelve hours, maybe more, definitely past the next sunrise, and with no idea how to hunt, or start a fire, I ambled the woods, the lakes, the marsh until I found this rotting shed. For sixteen sunups now, some notebooks, the squirrels and a rusted snowmobile have kept me company.

I think I'm in Canada, but by the time you read this, I think I'll be dead. I am so hungry I get dizzy standing. I am living off snow and distraction. Bird calls. Moose sightings. This memoir. Regret.

There's a tiny skating rink next to me.

Reflective. Sentimental. What I keep returning to, like my mother's voice, is worrisome. Are we simply fucked from the start?

I dropped the rosary beads in the woods somewhere. I don't need them anymore.

Nala is deported. Malik is dead. I am alive, but survived about as well as Malik or Mom. Same goes for Tom and Chris. They filled emptiness with fraternity, liberty, and a DUI. I succumbed to the nihilism that taunts those of us who lose the game. Hopelessness is just a rage-quit.

Am I proud of myself? Would my mother be proud of me? These questions, which sustained me through her death and my would-be suicides, through opiate highs and sexless nights, through withdrawal symptoms and laugh-light sets, are irrelevant now. Mom could not be proud of me because I could not be proud of me. She never knew me. I never knew me. And Stephen showed me that I never knew her.

Maybe only Addy knew me. Or maybe Malik. Sometimes I thought Nehemiah knew me and this is why I retreated.

A rustle outside. The flap of several crows. A storm, a hunter. Loons in the distance. I'll kill if necessary, me or whoever.

Hollow like a rotting log. So many people tried to love me and help me, but I was too far gone. Millions of Americans live like Mom. I worry that life is a war of attrition.

I miss her. I wonder if she would miss me, or simply the idea of me. Her oldest, brightest, saddest son, the one for whom she endured miscarriages and beatdowns and $9.00 an hour, the one who promised she'd be able to retire, which was true. As she withered those last few months, she could not work and we were all too hopeless to eat anyway.

The trees sway. Animals brush through the leaves and snow. I can see them through a hole in the baseboards. Something is coming. Vacant breaths.

I think of her every single day. Where does it end? This hole? Nobody but my mother ever cared if I lived or died. Nobody but my mother truly believed I mattered, that I could matter even more, that I could matter to people outside of her, an overly attached single parent with too much pain and sadness in her life for real-adult interests. Piano playing, beer drinking, chess. Comedy or writing or knitting scarves for grandchildren that will never exist, that she would never live to see. No, she only loved three things, and it was her three sons, and we found a way to fuck that up for her, too.

Shouts and marching now. Like a carnival. The barking, the chugging, the stamp of feet and crunch of boots. I decide to go outside. They won. They were always going to win. I should just surrender, but I can't. Call it whatever you want, but it doesn't come for everyone. Some of us have to live in it and with it, endure it over and over and over again, and it's a choice someone else made for us. Worse than when we entered. What is it? What is it? It's why I can't surrender.

They do what they do, and I do what I do, and then there's lots of yelling and popping and blood. All sorts of male bullshit. He's here even when he isn't. Voices and colors like the first seconds of summer break. I'm hollow, giggling, and sad. Walls and ice. An empty beaker. So, so sad. I don't even know who or what I care about. The bullying worked. Screwing, screwed. I just wish we could screw back. Hunger and foolishness. Busy and tired. And even though I have so many questions, my fogged eyes and empty stomach only allow for one.

"Is this some kind of joke?" I ask the face.

"Good one. Nobody's laughing."

AUTHOR'S NOTE

WHEN I CONCEIVED of this novel in the wee hours of November 9, 2016, I was drunk and suicidal in the New York University library. I'd been trying to write a story about foreclosure and economic desperation, but I was too emotionally foreclosed and economically desperate to properly calibrate it. Though it would take another couple years for me to iron all that out—if I ever did—riding the rails up to my shitty Harlem apartment, gone off Old Crow and uppers, I realized that the story of the election wasn't about people like me; it was about the people I'd lost. If, for instance, my mother's life had shaken out a bit differently, if she'd been a little less religious or a little less empathetic, she might have been one of the braying, red-hatted fascists we'd seen (and would continue to see) as the center of the political universe. This novel is about a lot of things, I guess, but on the 2 train at 5:00 a.m., I decided I wanted to write a story about empty people in the emptiest country on earth, and how they might make their lives a little bit fuller.

It took over 300,000 words of writing and editing to reach the 108,000 words we have here. It took grinding, meal-skipping poverty. It took the resilience I learned from my mom. I wish she was here to hold this thing—to tell me what she thought, to reflect on how all the misery we endured finally led to something tangible (and maybe even good)—but I'm still smoldering. So, short of having her here, I'll keep writing about her, and people like her, the people I've lost, who are struggling and complicated and hurting, but trying their best to be decent people anyway.

I never thought I'd live long enough to see this in print. As recently as March, I considered this a suicide note; my optimistic scenario was posthumous publication. The people most responsible for proving me wrong are Andersen Prunty and Wang Ping. Andy, thanks for taking a chance on me. Ping, thanks for insisting that I keep taking chances on myself.

For the last two decades, Fran, Bernie, Jessica, and Jerry have been maybe the only stable facet of my life. Jer, I know I'm an up-and-down friend, and I'll never forgive myself for failing you in summer 2018, but without your patience and commitment to me and all my bullshit, I wouldn't have survived this long. I love you. All of you. You aren't like family to me. You really are my family. Taylor, sorry that I am who I am, but that includes you, too.

Nolberto, you inspire me more than anyone I know. You're my hero. Thank you for your kindness, patience, enchiladas, and liquor. A bumbling oaf like me doesn't deserve having someone so selfless and courageous in his life. I'm so thankful we're friends.

Without the guidance of Marlon James and Peter Bognanni, I never would have made it out of Minnesota. Without the warmth of Anne Walsh, Nora Main, Catherine Westby, Elyan Paz, Jeff Allen, and Nancy Mackenzie, I never would have made it out of 2016. Without the friendship and thoughtfulness of Steve Gugliemo, I'd still be a well-educated manual laborer. Steve, I swear we'll get beer again sometime this century.

John, Joni, and Pat Bennett: you remain important people to me. Those dark years were a little lighter on your couch. And, Jeff Bennett, I couldn't have navigated the last few years without your advice. I'm awful at keeping up, but you've stayed with me despite the distance.

New York City has been a slog. Grady, I wouldn't have endured those first couple years without your help. No matter how lonely or mutually broke, you were the sturdiest, funniest, kindest person in NYC. I owe you, Jim, and Ty approximately one billion drinks.

Joe Dykema, you've been my rock for a decade. I wouldn't have hacked it here without your generosity and love.

NYU was no cakewalk either. This book wouldn't exist without the stewardship of Emily Barton, Darin Strauss, Jonathan Safran Foer, Katie Kitamura, Hari Kunzru, Nathan Englander, and David Lipsky.

And, well, what is there to even say about Dario Diofebi? We've chosen a wretched thing to do with our lives, but since September 2016, no one has been more vital to the writing—and living—process. Thank you for keeping me around. And for listening to me rant and blather and ideate. I'm honored to be friends with someone so driven, talented, passionate, and loving. We'll keep pounding.

Whether they know it or not, pretty much everyone I knew at NYU changed my life. I never thought I belonged with such brilliant people; I'm sure most of you felt the same way. You're brighter and more successful than I'll ever be, but I'm just lucky to have worked alongside you. Andrea, even if you're the nicest person on the planet, you've always been too nice to me. Felice, I would've quit on this novel long ago without your encouragement. Isabel Kaplan and John Maher, I'll never tire of drunkenly complaining with you two; you've both taught me so much about whatever it is we're trying to do here. Katie Bockino, you talk me off the ledge better than anyone. Hannah Gilham, Megan Swenson, Matt Chow, Razmig Bedirian, Mallory Imler Powell, Alexandrine Ogundimu, Ethan Loewi, Jordan Tucker, Francine Shahbaz, Carl Fulbrook, Lindsey Skillen, Crystal Powell, Amir Ahmadi Adrian, Adham Mahmoud, Alyssa DiPierro, Azzuré Alexander, and Hallie Newton endured more awkward conversation and self-conscious lacerating than is medically advisable. It probably meant nothing to you, but it meant a lot to me. Finally, Drew Grauerholz, I miss you. You're an older brother to me, so let's throw more family functions.

Despite now being a fancy, city-slicking, New York pseudo-writer, I will always be pathologically Midwestern. I am not nice, but I am Minnesotan, and my people back home have been putting up with me longer than anyone. Tammie, Rick, Tanner, Torie, Erik, and Ryan extend more grace than I deserve. Kevin, Todd, Chad, Erin, and Emmy don't see me enough, but I do hope they know I'm here for them. Nancy Rodgers always seems to sense when I'm at my lowest and builds me back up. Sue Landmark always gives me strength and fearlessness when I most need it; Mom could always count on you and the whole Pearson clan, and I can, too. Steph and Steve Schmit, you've always modeled compassion and wisdom, and without your help in 2015-2016, I'd be living in my car. Wanda and Phyllis are a true power couple (and my favorite people in the world). Colleen and Sandy, your warmth and energy always lifts my spirits.

There are so many friends to thank—the constant blessing in this grind of a life. Spencer and Carla care about my wellbeing more than

I do; you're my water wings whenever I'm about to drown. Jacob Peterson, I miss you and couldn't have white-knuckled through the last 10 years without your perspective and moral compass. Charlotte, you're one of the best things that's ever happened to me. Ali, no matter how bleak it gets, you keep me going. Tyler, as unfocused as those calls can be, you always keep us plowing ahead. Eli, you always help me keep the faith. As for the Thunderbirds and beyond—Dean, RC, T, C, Con, Mog, Al, Stuts, Randall, Bean, Sammy, Green, Lev, Duke, and Mycleach—you consistently see me at my worst but never give up on me. Thank you.

I hope to publish again soon. Ideally, this is only the beginning. But whatever happens—to me, or the United States—I have been in a very bad way with a very good crew. I owe you all everything. I'm not good at showing it, and I'm even worse at telling it, but if you're reading this, I love you. Yes, you, right now. We are in this fight together. The struggle continues.

SCOTT GANNIS is a former forklift operator from Minneapolis, MN. His work has appeared in various defunct Midwestern literary journals and unviewed YouTube channels. He cycles between the floors of Brooklyn and couches of Minnesota.

Other **Atlatl Press** Books

Heck, Texas by Tex Gresham
Along the Path of Torment by Chandler Morrison
The Joyful Mysteries by Pam Jones
Distant Hills by Lydia Unsworth
Murder House by C.V. Hunt
No Music and Other Stories by Justin Grimbol
Elaine by Ben Arzate
Bird Castles by Justin Grimbol
Fuck Happiness by Kirk Jones
Impossible Driveways by Justin Grimbol
Giraffe Carcass by J. Peter W.
Shining the Light by A.S. Coomer
Failure As a Way of Life by Andersen Prunty
Hold for Release Until the End of the World
by C.V. Hunt
Die Empty by Kirk Jones
Mud Season by Justin Grimbol
Death Metal Epic (Book Two: Goat Song Sacrifice)
by Dean Swinford
Come Home, We Love You Still by Justin Grimbol
We Did Everything Wrong by C.V. Hunt
Squirm With Me by Andersen Prunty
Hard Bodies by Justin Grimbol
Arafat Mountain by Mike Kleine
Drinking Until Morning by Justin Grimbol
Thanks For Ruining My Life by C.V. Hunt
Death Metal Epic (Book One: The Inverted Katabasis)
by Dean Swinford
Fill the Grand Canyon and Live Forever by Andersen Prunty
Mastodon Farm by Mike Kleine
Fuckness by Andersen Prunty
Losing the Light by Brian Cartwright
They Had Goat Heads by D. Harlan Wilson
The Beard by Andersen Prunty